MEDUSA & MOD's
ODDITY ODYSSEY

MEDUSA & MOD's
ODDITYY ODYSSEY

JEREMY BRUNDAGE

Cursed Dragon Ship
PUBLISHING

Copyright © 2025 by Jeremy Brundage Owen

Cursed Dragon Ship Publishing, LLC

6046 FM 2920 Rd, #231, Spring, TX 77379

captwyvern@curseddragonship.com

Cover © 2025 by Jeremy Brundage

Developmental Edit by Kelly Lynn Colby

Proofread by S.G. George

ISBN 978-1-951445-90-4

ISBN 978-1-951445-91-1 (ebook)

This book is a work of fiction fresh from the author's imagination. Any resemblance to actual persons or places is mere coincidence.

For Churstan, who has always believed in me even when I didn't believe in myself.

Contents

PROLOGUE

It was the first day. Emphasis on *FIRST*.

There were a whole lot of self-important, all-powerful beings there, at the beginning. Quite a few of the second-generation gods were there too, but they didn't get to participate just yet because they'd missed out during the first draft selection process.

Everyone wanted to be the first—and the only one credited with creation to boot. Set glanced around and shook his head. *Way to go, guys. Start everything off with a paradox, why don't you?* It was obvious to anyone that all the gods and goddesses assembled in the here and now had to have come from somewhere, so defining this moment as creation was a bit of a stretch. Even so, two dozen deities with the powers of creation stood shoulder to shoulder and postured and displayed the objects of their divine power (each of which they had created themselves, of course). When they told the story of this day to their mortal followers in some two million to six thousand years, each would claim to have worked alone and declare glory for themselves.

It's all in the semantics, I guess. Set leaned back on his heels and tucked his hands into his belt. It was still going to be a good show, no matter when or how you pinpointed the moment when everything really kicked off.

Set sighed, just happy to be a part of things. He backed away from the spectacle and those vying for position. He was just glad that Ptah, Grand Poobah and self-proclaimed creator among the Egyptian gods, had thought enough of him to bring him along. Set didn't want the credit the ones in front craved, and he wasn't going to put up with

1

the smattering of insufferable bores and overbearing personalities in the front row if he didn't have to.

Besides, now Set knew the real truth about creation. The small, bespectacled man driving the delivery truck gave the gods all the raw materials and plans for the universe, and everything would work out fine if they just followed the simple-to-use instructions, with pictures, that came with the product.

Pretty simple, Set thought to himself. *Follow the steps, and after a while, koala bears. How hard is that?*

The man from $\mathbf{A}$ to Ω Mart used a hand truck to wheel the twenty thousand pages of instructions to the group of the most important looking members of those assembled.[1]

"Bah. Who needs instructions? I can already see where these parts all fit together," Odin, All-father of the Norse gods, said.[2]

"I am not leaving the assembling of the universe to someone with no depth perception." Brahma, the Hindu god of creation, huffed and pushed himself between Odin and the delivery man.[3] "Why are you even here? We drew straws, and you didn't pick the long one."

Jehovah, Lord of Israel, held up his hands in an apparent appeal for some patience from everybody. "We don't need to rush stuff, Brahma. We should be able to take our time, and we should have everything sorted out and assembled in a week."

Ptah nodded agreement. "We all have bits and pieces we're more skilled at. I suggest we take a moment to divvy up the assemblage process so we can get it done with a day or two to spare."

Jehovah acknowledged Ptah's optimism. "A very insightful

---

1. $\mathbf{A}$(Alpha) to Ω(Omega) Mart! Your best place to shop for fantastic beginnings, cataclysmic ends, and everything in between.
2. Odin called himself the All-father, but Odin's father was Borr, and Borr's father was Búri. By my reckoning that meant at least two fathers had to have happened before the All-father came upon the scene.
3. The barter system in the nine realms was brutal. Asgard is where the phrase 'cost an arm and a leg' came from. Odin traded one eye to be granted wisdom and knowledge, and that was a pretty good deal. You wouldn't believe what they charged for a tankard of mead and a plate of cold mutton.

suggestion. We'll not feel pressured at all and should get it done in plenty of time. A bit of rest on the seventh day would be nice, wouldn't it? A break before the real work begins. I suspect we'll all be busy once this is up and running."

The delivery man held out a clipboard to be signed. "Proof of acceptance of delivery," he clarified.

Chiminigagua, supreme creator and ruler of the religion he intended to call the Muisca, reached out, scrawled something on the paper, and handed the clipboard back to the delivery man.[4] It was a signature that any future practitioner of medicine would be more than impressed by.

"Could you also please print your name legibly on the line just below the signature?"

Chiminigagua scowled, brought the clipboard back, and took his time spelling out his name in block letters.

The delivery man glanced over the form, nodded his approval, and tucked the clipboard neatly under his arm. "If you're missing any components or find any parts are missing, you can—"

"I'll be fine." Brahma waved the man with the clipboard away. "I wouldn't be god of creation if I couldn't deal with a little missing part or two, would I?" When that earned several reproving glares from his peers Brahma gave a sheepish clarification. "I meant to say that *we*, the *gods* of creation, could handle it."

Chiminigagua grunted in disgust at Brahma's lame attempt at damage control.

"I think a missing part and the ensuing workarounds are good in a way. They bring about the unexpected," Chaos, the Greek god of creation, said. "Who doesn't like to have the little thrill of panic and surprise when something essential goes wrong once in a while?"

Brahma narrowed his eyes and glared at Chaos. "No one let him touch any of the fundamental gearing," he said to the other gods huddled close.

---

4. The predominant main religion in the early South American Andes.

"That was uncalled for," Chaos muttered to himself. He folded his arms tight and took a step back from the assembly area.

"Service calls can take a while if you need one, just so you know." The delivery man shrugged. "Good luck. No refunds or returns on partially assembled items."

Brahma snorted, pushed the man aside, and started opening boxes.

The delivery man didn't look surprised, like he'd gone through this kind of thing many times before. The man got in his truck, turned the key, and blipped into another plane of existence.

Shoulda listened to the expert. I certainly would have, Set thought. *But when do the bigwigs ever listen to the guys they think are below them?*

It was no surprise to Set that when all the cogs and wheels were laid out for the universal machine that something was misplaced or missing. Of course it was a vital part, and of course there was no spare to be found anywhere, no matter how much the ones in charge huffed and fumed and tried to blame those who weren't involved.

"I say we search Chaos," Brahma threatened.

Chaos took a step back, settled his weight on his cocked hip, folded his arms self-righteously and arched a bemused eyebrow at the other god. "Go right ahead. I've been standing here the entire time. None of you omniscient beings saw me so much as twitch in the direction of the machine's components."

"He's right," Jehovah confirmed. "Chaos never went near the boxes."

"It would have gone better if you'd let me help," Odin said smugly.

"Quiet you!" Pangu, creator of Asian Taoism, snapped and wildly shook his giant axe in disgust at all of the others.[5] "We could

---

5. Pangu used one hack of his mighty axe to split yin(earth) from yang(sky). Why he had an axe before anything else existed is a mystery, but it did come in handy.

have just gone with the cosmic egg design, one crack and done, but no. You all thought the kit would be so much more—"

Jehovah cleared his throat and gently pushed Pangu's axe aside. "Careful where you swing that thing."

Pangu got quiet as everyone stared at him. He took a step back, tucked his axe behind him as if to hide it, and ran his free hand back and forth between the stubs of his small horns.

"It was cheaper, okay? We all agreed." Chiminigagua reminded everyone. "I mean, I'm filled with light, but I'm not exactly heavy in material wealth, if you catch my drift."

"They said our credit was good, and if you can't trust gods like us to uphold our financial obligations, who can you trust?" Brahma reminded the group.

"I understand the frugality and rationale of our choice, making sure we could pay off the purchase during the promotional period before the interest kicks in," Pangu said. "Still would have helped to have the whole mess come fully assembled."

The other gods grumbled and nodded and generally agreed.

"We all came into this fully apprised of what to expect. We deal with what we were given, yes?" Jehovah asked. "What exactly are we missing?"

Brahma pointed at the instructions, which he'd finally consulted after what had been a painfully awkward and frustrating amount of time for everyone. "A bearing, just a tiny, hard, little round thing that sits right here, rubbing up against the other bearings surrounding the pin in the center point of the main cog that turns and spins everything."

Chaos chuckled. "Adapt or improvise."

"Or put in a call to the company for a replacement part or a service tech that will know what to do," Jehovah said as he stroked his beard in thought.

Chaos chuckled again. "Good luck with that. I was on the advisory board that helped devise A to Ω Mart's customer service processes."

Brahma narrowed his eyes and glared at Chaos.

Chaos just grinned back, unaffected by the other god's withering stare.

Ptah's brows knitted in thought. "This bearing? About how big should it be?"

"Oh, about one *mutthi*."[6] Brahma pulled his attention off Chaos and held up a fist for the others to see.

All the other gods looked on as if the phrase, and the gesture, meant nothing to them.

Chiminigagua leaned over to Ptah. "Why'd he make an angry hand like that?"

Brahma was quiet for a moment before he lowered his hand. "Four and a half or five inches. The size of a fist?" he clarified.

"Ah, yes, I knew that, of course." Chiminigagua cleared his throat, lowered his eyes, and said nothing more.

Brahma scanned over the specs. "Made of a tough, rubbery material that weighs about 4333 *ratti*."

There was the same reaction to the pronouncement of weight as there had been to size.

Brahma sighed. "Fifteen ounces."

Ptah looked to be pondering the weight and size of the bearing. "Hey, Set, come here for a moment."

Set had been watching and paying attention to everything, but he hadn't expected any of those first-tier gods to want to have him in the way for anything. The summons caught him by surprise. "Uh, sure! What can I help you with, Ptah?" He was eager to help in any way he could.

"What help could this little dog-headed godling be to us?" Chiminigagua eyed Set up and down judgingly.

---

6. A *mutthi* is a unit of measurement in ancient India equal to one fist. With the variation of hand sizes available, the phrase "You short-fisted me again!" had to have been used at one point or another.

"There's more to Set than meets the eye," Ptah said to the other god.

Set beamed, his lips pulled back so far he displayed all of his canine teeth with his smile.

Ptah waved him closer. "I think you might have it in you to fix this problem. Come here and take a look." Ptah pointed at the large cog laying at their feet and the metal collar at its center with the obviously missing bearing.

"What am I looking for?" Set asked.

"Just lean in a bit more. It'll become evident to you pretty soon."

Set leaned over and felt a violent, stabbing tear as Ptah drove his hand into Set's back. Something was pulled from his chest. "What was . . .? Why did you . . .?"

Ptah bounced the heart in his hand. "Four and three-quarter inches and half an ounce shy of fifteen." He tossed the still beating heart to Brahma. "You think this will work?"

"That was brutal." Jehovah's eyes went wide.

Ptah shrugged. "One little thing was holding us up. If this works, we can get the universe up and running."

Ptah seemed so sure of what he had done that none of the other gods objected. Chaos even looked a little impressed.

"How could you do this to me?" Set staggered and fell to the side. He tried to feel the gaping wound in his back, but he couldn't quite reach it with his hand.

"Why use his heart?" Jehovah asked. "Any of our hearts would have worked, or we could have come up with something else the right shape and weight and size."

"True. Any other heart might have worked." Ptah shrugged and pointed at Set. "What's the point of bringing along spare and backup parts if you never use them?"

Set staggered and tried to back away from Ptah. He stumbled and fell. "Is that all I am to you? Bits and pieces to be used as you see fit?"

"Aren't you?" Ptah caught Set before he moved any further away.

"All your dramatic stumbling and tripping is a bit over the top, don't you think?"

"You try walking with your back shattered and no heart," Set whimpered and shrank from Ptah's touch.

"Oh, hold still, you *whiner*." Ptah brushed his hand over Set's back, and the ragged hole sealed over. "You're a god. You're not going to die. And if you're going to act like a weak little invalid, at least do it with a bit of flash and style." Ptah picked up an ornately decorated staff of office he'd left leaning against an empty crate and handed it to Set to lean on.

Set stumbled and gripped tight onto the rod. The ceremonial walking stick held him up. Set wondered how it would feel to rise up and bash Ptah over the head with the stick. When he tried to do so, the stitch in his back doubled him over, so he had to catch himself on the stick again to keep from falling.

"See? How much better is that? A bit of practice and you'll be the talk of the town. You'll look just like a venerable sage or a holy man or some such." Ptah wiped his hands on his skirt and urged Brahma to test the fit of the heart into the machine as he turned his attention away from his associate.

Brahma hesitated for a moment, but when he leaned over and squeezed the heart into the collar next to the other bearings, it fit perfectly. He dropped the center rod into the hole in the middle of everything. The main cog that drove all the mechanics in the rest of the universe started to spin.

"See? I'm not a bad guy," Ptah said. "I'm just a problem solver."

Set couldn't bring himself to look toward any of the gods. If any of them were like Ptah, his creator and betrayer, Set wanted nothing to do with them. All he could focus on was the thing that might fix the dark growing inside him. "My heart." Set leaned down heavily against the walking stick and reached a hand toward the cog.

Ptah slapped Set's hand away, almost bowling him over in the process.

"My heart." Set wept as he fell against and clutched the staff as if it were the only thing supporting him in the universe.

"Oh, fine. I'll contact customer support." Ptah pulled out a plaster-coated sandstone tablet and scratched at it with a three-sided gold stylus. "Heart switched with bearing. Do what you need to fix or repair the problem." He finished drawing the final hieroglyph and tapped the writing instrument hard against the tablet in punctuation. "There. They'll send someone out to fix it soon."

"How soon?" Set pleaded.

Ptah wasn't listening anymore.

None of the major gods were paying Set any attention.

Like it mattered.

Set knew now that their new toy worked, none of the other gods would take his side. They had a lot invested in this project, and they wouldn't see the heart of one, second-tier god as worthy enough to stop everything to replace a ticker that was just the right size and weight to fix a problem for something else. Or, newly burgeoning heavens forbid, see Set's misappropriated heart as something worthy of a trip to the store to actually pick up the right part.

At least Ptah had put in a work order.

Set was still crying, but now he was angry too.

Through his tears Set looked around for support from any of the other, lowlier gods and goddesses in attendance. None of them would look him in the eye.

The big gods had Set's heart, and there was nothing he could do about it.

Yet, Set amended as he wiped away his tears and picked himself up, leaning heavily on the worthless piece of wood Ptah had given him as a crutch.

The other gods had explained and pontificated about what a day, *this day*, would be like. No one knew the truth for sure until the first one actually happened.

If this is what a day is like, I'm all in favor of going back to the

Void. Set coughed and staggered and tried to push his way closer to his heart.

Chaos caught Set by the back of the neck. "This one's a fighter," he said, holding Set aloft like a prize fish or something for the others to see.

Set struggled to free himself from Chaos's grip with one hand and repeatedly whacked Chaos about the head and shoulders with the staff held in the other. He cast his eyes about and pleaded for anyone to help him retrieve what was rightfully his.

None of the other, lesser gods, came to his aid. They were probably afraid they would be next if they drew any attention to themselves.

Useless bunch of Adjawetets.[7]

He'd been so excited when Ptah had asked him to be here today. Maybe this is what Ptah had planned all along? It didn't seem like that was the case, but . . .

Set would never trust anyone again.

Ptah stood in front of the struggling god and cocked his head to the side. "Set, child, you don't yet understand what your small sacrifice has wrought here this day. Perhaps you need a bit of perspective to see what good you have done."

Set redoubled his efforts. He snarled, kicked, and bit at anyone who came near him.

"He's actually becoming a bit hard to hold." Chaos sounded impressed.

"He just doesn't understand." Ptah sighed. "I'll take care of it."

"Don't you come near me. I'll kill you!" Set lashed out, unconcerned with the damage he might cause, even to himself.

Ptah avoided Set's claws and teeth and put his hand on Set's

---

7. Adjawetet is the name of a dog from ancient Egypt. The dog was blind, deaf, and lame. *Adjawetet* translates roughly to *useless*, which the dog was. Still, his master, probably a child, loved him anyway, otherwise we wouldn't have a record of his name.

chest. "Go, experience the world you have helped bring to life. See the first day for yourself."

There was a pulse of energy, and Set wasn't in the center of the universe anymore. He was surrounded by clouds and sunlight and air. He tumbled through the sky, and below him a ribbon of blue cut through the sands of Egypt as the Nile made its way to the sea.

The view was breathtaking, but any beauty was lost on the injured god as he plummeted toward the world below.

The sands of Egypt rushed up to greet him.

He hit the top of a sand dune with the impact of a meteor and tumbled head over heels until he came to rest in the dust that shifted and billowed at the base of the mountain.

Set wanted his heart.

It had only been moments since he'd lost it, but he didn't like how he felt without it. He already hungered and ached for it.

Nothing else mattered.

They'd stolen his heart and tossed him from the heavens.

Ptah and all the others would regret that.

"Damn you, Ptah!" Set raised his staff toward the sky. "And damn all those who stood by and did nothing while this first crime was committed. You all created the Grand Machine, and in so doing, have tied your existences and fates to it. I swear by the void in my chest that none of you matter. The Grand Machine doesn't matter. Somehow you'll see what you've done."

His strength spent, Set's arms dropped to his sides, and he fell to his knees.

"Somehow I'll make you see." Set quietly wept to himself.

Hand over his left breast, knowing he couldn't sense the beat of a pulse from the empty void in his chest but hoping for it just the same, Set felt a cold certainty spread through him. He didn't know when, or how, but one day he would have his heart back.

And then . . .

Then all of them would pay.

CHAPTER 1

A DISQUIET IN HER DREAM

MEDUSA STARED AT DOUG, THE HANDSOME YOUNG MAN WITH the endearing lopsided smile. He wore a blindfold, just as he had on the day when he'd freed her from her curse. Only she wasn't happy to see Doug. Not like this. For some reason, the sight of him sitting on the picnic blanket before her was tying her stomach in knots.

"Do you remember?" Doug asked. "It was so easy to get rid of the curse, you'd just never thought of it before."

His tone stung a bit, and it seemed as if he had intended it to, which was totally unexpected. Doug wasn't that kind of person. He always showed concern for the comfort of everyone around him. He always tried to help others, even those who didn't really deserve it.

Like me, Medusa thought so softly in her own mind, she almost wasn't aware of the thought.

Almost.

"I mean, all you had to do was just ask," Doug pointed out with a light, mocking laugh.

"This isn't funny, Doug," Medusa folded her arms and glared at him. "I don't know what got into you, but I don't like it."

"It's your anniversary." Doug threw his arms wide for emphasis. Then he hesitated, and the spread of his arms and smile faltered a bit. "Is anniversary the right word, or should I have said birthday? What do you call it when it has been a year since a life-ending burden has been lifted and a condemned person gets to taste life and freedom again?" He shrugged. "I guess it doesn't matter. It's been a year since I saved you, and I just thought you'd be thankful to have a reminder.

"You are thankful, aren't you?" Doug threatened.

Medusa could feel tears welling in the corner of her eyes. "Why

13

are you talking like this? Are you drunk?" She'd never seen Doug so much as tipsy before, but the way he was acting now was way outside normal for him. "Is everything all right between you and Larisa?"

The name of Doug's wife brought the smile back to his lips, just not a pleasant one. "Me and Larisa in trouble? You'd like that, wouldn't you?"

Medusa gasped. She couldn't believe what he'd said, let alone imagine what he seemed to be insinuating. "Larisa is my friend! I would never—"

"Sure. Whatever makes you feel better about yourself," Doug muttered with a dismissive snort. "Larisa is fine and continues to adore me. Like, who wouldn't, right?"

He leered through the blindfold—at least, that was the way it felt.

Doug continued, seemingly oblivious to her discomfort. "Anyway, today marks a year since you had the curse lifted, so I put on this blindfold to see how you've been doing. It's a test to see if you're still worthy of the salvation you've been gifted."

Doug reached up to tug the blindfold from his eyes.

"No!" Medusa grabbed Doug by the wrists and wrestled with him. She was deathly afraid of what might happen if he were to see her. "This is wrong. This is cruel! Why are you acting like this?"

"Scared to look me in the eyes? Afraid of what it will prove?" Doug shoved her away.

He ripped the blinders from his face and glared at her.

Medusa tried to hide.

"As I expected." Doug's face took on a sour look of disgust. "Hiding, because you know you aren't worthy of forgiveness."

The color drained from his hair and skin. "And now you can add my life to all the others you've taken." The last thing he muttered before he finished turning to stone was lost as his lips petrified.

Medusa still knew what the word was, and it hurt more than anything else Doug could have said.

The final curl of his lips formed out a hint of the word *pathetic*.

"No." Medusa clutched at the unyielding stone statue before her. She clawed at Doug, unwilling to believe what she was seeing.

Her curse was back. She was about to scream when two strong hands grabbed her by the shoulders and shook her. The hands were firm yet gentle. Medusa lashed out at them anyway.

"Medusa," Three said as she easily grabbed Medusa's hands so she couldn't hurt herself. "You need to wake up, sweetie. You were having a bad dream."

Seeing her friend looking down on her with concern in her eyes, Medusa broke, sobbing. "Oh, gods, Three. It was so real. Doug did something to me. He gave me back my curse."

"It was a dream," Three soothed as she stroked Medusa's hair and held her close. "I watched you toss and turn for a bit. But when you started to thrash, I thought it would be best if I woke you."

Medusa slumped against her friend's chest. "It was so real."

"It was just a dream," Three repeated. "Your curse is gone because you never deserved it, and Doug would be the last person to do anything to hurt you." She patted Medusa's hair again as the final tremors of the nightmare worked their way out of the scared girl's system.

"You're right," Medusa said to her friend as they held each other tight. "Of course you're right."

But in the back of Medusa's mind, Morpheus had planted a variety of noxious seeds, and a few of the seeds had found places here and there to try to take root.

A final tremor ran the length of Medusa's spine, and she was awake.

Another uncertain day in the cursed/not cursed life of Medusa had begun.

CHAPTER 2
A TOY AND HIS MOTHER

Modifixeus felt the ocean spray on his arms and face, and he laughed at the feel of the mist as it quickly dried in the sunlight. The sun was warm. The slight breeze and the cool spray in the air kept the temperature perfect.

Mod felt the weight of his favorite toy in his hand. It seemed much heavier than normal. He raised it up to look at it and was surprised to see how big the toy looked when compared to the fingers that held it.

The hand holding the toy was the hand of a toddler.

On some level Mod was aware that this had to be a dream, so why not just go with it?

Mod raised up his unburdened hand and flexed it in front of his face. He noted the wonder of it as he splayed his digits out so far he could feel the skin between his chubby little fingers stretch, then he clasped them into a fist so tight, from the wrist out he felt nothing but pins and needles when he let it go.

Mod giggled at the joy of having tiny child's hands that worked this well.

He looked at his feet, chubby little toes poking out of the end of his sandals, and took a huge step that swung his foot wide. The foot fell back down on the cobbles with a loud slap.

Mod stepped again with his other foot.

Slap!

Giggle.

Then Mod put his feet together, crouched down, and gave a little hop.

He belly laughed because the hop felt like he had flown far above the earth.

"I fly." He giggled. Then he hopped again.

Hop. Hop. Hop.

Mod was a bit taken at just how happy he felt, and suddenly he hoped he might not be dreaming after all.

"Pretty little boy. Are you jumping?" someone asked.

His heart leaped to hear that voice.

Mod turned to search out the speaker, so familiar and comforting, before the woman had a chance to move far away. She stood closer than she'd sounded, right next to him. "Momma?" Mod looked up at the woman who towered over him. He tried to look at her face, but all he saw was a blur of her features with a halo of light surrounding her head.

"Momma?" he asked again, a bit hesitant.

"Who else would it be, silly?" The blurry-faced woman extended a hand. Her open fingers beckoned.

Mod knew it was his Momma, even though he couldn't see her clearly. Mod reached up his free hand and twined his little fingers with hers.

She picked him up and swung him by his arm. Now Mod felt like he was really flying. It seemed like he was high above the heads of the people on the docks before he floated back to the ground and landed with a thump.

"Again!" he shouted.

Momma with the blurred face shook her head. "There are more people here, and if I swing you about, you might bump into one of them. You just need to be patient for a moment. We can play again when the business of the day is through." She patted his hand and reassured him.

There were a lot of people.

Mod was suddenly worried about his toy, so he rolled his arm around it and pressed it to his breast. He was protective of it. Momma had told him it was special.

Mod looked about at all the other people, the ones he needed to protect his toy from. There were no other children, and all the other adults had blurred out faces too.

The spray from the ocean felt cooler, and the warm sun went behind a cloud.

Mod shivered, and not just from the sudden chill.

The crowd was thicker, and people bumped Mod and his Momma.

Mod tugged on his Momma's hand. "I wanna go."

"Just a minute, Modifixeus." Momma always used his full name when she was serious.

He was stuck. He wouldn't leave his Momma. Mod stopped tugging to pull her away from this place and clutched his toy a little tighter.

The knot of people on the dock grew even thicker, the noise and sound of the place was harsh in Mod's ears. He would have covered his ears if he could, but one hand clung tightly to Momma and his other hand held his toy.

He really wanted his hands free, so he could cover his ears.

If only I had a pocket I could put the toy in, then I'd have a free hand to cover my ear from what is going to happen next.

It was an odd thing to think because how did Mod know something bad was about to happen? And even odder because he realized he hadn't thought it in a toddler's voice.

"Mom?" he asked, in a voice that was very much a man's. "Why am I here?"

"You'll see soon enough." His mother turned and looked down at him as if he were still a little boy. The blur over her face was gone, and he could see her bright eyes and her dazzling smile. "It's all right, sweetie. I told you it would only be a minute more. You can be patient for a minute more, can't you?"

The halo around Momma's head flared and blinded him.

"Mom?" Mod blinked hard as he tried to clear his eyes. He

couldn't see her face anymore. His eyes filled with tears, and the pit of his stomach dropped away as if his gut anticipated something bad.

Momma's hand was ripped from Mod's clutching fingers.

"Mom!" he screamed.

Someone else screamed. More panicked voices joined in.

An army rushed the dockside, man-like creatures hacking and pillaging with weapons and nets caked with seaweed and barnacles. A rough, ugly man that stank of rotten seawater grabbed Mod's momma around the waist.

"My little, sweet one. It will be all right," she said, totally unfazed by the stinking barbarian stealing her away.

Mod screamed and clutched the air before him as he tried to grab his mother back.

"I'll only be—"

And then Mod woke up.

Mod's heart thundered in his chest. He stood there naked, drenched in sweat and breathing like he'd just run a marathon. He stood in the center of the room, facing the east, and held the toy from his dream in his hand.

The same toy he'd had since he was a child.

He studied the toy for a second, not that he needed to. He knew the make of the toy better than anything he'd ever come across. He used it as a type and measure of everything in his life.

The toy was present in the dream and here in real life.

Maybe Mod's mind was trying to tell him something?

Maybe he was just stressed from something he wasn't really aware of on a conscious level?

Maybe Morpheus smoked too much hemp and had started screwing with people's dreams.[1]

All Mod knew for sure was that he'd lost another night of sleep.

---

1. A son of Somnus, Morpheus appeared to men in dreams, to trick or guide them, in the shape of a man. He spans the space between the realms of waking and sleep, and between literary and mythological beings.

He could lay back down, but what would be the point? He'd been having this same stupid dream, or a version of it, for the past few weeks.

Mod gave a ragged swallow and blinked hard. He still was in a place somewhere between conscious and dream, but the toy in his hands was tangible enough. He took the thing in both hands and twisted and rotated piece after piece until the toy's size was half what it was. With all its pieces in place, it formed a perfect sphere small enough to be shoved in his pocket.

The small curtain of fabric that didn't quite cover the window was pulled back just enough to show the line of light brightening on the horizon. Mod yawned and tried to rub away the headache he got from lack of sleep. Massaging his temples didn't help, so he sighed and decided he might as well go about his day.

Dreams were just dreams, right? Mod would rather focus on things he could touch and manipulate and fix with his hands.

Another glorious day in the mechanical puzzle of Mod's life had begun.

CHAPTER 3

A MODEST, AND TOTALLY MISUNDERSTOOD, PROPOSAL

Medusa had searched for ways to deal with the dread and anxiety her dreams had created within her. She couldn't defeat the furies that flitted and scratched, worried and pecked at her inside her skull. She'd come up with plan after plan, only to have them fall apart before they could even give hope. Whatever she had tried hadn't worked, and she had grown more desperate by the day.

Her latest attempt for distraction and meaning may have been the one most doomed to fail of all of them.

The main component of this plan, oblivious to the damage he currently caused to Medusa mentally and spiritually, walked into the workshop where Medusa waited for him.

As Mod came into the shop he whistled, the newest gadget from Hephaestus & Co. bending to his will.[1] The knot of wooden blocks and twine fell apart as if they hadn't been assembled and then were just as quickly assembled as if they had never fallen apart.

No physical object is a mystery to him. It's just the rest of the world, and life, that he has no clue about.

Medusa sighed and glanced across the room to the mechanical woman who lounged on the couch against the far wall as she looked for moral support.

Three shrugged, shook her head, and said nothing.

Mod walked past Medusa. He brushed up against her shoulder as

---

1. This company is actually owned by a swindler, user, abuser, and lawyered up to the hilt *nyfitsa* named Apateónas. Heph doesn't like it, but he doesn't want to get mired in a legal battle with a morals-lacking weasel. Besides, Heph consulted with an oracle, and Apateónas will soon leave his position for a "new opportunity" in Hades. Heph and Hades already have several "retirement" ideas in mind.

he did so and somehow didn't notice her despite the contact. Not once since he walked in had he looked up. His focus was always on his hands or on a toy or on his feet as he made his way forward.

Mod hadn't even noticed Medusa was here. She still wasn't used to that.

But this is Mod, after all. What should I expect?

He put his new toy on the shelf against the wall, apparently already bored with it.

"Good morning," Medusa said in a flat voice.

Mod looked about until he zeroed in on who was speaking. "Oh, hey, I didn't see you there."

"Yeah, I noticed," Medusa said, her voice tight and drawn.

Mod walked over and rummaged through a few tools on a workbench, pushing aside the project he worked on yesterday. He nodded his head in the direction of the shelf. "I got a new toy. Wasn't very impressive, but you can look at it and play with it if you'd like."

"Oh, I'd really love that," Medusa said sarcastically. "But I don't care about *your* new toy."

Mod appeared not to catch the emphasis on the word *your* as Medusa waited in silence.

"No problem. What are friends for?" Mod started whistling again as he shifted a box to the side.

Three winced but said nothing.

"All right!" Mod must have found a part he was looking for. He tossed it in the air, caught it, and dropped it into his pocket.

"So you went by that tacky crap shop and picked up a toy this morning?" Medusa asked. Try as she might, she couldn't keep the edge from her voice.

The sharp tone of her words, like so many other social cues or niceties, blew past Mod without making contact. "There wasn't really anything good at AliBaba Express,[2] but then, there almost never is, so I went by H&C just to see if they got a new shipment in."

"Oh, that's nice." Medusa drug a fingertip along one of the clearer work surfaces. She was getting a bit frustrated, and that could quickly turn to anger. And she wasn't really angry with Mod.

That would be like getting angry at a toddler, wouldn't it?

"So just a leisurely morning of shopping. No plans. Just a normal, typical day?"

Mod stopped what he was doing. "Now that you mention it . . ." He looked up from the workbench. Two brass rods with hooks on each end twirled and spun between the knuckles of his right hand as he considered. "It seems like I'm forgetting something I was supposed to be doing today."

It was quite impressive the way the brass tools tumbled and twisted in his fingers like he was a drummer searching for a beat. His hands in motion, she could see the gears of his mind engage as he searched his memory for what he had forgotten.

Medusa's heart actually stopped for a second. A hope she hadn't realized was so dear rose up. She glanced in the direction of Three for confirmation, not willing to trust only her judgment on the matter.

Three didn't really help that much. The automaton shrugged back at Medusa and continued to watch the interaction between her friends, but she said nothing.

Mod walked around in a little circle. The brass hooks acting every bit of a mental propeller as they urged his memory to fly. The speed of the hooked rods spinning increased and decreased, increased and decreased until the sound of them fanning through the air was almost too much for Medusa to take. The blunt ends of the hooks slapped to a stop in Mod's free hand and his eyes went wide just as Medusa was about to snap.

---

2. The name was meant to evoke places and items exotic and mysterious, but it was chosen to mask the poor quality of the products offered. The company had staying power, though. They're still around, but they dropped *Baba* from the name once they started their online store.

"Oh, my gosh! How could I have forgotten?" Mod shook his head and pinched the bridge of his nose.

Three arched an incredulous eyebrow at Medusa and shook her head slightly from side to side, possibly to convey the message that while the signs were promising, Medusa shouldn't get her hopes up.

Medusa turned to Mod, her expectations tempered by previous experience yet growing nonetheless. *Maybe this time he'll remember? He'll feel sorry and find a way to apologize.*

"Ktesibios. I'm supposed to help him rebuild a water pump for Heph's new forge this afternoon." Mod beamed at Medusa before he turned back to rifling through the items atop his bench. "Thanks for reminding me. I'm going to need to bring along a couple other tools."

Medusa's heart fell. "Hopeless," she muttered with a scowl.

Three just opened her arms, palms upward, as if to say *what did you expect?* "Say hi to my dad for me,"[3] Three said to Mod.

Mod brightened when he heard Three's voice. "Oh. Hey, Three. Nice to see you. I will." He looked kind of excited. "Have you seen the pump your dad came up with?"

Three shook her head that she hadn't.

"It's genius. A screwing mechanism in a wooden tube uses mechanical displacement to force water up a thirty-degree incline.[4] Wild and wacky stuff. Your dad and Heph want to see if we can recreate the whole thing in metal." Mod grinned as he turned back to Medusa. "Want to come along? We might need someone to help grease the gears and bearings that interact with the screw's shaft."

Medusa continued to glare at him, speechless. It took a couple of beats before it looked like Mod realized there was a look of disapproval on her face.

"Do you not like talking about screws and shafts?" Mod asked.

The boy really is oblivious.

---

3. Ktesibios and Talos the mechanical giant created the automatons, so the two men are their fathers.

4. This device is called the Archimedes screw. Ktestbios did come up with the idea, but Archimedes was the first one to build a working prototype.

"A lot of people get testy around engineering terminology," Three said without a hint of sarcasm.

Medusa glared at Three.

Three shrugged again and turned her focus back to Mod. "If I were a better friend, I'd warn you that now would be the appropriate time to drop to your knees and beg for forgiveness, but I'm enjoying the show."

"Show?" Mod's brow furrowed as he attempted to figure out what he'd missed. He turned to the automaton. "When did the show start?"

Three pointed at Medusa. "Shortly after she got here. I tried to talk her down, but I can only do so much when the fuel igniting her fury throws more tinder on the flame."

"That was a nice turn of phrase," Medusa said to Three.

"Thanks. I've been getting coaching from Isocrates."[5] Three gave a nod.

Medusa folded her arms over her chest and turned back to glare at Mod.

Mod looked back and forth between the two women, obviously lost. "What are we talking about?"

Three indicated Mod with a hand gesture that encompassed him from head to foot. "The subject of the lady's ire. You performed just about as expected."

"Ire? Me? I thought we were talking about water pumps."

Medusa could see the young man had no clue what was going on. That fact did not endear him to her. She clenched her teeth down so hard you could hear them grind from across the room.

"What did I do?" Mod asked.

"Absolutely nothing," Medusa replied coolly.

"Danger, Zale, Robot's son. Danger!"[6] Three said.

---

5. Isocrates was an ancient Greek rhetorician and orator. Rhetoric is often noted for coming across as insincere, so you have to distract from perceived insincerity with flair. "Shock and awe, baby!" "Release the Kraken!"

6. Lucien of Samosata was renowned and credited with the first science fiction tale,

Mod blinked at Three. "I feel like I'm missing a part of the conversation that began before I was here."

"That was eerily and tragically accurate," Three acknowledged before Medusa cut her off with a withering glare.

Medusa stared at Three as she addressed her next comments to Mod. "So mucking about with Three's dad in the guts of a greasy machine is the only thing you've got going on today?" Medusa asked, the edge in her voice no longer hidden and growing sharper by the moment.

Mod stood stock still, unable to speak.

"This is painful. It's obvious he doesn't remember," Three said.

Mod looked back and forth between the two women. "Uh, yeah, sure. Of course I remember."

Three held up her hand, stopping him in his tracks. "Now's probably not the best time to practice a suave, social maneuver like confidence bluffing. You aren't very good at it anyway, and we both know you too well for it to work."

Mod must have realized what he tried to do. He looked sheepishly over at Medusa.

Medusa purposefully didn't look at Mod. It felt a bit mean, getting angry at someone with the social awareness of a goat,[7] but she was mad and disappointed and couldn't control herself.

After a long, awkward pause, she finally found the strength to speak. Her voice sounded high pitched and tight in her own ears. "Yesterday. It all started with me telling you about the new *tiganites*

A True Story, but it was not his only creation. His most recent attempt involved a group on a boat lost beyond the bounds of the known universe. The characters are a boy named Zale, a mechanical man who thinks he is Zale's father, and a sometimes endearing, ofttimes underhanded blacksmithing faun called Dr. Smith. Every time the group lands in a precarious situation due to Dr. Smith's bumbling, the mechanical man shouts a warning: "Danger, Zale, Robot's son. Danger!" The story is a huge hit with Heph and the automatons.

7. Goats, especially those closely related to the faun branch of the family, have close to zero social awareness.

place opening up in town?[8] And suggesting that we should totally go and check it out."

Mod spun the little metal rods in his hands. "I don't remember talking to you about breakfast. I mean, I can eat, but—"

Medusa rankled.

Mod stopped fidgeting with the tools. "How does this—"

"Hush!" Three directed his attention back to Medusa and warned him to be quiet.

Medusa's lips were trembling as she continued, "'Eos's Breakfast Cakes?'[9] you asked, 'Are you sure you want to start your morning with something that perky and sickly sweet?' Then you laughed."

"When have I ever described anything as perky and sickly sweet? And why would I laugh? Do I really sound like that?"

Mod, clueless as he was, actually chuckled.

Medusa's eyes bored into him.

Mod took a step back from her and clamped his mouth shut.

"I admitted naming a restaurant 'Morning Dawn Pancakes' was a bit much," Medusa recalled with a scowl. "And I told you that she didn't just make pancakes."

At this point something must have connected in Mod's mind because his brows knit and he cocked his head to the side. "Marshmallow monoceros?"

"Marshmallow monoceros," Medusa confirmed.

"Now I'm lost," Three admitted as she looked between the two.

"Does each order come with a pink frosted marshmallow monoceros as a side?" Medusa clarified so Three would get the reference. "It was a joke, from Mod, that was timely and funny and unusually appropriate in the instance."

"Ah," Three nodded and gave Medusa an understanding look,

---

8. Greek pancakes made with wheat flour, olive oil, curdled milk, and honey.

9. Eos was the personification of the dawning of a new day, bright and cheerful. She had a bit of a dark side too. She had several bad breakups, and the guys paid for slighting her. Eos gave as good or better than she got. Just ask Tithonus or Cephalus.

"like he was feeling something for who he was with." She reached over and gave Medusa's hand a little reassuring squeeze.

"Pink frosted?" Mod brightened and gave a snort. "I do remember saying that. You laughed and told me I was being mean to Eos."

He must have expected a smile back, but the look on Medusa's face made the grin slide from his.

"Eos was so bright and hopeful when she was young, but life happened." Medusa stared back, resigned now instead of angry. "I admire what she's doing. She had a rough patch and is making a fresh start of things."

"A fresh batch of pancakes sounds good," Mod said. "I like pancakes."

A single tear ran out of the corner of Medusa's eye. "I asked you if eight o'clock would be good." Medusa's voice sounded disembodied to her own ears.

"Oh, yeah. I remember." The grin returned to Mod's face. "I said that it would be. I usually eat breakfast about that time . . . You know, I didn't have breakfast today. I probably should have eaten something."

Three shook her head with pity.

Mod stood there, still clueless as ever. "What?"

The tremor in Medusa's bottom lip returned.

"Breakfast? This morning? It was a date," Three explained with a weary sigh.

"A date?" Mod asked like he didn't understand. "Me?" He pointed at himself. "With you?" He pointed at Medusa. "We hang out all the time. Why would you call it a date?"

Medusa wasn't capable of responding.

"So I didn't show for breakfast? What's the big deal?" He shrugged to Medusa. "I'll buy you lunch after we meet with Ktesibios. You can come, too, Three." Mod paused and thought about it for a second. "I still want to work on the pump though. Probably best if we grab lunch beforehand. Bearing lubricant clings to the fingers, and then you taste it if the slightest bit gets on your food. Cutting fluid is like that too."[10]

"I don't want to grab lunch, and I won't be going to help with whatever the hells machine you're working on with Ktesibios." Medusa didn't realize how much she was hoping for this date with Mod until all possibility of it actually being a thing was gone. "I put myself out there, in a way that was uncomfortable for me to do, because I thought there might be something."

"Something?" Mod asked.

The man is really and truly oblivious.

Having Mod ask the question made it feel as if Mother Gaea had dropped out from beneath Medusa's feet. She couldn't bring herself to answer him.

"A relationship," Three clarified.

"We have a relationship," Mod said to Medusa, as if he thought this entire conversation had been ridiculous. "You're my friend. I hang out with you all the time."

"It was supposed to be a date," Medusa said, her anger waning as she fought to hold back the fresh wave of tears that threatened to break loose. "I thought this friendship could turn into more . . ." She let the thought trail off. "I was obviously wrong."

"I couldn't be closer to you if you were family to me." Mod sounded like he was afraid he'd hurt her feelings and he was trying his best to patch it up. "You're just like Doug to me."

Somehow, that simple statement made it all the more clear to Medusa. She was never going to find what she was looking for with Mod.

"That's the problem, isn't it? I've taken the place of your brother, leading you around, hanging out with you as a friend . . . I'm not Doug."

Mod stood there, the little brass hooks held loosely in his hand,

---

10. I learned this through personal experience. Worst movie popcorn I ever ate, and I was too dense and stubborn to figure out why. I still ate the whole bag.

the slow look of realization of what he'd most likely just lost drawing on his face.

Medusa didn't say anything else as she turned and walked away.

CHAPTER 4

VIP TOURISM

THE TOUR GUIDE WAVED THEM ALL FORWARD. "EVERYONE HAS their name tags on?"

The group responded with a series of mumbles and grunts.

"We all have a tour buddy?" She peered around the group just to make sure.

The giant redhead in the group reached over to grab Set's hand, as Set was the giant's assigned tour buddy. Set slapped the oversized fingers away.

The giant looked a bit crestfallen as he rubbed his swatted fingers.

"Good!" The tour guide hopped in place and clapped her hands a bit too enthusiastically. "I'm Minthe, and I'll be taking you all on a journey to the center of the universe today. You're actually my second group,[1] and I hope we can all enjoy this journey of learning, discovery, and wonder together."

"How'd the tour go over with the first group?" someone asked.

There was a little twitch in the corner of Minthe's eye. She didn't answer the question as she motioned them forward with little come-hither hand motions. "And we're walking. We're walking."

---

1. Minthe, former girlfriend of Hades, was the guide giving underworld tours to the newly dead of the Greeks. The Greek queen of the underworld, Persephone, didn't like Hades having his old girlfriend as an employee. After Persephone caught the two hanging out by the water cooler and laughing, she wrote a letter to her husband suggesting it was time for Minthe to find a new position.

Minthe is very, *very* thankful to be leading this group instead of any of the other positions Persephone suggested.

Minthe just really hopes that nothing goes wrong with the tour.

A smattering of gods from several pantheons were present in the tour group.

The red-headed giant was Thor, the thunder bringer from the Norse, and Viracocha, the god maker of the Incas, creator of all things and from whom sprang all things, had his two-legged, leashed pet with him, who was, ironically, also named Thor.[2] Tagging along behind Viracocha was Unkulunkulu from the Zulu creation mythos, easily recognized because he rode a cow made of reeds and led along a rather dull-looking reed man on a tether. Frowning Buga of Siberia trudged along the path and dragged along his mangled lyre behind him. And bringing up the rear was a quartet of Sumerian gods: Anu, Enlil, Enki, and Ninhursag.

Set, the shapeshifting canid of the Egyptians, was in the middle of the group, his walking stick in hand. He tried very hard to look as if he wasn't ready to bolt or that he didn't hold violent disdain for everyone that surrounded him.

Set recognized some of them from the beginning, but to him, one god was pretty much like another. He hated them all, but didn't care what they did, as long as they didn't get in his way.

Set had stewed over the problem for a long time, unable to get to the spot where his heart was trapped because it was in the center of the world. The sands of Egypt were really hard to dig a stable, eight-thousand-miles-straight-down well in. Sure, there was bedrock and mantle and the core after a while, but it was the beginning of the hole that was really hard to get started. The sides kept caving in, and Set was too proud to go out and hire a Phoenician engineer to do it right.[3]

Set initially thought he may have been able to sneak into the

---

2. The Incan creator of the universe had booked the vacation for him and his plus one under the name "Con Tici." I have it on good authority that Thor Heyerdahl slept at the foot of the bed.

3. During the invasion of Greece, the Persian army had to dig a canal to bring the navy into striking distance of the enemy. The canal kept collapsing, except for the section constructed by the Phoenicians, who started digging twice the width at the top as the canal had to be at the bottom.

entrance that led right to the center of the universe that lay in Greece. But the lots drawn by the gods at the beginning, the lots that gave them rule and reign over this slice of creation or that one, made it almost impossible for a god to cross a border uninvited without all the other gods and goddesses tied to the workings of the Grand Machine—*all of them*—coming after the one doing the illegal crossing.

The only way to enter another god's territory was for them to invite you in. And gods and goddesses, being what they were, didn't often try to rub shoulders with their equals.

There was no way for Set to get into Greece without being invited, not without having every other being in existence contract-bound to stop Set from doing what it was he planned to do.

And all those gods and goddesses against Set? Not good odds at all.

If he was just up against the Greeks, Set might have considered it. That wasn't really a big enough threat to stop him even then, until the Greek gods started putting all the horrors and monstrosities they'd defeated into prison here and there near the core, which helped bar the path Set needed to take.

It was hopeless. There was no way Set would be able to go up against Echidna, mother of monsters and all her little monsterlings. And then there was Typhon. Set might be able to take Typhon in a fair fight, but Typhon didn't fight fair. Set could bring along a companion or friend to fight alongside, but being heartless, he'd already burned pretty much any viable bridges to comrades who might have helped.

So there was no way across the border of the Greeks without being invited in, the Greek gods and goddesses would fight him tooth and nail even if he did, and unbeatable monsters blocked the way and warded the path to the thing Set most desired.

Set was almost ready to give up.

Then Hades had all but invited Set right to the spot he needed to go for the paltry price of admission and the hopes of further spending on overpriced snacks.

It wasn't like Hades needed the money. The tour group walked past diamonds, silver, emeralds, rubies, and gold as they made their way deeper into the world. Hades had wealth in spades, but like every other rich being, he never would pass up a chance to make a bit more.[4]

The rich don't often think of consequences, at least not as they apply to them. But Hades wasn't like the other rich beings. This wasn't about money. This was something different. This was about *pride*.

Hades had the wealth of the underworld, but then, there were other rich gods in other pantheons. So one-upping each other by showing off your treasure was pointless. If wealth didn't matter, what could you show off that was so special, so unique that even other gods didn't have access to it?

The center of the universe was a pretty unique thing.

Even the other Greek gods couldn't lay claim to the path to the machine. It was Hades's shiny bauble and his alone. It was the one thing a god could possess that would truly allow him to thumb his nose at his neighbors. But how could Hades show off his very special thing to his peers if all of them were barred from your realm by ancient treaty?

Invite them in.

Hades, bless his shriveled, shrunken black heart, had decided to start having tours. And Set had jumped at the chance to be a part of it. He still wasn't quite fast enough to secure a spot in the first group, but being a part of the second group was quite an accomplishment. The concept of the tour had proved popular, and it was solidly sold out for bookings for the next few centuries at least.

---

4. A local radio ad has the tagline "I won't lose a deal over a dollar. You have my word on it!" I'm sure the family of the businessman in question starts to sweat when someone mentions he has a nice grandma. "What kind of deal can I make to send you home with this pristine, fully loaded Nana today?"

Being invited in by one with authority grants access past secure borders. Have them pay a small fee, using exact change in the denomination you specify just to frustrate and humiliate them a little bit, all so they can have a chance to gawk at the thing that makes you more special than they are.

Set had to admit, he was a little impressed by what Hades had done to stroke his ego. Set appreciated anyone that took any chance to put any god in his or her place.

Money or hubris, whatever the reason, it didn't matter. Set was closer to his goal than he had been since the dawn of creation. He grinned, revealing his long row of sharp, canid teeth. He could hardly contain his excitement.

It was a little humiliating and frustrating to be part of a tour group full of second-tier morons when all Set wanted to do was run ahead, steal back his heart, and watch the universe and everyone in it burn. Still, patience would serve him well. Though he had been to the center of the universe when it was created, he was unfamiliar with most of Hades's realm and the lands beneath it. Even though he was past the border of the Greek underworld now, if he left the tour group it *may* raise the alarms, and a wrong turn or unforeseen obstacle would be enough for the guards of the underworld to be set upon him.

Better to take his time, make his way to the center of the Grand Machine without unnecessarily wearing himself out, and be safely shepherded past all the pitfalls and potential traps that may lie ahead.

The tour guide stopped, and Set was so lost in his own thoughts that he almost bumped into the back of Thor, his tour buddy.

Thor's cape smelled like a goat, and not in a good way. Set took a closer look at the garment. It might actually be made from the remains of a goat, and not one that had lived a clean, unchallenged life. Set wrinkled his snout in distaste and took a step back from Thor's stench as Minthe continued to ramble on.

"And here we are starting to see the underpinnings of the universe. All the mechanics that run the great machines that keep all of your mythologies up and running." Minthe clung to her clipboard as she took the band of sightseers along through the dark tunnel that led further and further toward the center of the earth.

Set looked back over his shoulder. He was sure there was someone here that wasn't a part of the group.

Someone that followed him.

Against his better judgment, Set raised his hand. He tried to shake it back and forth to get Minthe's attention from behind Thor's bulk. It didn't work. Eventually Set dropped his hand and called out instead. "Miss?"

Minthe stopped and hopped around in a little half circle to face the group. "Yes?"

"Are we all the entities that signed up for the tour?"

She paused for a second. The question must have caught her off guard. "There are always situations that can't be planned for that change the itineraries of those who wish to experience a special day. Not everyone who signs up for something can always be there."

So the answer to his question wasn't yes.

"You wouldn't mind telling me who it was that couldn't make it, by chance?" Set asked nonchalantly.

Minthe waggled her finger at Set. "Oh, you! That would be proprietary information. I can't give that out."

"Just curious." Set held up his hands and shrugged as if it made no difference to him.

It would have to be someone from Egypt, but why would anyone back home tail Set on what appeared to most likely be a vacation? There was no way that any of the Egyptian gods, or any other god for that matter, would have any idea what Set thought or attempted to do.

But what if somehow someone did?

Set searched the shadows behind the group but found nothing for his efforts, his fingers turning white and bloodless he gripped his walking stick so tightly.

He saw no one.

The feeling was there, just the same.

Thor—the god, not the leashed pet—took a step back and bumped into Set. The hammer hanging off the belt of Thor's backside swung backward and popped Set in the groin with a wicked spark.

It didn't hurt as much as it could have, but the thump and spark from the hammer almost pushed Set over the edge. "Watch it, you overgrown hippo." Set whipped his staff around and the tip of the stick snapped Thor in the back of his head with a little lightning bolt of his own.[5]

"You are also a thunder god?" Thor smoothed his ginger locks back against his skull, clearly amazed there could be more than one god with such a power. "Forgive Thor, small, dog-headed manchild. Thor's shoulders are broad, and Thor is often unaware of the destruction Thor's awesome physique causes on Thor's lessers."

The length of Set's staff crackled with increased energy. "I don't know whether to kill you for your self-aggrandizing attitude or your clunky usage of third person when referring to yourself."

Minthe was between them in an instant. "Gentlebeings, there is still much to be seen on the tour. If you'd kindly refrain from killing each other until after the grand reveal?"

"What happens if Thor kills the little dogface before then?" Thor asked. "Thor is inquiring about this hypothetically, of course."

"Such a course of action wouldn't be advisable." Minthe clapped her hands together, hopped in place, and cocked her head to the side. "Master Hades would be called in to deal with any situation that resulted in harm to a member of another pantheon, of course. And don't go sharing any of your pantheon's secrets either. Master Hades frowns upon that as well."

"So If Thor asked little dogface how his people make mead or

---

5. When Ra adopted Set, he gave Set the powers of the thunder of the sky. Set used his newfound powers to scare the locals and frizz out Osiris's hair.

Thor decided to kill little dog-faced man, the dark, broody, scary Hades would scold Thor?" Thor asked.

"Master Hades's judgements are harsh but fair. He'd find a way to deal with the situation taking into account the guilt of all participants involved. You signed the waiver of rights to accompany us on the tour that granted him final powers over you, and those agreements are eternal and binding. Master Hades does not mess around." Minthe pointed up above their heads where the demi-god Deipneus, strapped to a rotating, burning wheel, was having his liver ripped out by an eagle with two heads.[6] Honey Maid, goddess of grain in some obscure Baltic country that only lasted three months, was being tortured in a similar fashion to her companion in crime.

"Members of the first tour group. They betrayed deeply held, proprietary trade secrets in Hades's realm." Minthe chirped.

"For the love of gods, goddesses, and grains," Honey Maid cried as a gore-soaked raptor poked her in the giblets with its beak, "all I did was share with him my graham cracker recipe!"

"Master Hades likes to make an example of the first ones to cause an infraction so all those that follow are sure to get the point. Master Hades is just and wise." Minthe beamed as she watched the beings being tortured above.

"Is Master Hades close by?" Thor asked as he shrank back from the sight above him.

Minthe shrugged.

Not the most reassuring of responses, Set thought.

Thor gulped. "Thor retracts Thor's inquiry, and Thor promises to observe all the rules of the tour."

"What an embarrassment," Set said of Thor as he shook his head and sneered.

Set wouldn't mind seeing what punishment Hades might concoct

---

6. The Greek god of the preparation of meals, specifically the making of bread. The Paul Hollywood of ancient Greece, if you will.

for Thor. But then, Set wouldn't mind seeing Hades and all the other beings in existence die horribly either.

Patience, Set reminded himself, *seeing that all happen is closer now than it has ever been.*

Minthe eyed Set suspiciously, so Set buried his current feelings deep where they couldn't be seen so he could accomplish his higher goal.

"You know what?" Set said as he feigned humility and a sense of compromise. "There seems to be a bit of tension between me and Sparkles here. Even though he is my tour buddy and all, I still think It might be best if I head back toward the back of the group to give Coppertone a bit more room for his bulging musculature." He pointed the end of his walking stick to the place in the group he intended to occupy.

"Coppertone?" Thor looked about, confused for a moment as he tried to parse out who they referred to.

"Names based on hair color may be a bit too subtle," Unkulunkulu said as he pointed his nose knowingly in Thor's direction. "He seems to be but a child in his understanding of things."

"Child? Who is this Coppertone baby you reference?"[7] The neurons must have finally connected because the light of understanding dawned in his eyes. "Thor does have luxuriant, flowing red tresses, doesn't Thor?"

Or maybe not, because Thor still sought to clarify.

"You speak of Thor, don't you, little dog-faced man?" The Norse god approached the Egyptian, the look on his face triumphant and conciliatory. "You mean to give Thor more room?"

There was no way Set would give into his immediate urges. Killing Thor would be a pleasure, but it wasn't worth risking Set's ultimate goal. The temptation was still there, though.

---

7. Anyone over the age of forty should know who the Coppertone Baby is. It was a pretty famous print ad. If Thor is the baby in the picture, Set would be the dog that bit the baby's shorts.

Set grinned a tight smile and nodded as he tried his best not to use his walking stick as a bludgeon.

Thor clapped Set hard on the shoulder. "By the golden spittle that drips to Thor's father's pillow during Thor's father's Odinsleep! You are kind and gracious for a coward."

The grin on Set's face took on the look and feel of a death rictus, but he maintained it just the same.

The muscle-bound moron will die by my hand as soon as I get my heart back.

Set nodded despite how his clamped jaw damaged his teeth. "I'll just be over here," he managed through gritted teeth as he pointed over his shoulder toward the back of the group.

Minthe narrowed her eyes at Set, but she didn't point out any flaw in his suggestion. She nodded to him and turned back to lead the group onward again.

"Once the Grand Machine was up and running, the gods and goddesses of creation agreed to draw lots, with slices of the heavens and earth associated with each lot giving absolute power over that small slice granted unto the holder. The Greeks just happened to draw the lot holding the center of the universe in their slice. Everyone had the same chance of taking the lot containing the nexus of all, but that lot fell to the Greek creator, Chaos," Minthe told the group as they worked their way deeper underground. "The lot of ownership passed from one god to another as the children of Chaos grew, supplanted him, and ruled in his stead. The gods of Olympus saw the immense responsibility of their lot and broke it up so the burden of creation wouldn't fall on one alone."

Viracocha, god and father of all Incas, rolled his eyes and poked his slave on a tether.

Thor Heyerdahl sighed, straightened up, and spoke in a courtly voice. "My master wishes to convey that he knows all of this. He was there, at the beginning."

Viracocha looked above the heads of all the rest assembled in a pious manner and smugly pursed his lips.

High on the back of the cow made of reeds, Unkulunkulu rolled his eyes and shared a *please* glance with Buga. Buga just shook his head, acted like he focused on tuning his mangled lyre, and let the scowl on his face deepen.

"You weren't the only one there when they turned on the machine, Viracocha," Enlil pointed out. "But like the rest of us, you weren't important enough to see what was going on in the center of it all."

"Second stringer," Buga muttered with a dark chuckle.

"So are the lot of you," Viracocha pouted and folded his arms over his chest in a huff.

"He gets testy when people don't realize how important he is," Thor Heyerdahl explained.

His master slapped the tethered slave upside the back of his head.

"Let's all be kind to each other on the tour." Minthe pointed above her head in a slowly rotating motion that hinted and felt of a thinly veiled threat.

The gentle reminder of the burning wheels in the sky got the message across.

"What of the horrors and killers that are imprisoned in the depths of Hades's realm?" Enlil asked. "Will we get to see any of them?"

Set's ears perked up. He was interested in the answer to this one.

"That is a very good question." Minthe beamed. "Most of the entities that call the depths of Mother Gaea home are usually just happy to be left alone, and so we follow a path that steers clear of most of them. Master Hades has negotiated deals with some of the others, so that they may benefit, and in some cases even work for him should the need arise. It is a very beneficial arrangement. To answer your question, this isn't a zoo, so you probably won't see any of the persons or things that call this place home. If you're lucky."

The last bit was added on with a hint of malice. Minthe smiled as perkily as ever, but Set was almost sure he caught a flash of evil in her eye.

I'm liking our guide more than I thought I would. Too bad I'm going to kill her too.

A sudden thought brought Set up short. Sure, Minthe and the creations of the gods would die when the Grand Machine broke apart, but what about the gods themselves? Quite a few of them were around before the universe was created. Set assumed they would be tied to the Grand Machine in some way, and that the Grand Machine's destruction would take them out with it. But what if he was wrong? He'd have to hunt them down and kill them one by one, which could be difficult if the universe was gone and there was nothing to hide behind anymore.

I guess I'll just deal with it when or if it comes up. Set sighed. *Why can't things just be simple?*

Minthe resumed the tour, and the group lumbered along in glum silence. She paused in the opening of a large cavern. "Over here you'll see a collection of basalt columns that look incredibly like the frozen visages of the damned."

"Where?" Thor turned around just a tad too quick and thumped his head on a protruding stalactite.

"Odin's soup-sodden whiskers!" The thunder god rubbed his tenderized temple. "How do you blasted mortals manage to navigate in such cramped quarters?" He peered at the basalt column with one eye closed. "Thor thrives in open spaces like the tops of clouds and the sky, and wide-open seas and plains." He backed up into a calcite column, and it startled him. "Thor doesn't like these low ceilings and narrow ways."

"Why did you come along with us on this tour, anyway?" Set asked from the back of the group.

The others nodded along that they also would like to know.

"'Tis embarrassing," Thor said.

While most of the god's assembled rolled their eyes, Minthe was encouraging. "We're all friends here. This is a safe space where you can share anything without being judged."

Thor Heyerdahl snorted.

Viracocha gave the man a light, reproving backhand that bowled his servant over.

"It's all right." Minthe looked on earnestly. "Go ahead."

"Tis just that, Thor's brother, Loki, hid Thor's hammer from Thor. He told Thor that Thor could find Mjölnir if Thor plumbed the depths to the places where the lights of the heavens dare not shine."

As a group, all the gods and individuals positioned behind Thor turned and looked at the hammer hanging off the back of the god's belt so it bounced back and forth between his right and left cheek.

"Don't tell him," Set said, as a broad grin creased his snout. "Good one, Loki."

"Yes, Loki, Thor's brother." The thunder god spun about and faced the Egyptian god, and the hammer swung freely from the tether behind Thor. "You know of him?"

Minthe gasped when she saw the hammer.

The prank was up. Now our guide, Horus Honor-buddy,[8] *will be duty bound to tell him.*

"Thor? About your hammer?" Minthe pointed to his backside.

Thor spun about several times before he saw what she was pointing at. "Thor's hammer!" he cried. He snuggled the weapon against his cheek. "But Loki said Thor must plumb the depths where the sun failed to . . ." His eyes widened as understanding dawned. "Oh, brother! Truly you are the best of jokesters, making Thor take such a quest as this to secure a tool nestled in Thor's mighty crack. Such humor!" Thor thrust the hammer aloft, broke off a large stalactite and promptly dropped the huge chunk of calcified stone on his head.

"He just killed himself," Thor Heyerdahl noted.

Unkulunkulu looked down from the back of his cow and directed his reed man to poke the prone god.

---

8. Horus Honor-buddy is the Egyptian equivalent of Goody Two-Shoes.

"He's not dead. Look." The reed man pointed at Thor's gut. "His stomach is moving."[9]

"You can't win them all," Set said.

Looks like I'll still have the joy of killing this one. I could explain Thor's killing as something done for the greater good of all, were I not about to kill everyone else as well.

While Set pondered this pleasant thought, Thor opened his eyes and brought his hand to his temple. "That must have been some good mead."

"No apparent damage done." Set shrugged. "Well, that was fun while it lasted. Shall we get on with the tour now? It's not as if we have all day to waste." He indicated himself and all the others assembled in a broad, all-encompassing gesture. "Gods, just taking a break, you know. Haven't got all eternity to watch Thor repeatedly bludgeon himself."

Unkulunkulu laughed from the back of his cow. "I could watch it a few more times."[10]

The Sumerian gods nodded that they wouldn't mind a repeat performance either. Even frowning Buga cracked a smile.

"That's not really what the tour is about," Minthe said nervously as she made the little come-along motions with her hands. "We're walking. We're walking."

It took a bit, but almost all of the gods and hangers-on soon followed their guide deeper into the earth.

Set hung back, just a bit.

He searched the way he'd just passed but saw no hint of motion from the presence he was sure followed him. Maybe there was nothing there? Maybe Set was just on edge because he was so close to his goal? It didn't hurt to be careful, though.

---

9. One of my favorite lines from *Strange Brew*. I love the McKenzie brothers.
10. A lot of people enjoy watching other people hurt themselves. There are hundreds of thousands of views on random YouTube videos of women slipping when they try the latest TikTok dance or guys on ziplines crotching themselves on trees.

With a final glance behind, Set looked forward to the close, and hopefully very brief, future.

Thor was the perfect distraction. No one would pay attention to Set with that idiot about.

When creation had happened, and Ptah had taken Set's heart and put it in the machine, Set had cared a great deal about getting his heart back. It was his, after all. Yet the more he got used to life without a heart, the less Set missed it. Set had originally wanted to get to the center of the universe to get his heart back, but now he just wanted to pull the pin holding everything together and watch the Grand Machine fall apart.

Doing so might just kill Set too, but no plan was perfect.

Set wished he could be there to watch the face of Ptah as everything the god worked for was erased with the destruction of the universe. It would be very satisfying to lean in and whisper, "Should have used a different heart for a bearing, old man."

It would be so very nice to have Ptah know what his unthinking actions had wrought.

Set hurried after the others, not wanting Minthe to notice his absence and really start to pay attention to him. He didn't want to risk any complications.

Not when he was this close.

CHAPTER 5

THE FOOD CART OF DESTRUCTION

MEDUSA TRUDGED ALONG THE PATH ON THE OUTSKIRTS OF THE city of Larissa, her mood black as she ever remembered it being and her jaw set.

Mod and Three followed her somewhere close behind.

"Medusa? Please?" Mod said.

Don't say anything to him. Don't say anything to him. Don't say anything to him.

"Medusa?" Three sounded concerned.

"I'm ignoring you both," Medusa said. "Go away."

For a moment she worried it might actually work. But Three was nothing if not dogged and loyal to a fault. And Mod? Mod was also dogged and loyal to a fault. *And* thick and clueless. That was one of his most endearing qualities. Labeling him as such actually endeared him to her more.

She contemplated stopping then, of talking to her friends about what was really wrong. Mod had disappointed her, but that wasn't the reason she wanted to walk away. Medusa had a hard time letting go of things. She had a hard time letting go of one thing in particular.

If her curse had been so easy to reverse, it could just as easily come back, right?

And Medusa had no idea when or if that would happen. Medusa shivered, wrapped her arms tight about her despite the warmth of the day, and trudged on in silence.

The others were still following her anyway. Medusa could hear the *thwip, thwip, thwip* of Mod's sandals on the path behind her.[1]

_____

1. Great idea for a comedy/horror film: *The Flip Flop Killer.* They heard the *fwip,*

46

"You were never any good at surprising Doug when you were younger, were you?"

The thwiping paused for a beat as Mod stopped in the road. "How did you know?"

"Lucky guess."

"It was a misunderstanding. I'm an idiot," Mod said. "Please, don't be mad. Things just don't penetrate my skull the way they should."

"True. He is an idiot," Three said.

Medusa stopped in the road and lowered her head in a huff. "Is there any way in Hades the two of you are going to leave me alone?"

"Friend is a funny word," Three said. "What I understand from my studies is that it is something like a 95 percent love, 5 percent hate relationship. But the only way to get past the 5 percent is sticking around until the 5 percent is over."

That was actually a fairly astute observation, or so Medusa suspected. She'd have to take Three's word on the matter. Medusa hadn't had many friends before. Any really.

Her mother and father and kin, Keto and Phorkys and their spawn, had been the family on the block that none of the good parents of respectable standing in society would let their kids associate with.[2]

Medusa could have hung out with her siblings, but then again . . .

The most appealing life she could imagine had been a solitary one, far away from the relations and family drama of the multi-gener-

---

fwip, fwip of the footsteps getting closer. They might outrun it if there was an open stretch, but there's nowhere left to run; the night stockers had blocked all the aisles with over-stacked pallets. "I've got you," the killer said. "No one knows the aisles of BigBoxMart like one born and bred of the hells of its loading dock. Prepare to be RollBacked®."

2. Phorkys and Keto were brother and sister (a common theme in a lot of myths) and had a bunch of kids that might have benefited had the genes been a little more diverse. Maybe. Monstrosities may just be a dominant trait, and the sibling-lovebirds passed on the best ones to their kids: the Gorgons, the Graeae (three witch sisters that share one eye), Echidna (the mother of monsters), Ladon the Dragon, and Jeffrey Tambor.

trailer park in the depths of Mother Gaea. A celibate life, dedicated to service and quiet contemplation in the temple of Athena, away from family and lovers and relatives, was the way to go.

And look how well that had turned out.

So when Medusa had been cursed, she'd half believed she deserved it just because of who she was related to.

Monsters, Medusa thought to herself. *I am related to monsters, so what else could I be? The lotus fruit never falls far from the tree.*[3]

Now, for the first time in her life, she had friends. People who loved her despite who she had been and who didn't give a rat's ass about who she was related to. She probably ought to give the only good things to ever happen in her life another chance.

But that didn't mean she had to like it.

She turned and looked at Three and Mod. Medusa bit on her lower lip and cocked her jaw to the side. "Fine." She glared at Mod. "You've stopped me in my forward progression. Now what?"

"Are we going to discuss the miscommunication about potential romance, or whatever other big thing it is that's bugging you?" Three asked.

The second part of her question took Medusa by surprise. Three must have known there was something else going on, even though Medusa hadn't said anything about it.

"Let's just deal with Mod for the moment," Medusa said cryptically. "I don't think I can handle much else."

"Fair enough." Three gave Medusa a look that hinted she would be there when Medusa was ready. Then Three grabbed Mod by the shoulder and gave him a little push forward. "It's all on you now, Slick."

"I'm sorry I misunderstood about dinner," Mod said sheepishly.

"Breakfast," Three corrected.

---

3. Lotus fruit: persimmons. Waxy, slimy, and not very sweet when they are ripe. Unripe, they are tart, stick to the roof of your mouth, and it takes forever for the flavor to wear off the surface of your tongue.

"The meal." Mod looked at his feet as he scuffed his sandals in the dirt. "I don't want you leaving while you're mad and hungry, because I do care for you. I can't take care of the mad part, but I can, at least, take care of the hungry bit." He paused and looked up, a look equal parts endearing and pleading on his face. "Can I buy you lunch?"

That was almost nuanced and smooth. Medusa was a bit shocked that it had just come out of Mod's mouth. "I guess it wouldn't hurt to eat something."

"And with that, I'm out." Three bowed and excused herself. "You two kids have a nice meal."

Mod looked a bit panicked. "You're not coming?"

"I don't really need to eat. As in, I only eat when I want to experience what it is you meat puppets experience." Three flexed, stretched, and jogged in place. "If I do feel a bit out of sorts, I treat myself to Greased Nike's Signature Service."[4] Three stopped jogging and craned her neck around while lifting the hem of her chiton so she partially exposed a sticker on the outside of her left thigh. "I've got a checkup in twenty-seven hundred miles."

Three waved at the two of them and power walked away.

Mod turned to Medusa and gave a weak smile. It was obvious he was uncomfortable with the situation.

"Don't make it weird." Medusa grabbed him by the wrist and pulled him toward the restaurant district of the city.

They walked in awkward silence until the shops and dining areas began to appear.

"We can go by your friend's place," Mod suggested.

"She's only open for breakfast," Medusa said.

Mod stopped and looked at a sign.

"Isn't this it?" Mod pointed at the food wagon. "I thought you said she made pancakes?"

Medusa looked at the sign and panicked a bit at what she read.

---

4. The Jiffy Lube of the ancients.

"Eos. My friend's name is Eos, and yes, she only makes breakfast. This is not a place run by Eos." She grabbed Mod by the wrist and tried to lead him away.

"Well it's afternoon. So this could work, couldn't it? Enyo's Gyros. Sounds spicy," Mod said. "What do you think?"

"Do you actually know Enyo?" Medusa asked. "Goddess of destruction? Have you heard of her?"

"Well, yeah, but why would a goddess be running a food cart," Mod asked.

"Stranger things have happened." Medusa eyed the wagon with a sense of growing fear. "Eating a destruction wrap isn't high on my list of desired experiences. Let's go."

"Calling them that doesn't mean the food is going to destroy you."[5] Mod actually chuckled and stood rooted in the spot. "I'm sure the name is just supposed to be edgy and catchy."

Medusa shook her head and tried to steer Mod back to town. "If Enyo has anything to do with this, we want nothing to do with it."

"Seriously, though? How bad can it be?" Mod tugged Medusa forward and the screen for the order window rolled up.

"Hello, soon to be satisfied customers!" Enyo beamed from behind the counter.

Medusa wasn't prepared to see two eyes and short-cropped red hair,[6] but she recognized the face nonetheless. For a moment Medusa froze. Seeing her sister, a monster from her childhood, right in front of her was almost too close to Medusa's growing fears. Someone from her past showing up now overwrote any thought of giving her sister a chance.

Better safe than sorry.

"Goodbye bowel-destroying monster," Medusa said as soon as she

---

5. You'll have to wait for the emergence of Taco Bell and their so-called "Tex-Mex" before a restaurant becomes proud of their ability to destroy its patrons.

6. As one of the Graeae, Enyo should have gray hair and one eye that she shared with her two sisters. She'd obviously had a bit of work done.

could talk again.[7] She latched onto Mod's arm and began bodily pulling him toward other options.

Enyo's face fell at the prospect of losing a customer, then a look of pure confusion took over. "Wait a minute. Medusa? Little sister?"

Medusa froze again. She'd hoped the interaction had been quick enough that she wouldn't be recognized. She took a deep, steadying breath and turned around, her hands still locked in a death grip on Mod's upper arm just in case she decided to flee. "Yeah. It's me. Hi, Enyo."

The look of confusion intensified. "The snakes, and the stony gaze—"

"Gone." Medusa nervously patted her hair and was relieved she hadn't touched a roiling mass of serpents. "Long story, but gone."

"Oh, I'm so glad! That was a terrible thing, and there was no way you deserved it."

"Uh, thanks." It was awkward talking to her older sister, and she really didn't want to prolong the visit if she didn't have to. "Nice to see you, but we gotta run." She started pulling Mod toward the local franchise location of Kyamites Legumarama.[8]

"Please," Enyo said. "You can't write me off until you at least try something on the menu. I just . . . I just really need for this to work out."

Enyo sounded so sincere. It sounded nothing like the older witch of a sister who used to torture the kids she babysat—Medusa included —when their parents would go out to paint the town red.[9]

Eos. Enyo. How many of the women from my past are struggling to

---

7. Enyo and Medusa went to the same academy, which is to say they were home-schooled. Medusa was voted "most likely to succeed" by their siblings, and Enyo won the title of "most likely to destroy a prehistoric civilization". The prediction for Medusa hadn't come to pass, while Enyo had succeeded several times.

8. Kyamites: the Athenian god of beans. I'm not joking. The humble bean is the breadth and depth and scope of his realm. The other gods let him pretend to lord over legumes and lentils, but he really only rules the beans.

9. Dates between Phorkys and Keto usually ended up with a burgeoning civilization being razed to the ground.

make a new go of it? Medusa admitted she'd have to add herself to that number. Medusa stopped trying to pull Mod somewhere else.

She turned to Enyo and committed to at least talk to her. "You look good."

Enyo actually blushed. Medusa never would have expected blushing from her witch of an older sister. "So how did you do it?"

"There was this sorceress I met at the witch's convention. Cosmetolia does amazing things with dyes and powders and such.[10] She concocted a powder to give my skin a smoother, healthier glow. She said my hair was pretty coarse and thick because it was gray, but as you can tell, she can work magic." She fluffed up her hair so you could see all the hues and highlights in it. The color looked unbelievably natural. "And the eyes? Well, there was this one time I was talking with Argus Panoptes at a community mixer,[11] and I mentioned what beautiful eyes he had, and he just up and gave me a pair." She blinked hard and fluttered her lashes to show them off a bit.

"Well, the eyes and the hair suit you," Medusa said. "I've never seen you look better."

Enyo seemed as if she didn't quite know what to do with the positive feedback.

"So how did you become proprietor of this fine establishment?" Medusa asked.

Enyo tried to smile. "Heh. Desperation?" She shook her head. "I'm trying to change so many things, and I thought I needed something to do, something concrete, so I wouldn't slide back into destructive habits."

---

10. Cosmetolia: goddess of cosmetics. She was first introduced to the world in the epic classic *The Twelve Trials of Doug* by Jeremy Brundage. I'm sure you have a copy of that literary masterpiece on your nightstand, and if not, you should buy one right now. Available in paperback and digital e-book!

11. Argus Panoptes: the hundred eyed guardian of the heifer-nymph Io. He's the focus in both the nightmares and the dreams of optometrists.

Oh, gods, goddesses, and demi-deities, my sister is saying the exact things I'm thinking.

"Self-destructive tendencies, huh?" Mod said in an apparent attempt to be part of the discussion.

"No," Medusa explained. "Enyo pretty much destroys anything and everything around her."

A bit of Enyo's enthusiasm bled away as she continued to deal with someone who knew her from her past. "It's true; I just wish that wasn't the case. If I could just change the way my talents were used, focus them a bit, you know?" She hung her head a little. "I'd always thought of how cooking and destruction are inexplicably linked. Can't make an omelet without scrambling eggs. Crush and grind a grain to powder and drown it and you can make bread or pasta. Smash a garlic clove, mix it with milk you've let ferment, add a cucumber you've hacked apart with a blade and you've got tzatziki. Sometimes good things can come from the destruction of others." She sighed and untied her apron from the back. "At least that was what I was thinking."

Mod nodded along with her explanation as if he agreed. "She's got a good point."

"Hold up," Medusa said to Enyo. "I guess we could at least look at what you got before I condemn you for it."

Enyo retied the knot on her apron and smiled. "Now you're talking! I'm gonna make you guys such a dish. You won't regret it."

"Doubtful," Medusa said. She steered Mod toward the solitary booth. "But it's not like I haven't taken chances on other hopeless cases before."

"Really?" Mod asked. "How did that work out?"

Medusa grumbled and pushed Mod down on the rickety bench, a sour, resigned look on her face as she did so. She sat down opposite him. She was with a guy whose social awkwardness measured on the

Santorini scale,[12] eating at a lunch wagon that screamed of impending botulinic health violations, and was in the presence of a woman who'd effectively ruined every childhood memory Medusa had growing up. "Bring it on, Enyo. Let's see what kind of twisted sense of humor the fates really have."

At least, Medusa thought, *the day can't get any lower than this.*

---

12. The Santorini volcano is the largest volcano in Greece. All destructive forces are measured against it. Like our current use of the Richter scale.

CHAPTER 6

THINGS NOT LISTED ON THE ITINERARY

WE'RE GETTING CLOSE NOW, SET THOUGHT.

The unmistakable smell of Set's smoking heart permeated the air. No one else had mentioned it, but Set noticed several of the other gods unconsciously licking their lips. Set didn't blame them. His overworked, misused heart smelled delicious[1].

The tour group came to the large stone doors that closed off the final chamber before they could proceed to the center of the universe. They were guarded by a bare-chested brute who had a razor-sharp sword in one hand and a bad attitude in the clenched first of his other.

The guy was easily the size of Thor and looked as if he were ready to pop at any minute. Set evaluated the guard, sure he could take him until he noticed the unhinged glint in the shade's eyes, then Set was glad that such a confrontation wouldn't take place.

A large vein on the side of the guard's temple throbbed an angry red pulse. "No one may pass without uttering the password." He grimaced.

"Odysseus," Minthe said in a perky lilt.

The muscle-bound giant ground his teeth and released the lever.

Set was pretty sure he just heard one of the man's molars snap under the pressure.

The doors swung open, and the group made their way inside.

---

1. Not so far-fetched. Astronauts have described the smell of space as burnt steak. If the universe can smell like overcooked meat, then why can't the center of it smell like bacon? Maybe Set's ball bearing heart has been overheating and has permeated to the far reaches of creation with the delicious smell of BBQ.

"Who was that?" Unkulunkulu asked. "He didn't seem very happy with his position at the gate."

"Him? Oh, he's no one special. Just someone being punished by Hades. He once was one of the most famous of all warriors in Greece, but in his anger he betrayed those he should have been loyal to in his heart. Physical punishment means nothing to a big strong man like him, so Hades had to come up with something different. We aren't even allowed to use his name, for saying his name would set him free, and he has to wonder if he was ever known by other Greeks at all. And the password? It's the name of his greatest rival. He has to hear the name of the one he hates most every time he opens the gate."

"His name is never spoken, yet he hears the name of his greatest enemy constantly? Good use of psychological torture." Unkulunkulu nodded in approval.

The tour group had finally arrived at the grand finale, the thing everybody had been waiting for, the center of physical existence. The wheel holding the whole of the universe together was surprisingly small, not much bigger than a chariot wheel. It had much larger cogs and spindles coming off of it, all moving in a very precise and accurate motion in a manner unchanged and constant since the very beginning of time.

And Set was about to, literally, screw it all up. Or maybe it was better to say unscrew or dismantle or *something*. The point was, the thing that is working and should have kept on working was about to stop working because of Set.

The other gods and beings oohed and awed and gaped about the chamber as if they had just come to a deep and fundamental understanding of the nature of everything.

To Set the center of the universe just looked like a clock and not a very complex one at that.[2]

---

2. See Tim Wetherell's *Clockwork Universe* exhibit at Questacon in Australia for reference. I'm sure he's proud of his work, but I expected more.

And to think, the whole thing is just held together with a simple pin?

It was finally time. Set just couldn't control himself, and he finally didn't have to anymore.

And Thor—the god, not Heyerdahl—flamboyantly flashy dresser that he was, just happened to be wearing a cape.[3] An actual, flippy-flappy, blowing in the breeze, superhero beach towel draped behind the neck and attached to his breastplate at the shoulders. The most snaggable, catchable accessory this side of overlong scarves and untucked ascots. The idiot actually wore a cape around gears, cogs, pulleys, and wheels full of teeth and spindles and lots of rotating, spinning bits.

To Set's eyes it was almost too good of a setup to pass up. So he didn't. A gentle puff of breath was all it took.

The sharp tooth of a greasy gear bit into the precious-metal threaded hem of Goldilocks's back draping, and Thor was swept off his feet.

It must have taken the god of thunder a bit to realize what had happened. He didn't look too alarmed until the other gods assembled called out that he was blocking the view, and then Thor panicked. That was when the god-toting gear rotated up into a crack just barely wide enough for the machine part to clear each side of the earth's core beside it by the barest of microns. And Thor, larger than life and dense as the planetary inner core, was a tad more girthy than the gear he was strapped to.

A high-pitched titter sounded, which apparently was what the god of thunder squeaked out when he was really nervous. He tugged at the cape in a frenzy, unable to dislodge it from the gear of the Grand Machine. The end of the cape slid up into the crevice, and there was a tearing sound. But the Asgardian homespun proved very durable. Thor tittered again as he clawed at the clasps holding his

---

3. Consider the words of Edna Mode from *The Incredibles*: "No capes!" Thor could have avoided being smooshed if he just wore a jacket.

cape to his shoulders. The titter was followed by a sort of wet, Oobleck-squishing sound as Thor's head, shoulders, and chest wedged deeply into the crack.

The gear couldn't advance past his mead belly. The high-pitched tittering continued as it took on a slightly more frenetic frequency.

Things other than the god of thunder started to squeal. And then to smoke.

Unkulunkulu laughed and started to clap. "Why didn't they include this in the brochure?" Unkulunkulu's reed humanoid hanger-on began to clap as well.

Minthe turned a pale shade of green. "I am so getting fired for this."

The quartet of Sumerian gods—Anu, Enlil, Enki, and Ninhur-sang—attempted to help Thor out of the crack he was wedged in. The thunder god blubbered and wailed like a newborn calf pulled away from its momma.

There was a buildup of pressure and tension, and the wheel holding Gaea in her designated rotation slipped. The wobbling at the center of the globe was noticeable in the chamber in the center of everything. Set could only imagine what it was like up on the surface, the sweep of a rotated line being so much more at the end than at the nexus point.

Perfect. Set smiled.

Set walked right up to the center pin—held in place by what was once his heart—and gave it a tug. It didn't budge.

Unkulunkulu looked at Set from his vantage point above his reed cow and questioned what the Egyptian god was doing. "Pulling the pin will not help Thor. In fact it may cause more problems for the lot of us."

Set ignored the other god. He jammed the tip of his staff behind the head of the pin and gave the lever a shove. The pin moved out a quarter of an inch. Set repositioned his staff to the side and pulled with both hands.

Unkulunkulu shook his head. "I'm telling you, this will not help your friend."

Heyerdahl looked at Set and tugged on his leash to get his master's attention. "I don't think he's trying to help Thor."

Set swore and threw his weight against his staff. He could see there were grooves and ridges in the pin, probably formed from wear and tear. The deformities of the pin were making it hard to pull out.

Set grit his teeth and dug in his heels. He pushed so hard against the lever he could hear his bones creak.

The pin moved out about halfway.

The whole world—the whole universe—shook.

The area immediately around the central pin was hit by a fresh blast of the aroma of frying bacon.

The bearings, including Set's heart, were working harder with the pin only half inserted. Set could hear his heart sizzling as it turned. It was the heart of a god, so Set's ticker was pretty durable, and was in no danger of giving out anytime soon.

God's heart bacon seasoned with a touch of nihilism, a big slab of the end of existence, and a side of hashbrowns please?

The staff slipped off the pin every time Set tried to seat it. So he tossed the thing aside in frustration and grabbed the pin with both hands.

The pin started to spin lazily in its seating, the head of the pin making a slightly bigger loop with each rotation as Set dragged it further out.

Minthe screamed.

Set almost had it. A few more inches of pin to clear and Set would finally be able to touch his heart. He cackled with glee and pulled harder, but his hands were sweaty now, and he had a hard time getting a better grip.

Then something hit him like he'd just been crushed beneath a 2500-pound bale of hay.

Unkulunkulu's cow put a hoof on Set's chest and pushed him to the ground.

"No! I'm so close. I won't let you stop me, stupid cow," Set screamed and started to tear at the straw bovine's leg with his hands and claws. It wasn't a powerful enough counteroffensive to dissuade the grass cow, so Set grappled for his staff to use as a club against the beast.

Unkulunkulu's reed man started beating Set around his head and shoulders with his legs and fists.

It's like I'm being thwarted by *&^%$* brooms!

Set managed to get his right hand on his staff. He thrust the end of the stick upward and twisted it into the middle of the reed man's face. With a final half rotation and a bolt of electricity he blew the head of the strawman into so much chaff that it fluttered through the air.

The headless scarecrow stumbled, let out something akin to a sigh, and fell on its chest in the dust.

Set grabbed the staff with both hands, wedged the length of it between him and the cow, and sent the last of his energy stored in the stick into the attacking hay bale. The cow exploded,[4] sending its rider arching toward the cavern roof far above.

Buga jumped into the fray and hit Set over the head with his broken lyre.

Set tried to defend himself, shoving his staff up in an effort to deflect the blow too late. He reeled from the strike but managed to get to his feet.

The bits of reed straw littering the air made it hard to predict the attacks. Buga still had the belly of his lyre hooked on the walking stick. He yanked hard and pulled the length of wood from Set's grasp. Set spun as he tried to hold onto his weapon and failed. Buga took advantage of the spin and batted Set again from behind. Set crashed to the ground, cursing and dazed.

Having freed Thor from the Grand Machine, Anu, Enlil, Enki,

---

4. I imagine it was akin to bull riding in the middle of a twister at the Kansas State Fair.

and Ninhursang turned their attention to Set. They dogpiled on the dog-faced god. Thor Heyerdahl grabbed Set by the legs, and Viracocha put Set's head in a chokehold.

Set had waited too long for this. He wasn't going to let a bunch of second stringers keep him from his goal. He screamed and pulled everything he had in reserve from deep in his core. The bolt of lightning threw all of the ones atop him to the far walls of the chamber.

Set rose shakily to his feet. "It's time for you wastes of creation to go back to the Void. All of you!" He swatted the air in a broad sweep of defiance.

Minthe tried to bar his way back to the machine.

"'Cept for you, lady. It appears you're already there." Set hit her across the cheek with a wicked backhand.

Minthe dropped to the ground, a darkened, subdued shade of ichor dribbled from the corner of her mouth. Set stepped over her and made his way back to the pin. He was about to grab hold of it when a voice came from the side.

"I say thee nay!"

Now he drops the third person narrative? Set snarled and spun around to face his new opponent.

Thor, god of thunder, much the worse for wear, was still able to swing his hammer hard enough that it tore Set off the ground and embedded the Egyptian deep in the wall of the large stone chamber.

"Thor has heard it said that one does not tug on Thor's cape.[5] It is a popular saying in Midgard." He pointed his hammer in Set's direction. "And thou, little dog-faced man, did more than just tug on Thor's cape!" Thor postured and wobbled and took a step forward only to pass out and plant himself face-first in the dirt.

Set worked his way out of the Set shaped divot in the rock.

The other gods had all gathered back together. Set was going to have to fight his way back to the pin to finish pulling it the rest of the

---

5. The saying is "you don't tug on *Superman's* cape." from the 1972 masterpiece,*You Don't Mess Around With Jim,* by Jim Croce.

way from its seat. Set needed to reach his discarded staff. If it had any charge left in it, he might still have a chance.

A large black owl flew into the chamber.

Minthe looked both terrified and relieved. "Master Hades!" She pointed at Set as the others all positioned themselves between the Egyptian god and the center of the Grand Machine. "I don't know what got into him, but I don't think we should validate his parking."

The giant Stygian owl turned its head toward Set and glared at the Egyptian god with its blood-red eyes.

A voice sounded as if it came from everywhere in the chamber at the same time. "I've already called security. The bouncer is on his way."

Something unbelievably immense could be heard heading toward the chamber.

Set wasn't exactly sure of the guard's identity, but he could hazard a guess or two. He wasn't ready to go up against the misshapen titan that almost stopped Zeus and his entourage of teenage Greek usurpers dead in their tracks.

The ragged and angered gods of the tour group blocked Set from grabbing his staff again.

Set's reserves were exhausted. He couldn't get to the one weapon that might aid him. Reinforcements far greater than those he'd just faced were on their way.

"*Khara!*[6] *Khara, khara, khara,*" Set screamed, frustrated to be so close and be denied his prize.

There was a hole in the group, right in the place where Thor had fallen. It somewhat registered that Thor was no longer lying in a heap, but the void revealed by Coppertone's absence might just be big enough for Set to break through the defenders.

If I could only—

So intent on the goal within reach, Set didn't even see Thor swing the hammer until it slammed into his face and sent him

---

6. A not so nice way to say *excrement* in Arabic.

pinwheeling head over tail out of the chamber and back down into the tunnel the tour had emerged from.

Set bounced hard off a wall, ricocheted into another tunnel, and fell.

CHAPTER 7
THINGS GET WORSE

Z EUS WAS IN THE TUB AS HE TRIED TO ENJOY A QUIET MOMENT in the hectic schedule of running the Grecian universe. The hot water, relaxing herbs and spices, and small bobbing cork duck worked their intended magic as they released the tension from the god's neck and shoulders.

"Ahh." Zeus slipped further down into the bubbles. "Just what I needed."

His dog, Goldy, lay beside the tub. The dog put his head on his folded paws and let out a contented sigh.

Zeus lowered himself deeper into the pool.

There was a clap, and a wave of soapy suds curled and splashed over the edge of the tub.

Goldy let out a wet yelp.

"Sorry boy." Zeus thought perhaps he'd moved a bit too quickly and created the mini tsunami by mistake. He didn't want to make a mess in the bathroom or soak the dog anymore, so he lowered himself a bit more gently.

The level of the suds retreated faster than the god could immerse himself.

The tub was suddenly empty, and Zeus could feel the instant fissure in the bowl that had formed under his butt. The crack began at the base of Olympus and ran in a haphazard line that led directly to the peak.[1]

---

1. I was referring to the fissure in creation and the firmament, not the backside of the master of the realm.

The dog poked his dripping snout over the edge and into the tub. "So much for a leisurely soak."

"Damnit, Hermes!" Zeus bellowed. "What have you done now?"

"Sure. Blame me," Hermes said in a sour voice from the other room.

Zeus searched about for a towel. He'd heard Hermes's muttered reply, but didn't believe him.

Athena popped into existence right next to her ne'er-do-well brother.

"Hey, Hermes. I like the neck monitor,"[2] Athena said.

"Shut up," Hermes grumbled. "I don't know what's going on, but I didn't do it."

Goldy offered Zeus a hand towel clamped between his teeth. "Biggest I could find," the dog said out of the corner of his mouth.

"It'll do." Zeus snatched the small patch of terry cloth and thundered in his children's direction.

"It wasn't him, Dad," Athena called out before Zeus could come into the chamber, thunderbolts blazing. "The real-time alerts you had me add to his collar show he was only working on official tasks. No side trips or detours recorded."

"I really hate that you're keeping tabs on me. How do you think you'd like this?" Hermes sneered as he ran a finger under the chain around his neck.

"I probably wouldn't, but I'll never know," Athena said. "I think about consequences before I do things."

Hermes frowned at the reproach.

Zeus entered the grand hall, hair sopping and the hand towel placed strategically to preserve his modesty. "Well if it wasn't him, then who the heck is mucking stuff up?"

"No idea." Athena snapped her fingers, and a robe appeared and

---

2. The jangling, enchanted necklace was placed around Hermes's neck by Hephaestus and the bear god Arktus. Hermes must wear it until the other gods are sure he won't try to overthrow the universe again. Unrepentant, self-righteous, and self-justified, it's going to be a while.

swaddled her father in something a bit more family friendly. "But old twinkle toes hasn't deviated from his prescribed schedule."

Zeus looked at the fissure. "To affect Olympus like this, it has to be something deep. Something fundamental."

"Something fundamental," Hermes said in a high-pitched mock of Zeus's words.

Zeus leveled an accusatory finger at his son. "I swear, Hermes—"

Hermes jingled the necklace around his neck. "Twernt me, Pa! I'm on a leash, remember? Whatever is happening, I didn't do it." Hermes dropped the chain and folded his arms tight over his chest in a pout.

"Dad wouldn't suspect you if you hadn't just tried to overthrow and replace the ruling gods," Athena reminded him. "You do remember doing that, don't you?"

"Of course I remember. I'm not stupid." Hermes narrowed his eyes at his sister.

Athena arched an incredulous eyebrow as if she weren't entirely convinced of her brother's assessment of his capabilities.

Hermes just couldn't leave well enough alone, so the shadow of suspicion would always and forever hover about him. "I would have gotten away with it too, if it weren't for those blasted kids and their dog!"[3]

"Arktus is a bear," Athena corrected her brother.

"Whatever," Hermes glowered.

The universe shifted again. Goldy yelped as a tile crashed in the bathroom. Olympus was in danger. Zeus looked beyond his home. Olympus wasn't the only place this was happening.

Zeus focused past the surface of the world, past the foundations of reality, deep into the bonds that held everything together. The effect of the crack was amplified the further away from the center of the universe it traveled. The mechanics of the universe still moved,

---

3. Line adapted from one spoken by Big Bob Oakly in the episode "A Gaggle of Galloping Ghosts" from the series *Scooby Doo: Where Are You?*

but there was a catch and a wobble to everything. He followed all the celestial cogs and wheels back to their base and starting point. "Oh, no. This is bad. And this is big. There's no way Hermes could have pulled something like this off."

Hermes looked up, offended. "Hey!"

"Not an insult, son." Zeus took Hermes by the shoulder and helped him focus.

Hermes's eyes went wide as he looked beyond what he could see and studied what his father had seen. He gulped hard. "Oh, no. This will take all the gods to fix. Not just the Greek ones."

Zeus tried to focus on the problem more intently when, suddenly, his view of Hades's realm went dark. He closed his eyes and tried again.

Hermes screwed his eyes shut and stumbled back. "All I'm getting is static. Am I doing it wrong?"

"Hades has just blocked our ability to see into the underworld," Zeus scratched his beard. "Why would he do that?"

"Let me check." Athena blinked out of existence, only to blink right back and immediately stumble to the ground like she had just hit a rubber wall. "He won't let me in."

"Never send a woman to do a man's job. I'll make it. Guide to the dead, remember?" Hermes said cockily. He blinked out of the air with a tinkling of bells, only to be thrown back bodily into the room he'd just left with a bloody nose. His now dented helm dropped from his head and skittered across the floor. Hermes brought his hands to his face to try to stop the flow of ichor draining from his broken nose.

Zeus handed him the hand towel.

Hermes used it for a second, then threw it aside looking as if he just realized what it had most recently been covering. "Eew. Not a pleasant thought." He pinched his nose with two fingers instead.

"There's a problem." Athena drew a rectangle in the air, created a screen, and brought up an annotated view of the Grand Machine for the others to see. Then she traced out the path anyone would need to take to get to the source of the crack, to the place where the system was breaking. "We all should have access to this in the Olympus archives, but someone with a higher level of responsibility has locked us out." There was a redacted section of the schematic in the center that kept her from completely viewing the path on the map.

"Restricted access?" Zeus balked at the warnings. "How can I have restricted access to something in my realms?"

"It's not in your realms," Athena pointed out. "It's below, in the place of power and imprisonment for those the gods have overthrown."

"Grandpa and Great-Grandpa and their kith and kin?" Hermes said.

Zeus shook his head and sighed. "And gods and monsters defeated and deposed by other pantheons as well, not just the Greeks."

"I told Hades accepting the condemned from other mythologies was a bad idea." Athena looked like she wanted to tell someone *I told you so.*

Zeus ground his teeth from side to side. "That's what all of us in power get for thinking we can solve our problems by throwing them in a hole."

At the moment the situation looked very bad. Very, very bad.

"Let's not panic yet. Let me see if I can come up with any kind of plan." Zeus had little hope, but desperation often led to inspiration. "It can't all end like this."

Hermes, for the first time in his life, looked really and truly defeated. He turned to his father's dog and lowered his head. "Dog, I am truly sorry for all of the ire and vitriol I have directed at you over the years."

Goldy took the apology for what it really represented. "Well, we're *&^%$*."

CHAPTER X

SECOND BASE?

THE BENCH FELT RICKETY WHEN SHE FIRST SAT DOWN.

The table was a bit off too. Medusa risked a peak under the tabletop and saw one of the table legs perched on a couple of thick pieces of pottery to keep it somewhat level.

The entire operation of Enyo's Gyros looked a bit cobbled together.

Medusa didn't want to judge. Enyo was obviously trying, and Medusa didn't want to cast any doubt on her sister's new endeavor before even tasting anything she had to offer. A lot of startups struggled to get everything up to standard before the business took off. Enyo, even being a goddess, still had challenges and limitations like everybody else.

The food did smell good. And it wouldn't hurt anybody, least of all Medusa, if this was a good experience for her, her sister, or Mod.

So Medusa sat down and tried very hard not to rock back and forth on the bench for fear of toppling it.

Enyo went to the portable oven at the back of the wagon. She pulled out a steaming pita from the small brickwork shelf on one side. A fan attached to gears and belts sat over the vent to the oven.

Of course, Mod was so intrigued by the contraption that he totally forgot he was here with Medusa.

"So you're catching the updraft from the oven to push a fan, which is attached to a series of gears to turn a belt, which in turn rotates the spit full of meat over an open flame just off to the side of the bread oven." Mod observed.

Enyo placed the first pita on a plate and started to carve warm, thin slices of meat onto it. "It seemed like a good idea. The fan keeps the rotation of the spit constant, and the meat is all the better for it."

"Could I look at the gearing?" Mod asked.

Halfway into filling the second pita, Enyo paused, cocked her head to the side, and put her knife wielding hand on her hip. "Here I am, cooking some of the most succulent meat known to gods and mortals, and you want to look at the roasting apparatus?"

Mod perked up, rising from the bench. "Yes, ma'am. Very much please."

As the business end of the carving knife drew little circles in Mod's general direction, Enyo swiveled her head to Medusa. "Is he serious?"

Medusa sighed and dropped her head to her hands. Much as she wanted to tell Mod to please pay attention to her, there was a new contraption in the area, and experience had already taught her that Mod's curiosity was an undeniable natural force. "He won't be able to even taste the food until he sees how the contraption works."

Enyo started chopping and placing fresh vegetables onto the pitas. She mumbled something to herself, shook her head, then pointed her nose in the direction of the simple machine. "Why not? Knock yourself out, sport."

Mod had his nose next to the machine in an instant. "The fan must have excellent bearings. Look how smooth it rotates." He looked above and below it, then checked it out from side to side. "The speed of the rotation on the fan is quicker than the turning of the spit. Reductive gearing?"[1]

Enyo shrugged at Mod. "I have no idea what you just said." She turned to Medusa. "Heavy on the tzatziki?"

"Please," Medusa said with a forced smile.

Enyo stirred a bit more crushed garlic into the yogurt and cucum-

---

1. Reductive gearing is used to decrease the rotational speed of an input shaft to an appropriate output speed.

placed a large dollop of the savory mixture on one pita, then a heaping spoonful on the other.

"So you didn't build this machine?" Mod asked Enyo.

"My talents don't really fall into the engineering category. I am, however, very good at figuring out how to use things for purposes they weren't designed for," Enyo explained. "I salvaged this bit of machinery from one of Ares's siege weapons."

Mod gasped like he recognized it now. "The automated boiling oil dispenser?"

"Yes? How did you know?" Enyo took a step back from Mod, a mix of shock and curiosity on her face.

After another bored sigh, Medusa raised her head, brushed back her bangs, and blew an errant hair out of her face. "He probably saw the schematic on one of his numerous trips to Hephaestus's forge," she said as if she spoke to herself.

The tone in Medusa's voice must not have been lost on Enyo. The chef presented the plate with the fully assembled lunch wraps to Mod and urged him to take it to his companion. "Enjoy your meal with *Medusa*. I hope you both love what I've made for you." She poked Mod with the platter twice before he got the hint.

"Oh, thank you." Mod did a little head bob to acknowledge Enyo, turned, and headed toward Medusa with a satisfied grin on his face. "It looks and smells delicious."

Medusa knew he grinned because he just saw something he cared about—something nerdy, geeky, and unique. The food might have helped, but the machinery was the real reason for his joy.

That is just who Mod is. That little epiphany of who he was at his core and seeing him smiling made Medusa feel just a tad better. She did care a great deal for Mod. She wanted him to be happy, and she was pretty sure he wanted her to be happy too.

Maybe this is a good starting place to build something from after all?

Medusa, feeling better and more hopeful than she had in days, smiled back at Mod and reached out to take the gyro from the plate.

The bench buckled, and Mod stumbled. Somehow Medusa ended up on her back. At first she thought she'd dropped her pita down the front of her dress. But a quick glance showed her intact, if a bit shook up, pita still in her hand.

Wide-eyed and panic-stricken, Mod stood above her, with the empty plate frozen in the air, sandwich nowhere to be seen.

Unless Medusa looked straight down.

The gyro wedged between Medusa's breasts smelled and looked delicious.

There was a contrast between the warmth of the bread nestled between her cleavage and cool, savory yogurt splattered across her clavicles. The ratio of meat to vegetables to sauce looked perfect.

I'm a mess, but at least I'm not on fire like the last time we had lunch together. Mod is handling this better than I expected.

Mod appeared to be hyperventilating.

"I'd ask for you to pass more tzatziki, but I think you've given me enough for a bit," Medusa said in a sarcastic mutter from where she lay on the ground.

"I don't know how it got there. It was in my hand, and the next thing I knew it was, um, it was . . ." He pointed at Medusa's yogurt-smeared chest and turned a shade of green.

Enyo clung to the side of her rocking wagon. "Did you guys feel that?"

"What?" Medusa asked.

"The earth moving?" Enyo clarified.

"Really? You think that was an earth moving moment for me? I'm not as impressed by him as you think." She looked up at Mod and gave a slight frown.

Mod, now close to trembling from head to toe, turned around slowly and apologized to Enyo. "Sorry about that. I fully intend to pay for it. I'm usually not that clumsy."

Enyo let out a frustrated huff. "How did the two of you both miss what just happened? She fell and you stumbled because, well, just look around." She pointed at all the things that had fallen off the lunch wagon.

"If you're trying to give a girl a memorable experience, there are probably better ways to go about it," Medusa said.

Mod went from apologizing to Enyo to again face Medusa. He leaned over her and extended a hand to help her up. "I am so, so sorry. It was in my hand, and then it wasn't. I don't know how it got . . ." He gestured in her general direction and turned a shade greener.

The universe jerked again.

Treetops whipped back and forth on the mountains behind them. Enyo's food cart rocked on its tire rims despite the chocks wedged under the wheels while she tried desperately to hold it still. The upright benches and tables in the dining area tottered this way and that.

Mod flipped through the air so hard he landed on top of Medusa, and they both went rolling along the ground.

"That wasn't me being clumsy," Mod said as pushed up off Medusa to take a look around.

It wasn't an apology, just a statement of fact. The frightened and embarrassed mannerisms of a few seconds before were gone in an instant. He seemed unaware of the sauce and bits of wrap littering the front of his chiton from where he had fallen atop Medusa. He leaned back on his haunches as he studied the effects of the tremors happening all around him. He looked at the horizon, then stared up. Medusa followed his gaze.

Mod started writing calculations with the tzatziki on Medusa's chest. He scratched out the first part of the scribble, added something to the part he hadn't mentally erased, and started mumbling to himself as he studied the equation spread across her collarbone.

The tumbling of the world discombobulated Medusa enough she didn't even slap Mod's hand away until he smeared out one of the digits to replace it with something else, and then it was only done out of a delayed feminine protective reflex.

The reproach appeared not to register with Mod.

The clouds shuddered in time with the tremors of Mother Gaea beneath them.

Everyone was silent until the tremor finally stopped.

Enyo's cart stopped shifting about. "That was what I was talking about. You both felt it that time, right? What do you think—" She stopped mid-sentence as her eyes fell on her customers.

Enyo cleared her throat and glanced off to the side. "Do you two, uh, need a bit of privacy?"

"What?" Medusa was a bit startled by her sister's voice. As she tried to make sense of what Enyo was talking about, she realized Mod was still atop her, his hand pressed down on her left breast.

Medusa was pretty sure Mod wasn't in the least aware of the awkward position he was in. She picked up his hand and moved it off to the side of her chest. "We're fine, Enyo." Medusa explained as she propped herself up on her elbows. "He's just switched into his default deductive reasoning mode."

Mod didn't even answer Enyo. Medusa could see probable causes and catalysts being considered behind Mod's eyes. He looked down now, staring at nothing, eyes unfocused, as the heavy thinking took total control of him.

Seeing how Mod was acting, Enyo nodded like she understood. "Just making sure. People can have weird responses when the world might be ending." She started righting some of the tools and supplies that had been knocked over in her kitchen.

"Ending?" Medusa tried to rise, but Mod was kneeling on her skirt. "That was just an earthquake. Greece has lots of earthquakes."

"Felt different to me." Enyo picked through her fallen plates and serving trays. Half of them were broken.

"It was different." Mod tapped his finger in the air the way he always did when the math in his head started to add up. "Something fundamental is slipping. Something that shouldn't be."

"How can you tell?" Medusa asked.

Mod pointed straight up. "The clouds moved at the same time

and tempo as the ground beneath our feet. For something to affect the atmosphere and Mother Gaea at the same time?"

"Not normal," Medusa agreed.

"Smart." Enyo gave Mod a small nod. "Smart is good." She turned to her sister. "This one's a keeper, Medusa."

"We're kinda in the midst of figuring that out, Enyo." Medusa turned her attention back to the man hovering over her. Medusa tapped Mod on the thigh. When he looked down, she cruelly batted her eyes up at Mod, who was still between her legs and kneeling on her skirt. "Comfortable?"

Mod froze. It looked like it took a minute for his brain to relay messages to his limbs. He was all herky-jerky but didn't make any progress as he tried to scramble away. He slipped and slid in the same spot, apologizing the entire time.

Mod gaped. "It's not . . . I just . . ."

Medusa sighed and propped herself up on her elbows. "Mod, if you stay there much longer, I might actually think you want to be there."

He hesitated, almost as if he did want to be there. A decision was made, or Mod's muscles finally started to work in conjunction with his brain again, and he got up. Then he extended a hand down to her to help her to her feet, but his head swiveled about as he once again took in what had happened around them.

The engineer just took over again, Medusa thought.

She might have had Mod with her for a second, and he might have actually been a man thinking of her as a woman for a portion of that, but just as quick, he was gone again.

There was a problem to solve, and Mod wouldn't be able to focus on anything until he had the answer. Medusa was just going to have to be patient until this new crisis was solved, and then be patient while she and Mod figured things out. Or she was going to have to decide to cut her losses and leave.

She didn't know what she wanted.

CHAPTER 9

A FUMBLE IN THE END ZONE

"You fool," the giant owl berated Thor as Set tumbled through the air. "He was here, cornered and surrounded, and all that needed to happen was for me to take him and give him his just rewards."

Set heard the unapologetic voice of Thor. "Well why didn't you tell Thor to stop before Thor batted the little dog-faced goblin out of the room?"

Set tumbled and rolled and was back on his feet and running as fast as he could.

The sounds of pursuit were close behind. And there was no one to help him.

With every action since he had his heart wrongly ripped from his body, Set had done his level best to make sure he wasn't in the good books of any of the gods of Egypt, or any other gods for that matter. Sure, it could be argued there was the one time he helped out Ra on the battle barque[1] to confront and repel Apep, Serpent of Chaos,[2] but that was a long time ago, before Set did all that stuff to Osiris.[3]

There was a lot of bad blood between Set and the other Egyptian gods because of the killing and dismembering of Osiris. That had been a pretty big one. If Set had to choose a singular thing he prob-

---

1. A barque is a boat. Ra was really proud of his boat and named it Mandjet, the Boat of Millions of Years. The planks were sewn together, and the seams and cracks were sealed and plugged using reeds, so I doubt Mandjet lasted half as long as Ra suggested it did.

2. It's an official title, though they misspelled it as *kaos* on Apep's business cards.

3. Killing your brother and hacking his body into bits pretty much ensures that you don't get invited to the next family picnic. (Introverts, I am not endorsing this as a viable option to avoid seeing your family.)

shouldn't have done, killing his brother would have probably been the one.

And then there was the subsequent usurping of the kingdom. And, well, there were lots of things that tended to reflect pretty negatively on Set. For some reason all the others focused on what he had done to Osiris.

I knew feeding Osiris's dangly bits to that jackal would come back to haunt me.[4]

A three-headed dog started barking somewhere behind Set in the tunnel he was in. Set cursed the dog and made a sharp turn down a shaft and into another cave ahead, trying to lose his pursuers. He actually liked dogs quite a bit and couldn't fault the three-headed fellow for performing his job well. Maybe in different circumstances they could have been friends?

Set doubted it. He and the dog, what's-his-faces, wouldn't be chasing aardvarks together anytime soon.[5]

What was the dog's name anyway? Not like it mattered.

He emerged into a larger cave and set off in the direction of the immense open area that housed most of the dead in the underworld. If Set couldn't lose those who followed him in the twists and turns of the tight ways and paths, perhaps he could lose them in the thick of the crowds of undead.

So close.

He couldn't believe he'd had to leave his staff behind. He'd had it

---

4. Isis managed to resurrect her chopped up brother-husband Osiris with the help of the goddess Nephthys. Osiris's penis was the only part of the god-meat puzzle they couldn't find. Which is okay, I guess, because Osiris managed to father Horus despite the mysteriously absent peener.

5. Set hates aardvarks. Some scholars think Set has the head of an aardvark, and Set would like to talk to those idiots about their assumptions. Set has all these different heads because Set is a shapechanger. Set is Set, and Set doesn't like to be defined or limited. Set has tried them all, which is why Set has been recorded as an aardvark (would not recommend), an African wild dog, a donkey, a hyena, a jackall, a pig, an antelope, a giraffe, an okapi, a saluki, and a fennec fox. And on very special occasions, Set has been known to look a bit like Liberace, but the scholars mistook that look too, and said it was a flamingo.

from the beginning. He'd put a lot of time and effort into the thing and had imbued it with magics and sciences so that it was an aid and an asset to him. It acted as an amplifier and a battery backup for his storm powers.[6] It was the most effective tool and weapon that he had.

Being fought to a standstill and stripped of his arsenal by Thor? How humiliating.

Why wasn't I strong enough to pull that damned pin from the Grand Machine? Set looked down at his ineffective hands and scowled.

He pictured the pin, trying to see what he'd done wrong. Several large tracks had widened into deep grooves in the shaft. The grooves were uneven and had burrs on the metal. Most of the wear had probably come about because the wheel the pin pushed through had a slight looseness to it, like one of the bearings wasn't exactly the right size.

My heart.

Set's heart not fitting in the machine right had formed the grooves in the pin. The grooves in the pin had been what had caused it to catch, the reason the pin couldn't be pulled smoothly and cleanly from its seating.

In essence, Set's own heart had just saved the universe from being destroyed by Set. *Oh, the irony.* Set cursed his own heart and kept running.

The sound of the dog and the others was getting closer, and Set hadn't made it to the wide-open spaces of the underworld yet. He would be caught in the caves and forced to fight.

Just then, a catch and hitch in the Grand Machine sent a crack

---

6. There is scholarly debate about the discovery of several odd devices in ancient north Africa and the Middle East that could have been galvanic batteries. Ceramic pots, copper coils, and iron bars have been found together in several locations, and when the items are combined and container filled with water, they have been able to hold an electrical charge. No one knows what they were used for, but several nearby tombs containing images of pharaohs and kings playing Game Boys and listening to what appears to be Walkmans may offer us some subtle clues.

running through the core of the planet. The path behind Set was blocked by a sudden shifting of stone. He could hear the frustrated howling of the dog and the muffled curses of the guards he now pulled away from.

It would give him mere moments, at best. The guards and warriors tasked by Hades to catch him were nothing if not determined. Still, Set grinned at his good luck.

Unfortunately, Set didn't get as long of a respite as he'd hoped. The three-headed dog bayed loudly as it once again picked up the trail of its quarry. There were sounds of other forces up ahead as well.

Set took off in another direction, following a path that twisted and turned and branched off in a hundred different places. It wouldn't be enough. The minions of Hades would catch up to him sooner or later. They were trying their level best to delete him from existence or force him past the borders of the realm. If he was forced from the realm, he'd never be able to make it back, and Set wasn't going to let that happen.

Set doubled his speed and headed toward the place where the sound of pursuit was most concentrated. He would change himself to appear as one of his pursuers, but there didn't seem to be a standard in the forms of the ones being employed by Hades, though they all seemed to know each other. Perhaps there was a way unknown to Set that they were marked so as to recognize their comrades in arms.

If he couldn't disguise himself as one of the searchers and protectors of the realm, perhaps he should try to appear as something else? What would go unnoticed in the land of the dead?

He could disguise himself as a rock, but that would severely limit his mobility. He could disguise himself as someone with a low level of authority in the underworld, but the closest thing he had seen to someone involved in middle management was that minty little tour guide, and her sheer, greenish-hued clothing wasn't very good at dissuading attention.[7]

He'd have to find a disguise. Something moveable. Something unloved and unnoticed that no one would think twice about ignoring.

Did Hades have unpaid interns?[8]

The path he followed finally opened up into the immense chamber of the underworld filled with all those who'd lost the fight against time.

Set found himself in the midst of a large group of wraiths and shades that stumbled and lurched about aimlessly.[9] If Set couldn't disguise himself as part of the organization, perhaps appearing as one of the mindless flock would work instead.

Set took the head covering of a slack-faced woman and stole an ethereal bag from a grandmother who'd been unable to release the thought of her worldly possessions when she crossed over. He considered taking the robe from the portly shade of a man who now blocked his way forward, but wisely chose not to as the stench the man carried in life seemed to be the thing this one particular wraith hadn't been able to part with when he transitioned from one state to the next. Even the crowd of the dead, who were beyond the need of inhaling anymore, made a wide berth around the fetid man.

Stinky was out, and the rest of the group seemed ready to fight for their meager belongings. The crowd thinned, with the last members of the group clinging tightly to the things the Egyptian god might take from them. Gleaning any other disguise supplies might cause too much of a disturbance and draw attention to the ones searching for him. Set would make do with what he'd just lifted from the others.

---

7. Minthe's standard work attire did increase the number of men signing up for the tour group though.

8. Supervisor: "Your job is feeding Cerberus."

   Intern (all excited and eager to please): "Great! What am I feeding him?"

   Supervisor (hands intern a large sprig of parsley): "You'll figure it out soon enough."

9. One can only hope this plan works better for Set than it did for Bill Murray in Zombieland.

He slowed his pace and tried to think of what he needed to do next, but that only made him think of the opportunity he'd just missed. Set had been so close. And he still was close. He just had to lose those tailing him and find a place to wait.

He could wait. He'd waited this long.

It didn't matter if he needed to wait a week.

Or a month.

Or a thousand years.

But it was going to be hard to wait knowing his goal, the end of everything, was so close at hand.

There was always the chance that the pin would sheer, and the wheel would spin and break, and the whole thing would come tumbling down anyway. But the longer it took, the more likely someone was going to find a way to fix it. And once it was fixed the likelihood of getting back to take a second shot at it was nil. If the powers that be managed to fix it, they'd also find a way to protect the spot and keep tampering from ever happening again.

The options seemed less and less possible.

Set changed his appearance into a doddering old woman, a disguise complimented and completed with the homespun shawl and the stolen bag. He would have changed his scent too, but he'd been around plenty of old women who smelled like a jackal that had been running a marathon in the desert.[10] So the aroma surrounding him would probably go unnoticed.

Set turned right at the next crossroads the dead traveled. And then turned right at the following junction as well. Now he was heading back in the direction he'd been running from. He calmed himself and tried to walk at a less fleeing-for-his-life kind of pace.

Several dead guards rushed past him. They didn't even slow

---

10. What did they call a marathon before Pheidippides ran the first marathon at Marathon? I have no idea. Great. Another pointless thing to keep my churning brain up at night.

down. Set was feeling pretty secure in his disguise. Then the freaky three-headed dog rushed past and slid to a stop in a spray of gravel.

Crap.

Set had momentarily forgotten that dogs tracked by scent, and the scent Set currently packed was pretty potent. He'd managed to fool the others, and he might have been able to get past the nose of one dog, or possibly even two, but three canid olfactory sensors?[11]

Set was part dog. Sometimes, at least. He knew the gig was up. Set's smell had given him away. *Maybe I should have stolen the fetid robe from the portly dead man.* He discarded any regret for the missed opportunity immediately. Some deceptions were not worth the cost.[12]

One canine head rose, its snout up in the air as it sniffed deeply.

Another nose tested the air from side to side.

The third head turned and zeroed in on the frail looking γιαγιά tugging her shawl down about her ears.[13]

Not that it mattered, but Set suddenly remembered the tour guide mentioning the dog's name: *Cerberus.*

A trio of slavering, toothy jaws revealed by lips pulled back and trembling, the huge beast turned and faced Set in his wrinkled grandmother disguise.

"Something Granny can do for you, Cerberus, my pretty boys?" Set asked in his most frail, endearing, matronly voice. "Can YahYah get a num-nums for my dearies?" Set pretended to root around in his bag, as if he might find something to dissuade the beast from their calling.

One pair at a time, the ears of the demon mastiff flattened against its heads. A deep growl rumbled to life in Cerberus's chest.

---

11. Dogs can smell things 10,000 to 100,000 times better than a human can. That means, on the low-end, Cerberus could smell in the 30,000 times better range, and the high end was off the charts.

12. There are examples of people disguising their presence using noxious smells all throughout history. The social and psychosomatic cost would be way too high for me to consider unless my life depended on it.

13. Γιαγιά: *Grandmother* in Greek. Pronounced *YahYah.*

It's too late to make friends with them now.

Careful not to move too quickly, Set pulled his hands from the bag and turned to face Cerberus head on. He dropped his disguise, resuming his dog-headed persona. "No show of solidarity for someone who also led a dog's life?" the jackal-faced god said to the three-headed guard of the underworld.

Cerberus lunged forward—or would have if the gravel hadn't spun out from under his feet.

Set had a bit of a head start, but it wouldn't be enough.

There was a river ahead. If Set could make it past it, he might just have a chance. The undead minions of Hades were drawn to the braying of Cerebus's three heads. The dog and the army were close on Set's heels.

Set found the narrowest part of the river. It was too far for someone to jump or even swim across. But Set wasn't just someone. And it wasn't as if he had any choice. The jaws of Cerberus snapped in the air mere inches behind him.

The next lunge and attack from Cerberus would be the end.

The Cocytus was close,[14] the pained sounds of its waters loud enough in Set's ears it could be heard over the sounds of Set's pursuers. The surface of the river came more into focus. The water formed into the shape of twisted limbs and distorted faces. The mouths of the waves shrieked and cried out for help or comfort or release that would never come.

It seemed to Set as if his pursuers had begun to lag behind, but he wasn't taking any chances.

Set jumped.

Being the god of thunder and desert storms came with skills and knowledge. Set collected just enough moisture from the tortured mists hovering over the lamenting rapids to create a cloud strong and

---

14. The Cocytus, or the river of lamentation. Its currents are made of every tear that has been shed in pain or misery, sorrow or loss. The guy famous for "Leave Britney Alone" personally added seven gallons of tears and liquefied mascara to the flow from the multiple takes of just the one video.

stiff enough to hold him. He fell upon it and used the raft to skim above the surface of the brackish flow. Set could taste salt in the mist, like spray from the sea. *A river of saltwater. Strange.*

He expected the minions of Hades to be right behind him, but when Set risked a quick glance over his shoulder, he saw the mass of Hades's guards had pulled to a stop yards back from the shore of the river. Almost as if the dwellers in the underworld feared the water.

"There aren't even crocodiles or hippos in this river. How cowardly these Greeks must be to be frightened of even getting wet." Set laughed.

The Egyptian god took a better look at the miasma of pain that swirled beneath his feet and decided perhaps these were waters he'd best avoid as well.

A portion of the mists of the cloud raft Set rode upon appeared to be trying to rise up and wrap around him. Thin tendrils clung around his ankles and calves. The strongest and most determined creepers reached for his chest as if they searched for his core, to strike at his center and cripple him with their power. Set, lacking a heart, was immune to their effects.

The mists continued to try, and Set slapped the snaking wisps of emotion away. The raft fell apart after it had served the purpose it was created for, and Set dropped down on the far shore.

The ones that had pursued Set were still on the other side. It was hard to see them that far away, but to Set's sharp eyes it appeared as if they had all turned back and had given up their pursuit.

Now Set just had to find a spot unobserved, and he could sneak back across to have another go at the center of the universe before it was too late.

He grinned and scanned up and down the river. There had to be someplace nearby where he might give it a try.

A fluttering above the river drew his attention.

The giant owl with blood-red eyes flew past Set's head and lighted on the branch of a dead tree not twenty yards away.

Something about the owl was disturbing, Was this Hades? Or

were owls like this common in the Greek underworld?

The owl was doing nothing but glare at him, so Set made sure nothing else was threatening.

The undead guards on the other side were all gone now. Bad training or instruction on the part of their master, Set supposed. They hadn't even left an undead watcher to make sure Set didn't just go back the way he'd just left.

Maybe that was what the owl was sent to do?

Set made as if to go back toward the river and the bird did nothing to intervene.

"Just a bird. Nothing more," Set whispered to reassure himself.

The guards on the far side were nowhere to be seen It was time for Set to go back. Set called upon his power, pulling at the mist above the pained waters of the river to make another raft to take him back across.

The mist rose up and came toward him, only to spread out in a flat sheet parallel to the shoreline as if it had come up across a pane of glass. Set let go of the mist and tried again.

The raft of gathered tears welled up against the same invisible dam again. No matter how Set called or compelled the mist, if could not get to him.

Frustrated, Set let go of his second attempt and launched himself toward the river. He hit the same force that had stopped the mist, only Set hit it from the other side.

His snout bloodied, he bounced backward and landed on his backside on the gravel shore.

Set used both hands to straighten out his nose in an attempt to return his face to its proper shape. It worked for the most part, but he couldn't draw a breath through his nostrils. He brushed himself off and stood up as he surveyed the invisible barrier and gathered his strength to try to jump over it.

"I wouldn't if I were you, or you'll just get more of the same," the ethereal voice that had reproached Thor in the inner chamber of the

Grand Machine said. "The way is shut."[15]

The owl seemed to weigh and measure Set with its blood-red, unblinking eyes.

"The way is shut. And the dead keep it."

It didn't look like the owl spoke, but there was no one else around.

Set straightened his robe and belt as he turned to face the owl. "It doesn't matter. Try to keep me out if you will, but I'll find my way back and finish what I started."

Probably a mistake to state his intent and purpose so boldly, but what did that matter? Set was going to have to find a way around new defenses and precautions anyway now. And his pride was too great for him to not try to get in the last word.

The owl cocked its head to the side. "The way is shut. All ways are shut."

The voice spoke with finality, and Set wondered if he had just let his sense of bravado and self-importance screw him out of the one thing he felt he truly wanted.

After the final pronouncement, the owl stretched out one wing then the other. The large bird turned its head from Set as if it were done with him and focused back to the center of the hells it had come from. It jumped from its perch and flew over the river as if the barrier that had just bloodied Set wasn't even there.

Set reached out a hand and pressed against the force that held him back. It was slick at first, but the harder he pressed the more his hand was pushed to the side. It was the same in all the places he probed.

The way, it seemed, *was* shut. But Set was still in Greece. He was stuck because if he ever stepped foot out of their borders, he would never be let back in. He was in unfamiliar territory. He needed information, supplies, and, as unlikely as it seemed and as unwilling as he was to admit it, help.

---

15. Obligatory LOTR reference.

Even Hades, with all his power and authority, wouldn't be able to close the entire border separating the underworld from the rest of existence. There was still hope for Set's cause. Set had been impatient, and now he was paying for it. He wouldn't make the same mistake again.

The tremors from the partially pulled pin would have sent reverberations to the far reaches of creation. So Set had a fair idea of where he might find information. He'd work out the other stuff along the way.

CHAPTER 10

DOES ANYONE KNOW WHAT'S GOING ON?

SOUNDS FROM THE INSIDE OF THE ESTABLISHMENT WERE TENSE and guarded. There was still talk in the bar, but it wasn't the usual, calming banter the king of the Greek gods was used to.

Earlier that day, the effect on creation must have been deeply felt. Isaac's bar at the top of the world was packed. You couldn't find an open booth, and the stools and chairs were all fully occupied. Some gods stood and milled about. It was noisy, and not in a way that sounded pleasant or patient. Zeus wasn't surprised.

When he entered the room, he was met with absolute silence. Every god, goddess, and entity present locked eyes on the king of the Greek gods.

"You all look to me as if I have answers. I don't. I'm just as locked out and oblivious as all of you." Zeus hitched his bag higher on his shoulder and cleared his throat. "I don't know what's going on either. The source of the disturbance lay below my realm, and I don't have access. I've tried to contact the one in charge, but he has yet to get back to me."

One by one the eyes in the bar and their respective owners turned from Zeus. Not all of those who had just heard him speak looked as if they believed him. He'd expected as much.

Zeus again hitched the pack a bit higher. When the lingering glances caught sight of what the pack contained, they took a hint and finally looked away.

With the temporary distraction addressed, many of the gods and goddesses present returned to whatever discussion or disagreement they'd abandoned at Zeus's arrival. The tempers of some of the patrons ran fairly short.

Du Kang[1] and Aegir[2] looked like they were about to come to blows, not about how the world might be ending, but how best to bolster their courage about what was to come.

"Rice," Du Kang growled.

"Honey. Far superior to your pale, weak, little grain." Aegir towered over the shorter Asian god.

"Puking insects gives you superior alcoholic content?" Du Kang sounded incredulous as he looked up defiantly. "And you would know, wouldn't you? I forgot you were the god of *whine*."

Aegir narrowed his eyes, his lower jaw jutted out. "There's an insult there, somewhere. I know it."

"Don't burst a blood vessel parsing it out, Longshanks," Du Kang said with a hint of disgust as he stepped forward and poked the Norse god in the belt with a stiff finger.

Aegir flinched and balled both hands into tight fists.

Zeus put a hand on the shoulder of both men.

They jerked and turned as if they might both now fight him, but Zeus held on tight. "Gentlemen, remember where you are."[3]

Both men looked like they had physical and verbal attacks cocked and ready. It was tense for a moment before first Du Kang and then Aegir nodded and backed down. While not quite apologizing to each other, they at least stepped back from the brink of violence.

Zeus released them both just as Isaac appeared beside them. "Sorry about the delay, gentlemen. We're dealing with the crowd and the situation as best as possible. I've ordered the overflow areas open so we can all spread out a bit and breathe. Gopher, Julie!" Isaac called out in a slightly shrill voice.

A perky, slightly disheveled young woman appeared. "We had a hard time getting the police box open, and the wardrobe was just a

---

1. Chinese inventor/sage of wine, and patron of the Asian alcohol industry.
2. Norse deity of beer, wine, and mead.
3. Isaac's bar is neutral territory. A meeting and gathering place connected to every realm in creation. No fighting is allowed there, kinda like no crossing swords on hallowed ground in the Highlander franchise.

wardrobe until the kitchen help you just hired showed us how they both worked."

"C.W.[4]," Gopher said, as if he had to clarify who Julie was talking about.

"He prefers to be called Murry. Good kid. Murry understands tesseracts better than most." Isaac grinned. "That was a lucky hire on my part."

Isaac turned about and addressed the room. "Ladies, gentlemen, primordial entities, the overflows are now open. Stretch out a bit, try to relax, and I will have a server with you shortly."

There were mutters and grumbles as the patrons decided if they wanted to go to the fantastical overflow or the more futuristic one—or if they were going to content themselves with staying where they already were. A disheveled herd pushed in the two directions. Here and there a dappling of patrons clutched their liquor-filled lifelines, unwilling or unable to give up a prize so hard won.

After a few minutes, most of the patrons had opted for the overflow areas which had far more space to spread out. Du Kang headed for the wardrobe, and Aegir very pointedly steered toward the police box.

Among those that stayed behind like Zeus was Satan at his end of the bar, perched straight backed on his stool, reveling in the misery of the others present. There was another god Zeus didn't know who gave off the feel of a stormy desert. Stormy tried to hide in the shadows in the far corner booth as he bullied the little black rain cloud that popped and sparked near him into submission. It was an obvious enough sign. He didn't want to be disturbed. A god with the

---

4. C.W. stands for Charles Wallace, the smart little brother from *A Wrinkle in Time*. He's still smart, all grown up now, and he prefers to be called Murry. He doesn't go by Charles Wallace anymore, because He feels a bit like he's outgrown the double name thing, and nobody uses it anymore except his sister and his parents., And the name is too familiar to IT, and nobody wants IT's attention. Not the IT from Stephen King, but the IT from space. Hold on a second—The IT from Stephen King came from space. So IT may be IT? Is IT IT? Holy cow! I think I just blew my mind.

horns of a stag sat facing away from everyone as he stared out the window at the mountain peaks that surrounded the bar and quietly wept into a tankard of mead.[5] Nang Kwak, Thai goddess of good fortune, slurred into the receiver of a cell phone. "I don't care what they thing-thunk-think. Sell it all. Screw the customers and the merchants. Inventory. Supply and demand. I don't want to keep track of it all anymore. I'm tired of the responsibility." She brought a coconut shell overflowing with *mekong* to her lips,[6] spilling quite a bit on its journey.

A somber crowd in here today, Zeus observed. *Must be something about the end of everything that just gets people down.*

Julie took out a receipt pad and headed to the wardrobe. Gopher sighed, tapped his pen on his little clipboard, shrugged awkwardly at Zeus and Isaac, and headed to the police call box.

Isaac stared at the mess on the bar for a second, when a call came from the back in response to his unvoiced question.

"On it boss." A twenty-year-old Murry came out of the stockroom with a large, flat bucket. He cleared off the empties and trash and stacked them all carefully. It didn't look like the mess could be stacked into one plastic tote, but somehow Murry made it work. He picked up the stable-looking stack and went back through the door to take care of the dishes.

"It's like that kid can read my mind or something," Isaac said.

"Seems like a solid, reliable young man." Zeus went over to a vacated barstool and set down his bag against the foot of the bar. The tips of several lightning bolts poked out of the top and crackled as they clanged against one another.

---

5. Cernunnos: Celtic god of wealth and life. He tries to be upbeat, but the constant living with stag antlers takes a toll. Kids say mean things. He also doesn't sleep well. Pillows and antlers don't mix. Throw in the end of everything, and you can see why he's having a hard day.

6. Distilled from 95 percent molasses and 5 percent rice, then blended with herbs, spices, and sweetened with honey. Generations of drinkers have called it whiskey, but most people call it "I can't remember where I left my pants" after drinking it.

Isaac made note of Zeus's bag before he made his way to the back of the bar. "Looks like you're loaded for bear."

Zeus grinned despite the way he felt. "Only bear I really know is Arktus, and he would smack my lightning out of my hand before I had a chance to use it. I felt it prudent to be prepared for any eventuality until I figure out exactly what is going on."

"So you really don't know." Isaac sounded tired and disappointed.

"It's even getting to Isaac? Ha!" Satan laughed, mostly to himself. "The end of the world just has everyone in the best of moods. Isn't it swell?"

The stormy desert shadow in the booth at the other end of the room appeared to perk up at that without giving the impression that he'd just perked up. Zeus watched Stormy out of the corner of his eye for a moment but figured it was nothing.

Julie came in and handed a bunch of drink orders to Isaac. He mixed a few, pulled a bottle or two out from under the bar, and sent Julie right back. Gopher came in a second later. He didn't look as steady on his feet with the load of drinks Isaac loaded on the tray. He moved carefully through the door into the overflow.

"You don't want to try out one of the other rooms?" Isaac asked.

"I prefer your company, and the main room." Zeus slumped against the bar.

"What can I do for you?" Isaac asked Zeus.

Zeus shook his head. "Take care of the others first. I need time to think, and I'm waiting for someone, I hope."

Isaac nodded, filled up a tray with varied drinks he knew some of his patrons would be wanting, and walked through the doors where Julie had just disappeared.

Zeus felt helpless, and it seemed a bit worse now that he was alone with his thoughts. He picked up his bag and moved over to a stool closer to the large, ornate fireplace that dominated the far wall. The fire that crackled in the hearth did nothing to ease the chill, but the light and shadow and sound soothed him somewhat.

I forgot how comforting a fire can be when times are hard. We shouldn't have given Prometheus so much crap about giving it to humans.[7]

Satan moved from his perch at the far end of the bar and selected a seat closer to Zeus that was just outside of the god's striking range.

Zeus's mood darkened. *Pleasant feeling gone.* Not that it would have lasted long, anyway.

"The end is nigh." Satan chuckled as he tossed a pretzel nub in his mouth, turned toward Zeus, and grinned like the Cheshire Cat.

"Something you find funny?" Zeus growled. *Of course the devil of Jehovah's chosen would be one of the few who didn't make his way into the other rooms.*

"The end. The big denouement. The apocalypse. Armageddon." Satan shrugged. "I'm just kinda looking forward to it. On account of my being cast out of my Father's presence and whatnot."

"Your Father is often here when you are," Zeus pointed out.

"Quality time spent with Dad in a bar," Satan mused. "No wonder I turned out so well. Fitting, I guess." Then the grin returned to his face as if he'd just thought of something really good and amusing that he wasn't going to share with anyone else. He stuffed several bread knots between his teeth and crunched them to pieces open mouthed. He giggled and spewed pretzel spittle across the top of the bar.

Just being near him was almost too much for Zeus to take. The king of the Greek gods could see why the host of heaven had tossed him out. "Don't you have anything else you could be doing, like tempting a young monk to break his vows or something?"

Satan ignored the question and popped another piece of bar mix into his mouth.

"And you're wrong about Armageddon or whatever you call it. There's no battle going right now." Zeus traced a finger along the bar

---

7. "Better to ask forgiveness than permission" didn't work in this particular instance. Prometheus greatly misjudged what his act of kindness would cost him.

top, his eyes trying to make out the pattern in the wood. "Just a crack in the mechanics of the universe or some such."

Satan chuckled. "No battle? Give it time. The other gods are frustrated because they can't get to the center of the universe to find out what's going on. And why is that, I wonder? Whose realm has the center of creation in its midst? You deny having power there, but I'm not so sure. Maybe that unresolved question needs to be dangled enticingly before a couple of jittery individuals, and we'll see what happens." He popped a couple more bread knots into his open maw, chewed melodramatically, and grinned at Zeus.

What if I just kill Satan a little? Would that be wrong?

Zeus wouldn't do it, but the thought was tempting.

A voice came from the door behind them. "It isn't Zeus's fault creation pivots beneath Olympus and beyond his reach."

The sound of the speaker's voice brought the first sense of hope to Zeus that he'd felt all day.

Mopsus stood in the doorway, his windblown hair frizzed out to its maximum capacity and his robe slightly akimbo. The reason for his disheveled appearance was pawing at the ground just past the doorway behind him. Pegasus had just delivered the seer to the meeting place.[8]

A disembodied voice said, "you have arrived at your destination," and then left with a tinkling of bells.

"Thanks, Hermes," Mopsus said as the sound of bells retreated. Mopsus then bowed slightly to the flying horse. "My gratitude."

The horse whinnied a response and flew off as well.

"Mopsus!" Zeus rose from his barstool to embrace the seer.

"My lord Zeus," Mopsus wheezed as the much larger being swept him up off his feet and crushed the air from his lungs. Mopsus still looked a bit pained as Zeus set him down.

---

8. Mopsus had never ridden a flying horse before. The novelty wore off after ten minutes, after which Mopsus wished he had listened to the man at the stables and paid the three drachma for the extra cushy horse blanket.

"You got my message, I see. I wasn't sure how well that would work, given the recent happenings and such." Zeus sat back down on the barstool and patted the stool next to him.

"Ah. I'll stand for a minute if you don't mind." Mopsus smiled awkwardly, took a halting step or two closer to the bar as if his inner thighs were a bit chaffed. "Hermes has been getting your messages through loud and clear. The bells he's adorned with took a bit of getting used to, though. I thought I was developing *emvoés.*"[9]

"Oh yes, the jingling and the jangling is a bit of a necessity at the moment, after he tried to take over all of creation and whatnot. I needed a way to keep track of the boy."

"I've gotten used to it." Mopsus reached for his own pack. "And speaking about the fate of creation, it hangs in the very balance again?"

Zeus nodded.

Isaac popped in for a second and noticed the crumbs from the poorly chewed bar mix on the counter. Satan looked eager for Isaac to confront him about the mess. Isaac, being a professional, wiped down the bar without saying a thing.

Satan appeared a bit put out when Isaac turned his attention to the newcomer in the room. "Why, hello, Mr. M. Anything I can get for you?"

"Oh, you know me," Mopsus said. "I don't imbibe."

"Oh, but I do know what you like, Mr. M." Isaac reached below the bar and took out a perfectly chilled bottle with a green-and-gold label adorned with the face of a happy little man in a hat.[10]

---

9. *Emvoés*: We call it *tinnitus*, which is Latin, but Mopsus calls it *emvoés* because he's Greek. There's a musical group called the Emvoes Ensemble, which advertises chamber music fusion. The Ringing in the Ears Ensemble. With a name like that, they must be good.

10. Vernor's ginger soda is best served in a glass bottle straight from the fridge. It will strip the back of the throat of whatever ails you. It was the official drink of the author in his hard partying, high school days.

"Chilled ginger soda in a glass bottle?" Mopsus reached out and took the offering by the neck. "Isaac, you are a gem."

"I try to please, Mr. M." Isaac winked at Mopsus and turned to take a tray to other customers.

The first sip of the ginger soda made Mopsus choke.

"That carbonation is the real deal. Not many men can handle a drink like that, Mr. M." Isacc nodded to the seer and was off before Mopsus had stopped coughing.

The seer took another tentative sip before he set the bottle on the bar. From his bag, Mopsus pulled out a rolled-up scroll. He hesitated for a moment, scouring the room for spies amongst the gods who were left. "Are we sure we should be discussing such things in the presence of others?"

Zeus's eyes widened. "You know what's happening?"

Mopsus's shoulders fell just a bit as some of his energy left him. "I thought you called me here to tell me what is going on."

"I wish that was so." Zeus sighed.

The fire in the hearth flared with a woosh behind him.

Mopsus sucked in a breath, and his eyes went wide. Zeus hardly noticed.

A black, four-foot-tall owl with glowing red eyes perched on the rail of the bar next to Zeus, a long, black, crooked staff held tightly in its talons.

Zeus wouldn't usually pay attention to the sudden appearance of the oversized bird of prey. Lots of animal deities and nature gods frequented Isaac's bar. But there was something familiar about this bird that Zeus couldn't quite put his finger on.

Zeus propped his elbows on the bar and rested his chin on his fists. "Seers have access to powers and knowledge the gods are hard pressed to imitate. I was hoping somehow a line between you and the underworld still remained, Mopsus. Hades isn't returning my calls."

"Given the nature of the happenings, I felt it best not to trust such information to a messenger," Hades said from the seat next to his younger brother. He took the staff he'd previously held in his talons and set it on the floor so the crooked head of it leaned over the bar top.

Zeus straightened up, noticing the sudden absence of the giant bird, and put two and two together. "I didn't recognize you. Nice disguise."

"Stygian Owl. Just something I'm trying out." Hades inclined his head ever so slightly to acknowledge the compliment.

Zeus spun on his stool so he faced the other god directly. "Brother, what is going on?"

"I made a miscalculation," Hades said. "There were and continue to be repercussions." Hades leaned in toward Zeus and spoke in a raspy whisper. "We need to talk."

Zeus looked over at Satan and glared.

"Jeez, really?" Satan rolled his eyes.

Zeus didn't waver.

"Fine. I know. I know. Get me behind thee." Satan picked up his drink and the bowl of bar mix and stomp-huffed to the far end of the bar.

CHAPTER 11

POTENTIAL PLOTS, PLANS, AND PITFALLS

ZEUS LOOKED AT THE SHADOW AT THE FAR BOOTH. THE DESERT god appeared to be asleep or in a stupor, or so Zeus assumed from the fact that the storm cloud had disappeared. He looked over at Satan at the far end of the bar, who pulled his finger over his heart in a cross-shaped pattern and batted his eyes as if the king of the gods had nothing to worry about from him. There weren't any other gods close enough to overhear anything Zeus, Mopsus, and Hades said.

Obvious misgivings aside, here and now was probably as safe a place to discuss the happenings of the breaking universe as anyplace else. "Tell me what is going on, Hades."

The god of the dead fidgeted, something quite out of character for him. "I made a mistake and led someone to the heart of the universe."

"Someone has attacked the center of the Grand Machine?" Mopsus asked.

Zeus looked over at the seer, just a bit impressed. He had no idea that Mopsus's insights ran that deep.

"It was foolish and vain of me," Hades continued. "I felt there was an opportunity to let a few select entities in to see the hub that ran creation, to share the wonders of the workings and underpinnings of the universe with certain parties of interest."

"To stroke your ego you let someone unqualified get near enough to the workings to break something?" Mopsus laughed and shook his head.

"They were supposed to be supervised." Hades blinked slowly as he folded his hands in his lap. He narrowed his eyes at Mopsus as if he didn't like the seer.

Hades had allowed someone or something close to the nexus of creation. Even if everything returned to normal, there was bound to be a family council called.[1] Zeus wouldn't be looking forward to that one.

Zeus took a deep breath and let it out slowly. "What happened?" There was a pause, and another question occurred to Zeus. "Is it broken beyond repair?" Another pause and another question. "Have you fixed it?" And then there was one more. "How are you keeping this from happening again?"

Hades looked like he wasn't used to being called on the carpet for anything. "It was a mistake. We learn from mistakes. We're only gods, you know."

Zeus sighed. "Hades?"

The pallid god looked at his hands. "The seer is right. I allowed tours to see the nexus of the Grand Machine, and one of those individuals took it upon himself to attempt to pull the main pin."

Zeus and Mopsus gasped.

The shadow at the far booth stretched, shifted on the table, and started to melodramatically snore. Satan perked up and stared at the sleeping man in the booth. Satan's focus of attention worried Zeus. He too looked at the sleeping man, trying to detect if the man was faking or not, but he couldn't tell.

"Whoever it was didn't manage to pull the pin from its seating in its entirety," Hades explained. "I had Thor try to hammer the pin back in place, but the pin bent, and the Grand Machine started to make a grinding noise, so we decided to leave it as it is for now."

"Thor?" Zeus asked.

"A Norse god," Mopsus said, "taking in the sites during a brief vacation, most likely. Not known for his finesse with a hammer when dealing with breakable machinery."

---

1. There was enough backstabbing and behind-the-curtains betrayal in a regular Greek gods family get-together to shock Machiavelli. There wasn't enough wine in all of Greece to make it through a serious family discussion criticizing Hades for a short-sighted business venture.

"It was a noble attempt," Hades growled. "We stopped before any further damage was done."

"Bent pin testifying to the contrary," Mopsus pointed out.

Hades glared at the seer. "The nexus point is held together, but the bearings on the wheel behind it have slipped, and the collar and hole on the other side no longer line up one with another. The main pin is worn and pitted and sliding it in without knowing what one is doing may cause it to shear. Someone with mechanical and engineering expertise is needed to put the pin back into place before more damage is done."

"I'll contact Hephaestus right away," Zeus said.

Hades flinched. "There have been further complications."

"We can't send Hephaestus?" Zeus asked.

Hades shook his head. "You know that the center of the universe lies below my realms, and that there are others there who would take offense at the presence of a god in their domain."

"The titans." Zeus rubbed his temples.

"And others," Mopsus added. "There have been many thrown into the pit since the dawn of time. Add to that the fact that Echidna and her mate Typhon have continued to sire children and there is no guarantee that the gods will prevail in a rematch."

Hades looked over at Mopsus and nodded as if he were in the presence of an expert. "There was an uneasy truce between those dwelling below and myself. I give them autonomy and certain concessions to keep them peaceful and content in their lands. I and my representatives are offered diplomatic passage at the whim of those in the Deep Under. To send a god other than me would reignite the war between the gods and titans."

"That would be bad," Zeus said.

"Especially with the nexus creaking, grinding, and threatening to give way. Not the best of times to risk an altercation with beings that can shake the firmament," Mopsus noted. "The options are getting more and more limited."

"I'm afraid there is more," Hades said.

Zeus and Mopsus turned to the god of the undead and waited.

"The borders of my realm have been shut, on both sides. No one is crossing into the underworld, and no one is crossing out. All official paths have been locked," Hades said.

"What exactly does that mean?" Zeus asked as he narrowed his eyes.

Hades stared back at his brother, not saying a thing.

"Even the dead?" Mopsus asked.

Hades stared back, his eyes as unblinking as the owl who had entered the bar.

"Well the fates are going to be ticked about that one, aren't they?" Zeus said.

"Unusual times," Mopsus noted.

Hades nodded in agreement. "In order to secure the site of the nexus, I was forced to broker a deal with the council that rules the Deep Under. Kronos and Typhon will allow no Greek god, not even I, to travel to the nexus ever again. We, and our powers and presence, are known to them. We would not be able to sneak by them even in disguise." He tried to add a bit of positive news by going a step further. "The only bonus of this is that the way is barred by our father and the monster we barely defeated the last time around. The saboteur can't return either."

"Small consolation as the tremors from the hub slowly shake the universe apart." Mopsus chuckled morosely.

Hades again glared at the seer.

Zeus ignored them both as he tried to find a way around the restrictions. "If we have to defeat Typhon, I still have the only weapon he fears." Zeus indicated his bag with the tip of a lightning bolt sticking out of the top. "Could we send a demi-god to do this?"

Hades shook his head. "We have to send a mortal."

"A mortal, holding the power of my lightning in a fight against Typhon?" Zeus scoffed. "This keeps getting better and better."

"If they make it that far." Mopsus pointed out.

"I almost overthrew my dad once. I can be pretty handy in a pinch," Satan offered from the end of the bar.

"Stay out of this, Morning Star," Zeus threatened. "Last time I checked you don't qualify as mortal anyway."

The smile on Satan's face drooped. "You didn't have to get all personal." He muttered to himself as he dug a maraschino cherry from the ice at the bottom of his fruit punch.

"So we need some mortal to fix the center of the universe, but we have to get them there first?" Mopsus said.

Hades looked as if he weren't telling everything he knew. He took a long, slow drink before he set the glass down and spoke with finality. "As I said, the way is shut."

Satan snorted from the end of the bar. "Heh, sure it is. Totally impassable." He mumbled in a sour whisper as he chewed on a mouthful of fruit-flavored ice.

Hades's stare bored into Satan.

Satan flung up his hands in mock surrender. "Oh, don't mind me. You're just basing your conclusion that your kingdom is impassable and impregnable off of the supposition that everyone plays by the same set of rules that you do."

Zeus turned to Satan and gave the devil a slight nod of acknowledgement for the insight. "He has a point."

Hades narrowed his eyes and glared at Satan. "What are you planning?"

"Me?" Satan laid his hand against his heart melodramatically. "Why would I need to break past your borders?" He turned, picked up his drink, and took a swig. "It's not as if I don't already have my foot in the crack of the door there anyway."

The color in Hades's cheeks paled a bit at the statement.

Satan rose from his seat and picked up his glass with a flourish. "Oh, don't be so dramatic, you old worry wart. I signed a contract, remember? And if you can't trust me, who can you trust?"

Zeus looked confused. "What is this about?"

"Nothing," Hades said with undisguised hate in his eyes.

"Jeezus! Lighten up, will you?" Satan said as he sauntered over to the other end of the room. "I'm not going to mess with your precious end of the world here. I'm just here to have a bit of fun and to make a new friend or two, you know, someone to *play* with for a while. I can see that you lot are a total loss, so I'll try my luck with someone who knows how to enjoy life a bit more." Satan slid into the booth with the desert god and poked him on the shoulder. "Hey, Stormy. Looking for a spot of company?"

The desert god mumbled something and tried to swat Satan away.

"Oh, I like you." Satan stuck his tongue out at Hades and the others and patted his new friend on the hand.

CHAPTER 12

HERO SELECTION

"Is Satan always that annoying?" Hades asked when he turned back to the others.

"He's actually quite the charmer," Mopsus said.

Hades arched a disbelieving eyebrow at the seer. "If you say so."

Satan laughed and spoke in soft whispers with his new friend, fully engaged.

To Zeus it felt like they could finally have a more private conversation. "Getting back to the crisis at hand, no one can get to the center of creation right now?"

Hades shook his head. "No Greek *god* can get there."

Mopsus was silent for a moment as he considered. "It falls on the creations of Prometheus to make the journey.[1] There will be challenges, and as such we will need a fearless, capable person who can deal with the horrors Mother Gaea hides from the upper world. This is not the time to deal with the egos of heroes."[2]

"We probably ought to send a woman. Or a eunuch,"[3] Zeus admitted reluctantly.

---

1. Prometheus created the first humans out of clay, then Athena breathed life into them. If they'd looked a bit more on the future and focused on some of the social media trends happening now, they might have reconsidered and made a couple of ashtrays instead.

2. What is it with the male ego? My son's friend said my son wasn't tough and manly and proceeded to punch him in the shoulder. There followed a punch to the gut in retaliation and at least one punch to an eye in the ensuing scuffle. After parents forced the little idiots to apologize, and a peace was brokered and sealed in the traditional sharing of chocolate chip cookies, the volatile alliance was mended.

3. Just a small snip and you have a man that is almost 100 percent aggression free. They still like to be scratched behind the ears though. Or a good belly rub.

"No need to find or motivate an emasculated adventurer," Mopsus reassured the god. "I have just the woman in mind. I have seen her react in the face of danger before and found her to be cool and level headed: Medusa."

"The familial connections might allow her access where others would be turned away."[4] Zeus nodded in approval. It was a good suggestion. "She is very capable, wise, and adaptable. I couldn't think of a better choice."

"But does she have the intuition to fix the machine?" Hades asked. "I'm unfamiliar with this Medusa."

"It's *that* Medusa," Zeus said. "There's only the one."

Hades looked confused. "Won't she just turn everyone she encounters into stone?" He stroked his bottom lip with a finger as he considered. "Actually, that could solve quite a few problems."

"She doesn't do that anymore," Zeus explained.

"Really? Since when?" Hades asked.

"You really need to get out more or at least pay more attention to the family group chat if you want to keep up with current events,"[5] Zeus said.

Hades pursed his lips in a frown. "So Medusa can't fix the Grand Machine?"

Mopsus shook his head. "We'll need someone else for that, I'm afraid."

"It feels as if we would need a proven hero for such a thing." Zeus stroked his mustache in thought. "Like the lad who rescued Medusa. Doug could do it. What about Doug?"

"Doug, brave and selfless as he is, doesn't have the skills needed."

---

4. Echidna, Mother of Monsters, is Medusa's younger sister. Medusa is basically related to half of the underworld.

5. The gods have access to something akin to the internet and digital messengers, but Hades just uses the tech to mostly look up funny fail videos so he can harass the ones who don't make it by customizing their punishment to reflect their final mistake. "I asked someone to hold my beer, and the next thing I knew I was pushing this boulder up the hill I tried cliff diving off of."

Mopsus pulled a rolled up scroll from inside the front of his robe. "I already consulted with Hephaestus and Kestibios about who we might use."

"Isn't that just a tad too forward thinking and too convenient?" Hades narrowed his eyes in suspicion at Mopsus.

"I'm a seer," Mopsus pointed out. "Forward thinking and too convenient is part of the job description."

Hades arched an incredulous eyebrow.

"I anticipated the need and considered the options. Most of the names they listed won't work for reasons we've already mentioned." Mopsus handed the list over and Zeus and Hades scanned it.

Zeus pondered the names for a moment.

"Fifth name on the list is the one you want," Mopsus directed.

"Modifixeus." Zeus grinned at the name. "Doug's brother?"

"The same," Mopsus said.

Hades shrugged. "I don't know this one. Not yet, at least. I know I'll meet him someday."

"We can't wait long enough for you to meet him like you do everyone else," Zeus said to his brother. The king of the Greek gods tugged at his beard for a second while he thought. "Raised by the same parents that taught Doug? Mod's the one. He's already connected to it somehow. I feel he is the right choice, as if Fate would have it be him."

Mopsus beamed. "You know how I feel about Mod. He's an excellent choice. It's just that . . ." Mopsus hesitated for a moment.

The silence grew for long enough that Hades became impatient. "Whatever it is, spit it out, man."

Mopsus blew out a breath and cleared his throat. "I assume they need someone to guide them along the way?"

"You want to go?" Hades looked a bit skeptical.

"Want? No," Mopsus said. "However, I will go if I am needed."

Satan raised his hand from the booth. "I'm more than willing if you're second guessing sending your portly Nostradamus with the group."[6]

Mopsus patted his gut and appeared slightly offended. "Who's portly?"

So much for privacy. Zeus scowled and gave the devil a wicked side-eye. "I'd prefer it be someone not trying to kill them or sabotage the mission every step of the way."

Satan pouted. "Where's the fun in that?"

Zeus's glare at the devil didn't waver.

"Harumph!" Satan snorted and folded his arms tight over his chest in a pout. "Spoilsport." He turned back to his booth companion as if he were ignoring Zeus and the others.

"They would need a seer as a guide, and I am a seer . . ." Mopsus began.

The desert god snorted loudly and woke up. He mumbled something as he rose and attempted to make his way past the gods and seer at the bar, whatever he was drinking held loosely in his hand. The man caught a foot on the strap of Zeus's bag and stumbled into the back of Zeus's stool. The desert god went down hard and managed to drench Mopsus from head to toe with his drink in the process.

"Clumsy of me." The man belched from below. "I beg your pardon."

Mopsus drug a hand over his face to clear away most of the drink then bent and helped the stranger to his feet.

The man exhaled in close proximity to Mopsus, and the seer immediately released him. "Imbibed a bit too much, have we?"

Even Zeus could smell the man's breath. It was tainted with the

---

6. Nostradamus was a hack. A prediction in vague enough terms can be applied to anything. Here, let me try:

Great strife will reign between the parties of rule and governance.

You will order the fish and lament, for chicken was your soul's desire.

A foul wind will blow, and a toddler shall wail. The receptacle of filth shall be discarded, but the air shall lay heavy with its memory long after it is gone.

strong scent of pomegranate wine.[7] Or was it fig? Given the current state of the man, quite possibly both. In large quantities. The man's tastes were expensive, and from his breath, his appetites were hard to quell.

"Clumsy. Excuse me. So sorry." The stranger apologized as he pulled away from the seer and the others. The stranger clung tightly to the folds in the front of his robe and shied away from the group he'd just stumbled against as he plotted a circuitous path toward the restrooms.

Satan laughed.

"What?" Zeus demanded.

"Nothing." The devil grinned to himself and acted melodramatically pious and innocent.

"If it must be, I shall lead the group, my Lord Zeus," Mopsus said.

"I was hoping you would be willing," Zeus said to Mopsus.

The stranger crashed through the entrance to the restroom. "Sorry. Excuse me. Sorry," he said to the ether as he disappeared through the swinging door.

Hades nodded along with his brother's decision despite the looks he'd given to Mopsus earlier. "I trust your judgment in this."

"Oh, who wouldn't trust his judgment? Nothing gets past him," Satan sniggered.

"That is quite enough!" Zeus leaped up from his stool, ready to give the devil his due.

There was the sound of doors opening and closing. Isaac came in and got more drinks at the bar. He filled new trays for Gopher and Julie, and Murry went in one of the overflows, then the other, and came back out with a dirty dish tray loaded to an almost impossible height.

---

7. The ancients bordering the Mediterranean mastered the process of winemaking in both red and white grape varieties, as well date and fig wine—akin to rum in their sweetness—and pomegranate wine with a bit of a zingy kick.

Zeus stood there, frozen. He didn't dare move until the bar help had gone back to their patrons.

"Remember where you are," Satan said with a justified smile as he leveled his gaze at Zeus and took a long, slow drink from his virgin strawberry, goji, pineapple daiquiri with a handful of cherries in the bottom. Satan had just turned the law of the bar back on Zeus.

Or had saved Zeus from making a terrible mistake.

The devil slowly stirred his drink with his straw before taking another long, drawn-out sip. His gaze never wavered from Zeus's eyes. It would have been more dramatic if his straw hadn't gotten clogged with a chunk of ice.

Zeus huffed and sat back down hard on his stool. When it was quiet again, he got back to their conversation. "Medusa, Mod, and you. A good group," he said to Mopsus as Zeus twined the end of his mustache between two fingers. "Now we only have to figure out how to get past an unbreachable border into the underworld."

Hades looked to his younger brother and then to the seer. "Well, the border may be officially sealed, but . . ." He reached into the opening of his robe, fished about in a pocket, and came up with a golden plate. He handed it to Mopsus.

The seer took the plate and looked at it uncertainly. "What is this?"

Satan sniggered over on his bench. "Someone bending a rule." The devil's whisper was just loud enough to make those at the bar turn around and glare at him.

The weight of Hades's attention was oppressive for those he wasn't staring at, but Satan made as if he were suddenly engrossed in a piece of fruit pulp on the rim of his glass like he didn't notice it at all.

Hades cleared his throat and turned back to his brother and the seer, his voice more guarded and hushed. "I've blocked all the main passages, essentially making it impossible to get to the center of the universe. All the usual paths in or out of the underworld are warded and impassable."

"So we need a path that is not official." Mopsus looked at the plate a bit more. "This is one of Orpheus's tablets."[8]

Hades nodded. "The most important one. This tells you how to get to the center of the universe and in and out of my realm when all other ways are blocked."

"To the left of the entrance to the land of Hades you will find a spring, and standing beside it, a white cypress," Mopsus read.

Hades dipped his head again. "All the other occurrences of this page of instruction tell the user to go left of the tree, or right to drink from the spring at the tree's base, or avoid it. Only this one tells you what you really need to do."

Zeus looked at the plate and saw nothing. "The plate is blank. I see no instructions."

"Gods can't see it," Hades explained. "This magic is aimed to aid only mortals."

"The innards of the tree will bring you down." Mopsus looked as if he didn't understand. "Take the stairs. A mushroom is key to finding the missing. Don't feed the fish. Give time what it has lost. Reblind the blind. Shake and bake for goodness sake. That last one doesn't make much sense." He paused and thought about it for a second. "Actually, none of them make sense."

"Clarification will come," Hades explained. "The instructions on the plate may change as need and situation dictate. Follow the new instructions when and if they come."

"But I will still have inspiration from you to help guide me, will I not?" Mopsus asked Zeus.

Zeus said nothing for a moment as he thought how best to approach this. "Hermes is bound by the same restrictions as the other gods. He may be able to approach you in the lands of Hades, but once past my brother's realm and into the lands of the titans and others,

---

8. These golden plates, though rare, have been found in the hand or mouth or deposited on the chest of the dead. They gave direction and instruction on how to find and succeed in your new reality in the underworld. A *What to do in Hades When You're Dead* if you will.

Hermes may not come and go without reigniting the war between the titans and the gods."

"Hermes won't even be able to get to you in my realm," Hades said. "The ways are blocked, and he doesn't know of the path and gate listed on Orpheus's tablets."

Mopsus looked a little uncertain at that. "No help then." He smiled and took a deep breath. "I shall find a way to make it work."

He didn't look as confident as he was trying to sound, of that Zeus was sure.

Hades reached around to the side and picked up the staff he'd brought with him. "This may aid you as well. It was a possession of the god that tried to undo the universe. The staff holds power, and just being in its presence may give you insight into who this person was and why he attempted such a heinous thing.

"More importantly, taking this with you will ensure that the weapon of the enemy does not once again fall into his hand."

Mopsus accepted the staff as if it were a heavy burden.

"I will give you something to aid you as well." Zeus reached below and pulled out the pack he had brought with him.

Mopsus's eyes grew wide. "Are these . . .?"

Zeus nodded. "Use them only if the situation is dire and no other option remains. No one has ever wielded them but me, and I am unsure of how things might go should such undeniable power be required."

Mopsus took the pack as if it might explode at any given moment, which it just might.

Bag over one shoulder, staff of power resting in the crook of his other arm. Mopsus turned a bit pale. "I think I need to use the restroom before I go. Maybe I can wash off a bit of this stain before it sets?" He picked at the front of his alcohol sodden robe. Mopsus went to set the staff and bag aside, but then thought better of it. "Guess I need to get used to doing things with these in tow." Mopsus bowed to the gods and headed through the swinging door into the water closet while fumbling to keep his new burdens from tangling and tripping him.

"We have faith these things, and this situation, are in the right hands," Hades called after him.

It was a desperate plan, but these were desperate times, Zeus thought. *And in such circumstances Mopsus had never failed the gods before.*

Zeus still felt uneasy as the door closed behind the seer, and the journey of Mopsus's lifetime began.

CHAPTER 13
AN UNEXPECTED DELIVERY

ENYO STEPPED BACK FROM THE MENU BOARD, PLANTED HER hands on her hips, and looked quite pleased with herself. "Work with what you're given."

The sign now read *Destruction Wrap Sale: The perfect gyro to get you through what could be a very challenging day!*

"Attention grabbing, for sure," Mod said, only half paying attention to the girls. "A bit wordy but that ought to sell a few sandwiches."

"It is kinda funny." Medusa ran a finger over the food on her collarbone and put it in her mouth. Her eyes went wide, and she smacked her lips. "This actually tastes even better than it smells. Not bad."

"Thanks," Enyo blushed.

There wasn't much panic going on in town yet. Greeks had quite a few volcanoes about. They knew what an earthquake felt like and looked like and was like.[1] Sure, there was a lot of variety within the definition of the happening, but initial shocks, aftershocks, landslides, and such in all their forms were pretty well known by everybody.

To Mod, what was happening didn't feel like an earthquake. It felt like something far different.

From time to time the ground would shake again, just not as violently as before. Mod had seen that lots of times, on small machines when a shard of metal fell onto a tooth of a gear, a grain of

---

1. Ask the average person who the god of earthquakes is and they would probably answer wrong. The correct answer is Poseidon. Poseidon is the god of earthquakes. And the sea. And horses. One of these things is not like the others.

sand worked onto a shaft, or a burr on the wheel rubbed against the axle the wheel revolved around. Most of the time the circular motion and the speed of the rotation took care of the problem.

Most of the time.

Then there were the other times when the bit of grit or debris in the wrong place caused the whole thing to seize, strip the gears, and explode.

The last time that had happened, a transfer plate had whizzed through the air, narrowly missing Mod's head and clipping off Hepaestus's beard on the right side at a thirty-three-degree angle.[2]

Mod had seen the effect of a small machine blowing up from binding and halting on the shaft, but what if the machine were far bigger? Like, say, the size of Gaea?

Mod frowned then brightened a bit as he looked over at Medusa.

She still dabbed at the residue of tzatziki on her collarbone and seemed to be creating quite a rapport with Enyo. The two women had stabilized the food cart, and Mod had helped them put everything back where it was supposed to be.

Mod frowned again.

It was dawning on him that the friendship he had with Medusa had changed, would change, is changing. She wasn't going to be just his buddy anymore, stating that she wanted more. The "more" altered the composition of the equation, and Mod wasn't so sure he would be pleased with the results.

Not that he wasn't curious, but Mod, by his nature, didn't like change.

And change was coming whether he liked it or not.

He'd managed to get through Doug marrying Larisa because Medusa had been there. He didn't know what he would do if Medusa

---

2. They knew it was a thirty-three-degree angle because everyone present had at least a slide-rule handy to measure the rise and run of the cut. They set out to recreate the explosion in the off chance it might be useful, and it worked nine times out of ten before they figured out cutting beards at thirty-three degrees really didn't have any practical application.

left him too. And now he didn't know what would happen if Medusa stayed either.

But to not follow through with the experiment meant the possible loss of the friendship in its entirety, which would leave Mod alone. He wasn't ready for that either.

The only constant is change.[3] Mod added his own twist on Heraclitus's words: *Mod's only constant is the fear of change.*

He looked over at Medusa and tried to smile. Medusa looked back, smiled for a second, then dropped the smile and looked away. Mod wasn't sure what that meant, but he was pretty sure it wasn't good.

I wish Doug were here. But Mod's brother wasn't there. Doug and Larisa were off finalizing a trade pact with countries in Northern Africa.[4] Mod, for good or bad, would have to work this out for himself.

There was a small buzzing sound that grew and clarified until the air was filled with the chimes of tinkling bells. Everyone around the picnic bench looked up, and suddenly Hermes was there. And there was a familiar face riding the messenger god piggyback.

At least most of the face was familiar. Mopsus's jaw was covered in dirt, and he had a nasty scrape on his cheek that ran across his face and past his bright red nose. His hair was also windblown in a chaotic explosion that made him look all the wiser for it.

Mopsus clung tightly to a long pack slung over one shoulder with one hand and a curious walking stick with the other. He had his legs cinched around the waist of Hermes, who didn't look any happier about the arrangement.

----

3. Mod hadn't cared about Heraclitus when he came up with the saying, and he pretty much hated Heraclitus and his oh-so-astute observation now. Stuck up, weepy philosophers and hard-fact engineers just can't understand each other.

4. Mod and Doug's father had made trade agreements with the Maghreb (the African lands bordering the Mediterranean) for grain back when both of the young men were toddlers. Because Doug had grown up watching his father do business, he had a natural understanding of balance, fairness, and diplomacy, which came in handy as he helped rule a kingdom.

Mod brightened. "Mopsus! Good to see you. May I ask why you're riding on the back of a messenger?"

"God," Hermes corrected.

"Sorry," Mod said. "I meant no offense."

Hermes ignored the apology and answered the question that wasn't directed at him. "We couldn't find the blasted horse again," Hermes grumbled. "Pegasus must have decided carrying lard-ass around earlier was already enough of a workout for the day."

That didn't really answer what Mod had asked, but he let it slide. He shifted his focus to Mopsus's mount, considered for a second, then thought it best to address the god as well. "Hermes," Mod said flatly.

Hermes grunted in response.

Mopsus dismounted Hermes. As he jumped down, the crook of his walking stick smacked Hermes upside the head and almost knocked his winged helm from his blond curls.

"Careful, fat man," Hermes growled as he righted his hat and glared at the seer.

Mopsus ignored the messenger god and looked to those he came to meet. Food was still smeared and smashed all over both Medusa's and Mod's chests and faces. Mod, in a rare flash of social awareness, wondered how this might look to someone who just got there.

Mopsus was quiet for a second as he appeared to process. He shifted his pack as if he were just a bit afraid of the bag's contents, and shifted the staff from side to side like it was heavier than it looked. While he was doing this, he tried to pat down his windblown hair to get it out of his eyes. Mopsus looked between the two women for a second, almost as if he didn't know who he was looking for. "Uh, hello, Medusa."

Medusa smiled and gave him a small wave.

The pause was a bit odd to Mod, but the seer had been riding piggyback on the messenger of the gods traveling at who-knew-what kind of speeds. His eyes were probably dried out, and he was having a hard time focusing. And his burdens seemed to be taking a toll.

Mopsus nodded to Medusa then turned to Mod. "Hello, Motefexus."

Mod had never heard Mopsus mispronounce his name before. "Modifixeus," Mod corrected.

Mopsus cleared his throat and tried again. "Modifixeus. Sorry. My lungs and throat feel like they're made of old dried figs, and not in a good way. Could I trouble someone for a sip of water?"

Enyo went over to the food wagon and came back with a waxed paper cup.

Mopsus drank the whole thing in a slow swig. "My thanks." He smacked his lips, cleared his throat again, and turned to the group, surveying them in with a long, appraising sweep. He looked hesitant to say anything but pressed forward anyway. "I hope I'm not interrupting anything."

Hermes looked disgusted by all of them. "These are the ones father is pinning the hopes of saving the universe on?"

Then Hermes's eyes passed over Medusa a second time with a long, lingering glance. "If you'd like to spend the end of the universe doing something, or someone, more worthwhile, I'm sure I could find many ways to console you."

"I'd sooner tongue kiss Charybdis,"[5] Medusa responded.

Hermes grunted as if her rejections made no difference to him, turned to Enyo, and arched an enquiring eyebrow.

"Not very picky, are you?" Enyo folded her arms, cocked her weight back on one leg, and stared him down. "Lucky for you, I have standards that you don't meet. I'd break you, Jingle Belle."

The second rejection made him look a bit put out. Maybe it was too much to have his offer rejected by two women? Or maybe he was just offended by Enyo's new nickname for him? Or by Enyo telling him he didn't measure up.[6] Hermes sneered at the lot of them.

---

5. What people choose to do with mythical, monstrous whirlpools is their own business.
6. We can't all be Priapus.

"Hopeless and worthless to the end, which I assume is swift in coming. I guess I need to get my affairs in order." With a jarring tintinnabulation of the bells around his neck, Hermes left without another word.

"Worthless? Hopeless? How rude. The three of you are fully capable, creative, intelligent adults." Mod huffed. "As for me, I'm just out of sorts. There has to be an explanation for what is happening."

"As to that, I think I've had about all I can handle for the day." Medusa walked over to her sister and gave her a hug. "Not a bad lunch, Enyo. I'll have to come back and try your food again on a day that is a little less unusual."

"I would love that, sister." Enyo hugged her back. "Are you sure you won't stay for a bit? I could put together something quick for you to take with you."

Medusa sighed and shook her head. "I'm tired and think it's about time I get on my way."

Mod had hoped he'd have more time to figure things out. It appeared that Medusa didn't think that was necessary.

A flush of heat hit Mod's cheeks, and he started to fidget.

"About that, if you would wait for just a moment," Mopsus began.

The world jerked again. Mod was a bit more prepared for it this time, so he wasn't thrown atop anybody. Everyone standing in the area felt like they were shoved a bit to the west.

The shift from whatever Medusa had intended to what Mopsus wanted rooted and calmed Mod a bit. "I'm forming a hypothesis. The jerks in the world are rotational, happen at a fairly regular interval, and seem to come from the center of Mother Gaea."

Mopsus nodded that Mod's deduction was correct and pointed at his own scraped cheek and swollen nose. "It wasn't just the world. It was bigger. Hermes stumbled while traversing the ether and dropped me, and that's how I got this."

"So Mopsus, why are you here?" Mod asked.

"The gods have need of you for something most urgent," Mopsus said.

"I guess I'll leave the two of you to it then," Medusa said as she turned to leave.

It sounded like she was just as scared as Mod felt, and Mod was sure it wasn't about the news the seer had brought to them.

"Medusa, the gods have need of you as well," Mopsus said.

Medusa halted and turned toward them slowly. She actually looked a bit relieved that she had to stay.

"I'll fill you in as we go. Zeus has made arrangements for us to meet someone just up ahead," Mopsus said to both of them. "There's not a moment to lose."

CHAPTER 14

TROUBLE AT THE CORE

THREE JOGGED UP JUST AS THE GROUP WAS GETTING READY TO leave. "You went to Enyo's? Bold choice. How'd it go?"

"It was nice," Mod said as he paid.

Medusa looked at Mod and wondered if he'd just attended the same lunch she had. "Aside from the fact that the world might be ending because we went on a date."

"I don't think the two events are related," Mopsus clarified.

"Oh, hey, Mopsus." Three smiled and greeted him. "When did you get here?"

"Ah! One of the mechanical people. Excellent timing." Mopsus nodded.

Three looked a bit confused at how he greeted her. "I'm not One. I'm Three."

"Of course." Mopsus bowed his head in slight apology. "I meant no offense."

"The other automatons, One and her brothers, are off doing who knows what right now,"[1] Mod said.

"We'll, except for Nine," Three said.

"Nine?" Now it was Mopsus's turn to look confused.

"The king?" Medusa said as if it should be obvious.

"Oh." Mopsus let out a tsk. "Of course. The king. I knew that." He looked a bit flustered and furrowed his brow. "Sorry. There is quite a bit going on, and Three's arrival forced my brain to shift gears

---

1. The automaton siblings were all introduced in the first book of the Not Quite Legendary series. They are One, Three, Four, Five, Six, and Nine (also once known as Two, now also known as Teutamides the king).

a bit. No time for pleasantries or chit chat." Mopsus urged them all to begin walking. "Time is of the essence."

Mopsus led the group back into the center of Larissa.

"We're going back into town?" Medusa asked.

"We need to get to the palace. Someone is waiting for us there," Mopsus explained.

Mopsus seemed to be having a hard time remembering people he should know. It made Medusa a bit worried. Mopsus was an old man and a seer. Seers tended to get a bit loose and eccentric after a life-time of consulting the vapors to divine the will of the gods.[2]

"I like the walking stick. Looks fancy," Three said. "And that's not the only thing that's new." She reached over to lift the flap of his pack.

Mopsus flinched away. "Careful. The pack was given to me by Zeus. The contents of it could be very dangerous."

Three let her hand hover near the pack. Her hair frizzed out the longer she let her hand stay close. "Electricity? In a backpack? How awesome is that?"

"Yes, awesome indeed. Just don't touch unless I say so." Mopsus nodded and continued forward. "I hold on my back lightning from Zeus. A weapon of last resort, and one I hope we will have no need of using." Mopsus shifted the pack gingerly as if fearing that it might go off at any moment.

Three pulled her hand back and twiddled her fingers in front of her face. "Feels tingly."

Medusa hadn't really noticed the stick or the pack until now. She was preoccupied with too many other things. She pointed at the walking stick. "So what's this? A thumping stick from Ares?"

It didn't look quite sturdy enough to be a bludgeon used in

---

2. The seer takes another long hit from the smoking hemp blunt. "The vapors are telling me to get another burrito."

The supplicant grows frustrated. "That's what the vapors told you last time!"

The seer pulls out a tortilla and some salsa. "I'm just a messenger, bound to carry out the will and whim of the gods."

dispensing death, and it was prettier than most instruments favored by godly, macho warriors.

"Did someone give Ares a Bedazzler or something?"[3] Three asked.

Again, Mopsus held the item away from everyone else protectively. "This is Egyptian. The god that caused this all left it behind when he fled. It is a curious device, and it may give some insight into the one who used to wield it."

"So all the gifts and surprises on the trip are just for you?" Three teased the seer.

Mopsus at first looked annoyed, but then he pursed his lips and gave a nod. "A fair assumption, given how I have been protecting the staff and the pack." He set the pack down and rummaged through one of its outer pockets. He produced a sheet of gold and held it out for Medusa and Mod to see.

"What's this?" Mod asked as Medusa handled the sheet of gold.

The seer shrugged. "Supposedly a guide to find a way into the underworld, or so Hades said when he produced the thing."

"An Orphic tablet?" Medusa's eyes went wide, and she held the sheet of gold a bit more carefully.

"That was what he called it, yes." Mopsus nodded. "Though aside from the metal it is made from, I haven't found it to be overly special."

The words *Not everyone gets me* appeared on the tablet in Medusa's hands.

"Holy sheep!" Mod leaned in and gaped at the golden sheet.

"This is amazing." Medusa held the tablet out to show the seer. "Had it shown you anything like this since it was given to you?"

Mopsus frowned slightly. His eyes searched the golden surface for a second. "Not as such, no. Orphic tablets are a curious magic of a type unknown to the gods and their servants." Mopsus closed up the

---

3.   No, someone did not give Ares a Bedazzler. He bought one for himself during one of those late-night shopping marathons on QVC.

pack and once more slung it over his shoulder. "I assume this means the tablet was meant for you or Mod." With that he took off again, as if the tablet meant nothing to him at all.

Medusa slid the tablet into the pocket in her dress as if it were made for it.

Mod smiled. "I knew there was a reason I made a pocket that size for you."

Medusa was forced to smile back. Feminine fashion was regrettably lacking in pockets, so Mod had taken it upon himself to give pockets to the clothing of the closest of his female friends. He'd done a good job of it too. Apparently engineering and tailoring both came naturally to him.

Then Medusa remembered that she was upset with Mod, or herself. The smile on her face faded. And so did Mod's happy look.

Mopsus cleared his throat, urging them all to be on their way.

"So what's in the basement?" Medusa asked.

"Someone we must meet with to take us where we need to go next," Mopsus explained somewhat cryptically.

"Sounds good," Three said. "Who wouldn't want to meet someone in a deep, dark place so they can send you on an adventure? Count me in!"

"I can't tell if you're joking or not." Mopsus narrowed his gaze at Three before he continued, "It is a bit convoluted sounding, but I think it necessary you know the reason we are in this peril. There are those who think that Gaea is the center of the universe, and the whole of creation revolves around it, with the planet as the nexus and center point."

"Gaea is not the center of the universe?" Medusa asked.

Mopsus nodded as he continued walking. "Gaea's center is not the center of the universe. The true center of the universe is roughly 137 feet from the center of our rotund Mother Gaea. Gaea's core sort of pivots about that singular spot like an unenthusiastic yet boringly consistent pole dancer."

Mod nodded as if he understood, then furrowed his brow because he apparently didn't. "Pole dancer?"

"Forget I said that." Mopsus shook his head and leaned into his walking stick a bit harder as he picked up the pace. "The planet is only pinned to the universal nexus rod in the one spot. The pole the earth is pinned to is riveted to a cog, and the cog connects to a bigger wheel. There's gears and pulleys, rods and wedges and cones, and a half a dozen rotating clock-like mechanisms that connect and spin off of this singular pole just to set up our solar system. Those in turn connect to other bits and pieces to create something akin to a giant mobile dangling all the other systems into a startlingly complex machine that runs the Milky Way.

"None of the gods can get there. The way is blocked by beings they can't deal with."

"That's not very encouraging," Medusa frowned. "Go on."

"That brings us to the reason you are necessary, Medusa. Zeus thought you might have special insights into thoughts and actions of the residents of the realms we must pass through," Mopsus said. "You could very well deal with the beings the gods are unable to interact with."

"Special insights?" Medusa narrowed her eyes at him.

"I shouldn't beat around the bush on this one." Mopsus shook his head. "Because of your birth and experiences, Zeus feels you will have a certain rapport and understanding of the monsters residing at the center of the earth."

"He thinks I can sweet talk the titans because I lived with snakes for hair most of my adult life?" Medusa didn't say the real reason Zeus thought of her. She was needed because she was a monster just like her mom and dad and family.

Mopsus appeared not to recognize Medusa's sudden discomfort. "I know, such a thing sounds like a stretch, but the situation is desperate and any incursion by a god could risk reigniting the war that almost ended creation."

"If creation is already hiccuping, the war route might be the only option," Three pointed out.

Mopsus shook his head. "War takes time and is unpredictable. Our reality is still healing from the last attempt to rewrite the rules."

"Thanks, Hermes," Medusa grumbled. She followed the seer, but she could feel a sudden urge to run the other way. Maybe she could convince Mopsus to take Enyo instead, after all, Enyo had almost all the same qualifications. She pushed the thought from her head. Even if Enyo and the others agreed, Medusa felt it would be wrong to send her sister in her place, and it would only make Medusa feel worse about herself.

Mopsus continued to address the group completely unaware of the mental wrestling Medusa was doing. "You will deal with the denizens of the pit, and I'll be there to help find the way. It will be difficult. There are unofficial paths, places where one might slip past the borders of Hades's realm, but they are dangerous and unknown to all but one or two. And the gods cannot pass through using those paths, or they risk war. Which is why I must go on this quest."

"Okay, so you've asked Medusa along because she understands monsters?" Mod asked.

Medusa flinched at that.

Mopsus nodded, oblivious.

"What about me?" Mod looked like he had a sneaking suspicion.

"You get to fix the machine." Mopsus said it so plainly, it was as if there were no question about the inevitability of celestial mechanics simply giving way to Mod's will.

"Can I be the screwdriver?" Three raised her hand to ask. "And not to point out the obvious solution, but can't Mod just use his portal, skip to the center of the world, and work it out from there?"

Mod stopped on the road. "Using the portal is complicated, and I have to have been to the place I'm programming in or I have to have a connection to someone or something on the other end. Just using it randomly could open a hole into the bottom of the ocean or put us in the center of solid rock. It's kind of an art, really. Besides, Mopsus hasn't really told me what is going wrong, so I don't know even if I can fix whatever it is. And wouldn't it be better to send Hepheastus or some other maker god to fix celestial machines?"

"Like I said, any incursion by a Greek god will risk reigniting the war with the titans. Plus, a few gods from other pantheons have already attempted to breach the firewall, with devastating results."[4]

"Firewall?" Medusa asked.

Mopsus explained, "A term for a ring of protection that will be used to safeguard proprietary technology in the far future. The technological meaning of the term is not applicable in this instance, but the term itself is still appropriate. Firewall in regards to us is pretty much exactly what it sounds like. No one, god, mortal, or the dead is getting in or out. It's causing quite a ruckus." Mopsus shrugged and got the group moving again.

"We're included in the groups that you just mentioned are excluded, if you hadn't noticed," Medusa pointed out.

"Ahh, but there still might be a way. Hades knows of at least one path to get there. And it is rumored that the Grand Machine's engineers put in a backdoor somewhere, a service entrance and tools they can use to fix the machine should the need arise."

"Uh, the need has appeared to have arrived." Three gestured around at the debris strewn by the repeating earthquakes.

Indeed, there were cracks in just about every building they passed. A few of the roads into town exhibited new bumps and rises. The citizens of Larissa seemed scared but were mostly quiet.

They've been lucky so far. It doesn't appear as if anyone has died. I wonder how long that can last?

Mopsus looked about at all the damage they passed. "Several gods have been trying to get a message through on the Grand Machine's company helpline, but so far they've all been placed on

---

4. Baal and Baalim gave it a shot. The fire proved superior. The olfactory result was worse than microwaving burnt popcorn and a dead fish on high in a closed office for forty-five minutes. The smell of burning Baals hung in the corner of the underworld long after the Baals left the toaster.

hold. It appears the one servicer trained in fixing this type of situation is currently unavailable because he's on another call."

"So the universe is going to be destroyed because there aren't enough trained repair persons available to fix the . . . What did you call it? The Grand Machine?" Medusa, in her current fatalistic mindset, wasn't in the least surprised. "That figures."

"I'm sure the repair of the Grand Machine will be mostly intuitive to someone mechanically minded." Mopsus gestured to Mod. "And we know where we need to go, the hardest part is just getting there."

"This is just bigger and more important than anything I've ever done before. I haven't seen the machine. I won't have my shop and most of my tools." Mod's pace slowed as he contemplated. Then he said the words Medusa had never heard him utter about working on a machine before. "I don't know if I can do it."

Medusa was a bit taken aback. Her being down was one thing, but Mod acting unsure about fixing something? She thought it best if she reassured him of his skills. "I know you can do this thing asked of you."

Mod looked as if her confident tone restored him.

"I still need tools." Mod glanced over at Medusa. He just as quickly looked away.

Three raised her hand. "I'm basically a walking, talking, all in one tool chest. We'll have what you need." To demonstrate, she popped back all the fingers of her right hand to reveal the screwdriver heads concealed under her nails. "They're ratchet geared." She gave her pinky a little twist, and you could hear the clicking.

"See. All the tools you should need to do the job." Mopsus clapped Three on the shoulder.

"We got you covered," Three said.

Mod nodded hard like he was up to the challenge. His renewed confidence appeared to waver when he looked over at Medusa. "Traveling together might give us a chance to figure things out?"

Medusa nodded back to him, resigned. *Well at least if we fail, the universe will end and we can all get out of this awkward situation. There's always a bright side if you look hard enough.*

FIXING THE GRAND MACHINE WAS ONE THING. TRAVELING with Medusa, who he was pretty sure was mad at him and who would probably want to talk about subjects that would make Mod uncomfortable, was another thing entirely. He'd rather focus on things that had nothing to do with relationships. He wanted to think of pleasant things like lubrication and rotation, shafts and pistons, incredibly tight-tolerance sheaths and interlocking multi-jointed sliding pieces.

Mod sighed. He felt like he was stuck going with the others now, whether he wanted to or not. And he had a pretty good idea that if you were trying to get to the center of the universe, Doug's house wasn't going to have a passage that would lead there. "So, we're trying to get to the center of the universe, and the path leads us through the palace of Larissa?"

"I know Doug and Larisa are gone on official business, but shouldn't we at least stop and say hello to my brother?" Three asked.

Mopsus paused for a second. "Your brother?"

"Nine," Three reminded him, "the king Teutamides."

"We really don't have time for pleasantries like a court visit." The seer led them through a small gate on the eastern side of the palace. "Besides, our path leads us not through the palace, but below it."

"We're getting to the center of the universe through the basement?" Mod asked. He'd been in the basement plenty of times, and he'd never seen a pathway to the underworld right there.

"This is just a stopping point," Mopsus said. "We're hitching a ride."

"Hitching a ride?" Medusa sounded confused as well. "Is there a chariot depot or a wagon station under the palace that I don't know about?"

"No. Nothing like that."

They walked into the basement, followed a hallway for a bit, and then started down a winding stairway. The light grew dimmer, until it began to be hard to make out the details of the walls and the tread of the stairs.

Three reached for a torch on the wall.

Mopsus stopped her. "We won't be needing that."

"Not for me," Three said. "To chase away the dark and help the others."

"The dark is here to help," the voice of the dark said.

"Erebus?" Mod asked.

The dark nodded. "Time is of the essence, so there is no time for your group to travel to Cape Taenarum."

"Cape Taenarum?" Mod asked, and then he remembered what Doug had told him. "The entrance to the underworld is in the cave there."

"There are other paths, but this one is the easiest for a group to travel, especially a group that can't breathe underwater," Erebus said with a hint of surety. "The path Doug used on his trip to Hades is the safest path for you."

"The official borders to the center of the universe are all closed down below, but we still have to use the same entrances to get from the surface to the underworld," Mopsus explained.

Medusa pointed down at the floor of the basement. "This isn't Cape Taenarum."

Mod smiled in anticipation because he was pretty sure what Erebus had planned. "Hold on. You'll understand in a second."

There was a thickening of the air around them. The dark coalesced into a tangible thing. The spirit of the dark, made corporeal, picked them all up. The sensation of being weightless was still a bit unsettling, but Mod laughed at how it felt the second time he'd ever experienced it.

"The dark is comforting." Medusa sounded a bit surprised.

"Erebus is kind and more gentle than most know," Mod said.

"You're making me blush," the deep, soothing voice of the Dark rumbled.

The warm support of Erebus set the feet of the group down on the floor of the cave in Cape Taenarum. Erebus pulled enough of his substance to the edges of the cavern to reveal the cave floor and its surroundings in a sort of absence of darkness. It wasn't quite the same as lighting and illumination, but the group could all make out the details of the world around them.

"Thank you, Erebus," Mod said.

"Thank you," the others echoed.

"I would have taken you further, but there is something here that I believe may need you, and it may turn out to be a boon to you as well," Erebus said.

"Are you sure we have time for this?" Mopsus asked.

"I do not make decisions in haste, child," Erebus chided the seer.

Mopsus grumbled and folded his arms.

"Could you just please tell us what this boon is?" Mod asked. "Not to be rude, but I've already had enough surprises for the day."

"It is another companion," Erebus explained. "One who has much need and may prove helpful in your quest. I would approach closer, but the beast is afraid of me."

"Beast?" Mod questioned.

"Good luck," Erebus said as he retreated, and the group was left in the absence of light that filled the cave.

They hadn't gone very far when there was a sound of something moving up ahead.

Mod slowed. "It sounds a bit like an animal."

There was a gentle whimpering from one of the shadows off to the side. The animal sounded tired, scared, and hopeless, as if it had been lost and alone for quite some time.

"It sounds like some sort of dog," Mod said.

As they came closer, the whimpering quickly stopped. It was a small dog, just as Mod had suspected. He got close enough to the animal to pet him, and the dog welcomed the physical contact and looked relieved to have someone here he could trust.

"I've never seen a dog like this," Medusa said.

"Nor I," Mod said, "It's unlike any dog that I've ever known or seen before. It's not a molossus, nor is it an alopekis, a Cretan hound, or a kokoni."[1]

"You know all the types of dogs in Greece?" Three asked Mod.

"There's only really four types, and yes, I know them all. I grew up on a farm. Dogs always helped us herd the livestock." Mod shrugged.

"Surely this short-legged runt can't be the companion Erebus told us about." Mopsus scoffed.

The pocket in the front of Medusa's dress started to glow. She opened up the top of it and looked inside. "The light is coming from the Orphic tablet."

Everyone, Dog included, was intrigued as Medusa pulled the tablet out. They all gathered round. The surface of the plate shifted and shimmered until words appeared on the surface.

This is the one Erebus spoke of. His name is D'artagnan. He is far from his home and his time. He misses his master, who is the captain named for a bowman on a ship that flies through stars.

Mopsus stared at the glow and appeared flustered. "Is this supposed to help?"

Three leaned in. "I like the light."

"It just told us the animal's name, and that he's lost." Medusa looked confused as she pointed out the lettering on the tablet.

"Anything else you can tell us about him?" Mod asked the tablet.

He's a good boy.

---

1. All ancient breeds of Greek dogs.

"There wasn't ever a question of that, right, D'artagnan?" Mod scratched the dog behind the ear. The dog came closer and hid his nose against Mod's leg.

"Poor thing," Medusa said. "Do we know how to get him back to his family, or back to his home?"

The magics that brought him here are beyond my abilities and understanding. I'm afraid D'artagnan is stuck in this time.

"Well, we'll try to take care of him as best we can." Mod tucked his hand under the dog's chin and gently raised the dog's face up so he could look him in the eyes. "So it looks like you'll be heading into danger with us. Sorry, buddy."

The dog didn't seem to mind.

Mod's fingers scritched the dog on the side of the head and around to behind his ear. "Now we only need know which way we should go."

D'artagnan barked and stood up.

"I'm the guide," Mopsus said a bit testily.

The dog pointed down the cavern at the same time the seer did.

"How does the dog know which way to go?" Mod asked.

The tablet flashed in Medusa's hand. "The images of *bacon* and *down*," she read.

"The center of the universe smells like bacon?" Three asked. "I wish I could smell bacon. It is one of the smells many mortals speak of with great reverence." She pointed at her mechanical nose, a look of longing on her face.

"Why would the center of the universe smell like bacon?" Mod asked.

Mopsus did not look pleased.

"Doesn't matter. All this means is that we now have a guide to lead us." Three gave a polite nod to Mopsus. "And a backup should it become necessary."

When the light from the tablet faded Three handed out smoke-less torches to all the members of the group.

Medusa, Three, and the dog started working their way downward.

Mopsus pulled Mod aside. "Careful, young Modifixeus. There is a god behind this all. He attacked the center of the universe, and he will attempt to finish the job should he get the chance." Mopsus inclined his gaze at the retreating dog. "Who knows what shape a desperate god might take?" Without another word, the seer followed the others.

The good feeling of bonding with the dog was gone. Mod watched until the light of the others had begun to grow dim in the distance, and then, reluctantly, he forced himself to follow.

CHAPTER 16

ONE OF THESE TREES IS NOT LIKE THE OTHERS

THEY WALKED IN SILENCE FOR A WHILE, THE WAY ILLUMINATED by the torchlight, the group quiet but for the shuffling of their feet and the steady, rhythmic click as Mopsus's walking stick kept time on the stone floor.

Mod wondered where the Egyptian god Mopsus had spoken of had gotten the thing and why such a fine piece of workmanship had been left behind.[1] It looked like some of the carvings Mod had seen that had come from the Maghreb or Ethiopia or such. The thing was roughly as tall as Mopsus with a crook at the top. The staff was ornamented with some sort of tough alloy metal foot at the base and a long, polished shaft ringed about with a gold and precious gem inlaid hand grip. The stick was impressive enough just on those elements, but the head of the thing was as fine a work of art as Mod had ever seen. The curve at the top had the head of some aardvark-like character at the highest point. The aardvark lorded over an upside-down snake-headed man carved into the end of the crook. All in all, the staff looked rather sturdy and grotesque.

Mod had never seen any seer or philosopher with such finery ever before. Mopsus looked comfortable enough carrying it.

Do seer's get paid?

Mod shook the unexpected question from his head. What a silly

---

1. Walking sticks, canes, and crooks were a high-end collectable in the ancient world. King Tut had a collection of no less than 130 staves buried with him. I guess he must have chosen his accessory by mood or what went best with his outfit. So every time you pick up a branch to take a walk with, and keep it, you become a part of an ancient and noble tradition.

thing to be wasting time on, wondering about Mopsus's fashionable walking accessory. Too many other things took precedence.

Walking in the dark of the underworld, there was a lot of quiet time to think and rethink over what was going on, what had happened, and what might happen still.

That wasn't necessarily a good thing.

It might just be the end of the world, and all Mod could think about was how he had somehow ruined things with Medusa. He still had no idea what it was he had done.

There had been times when she'd been upset with him before. There was the time she'd wanted to go out, just the two of them, and he'd accidentally set her on fire. He'd actually set her on fire twice, if you counted the saltpeter incident. The point was, he thought she understood who he was and what to expect from him, but it seemed she wanted to rewrite the rules of engagement.

And Mod was really bad at change.

The main reason Mod was so bad at social interaction was because he didn't feel it was worth the effort to do something to impress someone he really couldn't care less for. He didn't care about social status. He didn't care if people thought he was weird. He'd put on his best behavior when it mattered to his parents or Doug or his other friends, but the other stuff just didn't matter to him.

Acting in a manner to try to impress someone? What was the point?

He didn't like the feeling he got when he was put in a situation he didn't know how to handle, which is part of the reason he'd always followed Doug around. Doug was great at listening to people and making them feel wanted and needed. Mod just fixed things. Their talents complimented each other. Doug had never expected Mod to change. He knew Mod had always approached everything as a puzzle to solve or a problem to be fixed, and as long as Mod had Doug or someone like him to sort out the social niceties, things always worked out fine.

Doug wasn't here anymore, busy with his relationship and life with Larisa—as it should be.

Mod had sidled up to Medusa in his brother's absence. It seemed to be a good pairing as a friendship, and Mod would have thought it could have gone on forever that way had Medusa not told him his supposition was wrong.

Mod hadn't realized he was using the wrong science to apply to the situation between him and Medusa. He'd thought their friendship was simple mathematics, but it turned out it was chemistry. What he thought had been a simple matter of the addition of two parts becoming greater than the sum of the parts had turned out to be a far more complex chemical composition, and he didn't know the right variables to plug into the formula. If he put the wrong items in or added them in the wrong quantities, he would ruin the solution.

Mod had never been very good at chemistry,[2] and the social version of the science was almost incomprehensible to Mod.

One thing that Mod and Doug's parents had often said while the boys were growing up was that you couldn't control when bad things happened but you should never hide from them when they do.

Elpis, Mod's adopted mother had said, "I beg you to take courage; the brave soul can mend even disaster."[3]

And Mod recognized it for the deep truth it was.

Their parents had taught the boys well, not just in word but in deed too. There were times to think about the best course of action, but when no clear course presented itself, it was time to wrestle with the problem.

Aoug, Mod's adoptive father, had said, "No pig ever got back in

---

2. The saltpeter and guano torch experiment ended as a promising disaster. Hephaestus said there were possibilities for the compound but not as the reliable nighttime illumination device Mod envisioned. They could try again, but it would take time to remove the blast shield fragments from the walls of the caldera. Still, a good experiment because no one important was harmed, and summer interns were replaceable.
3. If you look up this phrase it will be attributed to Catherine the Great, but she found it in an ancient text about the benefits and pitfalls of raising pigs in ancient Greece.

the pen without someone getting covered in *&^%$*." He wasn't always as refined in his speech as his wife.

The longer something that appeared to be going wrong was left alone, the more it had a chance to become something permanent or unfixable. It was best to deal with things now.

Another good-sized tremor rocked the world. Everyone had to stand still for a moment until the shaking of Mother Gaea had stopped.

It reminded Mod that he was in the midst of dealing with more than one thing.

Mod didn't know what he was doing, but the engineering scientist in him reasoned every failure would only help him gather more data.

Just contemplating what he was about to do made his armpits break out in sweat. He could feel the heated flush of blood rising to his ears. Mod hated wet pits, but since he'd already panicked this far, Mod approached Medusa. He felt a lump rising in his throat as he thought of speaking, but he pushed it down and pressed forward. "Hey."

Medusa looked over at him and did nothing but nod her head a bit to let him know she'd heard him. Not the open and inviting reaction Mod hoped for. He could feel a fresh welling of sweat roll down his sides.

He'd air his pits out later. Mod forged ahead. "The stuff we were talking about before Mopsus appeared?"

Medusa shook her head. "We're off to save the world. I don't think now is an appropriate time to discuss how we both screwed up, is it?"

How we both screwed up?

Mod was quiet for a second. He literally had no idea if now was a good time or not. "I have no idea what I'm doing or talking about, but you are my friend. I'd like the chance to see how we can fix things to go back to how it used to be."

Medusa said nothing, but her posture took on a more defeated feel.

I've said the wrong thing.

"I'd like the chance to talk more about this later," Mod said.

Medusa just concentrated on putting one foot in front of the other.

"Good. Good talk." Mod gave a smile that jerked and ticked then dropped back before the sweat from his armpits reached his waist. *I'll just take up my place at the end of the group again.*

Before Mod could think any more about it, Mopsus said something that kept him from dwelling on what he had done wrong. "Our first obstacle is coming up shortly. Hades has barred the way, and we must get past his barrier."

Mod wasn't sure what to expect, but Mopsus was leading and Medusa had the golden plate with the cryptic instructions on it to aid him.

Mod glanced over at Medusa, but she never even looked in his direction. She looked as if she was actively ignoring him now.

Great. Well done, Mod, he thought sarcastically.

Mod assumed his mood was the thing making him feel worse and worse as the cave opened up into an enormous chamber. But it wasn't just his mood. There was a low, disconcerting tone that permeated the undercurrents of the air. It got more and more distinct and discomforting as they walked onward.

The note clarified into the wailing of thousands of voices that filled the air as if they were the sounds of a tumultuous river.

The waters creating the sounds came into view shortly thereafter. The barrier keeping them from moving forward seemed to be a huge river. Now Mod was confused.

That was the same barrier to Hades as always, right?

Mopsus stopped at the edge of the waters. Medusa, Three, and the dog walked up next to him. The mists of the river groaned and cried out and tried to lash themselves about the people standing just yards away on the shore. D'artagnan yelped and ran back to tremble next to Mod.

Mod knelt down and petted the dog. It was nice to have something else to focus on beside his increasingly dark thoughts. "It's all right. The river can't get you." He wasn't really sure of that, but it felt like the right thing to say.

It didn't stop the waters from trying. Tendrils of the flow lashed out, only to splash themselves apart as they hit the barrier that kept them from the shore.

The barrier isn't the river, it's something else. What it was, Mod had no idea. He'd seen plenty of glass before, and transparent rocks and gems, but never anything quite like what now encircled Hades. It was huge and cut through the air in a straight line. Mod could plainly see the lashing spray of the river break all along the base of the invisible wall with no signs of the mist and moisture making it past. He patted D'artagnan again, a bit more surety in his voice when he spoke. "We're safe here boy."

The others didn't hear him. The group's attention focused on the river.

"Misery loves company, I suppose," Three observed.

"Misery needs company. The only salve that would seem to treat such wounds as Misery carries can only be soothed by the suffering of others. Misery only wants those who don't hurt to be pained as it is, no matter the cost," Mopsus whispered almost to himself as he looked at the whitecaps of the rapids with disdain.

It sounded like he truly understood the principle he'd just talked about.

"How do we get across?" Medusa asked.

Mod expected the answer to be a boat or ferry, such as the skiff Charon piloted, but he saw no such craft in sight.

Mopsus leaned forward on his walking stick, his hand outstretched and fingers wide, and fell toward the river. Three and Medusa gasped as they rushed forward to catch him, both having to know that it was already too late. But the seer's hand slapped against the barrier and sent a pulse like a ripple that ran away from him on either side. "As I said, the way is blocked. I was just checking to see if the force was still in place."

"There had to have been other ways you could have proven that!" Medusa looked like her heart had almost stopped.

"That wasn't very nice." Mod shook his head.

Mopsus chuckled. The sound was darker than Mod had expected from the seer. *Must be the setting we're in.*

"This is the Cocytus, river of lamentation," Mopsus explained. "I was just having a bit of fun at your expense, since I knew we couldn't touch it because of the barrier Hades had erected." He tapped the barrier with the crook of his stick.

"Impenetrable, huh?" Three leaned forward and punched the thing hard. This resulted in a clang a gong made of meat would make after being struck with a hollowed-out skull.

The audible vibrations bounced about the surrounding area and echoed off the walls near and far for quite some time.

Mod turned a bit green at the sound. "Please don't do that again."

"How do we get past it?" Three asked as she patted the invisible barrier.

Mopsus looked this way and that. "At the moment, I am at a loss."

"The tablet." Medusa pulled the golden plate from her pocket. Its surface rippled and swirled.

The innards of the tree will bring you down.

The group all stared at each other as if none of them understood what it might mean.

"Are we supposed to start chewing on the pulp of a cedar to depress ourselves? Because I don't need a bit of fiber to help me in that endeavor," Mod grumbled.

Medusa actually looked a bit sorry at that.

Mod hadn't realized he'd just spoken out loud until he saw her glance in his direction.

Three clapped him on the back. "Well, you're certainly in a chipper mood."

"There isn't a lot of plant life this side of the rivers ringing Hades, so finding a tree as a starting point shouldn't be that hard of a thing to do." Mopsus started off to the left in a brisk walk as if he already knew which way he needed to go.

"Follow the seer, I guess?" Medusa said sheepishly to the others before she headed on her way. Three followed her close behind.

The dog looked like he didn't want to go near the river.

"We don't have much choice, do we?" Mod asked D'artagnan. "If it makes you feel any better, I really don't want to be here either."

The dog leaned into Mod's leg in an apparent act of solidarity and mutual support. After a quiet woof of acceptance he loped off after Three and the others and only looked back once to see if to encourage Mod to follow.

Off in the distance a large twist of dead branches reached for what passed for the sky of the underworld.

There were thousands of trees.

"How do we know which tree to go to?" Three asked.

"The tablet told Medusa that the innards of a tree would bring us down," Mod said as a possible interpretation occurred to him. "What if the tree were hollow?"

"Fair enough," Three looked about at all the trunks surrounding the group. "But what tree?"

"One big enough for us to climb within," Mod guessed.

There were quite a few trees large enough to qualify.

"Searching all these is still going to take a long time," Medusa looked to the tablet for more instruction.

Three and Mod leaned in to see if anything else appeared on the shining surface.

Nothing.

Mopsus didn't even try to lean in with the others, as if he knew it would be futile. "I seem to remember the gods discussing it." The seer closed his eyes. "In the land of Hades you will find a spring, and standing beside it, a white cypress," Mopsus said as his eyes popped open.

"Look for a stream," Medusa instructed the others.

Three was the first to spot the small trickle of water. The group followed it through the shadows of the eerily quiet forest.

The huge cypress grew on the banks of the Cocytus, a stream pooling against the base of it.

The tree's branches spread tall and wide. White bark and needles were strewn with ghostly mosses and gossamer threads of vines. The trunk was ancient and gnarled and easily ten paces across at the base.

"This tree is large enough to put a house in," Three said as she surveyed the oddly bleached conifer.

Medusa arched an eyebrow and looked askance at the mechanical woman.

"What? I'm not saying I want a summer home treehouse here, where you can hear the comforting sounds of the damned sweeping by at all hours of the night, but the size and look of it is quite lovely. If I were a nymph untimely brought down to Hades, I could do a lot worse than holing up in here."

Now everyone stared at her.

"Sometimes I think of things like that. Is that a problem?" Three asked.

"You're fine, Three," Mod said. "We all have thoughts other people don't always get. Everyone is entitled to their own understanding."

Medusa sighed. When Mod turned her way, she wouldn't look at him. *What did I say?*

Three patted the side of the tree to see if the invisible barrier connected with it. The force kept her hand from sliding halfway back on either side of the trunk.

The stream must have run into the river once, but now the barrier guarding the underworld barred the water's way forward. Water flowed to the left and right, running half a foot deep against the invisible barrier holding it on the shore. They were all wading in it up to their ankles, all except for the dog, who was soaked most of the way up to his knees.

"Well apparently following the creek into the underworld isn't the way to go," Three observed.

Near one of the larger roots, a small whirlpool swirled and sucked water down below the base of the tree.

Mod studied the way the water pooled and swirled. Still thinking of Medusa, his mouth operated independently of his brain for a second and he pointed out the obvious place to start. "The innards of the tree will bring us down. We need to get inside the tree."

Three studied the trunk. "I can't very well cut it down if I can only get to one side."

Medusa chimed in. "No. No. I don't think that's what Mod is saying. This is a pretty old tree. Are there any openings or hollows you can see?"

Mod grabbed a protruding burl and pulled himself up onto the rough bark. His wet sandals kept slipping against the bark, but there were plenty of handholds. He didn't have to climb very high. "There's a hollow right here. I think we can all fit inside." Mod thrust his hand into it and stretched out as far as he could. "Nothing seems to be holding me back."

Mopsus brightened. "There's the breach in the barrier we were looking for. A small thing, I admit, but a significant step toward me achieving my goal." The seer suddenly looked a bit relieved, possibly even excited.

We found a way into the land of the dead. What a crazy thing to be excited about. The whole world had gone crazy if this was the type of thing they now had to look forward to.

Three actually did look a bit excited to be here.

At least that makes two of us, Mod thought.

Mod was out of sorts. Medusa was out of sorts. They were taking care of a dog that had been torn from its home and displaced in space and time. And the group of them was in the midst of treading into the hells in an attempt to get to the center of Mother Gaea to try to prevent the end of the universe.

Mod should really just cut everyone involved in this whole debacle, himself included, a bit of slack.

So that is what he decided to do.

Then he busied himself helping the others climb into the tree.

IT WAS A LOT ROOMIER IN THE HOLLOW BURL OF THE TREE THAN Medusa had expected. There was the opening they had all crawled into on the one side of the barrier that led to a wide wooden ledge inside. Another opening about twice as wide as the one they'd used gaped on the other side of the tree. The opening hung over the rapids of the wailing waters.

Three craned her neck from her position in the back of the group as she tried to peer out over the edge.

Mod could see things more clearly from where he crouched down. "I wouldn't get too close."

The mists from the river snaked up the side of the cypress facing the water and peeked their ghostly fingers over the lip of the opening.

"The waters reach for us," Mopsus said with surety. "We have breached the barrier that kept us from Hades's realm."

They all tried to step wide of the feelers of the Cocytus. It was dark inside the tree, and the shelf was cramped with all of them there. Pressed shoulder to shoulder Medusa knew they wouldn't be able to avoid the mists forever.

"Now what?" Mopsus sounded impatient.

"Says the seer," Three grinned at Mopsus and fanned away a tendril of mist that couldn't figure out what to do with her.

The only one with enough space to move was the dog. D'artagnan wormed his way forward to the edge of the ledge and pointed his nose down into the hollow. His bark made Medusa jump.

Mopsus frowned at D'artagnan as he looked down into the dark. "Quiet, dog. We're trying to think."

"Maybe he's trying to tell us something." Three said before she turned to the dog. "What's that D'art?"

"D'art?" Mod asked.

Three smiled and managed to scratch the dog between the ears despite the close quarters. "Shortening long names is a sign of affection or closeness, *Mod*." She laughed, and Mod smiled back. "It helps form a bond of friendship. Right, D'art?"

The dog's mouth spread into a grin at the attention, and he broke out in a happy pant.

"See?"

Mopsus gave a derisive snort and moved on. "So, following the direction of the dog's nose, he expects us to just jump down into the tree?"

"Maybe, maybe not. We'd need to consult a seer, you know, just to verify," Three joked. "So, Mop, where are we off to next?" She grinned wholesomely at the seer as he turned and narrowed his eyes at her.

"Mop?" the seer looked annoyed.

"Worked with the dog." Three shrugged.

"I'm never sure if you automatons are sincere in your teasing of others or not," Mopsus said. "If that was a genuine attempt to connect with me, I'm flattered, but I prefer my full name. I am much more than a simple dog, thank you very much."

Three batted her eyes and feigned innocence.

They were wasting time, and Medusa felt pressed to get them back on track. *"The innards of the tree will bring you down."* She reminded the others. "That's what the tablet said."

D'art whined and scratched at the ledge. He pointed his nose down and barked again.

"Just where D'art was pointing, weren't you? Are the yummy smells from the center of the universe telling you where to go?" Three ruffled the dog behind the ears, and D'art wagged his tail in confirmation.

"We knew we had to go down at some point." Mopsus frowned. "I could have told you that."

"Now seems a good time to start. And we aren't expected to just jump to get there." Medusa pointed at the hand and footholds she noticed carved inside the tree that descended in a wide spiral.

The seer was the closest to the path. Mopsus took a step out and placed his sandal in the toehold of the first step. He struggled to make it work with the weight of his pack while holding his staff at the same time.

"I could help with the stick," Three offered.

Mopsus didn't look as if he liked that suggestion. "I can manage."

After a brief wait while the seer found his descending rhythm, the others followed him down the odd spiral ladder inside the tree. Mod stepped out onto the ladder right after the seer. Three wrapped a spare piece of fabric over her shoulder to create a sling, nestled D'art close to her chest, and climbed down with the dog.

Medusa went last.

The space inside the tree grew wider the further down they went. The innards of the tree took on a more humanly structured feel as they descended. The foot and handholds gradually morphed into steps and then into a spiral trail. The circular ramp had the nubs of a lip appear on the edge, which gradually turned into a railing and banister. Pretty soon the trail had transformed into something akin to a grand spiral staircase that was way ahead of its time.[1]

Three was able to put D'art down so the dog could walk on his own. He took a bit of time to walk along with everyone, and everyone seemed to enjoy having the happy dog alongside except for Mopsus, who repeatedly shooed off the dog every time D'art got too close. It didn't stop D'art from trying.

Mopsus had just chased off the dog again when he peered over the side of the staircase to see how much farther they had to go. The

---

1. In fact, it was the infernal inspiration for the pontifical gallery staircases that would be designed by Giusseppe Momo in the 16th century.

look on his face made it clear to Medusa that he wasn't pleased with what he saw.

"Who makes stairs this deep? Two and a half steps forward, one step down." Mopsus frowned, his walking stick clicking along at an odd stutter while he used his free hand to rub his sciatic nerve.

Three shrugged. "I kinda like it. It's almost like a dance." She took two steps, then gave a little bounce hop. Two steps, and then another hop.

"Gods save us from the *perkiness* of mechanical youth." Mopsus moved along as he continued to massage his butt.

There was a tint of resentment or annoyance in the way Mopsus said it that bothered Medusa. "She can dance if she wants to."[2] Medusa smiled at Three. With all the things happening, it was a small mercy to have someone along that didn't appear weighed down by the end of the world or stressed from the possible end of a relationship or in a snit because a dog was helping them find the center of the universe.

Medusa didn't know Mopsus as well as Mod did, but he never seemed to be the sort to be short with people or animals before. Maybe he was acting this way because he was old and hurting. Pain, emotional or physical, can make you blind to a lot of things. Medusa knew that better than most. She shifted her gaze from the seer to Mod. Mod didn't have the same spring in his step that she was used to seeing. Medusa knew who to blame for that one.

It seemed to take a very long time before they reached the bottom of the stairs, where a wide landing opened into a grand reception hall.

Mopsus let out a huge, weary sigh as they stepped out onto the landing.

Medusa was glad for the end of their spiral descent as well. Except for Three's little dance and the short conversation around it,

---

2. If you heard Men Without Hats singing *The Safety Dance* in your head as you read that, you most likely are wearing bifocals.

the walk had been too quiet and had given Medusa far too much time to think.

A tremor hit in time with their arrival, hard enough that the entire group had to stop for a moment until their footing had stilled.

"As if we needed a reminder of why we needed to make haste." The look on the seer's face soured.

Medusa watched as a bit of dust and debris rained down from above. It was enough that she had to shield her eyes from the falling grit but not enough to stall the activity of those in the hall.

There were small rooms that opened when the dead approached, and closed once the dead were inside. When the doors opened again, the previous occupants were nowhere to be seen. A stair descended off to the side of the small room. People were lined up before the large closets with the opening and closing doors. No one was taking the stairs.

There was a sparse number of the dead milling about. With each group that left, the number filling the hall dwindled as no new dead arrived to take the place of the newly departed.

"If the way to the underworld is blocked, how did all these dead come to be here?" Mod asked.

Medusa had just wondered the same thing.

"Perhaps they have been here since before the border was sealed?" Mopsus suggested. "The hall seems capable of holding a great deal more than what we see here, and once one is gone, there seems to be none coming to add to the number that are leaving."

"How they got here doesn't really matter. Where they are going does." Medusa pointed at an information desk off to one side, occupied by a slack faced denizen of the underworld. He was wearing a vest that set him apart as a member of the staff, and he had a name tag. "Maybe we can find that out over there?"

Medusa approached the desk. "Hello"—she squinted and read the writing on his name tag—"Thespis?"

Thespis gave a snaggle-toothed rictus in response, obviously happy to be called by name. He looked as if he tried to enunciate very precisely, which must have been hard because he looked to have been dead for a very long time. "'Ow meh I helb you?"

Medusa smiled back at him. "Could you perchance tell us where we are right now?"

Thespis grunted and slowly reached for a brochure. "The Dunteh center fo' brogressib bunishment. Welcom."

Medusa looked at the pamphlet. "The Dante Center for Progressive Punishment?"

Thespis's brow furrowed, and he nodded in the affirmative. "Tha's wha I just said."

Apparently the man in the kiosk was far enough gone that enunciation wasn't happening very well anymore. Luckily, the relevant information was included in the handout. Medusa continued to read, "Part of the Infernal Creations Expositions: an alternative view of afterlife organizations, with interactive demonstrations so you can experience firsthand what reward or punishment might work best for you. What could the future of spiritual punishment hold for those lucky enough to experience it? Imagine the possibilities."

The man behind the counter spread his arms wide in a slow, dramatic sweep. "Welcom to the world ob tumorrow!"[3]

"I'm just impressed they fit this all inside of a cypress," Three said.

"Yu haben't seen nubbing yet, sister," the dead man said. "The center has nine lebels!"

He was enthusiastic but translating what the dead information clerk was spouting might give her a headache. "Thank you for your time," Medusa said as she turned back to her group. "According to the pamphlet, the opening and closing closets are called elevators, a means of transportation to travel up and down in a straight line. There are emergency stairs to the side of the elevators, and then there is the express."

---

3. "Welcome to the world of Tomorrow!" Phil Lamarr wrote that quote from *Futurama* on a piece of art for me. I have it hanging in my office.

"The express?" Mopsus asked.

The clerk signaled to another member of the staff. "Eggbress demonstration!"

A vest-wearing dead woman grabbed a shade from in front of the elevator and threw him into a gaping pit off to the left. The ghost screamed as it plummeted down the shaft.

Thespis threw both hands out in a flourish. "Tuh-duh!"[4]

"Thanks for the demonstration." Medusa smiled at the dead man and nodded to his assistant.

Thespis smiled and gave a thumbs up to his coworker, an act which caused his thumb to fall off. "Awww," he lamented as he bent over to pick up his fallen digit.

"Just to clarify, I do not plan to take the express," Mod said.

Three's face cocked to the side in a contemplative grin. "Could be kinda fun."

"We'll take the elevator," Mopsus said as he stretched his back. "I'm tired after the climb down the tree."

Something about taking the elevator didn't sit right with Medusa. "The Orphic tablet said we should take the stairs."

"We already took the stairs," Mopsus pointed behind them. "Lots of stairs. I don't want to look at another stair. We'll take the elevator," he said with finality.

---

4. "Tada!" Thespis hadn't had an appreciative audience for a long while. The guy was showing just a little bit of fanfare for the demonstration, a bit of extra effort he was sure the public appreciated. Once a showman, always a showman.

CHAPTER 18

NINE LEVELS,
STRAIGHT TO HELL

MOD DIDN'T LIKE BEING IN THE BOX WITH THE CLOSING DOORS. The ceiling was a bit too low, and he felt like he had to stoop to not hit his head. All the important things, like the cogs and wheels and pulleys that operated the machine, were outside the box where he couldn't study them. There was a hatch just above his head that read *maintenance* in bold red lettering, but Mod was pretty sure if he opened it up to study the gearing and lift mechanism, the operator and his companions would disapprove.

Mod studied what he could from inside. A small light to the right of the doors indicated they were currently on a level labeled *lobby*. There were nine levels underneath. "How do we know which floor to get off on?"

Mod looked over at the seer for a bit of direction. Mopsus looked unusually nervous and sweaty. The seer fidgeted. "I'm pretty sure we'll know it when we get there."

"Maybe the tablet will tell us?" Medusa pulled out the piece of gold and looked at it. "How long do we take the elevator?" The Orphic tablet shimmered and morphed in her hands.

Follow the nose.

Mod felt a bit disconcerted as he read over Medusa's shoulder. "Which nose?" Mod could swear the tablet gave an exasperated sigh before it morphed again.

The dog knows the scent. Follow the dog.

Mod looked at D'art, currently plopped down with his head resting on his front paws. The dog looked like he was set for the long haul. Mod nodded to the tablet. "Thanks for the clarification."

The tablet gave a thumbs up sign.

Mopsus folded his arms against his chest and mumbled under his breath. "A bacon-loving stray and an eldritch Etch A Sketch directed by the spirit of a dead poet—what could you *possibly* need a seer for?"

When Mod turned an inquisitive eye at Mopsus, the seer looked a bit surprised anyone had overheard him and hastily glanced away. Mod really wanted to know what an Etch A Sketch was, but now was probably not the best time to ask about it.

Mod turned his attention back to the room they were riding in. The elevator was hand cranked, with two vested workers turning the wheels at an almost machine-like pace. Another two workers stood in the back corners of the elevator and sang in an unending loop.

"Duuuh, duh duh duh, duhduhduh duh duh, duuuh, duh duh duh, duhduhduh duh duh, duh, duh duh duh, duhduhduh duhduh duuuuh."[1]

"Do you think that might get annoying after a while?" Medusa asked.

"I find it somewhat soothing, especially given the current circumstances." Mod really did like the music and found himself humming along to it. He pressed his head against the glass and watched for the first level the elevator headed toward.

The bell set above the elevator doors dinged and shocked Mod enough that he stopped humming. The elevator lurched to a stop.

Mod tensed up as D'art rose and sniffed the air. Everyone else seemed to be watching the dog. D'art yawned, stretched, and laid back down.

Mod felt his shoulders relax as he let out a sigh of relief. He hadn't realized he'd been holding his breath.

---

1. A pretty fair imitation of Herb Albert and Tijuana Brass Band's version of "The Girl from Ipanema."

"Level one. The unbaptized and virtuous pagans," the attendant announced. His diction was perfect. He obviously hadn't been here as long as Thespis had.

The doors opened, and Mod was treated to a view of a melancholy hoard milling about.

"Is anyone getting off?" the attendant asked.

"That wasn't our stop," Mod said as Mopsus gave the dog a side eye.

"I think I recognized two or three of those guys in the crowd out there though,"[2] Medusa said.

"What does baptized mean?" Three asked.

"A ritualistic practice where one is immersed in water as a sign that one has accepted God," Mopsus explained.

"Sort of like bobbing for salvation?" Three guessed, before she knit her eyebrows in concentration. "So what does pagan mean?"

"A non-believer. One who is not embraced by the love of God," Mopsus said.

"If you swear fealty to a certain god you're saved, but if you were a virtuous Greek you just get lumped in with the unbelievers?" Three gasped.

"Doesn't seem fair, does it?" Mod deadpanned. He pressed his forehead back against the glass and waited for the next level to appear.

"Duuuh, duh duh duh, duhduhduh duh duh—"

Ding!

The elevator lurched to a halt.

"Second level. Lust!"

The doors opened.

While the others gaped out the open doors, Mod glanced over at

---

2. Dante included the likes of Virgil, Homer, Ovid, and others as a way to poke at those he considered to be good men, just not good or lucky enough to share his views and without outright saying they were going straight to hell for it.

the dog again. D'art raised his nose and gave the air a sniff before lowering it back to his paws.

Beyond the elevator, a violent storm full of gusting wind filled the air with bits of torn and soiled clothing. A beach umbrella rolled past the front of the elevator. There were two people holding onto it, at least that's how it appeared at first.

Three's eyes went a bit wider. "That was educational."

"Lust never fails to shock and amaze, does it?" The attendant must have assumed no one was getting off because he closed the doors and started the elevator moving again.[3]

The last view of the level was of a group of well-meaning and ill-informed patriots firing weapons at the storm to slow it down.[4] One of them got pinned to the beach by his own javelin, right before two more javelins and a heavy stone ball thrown by a shot putter hit him.

"They should learn not to throw things into the wind," Mod observed.

"They never learn. At least it's just weapons this time." The attendant didn't explain further. He had probably seen it enough without needing to rehash it, and Mod was thankful for that bit of ambiguity.

"Duh, duhduhduh, duuuh, duh duh duh, duhduhduh duh duh—"

Ding.

"Third level. Gluttony."

The doors opened. Cold air from beyond the boundary of the elevator hit Mod's sinuses with the power of sun-ripened roadkill in the summer.

Medusa, Mod, and Mopsus covered their noses. The world was chill and filled with the stench of foodstuffs gone past the expiration date.[5] The occupants of this particular circle of Hell were trapped in

---

3. The couple clinging to the umbrella, among other things, were pretty close to getting off, but that's not what the attendant meant.
4. Just a normal, everyday occurrence in Florida during hurricane season.
5. My kids found a "treasure chest" buried out on state land once. It turned out to be

the semi-solid slush, and Cerberus hopped around gleefully chomping down on whomever he chose.

Mod spared a glance through watering eyes at the dog. D'art licked his chops but didn't rise to his feet.

Mod turned to Three. "I envy your inability to smell."

"Tragedy of my life," she said as she tapped the end of her nose. "D'art seems to like it, just not the smell he's looking for." Three crouched down and scratched the dog behind the ear.

D'art thumped the tip of his tail in response.

"Cerberus works here?" Mod asked as he pointed out the huge three-headed canine presently rolling in the remains of something. Mod didn't really want to know what that something might be. "I would have thought Cerberus would be stuck with the Greeks?"

"The boss contracts out sometimes. Pull a little bit of torment from here, a little bit from there, and it becomes a more inclusive experience no matter your upbringing," the attendant said. "The dog seems to like the work, and he gets time and a half."

"Fair enough," Mod said.

"Duuuh, duh duh duh, duhduhduh duh duh, duh—"

Ding.

"Level four. Avarice and Prodigality."

Mod noticed that D'art didn't even bother raising his head to take a whiff.

The door opened on a scene of men and women pushing great weights about so that they would crash together. Then they would gather up the broken pieces, take as much from the others as they could, form the disparate pieces back into as big a ball as they could manage, just so they could smash them into someone else.

"It's not the having, it's the getting,"[6] Medusa observed.

---

a discarded icebox full of long deceased fish. The subsequent opening traumatized them for years and cleared out all the wildlife in a three-county area for a good month and a half.

6. I remember this from a Garfield comic where he was chasing mice and letting

Three furrowed her brow. "And this is worse than the infidelity level, how?"

"Ask Midas for a demonstration the next time you see him," Medusa said.

"Duuuh, duh duh duh, duhduhduh duh duh, duh, duh—"

Ding.

"Five! Level of wrath and the sullen."

The doors opened up. Mod checked the dog. D'art wasn't interested in anything going on beyond the doors. Mod still looked up and locked eyes with a man slouched in a squat with a participation trophy clutched loosely in his hand.

"Leave me alone," the man grumbled to Mod.

"Sorry," Mod stammered. "I didn't mean to intrude."

The man huffed like he didn't care what Mod thought. The squatter regarded the hollow symbol of achievement in his hand with obvious disdain and threw the trophy into the slow flow of the river before him.

"Well this is a cheery place, isn't it? What river is this?" Mod asked.

"Is today Tuesday?" The attendant answered Mod's question with a question.

Mod wasn't sure what the day of the week had to do with it.

The attendant checked a schedule tacked to the side of the elevator. He nodded when he confirmed what he was looking for. "This is Tuesday, so the river before you is the river Styx."

"I thought the Styx was up there?" Mod pointed above his head.

"The layout and architecture of the underworld is malleable," the operator said. "Damnation goes where damnation is needed."

There were men and women battling with double ended clubs on platforms perched over the river. Every time one would strike a blow,

---

them go, but apparently the quote is attributed to Elizabeth Taylor. The more you know!

the loser would be flung into the waters to sink slowly under the waves as they shot the winner with the stink eye.

"They continue to sulk under the water after they lose. And everybody gets a chance to lose." With that, the operator closed the doors.

"So how is this version of eternal torment different from, say, the Greek version of the underworld?" Mod asked the attendant.

The attendant seemed to like the attention, or maybe he didn't get many talkative passengers on the elevator during his normal shifts. In any case, he was more than eager to explain. "It's the groupings by category I see as the main difference. In Hades, punishment is random, decided upon by the whim of whichever god is most ticked off at the accursed, and carried out by Hades in a manner both specifically targeted and theatrical. This version, which we like to call the Inferno, is corporatized and homogenized so the condemned can expect the same sort of punishment as every other degenerate that shares their fetish."

"Sounds fair enough," Mod acknowledged with a bit of consideration, "but I think I can see benefits and drawbacks to both disciplines."

"No system is perfect," the operator admitted.

"Duuuh, duh duh duh, duhduhduh duh duh—"

Ding.

"Circle six! Heretics in flaming tombs."

D'art gave a little sneeze and wrinkled his nose.

To Mod this level smelt somewhat of the last vestiges of a dying bonfire made up of barnyard weeds. There was some other scent in the air as well. The crackling and snapping of the fires might be the source of the smell, but it was more likely coming from the ovens where those who practiced religious heresy shrieked and called out as they were baked like a loaf.

"Well I just got a few ideas for the self-regulating *testum* I was planning to build,"[7] Mod said as he turned a bit pale.

"If your *artolaganon* is making sounds like that when you bake it, you probably shouldn't eat it,"[8] Three said.

Mod's stomach knotted just a little bit more.

"Duh, duh duh, duhduhduh, duh, duh. Duh, duh duh, duhduhduh, duh, duh—"

Things were quiet in the elevator for a moment except for the music. The last scene was a bit unsettling.

"Nobody planning on getting out on the next stop?" the operator asked. "I'll make it a quick one unless I have to stop a bit longer."

"No. We're going to the end of the line," Mopsus clarified for the first time since they'd boarded the elevator. Mod noticed that the attendant looked a bit sad at that. He also noticed that Mopsus looked more and more tense. *What's at the end of the line?* He wondered.

"Duuuh, duh duh duh, duhduhduh duh duh—"

Ding.

"Level Seven. Those who have committed violence against people and property, suicides, blasphemers, sodomites, and usurers," the attendant said.

D'art's ears perked up. He rose up and slunk over to hide behind the employee turning the crank on the right. Mod paid attention to what the dog had done, then motioned for the others to stand clear of the opening doors as well. Mopsus had already hidden himself in a corner before any of the others.

"That's a pretty broad spectrum of sins there. They all had to go on the same level?" Three asked.

"How many levels did you want us to have?" With that, the attendant threw open the door.

No less than five spears and a double-bladed axe flew past. One

---

7. Testum: A domed clay oven, open in the front, with the fire or coals in the back. My buddy Doug (no relation to Mod's brother) makes great pizza with a small, gas-fired one.
8. Artolaganon: a round loaf of sourdough, coated with olive oil and then baked.

of the singers was perforated by two of the projectiles. He slumped to the floor and stopped singing.

The attendant closed the door as rapidly as he could. "I don't like stopping on seven," he said. "I don't feel anyone should be left to deal with a used-chariot salesman if I can help it."[9]

The loss of one of the singers didn't change the quality of the music, but now it didn't have the surround sound quality.

"Duh, duh duh, duuuh, duh duh duh, duhduhduh duh duh—"

Ding.

"Level eight. Panderers, seducers, flatters. Sorcerers, false prophets, liars, and thieves."

The door opened.

D'art came out from his hiding place. He sniffed the air but made no move to step forward.

Mod looked out the open doors with the others. He was surprised to see quite a few whom people would consider great leaders trying to lord it over one another.

Medusa's eyes grew wide. "Is that Odysseus and Diomedes over there in the two-pronged flame?"

The attendant shrugged. "The Trojan horse and the theft of Athena's statue are the big reason they're stuck here. They also made some princess cry, but hey, who hasn't?" He gave them all an open-mouthed grin while he waited for their response.

The attendant's attempt at humor fell flat. "Moving on." He closed the door. "So it's been a pleasure serving you today. So sorry that I have to leave you at the drop off for the last circle."

"That's actually where we were trying to go," Mopsus explained.

"Really?" the attendant sounded dumbfounded. "Right out there where Satan can see you?"

Mopsus paled a bit at the mention of Satan. Mod had no idea

---

9. Honest Heromenes's Used Chariots, 33 percent weekly compounded interest, a shockingly high down payment, and a Spartan debt collector should you fall behind in your payments. Remember our motto: "Sure, We'll Take You—For a Ride!"

who this Satan was, but Mopsus often knew things about other places and times that were clueless to the non-seers in the group.

"What's wrong with this Satan person seeing us?" Mod asked.

The attendant's jaw fell open. "You really have no idea, do you? This is the end of the line. No one gets past Satan."

"I should be fine," Mopsus said. "Satan swore in front of Zeus and Hades that he wouldn't interfere with the end of the world."

"Satan is renowned for keeping his word," the attendant said. "He plans traps and pitfalls in any and every agreement so he never has to lie."

Mopsus paled a bit more. And he began to sweat.

"But we have to pass through this level on our way to somewhere else," Mod tried to explain to the attendant.

"Then you probably didn't want to be dropped off on the elevator platform, because now Satan is definitely going to see you. If you wanted to slip past him, you should have taken the stairs," the attendant explained as he shook his head back and forth in sorrow.

Mod, Medusa, and Three all turned and glared at Mopsus.

"Isn't that what the Orphic tablet told us to do? Take the stairs?" Medusa demanded.

"Hindsight is twenty-twenty," Mopsus said as he cowered back from them, his staff held protectively between him and the rest of the group.

"Duh, duh duh, duhduhduh, duh duh, duh."

The last *duh* sounded with finality.

Ding.

A substantial tremor hit the level, hard enough that it shifted the elevator back and forth several inches within its shaft. The metal of the small room screeched and groaned. The cables holding the box in place twanged and vibrated.

The elevator operator looked decidedly uncomfortable. "Last stop! Everybody out," he called in a shrill voice.

"Which way to the stairs?" Medusa pleaded.

"What should I do?" Mopsus twisted his grip on his staff in frustration.

The doors slid open, and there was a pause, as if the universe were holding its breath.

Mod had seen gods and monsters before, but he had never seen anything like this. The outline of the beast stood partially lost and obscured in the high mists and smoky air of the impossible cavern. An endless lake of fire and brimstone stretched in every direction before them, crying heads of men, women, and children and their frozen, burning, twisted limbs littering the surface. The screams and cries that emanated from the vast lake surface below were muted and unreal until the arms of the giant above the clouds swooped down, raked the frozen field, and rose with a harvest of the damned. Sobs and wails drowned out all the others, more focused, heartrending, and personal, until every corner of the void filled with their sounds. Satan flung his newly picked crop into the air where they tumbled and flailed until they fell back into his cavernous, gaping maw. When his jaws shut with a sickening clack, the terrified screams were cut short, the silence that followed all the more terrifying because of the abruptness of it.

No one in the elevator moved.

D'art recovered first. He sniffed the air, let out a low, quiet yelp, then banked left and took off as fast as he could.

The movement of the dog was enough to almost pull Mod from gaping in fear at the sight above him. "Follow the dog!" Mod hissed. Even having been the one to give the instructions, Mod couldn't get his feet to work.

Three grabbed Medusa and Mod each by a shoulder and pushed them to the left. "Run." she whispered in a tone that could not have been more commanding. "Run!"

Mopsus stood rooted to the spot, unable to move.

Three grabbed the seer by the front of his robe and hauled him out of the elevator.

"There is a grand exit by those arches." Mopsus pointed forward with his staff. "We must head that way as quickly as possible."

Mod could see the exit, but it was a very, very long way off. *We're never going to make it.*

The group rushed now, hurrying along the edge of the frozen pit as fast as their legs could take them. Mod tried to run in a straight line but couldn't quite make himself because he couldn't tear his eyes away from the horror he was running from. Mod's stomach dropped as Satan turned slowly toward the group and smacked his lips as if savoring his snack then appeared to study the would-be heroes running for their lives.[10] He focused on one, then the next, until he came to the front of the group.

"You!" Satan gasped happily. "I'd wondered when you might finally get here. Want to play?" The smile on Satan's face crackled like a ragged red lightning bolt stretched across the sky.

The seer stopped, like a deer in a spotlight, and then he turned and bolted faster than anyone could have ever expected him to run.

D'artagnan ran between Mopsus's feet. "Worthless beast!" The seer stumbled and lashed out with his staff.

The dog tumbled to the side, almost falling into the burning frozen lake. Three snagged the him by the collar, clutched him tight to her chest, and kept running without even losing a step. D'art writhed out of her grasp and hit the ground running. He made his way in front of everyone then banked sharply from the obvious way forward toward a small recess set in the wall less than fifty yards away. The recess had a guard rail blocking half the front of it and a red neon sign that read *eísodos ypiresías* hanging just above it. D'art skidded to a stop and turned, beckoning them to follow him.

---

10. Satan, in all his horrifying and terrible glory, turned around here and on his barstool in Isaac's bar. Satan can be present in multiple planes of existence, and multiple places, at the same time. It still takes a bit of focus to single out one particular happening even for one as skilled as the Morningstar. He sucked on a piece of frozen strawberry from his virgin daiquiri and narrowed his eyes, and was quite happy to see fat old Mopsus had come for a visit.

Mopsus slowed down, as if confused about which way to go. The others hesitated as the seer contemplated.

The red lightning grin in the clouds went away. "You can't leave yet. That would be rude. Think you can come into my sovereign territory and just leave without a proper bit of play with your host?" Satan called out.

"Follow the dog!" Mod cried as he pushed Three and Medusa to follow D'art. He grabbed Mopsus by the collar and bodily pulled the seer in the new direction.

"Deadline. Can't stop. So sorry to disappoint," Mopsus wheezed over his shoulder as Satan's scowl seared the sky behind them.

"You think Zeus or Hades will protect you because you're on their little errand?" Satan called, his voice deep and full of menace. "You know what it means to be here. I told you in the bar. The devil must be given his due." He stabbed a finger at Mopsus.

Mopsus took the lead again. The flap on his backpack came unlatched and almost lost its contents.

"Could this be an appropriate time to utilize the power of your staff or the contents of your pack?" Three asked as she refastened the flap on the seer's bag while she jogged easily alongside him.

Mopsus flinched at the touch but said nothing. Bigger things than addressing the automaton touching his bag were going on.

"I think this would be the best time to run as if we have hornets in our chitons," Mod wheezed from the back of the group as he sucked breath hard into his lungs.

It was unnecessary. Pretty much everyone got the idea.

Satan's reach was vast here within the bounds of his prison. No place was safe or secure. The fallen Morningstar's great claws raked the air above the frozen lake, eddies of burning ice erupted and swirled in the wake of his reach, a storm of terror and pain whipped up by the passage of his great limbs and his ice-caked, leathery wings as they flapped and cracked and sought to capture the things he now wanted above all else.

The ether screamed.

Betrayers were tossed asunder and ripped apart, unable to die, condemned to fresh and unending torment by the renewed fury of the dragon as he clawed after those who fled him.

Because D'art had led them all on the shortest route possible, the Devil's efforts came just a fraction too late.

The group made it to the landing of the service entrance just as the force and debris of the assault nipped at their heels. They ducked the shockwave as they threw themselves bodily down the next flight of stairs. Even then they didn't stop. They stumbled and fell over each other and tried for the life of them to get as far away from Satan's reach in his horrible prison as they could.

Physically, they were beyond him now, but the words and tone of the one trapped in the pit cut deep and scored them to the bone.

"Betrayer! Deceiver! Do you think Zeus would protect you if he knew the truth?" Satan called after them. "I'm gonna tell."

CHAPTER 19

A STUNNING VARIETY
OF MUSHROOMS

"WHAT WAS THAT?" MOD ASKED MOPSUS AS THEY RESTED ON A level several flights of stairs below.

"All that matters is that we are past it, and well on our way to the depths of Tartarus." Mopsus leaned a little heavier on his staff, and the harshness of the trip was beginning to show.

"The big scary bat seemed to know you, and not in a manner where he seemed pleased to see you," Three pointed out.

"Unfortunately, for one with my gifts and callings, running afoul of dark powers comes with the territory." Mopsus sounded weary and guarded. His head shook as he pushed on, the staff held tight before him in both hands.

The rest of them followed in silence.

The stairs were gone, and they were back to following cavern systems as they gradually worked their way downward. The light of the previous realms was absent too, so they had to go back to the lanterns Three had provided to light the way. The humidity had risen, and the air had gotten thick.

They'd walked for a long time. The group was pretty far down in Gaea by now.[1] Mopsus led the way, D'art sniffing the trail and the air not far behind him. Medusa and Three were in the center, and Mod trailed quite a bit behind.

---

1. Hesiod wrote that if you dropped a bronze anvil from the heavens, it would take nine days for it to fall to earth (what an anvil was doing up in the heavens is beyond me). He went on to say that it would take another nine days of falling for it to get to the realm of Tartarus. Mod and company are about at the eighth-day level of the second nine-day drop.

The path since escaping Satan had been fairly uneventful. The universe felt calmer.

But then, after having seen the dragon of the pit pop his cork, pretty much anything would seem calm by comparison.

Mod hadn't been in much of a talking mood and made it fairly evident, so after a while Medusa and the others had sort of drifted off and left him to his own devices.

Or lack thereof. Mod scowled.

He couldn't believe how helpless he felt without his tools and gadgets and . . . Those things were all distractions. He hid behind them, using rods and wrenches and screws as diversions to keep him from interacting with the real world.

Mod felt bad about how everything had been going. He shouldn't have freaked out so much about having to leave all his tools and gadgets, and he knew that his fear about it and inability to cope had changed the way Medusa looked at him. He just couldn't help it.

That's why he was letting the others walk so far ahead. No opportunities to embarrass or belittle himself if he didn't interact with them, right?

Real mature, you moron, Mod thought to himself.

Mod pulled out his first toy from his pocket and gave it a hard look. Of all the things he carried with him, this would be the hardest for him to ever let go of. It was part of all his earliest memories. He'd held it when Doug and Doug's parents found him and took him in. It looked as new as the first day it was made, tight and exact in its machining, despite the near constant attention and use Mod had given it over the years.

Mod twisted it and turned it. One ring popped off, then another. Mod unscrewed it layer by layer down to the core then put it back together. It took about five times of disassembling and reassembling the gadget before he was calm enough to feel like he wanted to walk with the others again.

The others stopped walking just ahead. The lack of forward motion caught Mod's peripheral attention, and he reassembled his toy and put it away. When he finally did look up, three tunnels branched off from the path they followed, and Mopsus and D'art both looked lost about which one to follow. Medusa glared at the tablet and shook it. "All roads lead to Rome?[2] What in the hells does that mean?"

Mod noticed the dark recesses and corners of the tunnels had grown brighter, something the others didn't seem to notice, because they were trying to figure out which way to go. Mod came to a stop several feet behind them and flipped off the lantern hanging from his pack. The light around him stayed constant and bright. "Hey, everyone? Did you see this?"

The rest of the group stopped debating and turned.

Mod gestured to his now extinguished lantern, then to the brightness surrounding them.

Mopsus chuckled. "As focused as I was in putting one foot in front of the other, I'd not realized that the lights we carried were no longer necessary." Mopsus doused his lantern.

The reaction from Mopsus actually put Mod at ease. Hearing the seer chuckle was one of the first times on this trip that Mopsus had seemed like the seer Mod remembered. *That Satan had sure seemed to know Mopsus though and was not overly fond of him.*

It made Mod wonder how much he really knew about the seer after all. Mod had only been in the seer's company for a brief while during the twelve trials Doug needed to complete to prove his worth to marry Larisa. Mopsus surely had a life where he had done many things before that and had accomplished and done many things since.

People had lives and wants and needs that went far beyond what Mod understood, expected, or had experienced.

Mod was starting to see that now. He'd been having a lot of deep thoughts lately. What with the unexpected trip to try to fix the universe and the weird dreams Mod had been having, and things going on with Medusa.

---

2. A joke a couple hundred years ahead of its time.

Medusa's life had been far different than Mod's. He looked over at her and tried to smile. She arched an eyebrow in Mod's direction, like she wasn't quite sure what to make of him looking at her.

Three reached up and cut off the fuel supply to the last lantern. The light in the area didn't dim at all.

Mod would have pondered more about what was happening between him and Medusa, but the nerd, and a desire for a safer topic, called out and overpowered his train of thought.

"I wonder where the light is coming from?" he asked the others.

Mod walked over to a small outcropping of rock and pointed at the small growths atop it. "Mushrooms. Thousands of them. See how the light comes forth from them."

"*Helios mantári*.[3] They're all about in this part of the Under," a small voice said from off to the side.

The group turned and looked at the youth with the mushroom cap pack sitting perched on a frozen mudflow.

"Hi," the young man said, "I'm Anoup. Who are you?"

Mod was still somewhat shell shocked from the Inferno experience, so the unexpected appearance of someone new took him by surprise. Mod looked at the others, and their reactions were the same as his. They stood in silence for a moment as everyone took stock of one another.

"This being does not appear to be one of the dead," Mopsus said.

"No," the boy laughed. "I'm alive. There are other people alive in the Under too. Would you like me to take you to them?"

"A bit of a tour from a local wouldn't be a bad thing," Mod said.

Anoup squirmed a bit at that.

Mopsus laughed Anoup's discomfort. "This boy is not a local."

Mod turned to Anoup with a question in his eyes.

---

3. Greek for *Helios's mushrooms*. The mushroom's brightness was actually tied to the titan's waking and sleeping, so the light was fairly bright and constant when the god was awake, which worked out well, except when the aging god took an afternoon nap.

"He's right. I'm not local, but I've been here a while. I think." He looked down at his feet. "I could still show you around, though."

Mopsus looked skeptical, nevertheless the seer bowed to the boy first. He leaned heavily on his staff to do so. "I am Mopsus." He rose and pointed clockwise to the others. "Medusa and Three, Modifixeus, and this is D'artagnan."

Anoup's eyes took in each member of the group as they were introduced. His eyes lingered for a moment on Mopsus's stick, but they rested for the longest time on the dog.

D'art stared back at Anoup, and the tip of the dog's tail started to thump just a bit. He seemed comfortable enough with the youth, which in turn made Mod just a bit more at ease in the young man's presence. Not everyone seemed to share that feeling.

Anoup's gaze went back to Mopsus, and the seer eyed the youth with thinly veiled suspicion.

Mopsus doesn't trust him, Mod thought.

D'art must have recognized something in the air. He looked between Mopsus and Anoup, and the tip of his tail stopped wagging. The dog backed away from them both, placing himself in the protected space between Medusa and Three. Once the dog was settled, he looked up at Anoup again and whuffed at the boy, expectant, almost as if he was calling the young man to his side.

Three smiled and bent over to scratch the dog between the ears. "I believe he's asking for a bit of cheese, should you have any. We seem to have run out of treats for him a while ago."

"Cheese?" Anoup asked. He spoke the word with a hint of fondness. "If I had some, the dog could use it as a squeaky toy.[4] We don't get much dairy around here, and I ran out of what little I did have a while ago. I have some of what the locals call *spasmodikós mantári* if

---

4. Five thousand years ago, an Egyptian cheese called halloumi, made from goat and sheep's milk, was described as being tough and having a squeaky texture. I'd like some squeaky cheese, please?

he'd like a bit."[5] The boy reached behind his back and pulled a small, dried stick from a satchel at his waist and tossed it to the dog.

D'art glanced at the stick as it clattered on the rocks before him. He did not look impressed. The dog sniffed at the stick a couple of times, picked it up in his mouth, then quickly spat it back out.

"So what are you all here for?" Anoup asked the group.

Mopsus didn't look like he was going to answer. He signaled the others to be on their guard.

Mod stepped forward anyway. "We're here because—"

"To see the mushrooms, of course," Medusa interrupted.

"Beautiful mushrooms." Three nodded, following Medusa's lead. She pointed at the packs, the lanterns, and the spelunking equipment. "You can see by our gear we're avid mushroom enthusiasts. I bet you have mushrooms of a size that rivals Olympus."

"Olympus?" Anoup asked, looking like he'd never heard of the word before. The youth hopped down from his perch. "Oh, you mean big. Sure, I could show you some big mushrooms. Follow me this way."

"As I said, not a local," Mopsus whispered to the others as they started after the boy. "Egyptian, if I guess correctly."

The boy froze as if he had heard everything.

Good ears, Mod thought.

Now that the suspicion had been voiced, Mopsus pressed ahead to confirm it. "How did an Egyptian come to be in the underworld of Greece?" Mopsus asked.

"The underworld of Greece?" The youth scratched his head and gave a nervous laugh.

"We're below Hades, though I'm not sure how far that elevator dropped us. Are we in Tartarus?" Mod said, unsure why he suddenly felt the need to protect the boy from Mopsus.

---

5. *Spasmodikós mantári* means *jerked or dried mushroom*, not to be confused with *spasmodikós malakas* or *mushroom jerk*, which is an unflattering term for a man of questionable character with a fungal problem.

"I think we're below Tartar sauce, but I'm not really sure. The locals just call it the Unders." Anoup pointed the way forward. "We need to turn up ahead."

"Where we are is not as important as why you are here." Mopsus ignored the youth's directions and blocked the path before him. "You are far from your home, boy."

"And you're not?" Anoup said defensively. He rose up to his full height and tried to stare down Mopsus, but when the seer wouldn't back down Anoup deflated somewhat. "I was trying to follow some-one." Anoup admitted as he slowly turned to face the rest of the group. "I lost their trail and then I couldn't find my way out again."

"Sounds plausible," Mod admitted.

"Sounds suspicious," Mopsus amended. "To be here where he doesn't belong, at a time such as this?"

"I'm not the only thing from Egypt here, you know." Anoup pointed at the staff in the seer's grasp.

Mopsus arched an eyebrow and glared down at the boy. "I don't need to explain myself to you, boy."

Anoup balled up his fists at that.

Mod stepped in between the two and held up his hands for some calm. "Hey, can we just take a step back for a second?"

It took a moment, but then both of the men backed down.

"That's better."

What did I just do? Mod thought about it a second, and realized he'd just done what his brother would have if he'd been there. *So how would Doug handle this now?*

"So, it's always a bit of a shock when you run into someone you aren't expecting on the road, right? Always seems to turn into a fight,"[6] Mod said. "No need for that here." He turned to Anoup.

---

6. Every meeting on ancient roads had the potential for violence. In the story of Oedi-pus, when he ran into his father, whom he had never seen, it turned into a scuffle that ended with the dad dead and Oedipus king of his father's kingdom. Believe it or not, that's the happy part. It all goes downhill from there.

"We're glad to meet you." Then with a pointed glance at Mopsus, he added, "aren't we?"

Mopsus took a second before he gave a slight nod.

"There, see?" Mod could feel the sweat in his armpits running down his sides. "All good."

"Sorry if we almost got off on the wrong foot," the youth said. "Welcome to the Unders." Anoup turned to lead them on again and changed the subject back to a more neutral topic. "Great place to look at mushrooms, ain't it? There's all sorts and shapes here in the gardens and in the forest and in the mushroom sea. Course, they ain't letting many go poke around much, because of the end of the world and all."

"The end of the world?" Mopsus asked.

If Mod hadn't known better, he would have thought Mopsus had no idea what the boy was talking about. The acting took in Anoup as well. The boy looked confused, as if he'd suspected something only to have his suppositions rather abruptly proven wrong. "So if you're looking for the mushrooms, I guess we need to take you to the Mushroom Boss. He can tell you all about them."

"The Boss. Good." Mopsus smiled and nodded, his harsh tone of just moments before discarded or forgotten. "We would very much like to visit with him about these wonderful mushrooms."

"This way." Anoup led them down a branch of the tunnel that veered off to the left, the youthful spring in his step missing, though it appeared he was trying to mask it.

"Follow, but be wary," Mopsus whispered over his shoulder to the others.

"Some of the bigger mushrooms ain't mushrooms at all," Anoup said in way of conversation as they traveled along. "There's a land of the dead just above the Unders, and once in a while some of the dead wander down this way."

"Interesting." Three sounded as if she wanted to hear more. "Please, go on."

Anoup shrugged. "Not much to say. They wander in and out

mostly. Every so often one might get stuck and wind up staying too long, and the fungus takes over and tries to cover the shape of the man or woman that was."

Mod looked at a particularly large grouping of mushroom buttons. The cluster did look an awful lot like a face.

A small tremor of the Grand Machine shook the ground. Small, but still big enough to feel the rumble. The mushrooms before Mod undulated in a wave, making the fungal face roll back and forth in the swell. The eyes opened one at a time as if they'd been shaken from their slumber and blinked at Mod.

"Terribly sorry. Didn't mean to stare," Mod whispered in a stammer.

The tall, thin shade covered in button mushrooms coughed out a cloud of spores. "Haven't seen a discus golf disc about, have you?"[7]

"Uh, discus golf?" Mod asked, having a vague idea what the man might be talking about, but not being a sports person, he wasn't really sure.

Anoup was there in a second, pulling Mod back from the outstretched hand that had suddenly appeared by Mod's shoulder. "Don't talk to the mushroom shades. Once they're stuck, they have to find someone to take their place before they can leave. Mushrooms like it when they get a taste of what it's like to be part of something that moves about on feet. Then they get addicted to the feel.[8] The mushrooms won't let the shades leave."

Anoup glared at the shade as the mushroom buttons drew back to the wall. "Have you seen my kite?" The shade coughed again.

---

7. This deceased mushroom man is a disc golf enthusiast friend of mine named Tim, and his obsession with the sport was probably influenced by the deadly bowler hat welding psychopath Oddjob from the James Bond franchise.

8. Yes, they knew about addiction even back then. The common addictions in ancient Greece were to opium and hemp, though mushroom addiction was not unknown. It's not a new problem. The twist here is that it's the mushrooms that are addicted to the people and not vice-versa.

"I haven't seen any kite." Mod was a bit unsettled by this interaction.

"Tell Sara to feed the dogs." The shade slumped a bit more, the features and form of a man returning to a camouflage of caps and buttons and stems.

"I'm sure he was a good enough chap in life, but he ain't alive anymore. No more walking off the path." Anoup pulled Mod back to the center of the road and placed him next to the girls. Then Anoup made his way back to the head of the group, so he could once more guide the way.

"I hope the dogs get fed." Three reached down and scratched D'art between the ears. "Should we happen across someone named Sara we'll pass the message along."

"Woof!" D'art agreed.

Mopsus looked askance at the dog. "We should all take care of what walls we touch from now on."

"Yup," Anoup said. "You ain't even seen the cave worms yet."

"Cave worms?" Medusa asked as the group began to move again.

Guess I've got to be more careful. Mod followed the others but couldn't help a quick glance over his shoulder. The mushroom-covered shade had faded back into the wall. Mod couldn't even tell where it had been.

Anoup stopped up ahead, looking like he was unsure of which fork in the road to take. D'art came up next to the youth, sniffed the air, then headed down the left tunnel. Anoup watched after the dog for a second. "He seems rather sure of himself."

"The correct way forward smells like a treat to him," Mod explained.

Anoup nodded and trotted after the dog to catch up. D'art waited for him, then the two of them led the way together.

"The dog seems to trust him," Mod pointed out to the others.

"Why pay attention to the seer tasked by the gods to take you to your destiny when you have a dog and a lost teenager to show you the way?" Mopsus grumbled under his breath.

The proliferation of mushrooms was astounding. It seemed like every step they took brought the group further and further into a living world, the likes of which was unimagined on the surface. Not all of the mushrooms glowed like the Helios kind, but the variety on display was astounding. There were flowing mushrooms that seemed to be painted gold and silver. Some looked like gems and glittered as if they had facets as the light played over their surface. There were soft looking mushrooms, and mushrooms as hard as if they were made of the hardest stones and metals.

It was a lot of mushroom variety and information to take in. One thing was sure, though. The overwhelming shape of the things followed one pattern.

"Walking through a phallic collection the likes of which I have never seen," Three noted with a smile. "I like it here."

"The variety of colors," Medusa giggled.

"Oh, my gosh, can you even imagine?" Three laughed and leaned against Medusa in a well-meaning hug.

Mod pulled down the hem of his chiton a bit, blushed furiously, and held back just a step from the others.

The mushrooms were getting larger. Some of them looked to have been hollowed out and had small lizards and other odd animals living inside them. A lizard popped out of the top of a somewhat suggestive growth, and Three and Medusa actually clapped.

"How unexpected!" Three gasped.

"This is gonna haunt me in nightmares for years to come," Mod said.

At least the girls looked like they were enjoying themselves. Mod looked at the girls for a second before he noticed that something seemed odd about Medusa's clothing.

Her pocket was glowing.

"Hey, Medusa, what's that?" He pointed at her dress.

It took her a second, before she slowed and figured out what he was pointing at. "It's the Orphic tablet." She reached into her pocket and pulled it out. "It has a message."

She took it out and read the message on the surface. "A mushroom is key to finding the missing." She paused. "Okay. Which mushroom?"

"You do have a few to choose from," Three admitted as she swept her arm wide to indicate the bounty around them.

Mopsus, D'art, and Anoup kept walking ahead.

"Figure it out soon, or we're going to lose our guide." Mod thought about it a second before he amended the statement. "Guides."

The message of the tablet changed and morphed.

The tiny blue one with the purple spots. It's called the spotted vautia.[9]

"Well, that was oddly specific," Mod said, then added with a hint of sarcasm. "I wonder what this mushroom does if you eat it?" The sarcasm appeared totally lost on Medusa.

"I'd have to guess it was named what it was for a reason. Pity the poor fellow who figured it out. Mushrooms aren't things to mess around with. Some of them can start to kill you before you even realize you've been poisoned." Medusa found a small mushroom matching the description given by the tablet and picked it up.

"With a name like that, I wouldn't lick my fingers until I had a chance to wash my hands," Mod suggested.

Medusa pulled a scrap of fabric from her pocket, wrapped the mushroom in it, and placed it in her pocket with the tablet. Then she looked at her hands as if reconsidering what she had just picked. "I guess we'll find out why we need it later?"

They all hurried after the others, who were almost out of sight.

The path they followed opened up, and the roof rose high above them. The mushrooms started looking more industrial and purposeful, now appearing more like buildings and towers and such.

The women went back into taking in the sights.

---

9. Pronounced *naftia*, which means *nausea* in Greek.

"Look at the big brown one over there." Medusa pointed at a tower-like fungus that rose high above the others.

"The women really seem taken with the sights," Anoup noted.

"As we said, mushroom enthusiasts," Mopsus reminded their guide as he shot the women a sidelong glance.

After a while, sounds of work, of children playing, of life, filtered to the group traveling through the cave.

They entered into an immense chamber, with three of the largest Helios mushrooms Mod could even imagine hanging from the roof of the massive cavern. Not that he'd seen any before today, but these were huge. The mushrooms glowed like triple suns, brightening the day.

It might have been psychosomatic, but Mod could swear he could feel the heat of the sun radiating from the mushrooms above.

Anoup swept his arm out as if inviting the group into his home. "Welcome to the mushroom kingdom!"

CHAPTER 20

THE FUNGAL PALACE

MEDUSA FOLLOWED CLOSELY BEHIND ANOUP AS THE YOUTH LED them all into a crowded square. The sounds of the city went silent as the newcomers came into sight. Not just the spot where Mod and his group had entered, but the whole city. The men, women, and children all looked at Medusa and the others, unsure of what to make of their sudden appearance.

Three wiggled her fingers and flashed a smile at a group of children. They gaped and oohed and awed at her. "The people seem nice enough." Three just possessed a natural way of putting people at ease.

Medusa didn't have quite the same skillset. She tried to put on a friendly face, even going so far as to wave at a nearby child. The child swallowed hard, her bottom lip started to tremble, and she let out a glorious wail before her mother scooped her up and soothed her.

Three patted Medusa on the shoulder. "Good try."

"Bite me."

Three gave Medusa a good-natured hug.

A commanding woman in the crowd straightened, clasped her hands in front of her skirt, and studied the newcomers as if she weighed their intentions. "Visitors." The woman stood over all of them, taller than a tree. "We don't get many visitors."

Anoup took a knee and bowed his head. "I thought it best to bring them to you and the Boss Man, my queen."

A stout giant of a man walked up behind the woman. He was a head shorter than her and walked somewhat as if he had once been chopped into bits and put back together, or had been a horse, or both. "What have we here, my love?"

180

"Visitors." The tree woman eyed them all with an icy glare.

Mopsus bowed, and so did Medusa, Three, and Mod. Even D'art took a knee.

"Well-mannered visitors, to be sure." The man beamed. "Welcome! I am Kronos."

Mopsus appeared to stumble and choke at that. He reached behind him and tugged down the flap on the backpack so none of its contents could be seen poking out.

Zeus's dad? This could be good or bad. Medusa thought. "The man who castrated his father to overthrow him, and was castrated by his son in turn, now lords over a phallic shaped kingdom,"[1] Medusa whispered so only Three should have been able to hear.

"We don't know the kingdom is phallic shaped, only that most of the objects within sure are," Three whispered back.

Medusa watched Mod's eyes go wide as she and Three spoke. *Apparently I don't whisper as quietly as I think I do.*

"We are here to find and fix the tremors that are shaking the firmament, mighty Kronos," Mod said a little more loudly than he needed to.

"You are come to aid me, my wife, and our children. Welcome! Let us know more of what you intend, and we will see what we may be able to do to help you." Kronos beamed and nodded to his subjects. The normal sounds of a bustling city returned, although a tad more subdued than Medusa suspected would be normal.

"And as for you, my young friend, you shall be rewarded for bringing these allies to us in a time of need," Kronos patted Anoup on the shoulder. He motioned for his wife Philyra to lead then followed after her.

"Please, my new friends, this way." Kronos talked pretty much nonstop as they traveled down a road made from rock and living

---

1. Kronos used a stone sickle to lop his father Uranus's two veg from the stalk. Then he tossed the still-potent members into the sea. The blood that spilled to the ground resulted in the races of the Gigantes, the Erinyes, and the Meliae. The resulting foam also gave birth to Aphrodite. Damn! Uranus was like the original Nick Cannon.

fungus. "I mean, Prometheus made the first batch of men out of clay—"

"Slurry," Philyra corrected.

"Mud," Kronos compromised. "And when we got down here, it was somewhat lonesome. We wanted children and subjects, but"—he gestured at his groin—"the equipment isn't in pristine condition, if you know what I mean? Not for lack of trying, though." He tapped his wife in the ribs with his elbow.

"I'm sure they understand, dear." Philyra looked a tad embarrassed that he'd brought up the subject.

"Sure, there was clay—"

"Slurry."

"Mud." Kronos furrowed his brow and continued, "Didn't want to make a new batch and wind up with the same problems as the last time, so I thought, why not work with fungus? I mean, it's halfway there when it comes to breathing life into it."

"Slime molds never really achieved the higher level of enlightenment the fungi did," Philyra explained.

"Good at construction and administration, though,"[2] Kronos noted.

There was an ease in their back and forth that made Medusa think Philyra and Kronos really cared about each other. It made Medusa think of her own parents, and how she had never heard them talk to each other the same way, and how because of who she was and where she came from, she probably wasn't even capable of having a good relationship with someone either. Then there was the kid that had just screamed because Medusa had looked at her—

Medusa looked over at Mod, a knot in her gut, and immediately wanted to find something else to think about.

She used the streets and the architecture as a diversion. They were like nothing she had ever seen. It was a pretty city, or at least interesting. She wouldn't want to live here, but it was nice and felt

---

2. Where slime molds really excelled was multi-level marketing and used-car sales.

close without being too claustrophobic, which was an accomplishment this far down into Gaea. There was a lot of seismic damage visible as they walked through the city. Many of the walls and structures Medusa could see being repaired had a pulsing, veinlike something clinging to the walls and foundations, holding things together despite the damage. A ripple of pulsing flesh grabbed a large stone brick, carried it on a wave of veins up the side of the building, then mortared it in place.

Must be the slime molds Philyra talked about.

They seemed to be doing a good job.

Another small tremor rumbled through the city. The slime molds paused in their work until the shaking had passed, then resumed. They seemed to be making slow progress as they kept the worst of the damage at bay.

"Lots of repairs going on right now because of the hitch in Gaea's rotation and all." Kronos looked around and seemed happy with what he observed. "Knocked a lot of things loose, but everything seems to be going back into place just fine."

"Life continues despite the tremors?" Mopsus asked.

Kronos nodded. "Can't stop because you've been shaken to the core. My people are a resilient lot."

Medusa looked at some of the other people working, playing, or just going about their lives. They would freeze when a big tremor hit, but just went about their business when the smaller, more frequent rumbles vibrated the ground.

Medusa was surprised to see how many of the residents of the mushroom metropolis had mushroom-like features—or might actually be mushrooms themselves. The creation process used to make people must not have drifted very far from the original building material.

Kronos rounded a corner and almost tripped over a red-and-white-cap-headed child playing in the street.

"Your majesty." The mother of the child bowed and quickly snatched her toddler from the ground in the same motion.

"You look lovely this morning, PortaBella." Kronos nodded to the mother and reached out and pinched her little one on the cheek. "My, how little Frýnos[3] is growing."

"Yes, my king." PortaBella beamed. "He's all hopes and fantasy, this one is. Always looking for adventure."

"You've been telling him stories of the Vasiliás Chilónas again?" Kronos asked with a smile.

"Turtle King?" Mopsus asked.

"The Turtle King, ruler of the Turtle Kingdom. The most ancient of which holds absolute power and supports the world on his back,"[4] Kronos explained. "I don't know where the story comes from, but there are many variations."

"He so loves those stories." PortaBella bounced the little toddler on her hip. "Someday he'll be a great protector of the kingdom." She leaned her head in close and tickled the child. "Who's the little hero that will save us from the turtles?"

Frýnos swatted at his mom's hands and gave a belly laugh.

"I could see that happening." Kronos patted the child on the cap. "A protector of the kingdom who works closely with the royal family in the palace."

A gap-toothed smile spread over the child's face. He hiccoughed, burped, and spit up just a bit on his chin. Then he stuck his finger up his nose.

"Human, mushroom, whatever. All kids are gross," Three said.

"My mother told me it's endearing when the child in question belongs to you," Mod explained, then looked at PortaBella as her shoulders slumped as she searched for a clean spot on an already soiled burp rag. Mod amended his statement. "Sometimes."

Frýnos threw his arms around his mother's neck and buried his face in her shoulder. PortaBella hugged him back as if the frustration of a moment before was completely forgotten.

---

3. The kid's name is Toad. He *will* become a mighty and brave adventurer someday.
4. This myth of creation and power exists in the folklore of India, China, North America, and the Nintendo Mario franchise.

"Come, friends, my home is just ahead." Kronos led them on.

Medusa's eyes lingered on the mother and child as Kronos led the group away.

They had wandered about long enough that the large mushrooms in the sky had gradually started to dim. "Let us give you rest, supplies, and make sure you can be on your way at first light," Kronos suggested.

"We're in a kind of rush—" Medusa began.

"Nonsense. I'd be offended were you to reject my hospitality." He once again clapped Anoup on the shoulder. "I must insist."

The city was separated into upper and lower districts, with the palace and the ruling class seeming to occupy the upper reaches, or so Medusa assumed from the grandeur of the fungal facades she was now passing by. There was more space around the buildings as well, to give breathing room to the sculptural landscaping, lichen topiaries, and mildew-like succulents and trees arranged here and there by obviously well-trained and expert gardeners.

The sculpture gardens were a little hard for Medusa to look at. It had been different when she had been joking about phallic shapes with Three, but now that Medusa was stuck in her own mind, the shapes reminded Medusa too much of things from her past that she'd rather forget.

You'd need multiple sessions with Aristotle or the Oracle at Delphi to even identify all my problems, and none of those things matter right now. What does matter is fixing the Grand Machine. As she thought it, she clung to it, the lifeline of distraction she'd looked for. Because she hadn't pressed the group to move faster, they might now have lost more time they couldn't afford to lose.

That wasn't the only thing that bugged her, though. Something else about this didn't feel right. She never expected to get this sort of welcome from Kronos, who, arguably, didn't leave the surface world under the best of conditions and feelings with those who took his place.

So why would he be so welcoming now?

She studied the king and his wife as they walked, sure that her sense of unease stemmed from them.

The rest of the group seemed intent on taking in the sights—all except for Mopsus, who was fidgeting and biting his lower lip as he trudged along. The seer looked more anxious to get going than Medusa was.

The palace was a testament to multi-towered phallic architecture[5]. There had to be at least a dozen spires reaching up toward the dimming faux suns in the sky.

"You will be given the finest lodgings. Rest. We will send you off in the morning with all that you need."

"Time is of the essence," Mopsus said in an urgent voice.

"Nonsense." Kronos gave the seer a look that suggested his objection was noted and rejected. "The world has not failed, and I cannot foresee how it could be torn asunder by you and your companions getting a good night's sleep and being stocked with provisions."

The queen interjected. "If they feel that time—"

"Enough about *time*."[6] The king sneered as he said the word. "I never liked him, and I hate that beings are always conflating and confusing me with him. He is not the king of this land. If I am not mistaken, that would be me."

"My king." The queen bowed.

The rest of the group joined her.

The king nodded his head as if the matter were settled. "I will not send our saviors out ill-rested and unprepared." He clapped his hands together. "That's the end of the discussion. My wife will lead you to your rooms. And you?" He placed a hand on Anoup's shoulder. "I have a special thanks in mind for you. Come with me, lad."

Anoup looked hesitant to go, but when D'art went up and

---

5. Think of the castle illustration on the front of the VHS release of Disney's *Little Mermaid*. Caused quite the uproar at the time.
6. Chronos, the embodiment of time, came into existence along with other primordial deities such as Chaos, Erebus, and Nyx. Kronos, as one of the titans, is just a kid compared to his great-uncle.

wagged his tail beside him, intent on staying with the youth, Anoup relented and allowed Kronos to direct him to another part of the palace.

Medusa noticed a questioning look the queen gave her husband. She appeared as if she might object. No one else acted as if anything were amiss, and it bothered Medusa. *Maybe I'm just being paranoid.* But hadn't she been chosen because she knew how to deal with gods, monsters, and their unexpected ways.

Philyra held out a hand and motioned for the group to follow as she led them to the group quarters.

"Rest," Kronos called over his shoulder with a good-natured laugh. "I will send you off to your great destiny first thing in the morning."

As Medusa followed her hostess, she was certain of one thing. *I'm not going to get any rest at all.*

CHAPTER 21

BRINGING LOST FRIENDS BACK TO THE TABLE

WHAT MEDUSA COULD ONLY ASSUME TO BE A MUSHROOM rooster crowed in the dawn somewhere out in the city. It could have been a normal rooster, but the strangled warble sounded off, and Medusa hadn't seen anything resembling a regular bird in the underworld so far.

The ground beneath their feet rumbled and shifted.

Mopsus chomped at the bit in the morning. The seer didn't look like he'd slept at all. Mod could hear Mopsus grinding his teeth at the tremor from across the room.

That was probably why Mopsus hadn't slept. If he keeps this up, his molars will be nothing but nubs by the end of this.

"All this waiting for nothing is infuriating." Mopsus gripped his staff so hard his knuckles popped and cracked.

"The king all but ordered us to stay," Medusa said. "You wouldn't want to suffer the wrath of a titan[1]."

The seer grumbled. "What is taking them so long?" He paced back and forth in the hallway shared by the rooms each of them had used during the night.

"The mushrooms in the sky are just barely starting to brighten." Mod pointed at the huge arched window that looked down over the city. "I'm sure someone will come to gather us up soon enough."

As if on cue, a slight and sprightly mushroom maid appeared. She counted the people present and nodded. "I've been asked to gather

---

1. I was disappointed in the movie and its prequel. They both made me long for the days of stop motion by Ray Harryhausen and the acting chops of Harry Hamlin.

you so you may break your fasts with my lord and lady." She motioned for them to follow.

Mopsus muttered something under his breath, hitched his pack higher up on his shoulder, and headed after her. Three sauntered after them. Mod was just about to follow when Medusa put her hand on his shoulder. Being touched by her immediately got his attention.

Medusa dropped her hand to her side and started after the others, holding back just enough to keep out of earshot. Mod fell into step beside her. "I thought you were mad at me."

"Later." She had something else on her mind that was more pressing. The night's stay had been pleasant enough for Mod; he looked to be well rested. She'd been up all night pondering things he probably hadn't thought of. "Something is wrong here."

Mod nodded. "If you say so, I believe you."

"Have you seen Anoup or D'art?" Medusa asked.

Mod shook his head. "I figured we'd see them when we get to breakfast."

"That they weren't with us last night makes me worry," Medusa said. "I know we haven't known them long, but—"

"If they aren't there, we won't leave until we find them."

She looked a bit shocked that Mod had agreed so fast. Medusa searched Mod's face for a step or two before she turned her eyes back to the servant they followed. "The king . . . There's something off about him."

"He seems nice enough to me, but I often wonder what I might have missed when it comes to social interactions." Mod pursed his lips and shrugged. "I'm not always the most observant, so it could be a lot of things. Whatever it is, you'll figure it out. Like I said"—his lips turned up at the corners of his mouth—"I trust you."

Medusa was a bit shocked at how easily he said he trusted her. She grinned back, and the two walked in silence the rest of the way.

The mushroom maid led them past the grand rooms and halls on the main floors, to the high tower that was the royal private living space. The young woman opened the door to a receiving room that was large yet intimate and motioned for them to follow her inside. The room was open to one side, with a wide balcony that looked out over the city.

"Shall I get a hot morning fungal cider for you as you wait for the king and queen to arrive?" the serving girl asked.

"While we appreciate it, I fear there is little time," Mopsus said. "Our quest is vital, and it has taken us much time to get this far. The night's stay was an unexpected delay."

Probably not sure how to answer the seer's urgency, the girl bowed. "Your hosts will be with you shortly." And she left.

Mopsus huffed and began to pace the length of the balcony, his staff making an angry, rhythmic tic, tic, tic.

The sounds of the king and queen came from the corridor just as Mopsus was about to drive Medusa nuts with his pacing.

Kronos and Philyra entered the room. Anoup and D'art were not with them. Medusa looked over at Mod, and he just nodded back, a signal that he was ready to act no matter what she decided.

"Sorry to keep you." Philyra inclined her head. "My husband had a hard time getting up and about this morning."

"I spent quite the night talking and bonding with the young lad and the dog," Kronos said. "In fact, we had a good enough rapport that they both decided to go to work for me. I sent them off on a very important errand in the middle of the night."

That didn't sound suspicious at all.

Mod looked over at Medusa again. Medusa gave a very slight shake of her head to wait just a bit longer.

Philyra arched an incredulous eyebrow at her husband as if the youth and dog working for him were news to her.

"Let us all have breakfast, shall we?" Kronos clapped his hands.

Serving maids came in bearing bowls full of unknown fruits and cakes. The last girl entered with a platter filled to the edges with some kind of eggs served sunny side up. The whites of the eggs appeared clear, and the yolks seemed to be a yellowish-green color.

Medusa suddenly wondered what the rooster that had announced the coming of this morning and his little harem of a flock must look like if the eggs had originated from them.

The food smelled good though.

Mod looked across the table to Medusa to see if she thought the food would be safe to eat.

Medusa's eyes followed the serving girl with the platter. When the girl got to Kronos the king held up his hand and declined the egg dish. "I think I'll just nibble on some fruit this morning. I had snacks late last night."

The queen's eyebrow raised again, but she said nothing.

Medusa signaled Mod not to eat. She got Mopsus's attention just as the seer was about to raise a forkful of food to his mouth. "It would be impolite to eat before our host has had anything," Medusa said. Mopsus grumbled and placed his fork back on the plate.

"Ah. How rude of me. Forgive me." Kronos held his hand over his heart in apology. "Perhaps a spot of morning juice, a sweet drink to share with our new friends and wish them a swift and successful journey."

The serving girl nodded, and another girl went to the juice bar to prepare drinks for everyone.

"Please. Allow me." Medusa rose, her hand sliding quickly in and out of her pocket as she did so and made her way to the drink station. "But given the nature of what we embark on, I feel wine to be far more appropriate as a drink."

Kronos smiled at Medusa's way of thinking. "The wines are over there." He inclined his head off to the left.

Medusa lined up a number of earthenware bowls, the most ornate of which she placed at the end of the line for the king and queen. She went to the open wines and gave each one a whiff.

"I have white, and a black from Rhodes, very hard to come by, and—"

Medusa took the top off of a final container and gave it a sniff

191

before she nodded appropriately. "Melogion."[2] Medusa made her selection.

"You know of it?" He chuckled. "Quite the connoisseur." Kronos sounded intrigued. He turned around to watch Medusa as she worked.

"I know my way around gods, and you, being of the generation that came before the gods, should be given that much more honor and reverence, hence a special drink because you allow us into your presence," Medusa answered.

Kronos looked pleased to have a mortal put the gods in their proper place. "I like you. Please continue."

Medusa filled a serving platter with the wine bowls and poured a measure of melogion into each of them. She made her way to the table and placed a bowl in front of everyone there, left one in her spot as she passed, and ended by giving the ornate bowls to the queen and king.

Medusa went back and took her bowl in hand and raised it toward her host.

Everyone else took their bowls and pointed them toward Kronos.

"To the long and lasting reign of Kronos over his kingdom," Medusa said.

"To Kronos!"

They all drained their bowls.

"Ah! A perfect toast to start my morning. I must say, I'm honored." Kronos smacked his lips. "Very . . ." The king's brow turned down, and a frown formed at the corner of his lips. "Very . . ."

A small, perfectly timed, disconcerting jump from the Grand Machine was enough to push the titan past the point he could cope.

Kronos threw up all over the table.

Mod watched as the chunky wave washed over the tabletop. It obliterated the fruit, cakes, and eggs.

---

2. Artemidorus described this as a drink made by boiling honey with water and adding herbs for taste. It is rumored to be far more intoxicating than wine.

"Well, so much for breakfast," Three said.

"I told you we should have left earlier," Mopsus whined as he diverted a rivulet of spew with his plate.

The pile of vomit rolled and settled. As soon as the shock wore off, Medusa noticed two figures emerging from the middle of the largest lump of ejecta. Anoup and D'art lifted their trembling heads up from the sludge.

"I suspected as much," Medusa said as she cast a reproving glance at their host.

"Spotted vautía in his wine?" Mod asked Medusa.

"Spotted vautía in his wine," Medusa confirmed.

Anoup reached out with a trembling hand. "Does anyone have a towel?"

Three handed the youth the napkin from her lap.

Philyra rose up in fury. "You ate the child!"[3] she yelled at her husband.

"I was stressed. I needed comfort food." Kronos hacked and cleared his throat.

"Comfort food!" Philyra was having none of it. "What in the bowels of Chaos do you need to partake in comfort food for?"

"Please don't say bowels," Anoup begged.

"I can explain. The world might be ending. I was feeling stressed." Kronos held his hand out to her as he wiped the puke stains from his beard on the back of his sleeve.

D'art pulled himself out of the slime with a sucking sound, then, to Mod's great horror, shook himself to get the sludge off of his coat. Everyone at the table was sprayed with a mixture of chunky spew infused with the essence of wet dog.

---

3. Kronos learned of a prophecy that he would be overthrown by his child, so he ate Demeter, Hestia, Hera, Hades, and Poseidon. Only Zeus was saved from his father's gullet. Later, Kronos was given a potion that made him regurgitate his gobbled offspring. Zeus led a revolt backed up by his father's spewed spawn, and the victorious gods took their rightful place on Olympus.

"You ate the child and his dog!" It was clear to anyone watching that Philyra was livid. "You said you would never eat a child again."

"I promised I would never eat one of my, er, our children." Kronos stood up and tried to calm his wife down. "This child and this dog are not ours."

Philyra shot Kronos with a look that even Mod recognized.

If Kronos hadn't been gelded before, there was a sure bet he'd know that kind of pain and loss soon.

CHAPTER 22

STARTING OFF AGAIN ON THE WRONG FOOT

GETTING D'ART AND ANOUP BACK HAD NOT IMPROVED THE group's overall disposition. Medusa looked resigned and depressed to have been proven right, even though she'd saved the boy and dog from a fate Mod would rather not think about. The brief alliance and closeness Mod had shared disappeared the second the boy and dog emerged from Kronos's hurlings. Anoup and D'art were mental wrecks for obvious reasons. Mopsus had no mercy for those trauma- tized by the morning's activities and insisted they now redouble their efforts to make up for lost time, only relenting long enough to let everyone quickly wash up and change into vomit-free clothes.

And this is the group that's supposed to save the universe?

Just when Mod was about to give in to despair, Three walked by. She whistled and smiled and seemed unaffected by everything going wrong.

That made Mod smile. Maybe things weren't as bad as he thought after all.

Philyra and Kronos declined the opportunity to see Mod and Medusa and their little band off. Philyra had her servants make provi- sions and gear ready for the travelers. With few instructions and a curt goodbye, the queen had them escorted to the edge of the kingdom.

Medusa's mood had turned dark as she walked along the path. "I don't think we'll be welcomed if we come back this way again," Medusa said.

Mod had to agree with her assessment. "I'm sure we'll figure something out if we get that far." It was probably best if they left as soon as possible.

Anoup rubbed his temples as he walked down the head of the trail. D'art walked right beside him, his head down and a little less pep in his step than normal. The experience of being eaten and regurgitated by a titan seemed to have made a bond between the two, which is not to say the both of them came away from it unscathed.

The youth had a faraway look in his eyes and kept squinting against the light.

Mopsus pulled a pinch out a pouch of something from his pack and offered it to the younger man. "Dried willow leaf,"[1] he explained, "for tea, but the effect is more potent if you just stick a wad in your cheek and suck on it for a while."

Anoup put the pinch of dried leaves in his right cheek and flinched at the bitter taste. "And this will do what, exactly?"

"Pain suppressant." Mopsus tied up the pouch and put it back in his bag. "The bright lights and stabbing pain behind the eyes will go away in a little while."

"Got anything to make me forget the experience?" Anoup asked.

"How many can say they went through what you just did and survived? Focus on that."

"I'd rather not." Anoup held out his hand for more of the dried leaf.

The seer gave him a questioning glance.

"For the dog," Anoup explained.

Mopsus arched an eyebrow at the canine, clearly annoyed at anything that didn't mean moving forward. He opened the pouch again and handed a pinch of the leaf to the youth anyway. "Anything if it will help get us on our way."

D'art didn't like the taste. And the sound of him retching to clear the leaf from his tongue looked like it was just about enough to give Anoup shellshock. D'art gave a final hack and then stared up lovingly at the boy.

---

1. Aspirin, derived from the willow tree, has kicked back the effects of hangovers and headaches since before Dionysus went on his first rager.

The smell and sound of the dog retching was almost enough to make Mod lose his breakfast as well. "The quicker we move the sooner we put all of this behind us." Anoup picked up the pace in a quicker trudge down the trail, D'art close to his side as he sniffed the way.

Mopsus cursed. He brushed past them and established himself as the one to follow once again.

"Mopsus?" Medusa called out after the seer. "Is there something wrong with letting the boy and the dog lead for a while? They looked pretty certain that they were headed in the right direction."

Mopsus glanced at those following him over his shoulder. He did not stop walking. "As far as I remember, only one was tasked by the gods to be a leader of this expedition, and the dog and his boy were not mentioned in the discussion. How do we not know that one or the other might not lead us into a trap or danger laid out so only a seer might see?" He turned his head a bit further back and glared at Medusa out of the corner of his eye.

"Well that was a bit of a self-important answer, Mr. More-important-than-thou," Medusa muttered to herself.

The look the seer gave Medusa bordered on hostile. The glance she shot back all the more so.

Mod jogged forward to close the distance between him and Medusa while he watched Mopsus to make sure the seer didn't turn around. "Mopsus is taking this a bit seriously. I'm sure he means well. He's more driven than any of us to make it to the center of the Grand Machine, and the extra night spent in mushroom town put him on edge."

"Look at Mopsus. He doesn't care about the trauma the boy and dog just went through," Medusa muttered. "Does Mopsus seem off to you?"

"End of the world is getting to him, I guess." Mod shrugged. "Although it didn't get to him this way last time, but last time Mopsus wasn't responsible for a major part of the heroic effort. He is acting different, but . . . I don't know. He did give Anoup and D'art some of that leaf to help with the headaches," Mod pointed out.

Medusa looked like she wasn't impressed that Mod was defending the seer.

Then Mod turned to Medusa to make sure he had her attention. "Maybe you shouldn't question what he's doing?"

Medusa's eyes flared, and she shot Mod with such a look.

"That came out wrong." Mod held up his hands. "I didn't mean— Listen, something is still off here, and I just don't want to see us fighting with each other when we need our friends the most. I don't think we can do this alone."

The fire in Medusa's eyes cooled, and after a bit, she nodded.

"Just—" Mod glanced up to the head of the group, then back to Medusa. "Just be careful. I don't want anything to happen to you." He smiled and tried to get across the intent that he was sincere, but he had no idea what she now thought of him.

After a bit, Mod let her pull ahead and he took up his place at the end of the group again.

Both Anoup and the dog had looked a bit put out when Mopsus pushed them out of the way. But Anoup bent down and scratched D'art behind the ear as they walked, and he told him what a good boy he was. That put a bit more bounce back into the dog's step.

Mod thought if all of them learned to tiptoe a bit around the seer, maybe things would calm down and be all right. He wasn't going to suggest it, though.

They were almost to the edge of the huge chamber that encompassed the Mushroom Kingdom. The cavern tapered off at the wall, and cracks appeared near the base. The group was heading toward one of the bigger openings.

Mod saw the path obscured and covered by rock falls here closer to the cavern wall. There was a large mound of rubble at the base of the crack, and Mopsus, determined to lead the group, had to lean heavily on his staff to navigate it. The footing was hard, the way forward broken and rough.

"Are you sure this is the way?" Medusa asked.

Mopsus ignored her and looked annoyed when she repeated the question. He snorted and held his staff close to his chest. "Ask the dog and the boy if you doubt me."

The dog sniffed the air ahead and his tongue lolled out of his mouth. Anoup nodded and turned to the others. "D'art can smell that we're getting closer. The center of the universe is getting nearer."

"Satisfied?" Mopsus turned and continued onward. He didn't spare a glance back to see if the others followed. The way he had chosen was dark and dim, and though the floor started to level out, the walls and roof of the passage looked suspect.

D'art, Anoup, and Three walked close behind him.

Medusa held back, separating Mod and her from the rest of the group. She looked at the stone above her with nervous eyes.

Mod looked up at what she was studying. The rock shifted and moved as a new tremor from the center of the universe rocked the planet. Grit and dust showered down. He had to shield his eyes from the falling debris.

Mopsus slowed, as if somehow aware that not all of the group was following. "Confound it, woman!" He shouted as he made his way back to Medusa. "I told you the way was safe. Can you not see with your own eyes?" He stretched out his staff and tapped the arch of stone just above Medusa's head to illustrate his point.

Mod could see how all the broken shards of rock were holding each other in place. Mopsus just happened to choose the one spot to tap that would shift the interlocking shards just enough to release the pressure keeping everything together.

The whole section of cave came down.

Medusa and Mod may have both been crushed, but Mod saw the sudden increase in the falling grit and understood what it meant. He tackled her from behind, throwing both of them clear of the rockfall that would have killed or separated them from the others.

Mopsus was still holding his staff aloft, the pile of rocks from the cave-in ending right at the toe of his sandals. "I didn't expect to be disproved in such a dramatic manner."

Mod had shielded Medusa from some of the smaller rocks with his body. He scrambled up from atop her and helped her roll over so he could see that she was all right.

She coughed and rubbed the dust from her eyes.

"Sorry about that," Mod said. "There wasn't a lot of time to try to do that more gently."

Medusa let her eyes dart ever so briefly to a sheepish looking seer, and then gave a thin smile and nodded at Mod. "Second time since this has begun that you've found a way to put yourself on top of me."

Mod blushed. He offered a hand to help her to her feet. Then pulled his hand back as he second guessed if helping her up was the right thing to do, then held his hand out again.

"I can manage by myself, thank you, Mod." She stood and brushed off the front of her dress. "How 'bout we forego the demonstration of the stability of the rock we're standing under next time?" She arched an eyebrow in the direction of the seer.

Mopsus cleared his throat and tapped the new rock wall with his staff. "As I was saying, the way we follow is the correct way, and now it appears it is the only way forward."

"So it would seem," Medusa said.

Mopsus cleared his throat again and made his way to the front of the group again.

Mod came close to Medusa and touched her gently on the arm. "Are you all right?"

Medusa pulled her arm away. "I'm fine. Thanks for the rescue." Without saying anything else, she turned and followed after the others.

Her words didn't ring sincere, but she was probably just in shock. *Or she just really hated me now.*

A bit less spring in his step, Mod followed after the others and wondered why even when he saved a friend's life it seemed like he couldn't ever do the right thing.

CHAPTER 23

MIND IF I PUT A BUG IN YOUR EAR?

THE CAVERN WIDENED OUT CONSIDERABLY AFTER THAT, AND flora and fauna, if you could call it such, began to fill the space between the path and the far-reaching walls lost in the distance.

Medusa wasn't paying much attention to the beautiful and strange sights that appeared to either side of her. Her mind was occupied by other things.

Mopsus was a seer and should have warned them of the danger the titan posed, but the seer focused so much on the end goal that he said nothing. Three was still young enough that she didn't have the experience to know danger when she saw it, that, coupled with her being nearly indestructible gave her a skewed sense of mortality. And Mod? Mod was somewhat clueless, but he'd also been raised with a family that somehow always saw the good in everyone, an enviable trait that does not protect anyone should darker natures rear their ugly head.

Kronos wasn't technically a monster, but only Medusa seemed able to anticipate the evil things he would do.

I was invited along because I understand the monster in beings more than any of the others do. What does that say about me?

Medusa had no idea why she was talking to Mod the way she was. He'd just saved her life and taken a beating in the doing of it, and in return she'd been cold and sharp with him.

Medusa looked over at Mod. The poor boy didn't know how to act around her now. He actually had to think about his actions, and she was giving him nothing but hell for any of his efforts. At the beginning of this trek, she'd turned his world upside down. She wasn't sure if she'd been cruel or not, but she'd definitely been cruel in the times since.

Her world had been turned upside down many times, but that didn't mean she had the right to do that to someone else. She'd been given a second chance at a normal life, and what was it that she had done with it?

She didn't really have an answer.

Medusa twined the end of her braid in her fingers. There was a bit of fear every time she went to do so. Her heart skipped a beat in anticipation of touching fang and scale, instead of the soft brown hair she'd been born with.

Her hair was just hair now, and her visage no longer turned living things to stone.

She wasn't a monster anymore.

Or was she?

She risked a peek at Mod. His brows were knit in thought. He was probably trying to solve the situation with her like it was some sort of logic puzzle. The heart had nothing to do with logic, poor boy. He'd been given a life too easy for him to understand.

That wasn't really fair of her to think that. Mod had had his share of challenges in his life too. Though it didn't change the fact that in many ways he was naive and innocent.

And Medusa wasn't.

She thought back to when she'd been cursed. What if she had been the one to allow it? What if her belief that she'd done something so unforgivable that she was damned, and that the condemnation was only just, was the only reason she'd stayed cursed for so long? If lifting the curse had been as simple as raising her arms to the heavens and asking for it to be removed, she could have done it at any time.

But who, in the entire history of the world, had ever had the innocence and purity of heart to even think such a thing?

Medusa only knew of the one person, and it certainly wasn't her.

She missed Doug. And she missed Larisa too. They were a

package deal. You never found the one without the other. They were off taking care of their kingdom and their people and living a true life.

Medusa was glad for them and more than a little envious.

If Doug hadn't been so utterly devoted to Larisa, Medusa might have considered trying to build a relationship with him. But in all the people she'd known and heard of and seen in her lifetime, she'd only seen one couple that had been so devoted to each other that other people need not even exist.

Doug and Larisa were so complete together; Medusa wanted to experience that wholeness. Perhaps that type of wholeness, that type of relationship, would make up for the hurt and pain Medusa had dealt with all her life.

Hard to find that kind of acceptance when everybody you've ever met viewed you as an abomination.

Almost everyone, she corrected internally.

Doug never saw her as a monster. He would have been perfect. But there was only one Doug, and he was spoken for, now and forever.

But Doug did have a brother. She looked over at Mod again and felt a twinge of guilt.

Mod wasn't Doug. He was a good man in his own right. She shouldn't be pushing something onto him as an experiment to see if she might be able to replicate what Doug and Larisa had. Especially since she wasn't even sure if that sort of thing was what she wanted.

Medusa, you are screwed up.

But feeling the guilt of killing hundreds who need not to have died tended to do a number on a person. Maybe she was looking for something too grand or working on the wrong thing. She had no idea. She was totally lost.

Mopsus coming along at the time he had was a blessing. Any distraction, doing anything positive, was welcome. Maybe she'd find out what she needed when she was focused on something else. She hadn't so far, but she'd been focused on digging at Mod and figuring out what the hells they were even doing here.

Poor Mod. She glanced at him and could see her most recent slight had shaken him. *At the time you should be the most confident and sure of yourself, I'm causing you to doubt everything. I'm sorry I ever considered you to be the solution to my problems.*

Mod stumbled, probably too lost in his head to consider his feet. When Medusa saw him stumble again she called out to the others. "I think we need a few minutes to rest. We've been walking for quite a while."

Mopsus looked annoyed at the suggestion, but everyone except for Three appeared to be too tired to lift their feet. "Ten minutes to rest, then we need to get going again," he offered.

Medusa nodded that it would be enough.

"If you need to go into the jungle to relieve yourselves, just don't go too far," Anoup warned the others.

Grumbling and stretching, the members of the band all headed off in separate directions.

Medusa found a soft spot of dirt off the path by herself. She'd just sat down when a bug flew in front of her face and landed on her shoulder.

"Hey," the bug said in a tiny, surprisingly low-pitched chitter. "You Medusa?"

Medusa stared at the cicada.[1] She couldn't quite believe her eyes and ears. But, as had often been pointed out before, this was ancient Greece, and things that weren't supposed to talk gave monologues and had in-depth conversations all of the time.[2] "What?"

The cicada reached up with one of his forelegs and pulled a

---

1. Tithonus, beloved of the god Eos, was granted eternal life because she loved him so much. He got eternal life, but Eos forgot to request eternal youth for the man as well. Tithonus shrank over the years, growing smaller and smaller until he achieved the size of the insect currently resting on Medusa's chest.

2. I blame Aesop for that one. The guy anthropomorphized everything to the point that the whole world believed it. And all of a sudden you had talking ears of corn, badgers leaving reviews on Yelp, and the local ass discussing politics with the local tyrant (who was also an ass, just a different type).

proportionally large cigar from the corner of his mouth. "Did I stutter? You Medusa or ain't ya?"

She was a bit taken aback. "Yes, I'm Medusa."

"I figured." The cicada chomped back down on the cigar and took a puff. He blew out a tiny huff of smoke and pulled the cigar from his stylet once more. "Satan sends his regards."

Medusa arched an eyebrow and looked about. No one else was paying attention, so she scooted around to the side of a large mushroom just enough so she wouldn't be exposed without being too obvious. "And you know Satan how?"

The cicada took the cigar from his mouthparts and rotated his head as if unbelieving. "Does it matter?[3] Point is, he has information, and he thought you all should need to know."

"I'm not really on speaking terms with Satan—"

The cicada spread his arms out wide, his little cigar glowing like an errant spark as he waved it about in frustration. "Oh, for the love of—listen, sweetheart. Satan knows something. Big enough news that he told Zeus, and the big guy panicked and tried to find a way to get in touch with you. He couldn't send that messenger, JingleBelle, 'cause Hermes is a god,[4] and I guess it would rile up the locals. You all had passed beyond Hades's realm, so he couldn't tell his older brother, Gloomy, to have him pass along the message.[5] Satan offered to come down himself, but Zeus outright forbade it, like he don't trust the prat or something.[6]

---

3. Tithonus, because he is basically an eternal insect, gets along really well with Beelzebub. They have quite a few things in common no one else can easily understand. Tithonus is friends with Beelzebub; Beelzebub is a work buddy with Satan. Not too hard to see the connection.

4. Hermes's new nickname is catching on, much to his chagrin.

5. Hades would be appalled to hear this. He thinks he's edgy and mysterious, but the cicada thinks otherwise. Anyone else would be terrified of offending the god of the underworld, but Tithonus just doesn't care. Tithonus is the original grumpy old man that tells it like it is.

6. Around the 1960s they started using the word *prat* to mean an *idiot*. Before that it was an old English word for *buttocks*. The cicada is using the archaic version of the word's usage.

"They could'a sent a mortal messenger, but none of them union guys was willing to do a one way trip, and so they put their brains together and they came up with yours truly. I ain't a god, so me traversing about in the Deep Under ain't gonna tick off the titans. Besides, I'm a bug what spends seventeen years at a time underground. I'm the perfect messenger for those heading to the center of the universe, see?"

"Hades is blocked." Medusa narrowed her eyes at the bug. "How did you get in?"

"You done took the elevator, didn't ya? The back door through the cypress which was created and maintained by da one which don't care if he breaks a rule or three. Same path, sister, but *I* took the stairs." The bug sounded exasperated. "Sent by Satan? Which path do you think I took?"

"Fine," Medusa said in a complacent whisper. "Sorry to get you all riled up. Why did Satan send the message to me?"

"It was actually Zeus what sent the message," the bug explained. "Satan was just the intermediary. Satan hates Zeus because Zeus is rude to him all the time, but when the times is tough you do what you got to do." The bug shrugged as best he could in his chitinous skin. "Zeus was desperate. Satan had an in. Now Zeus owes Satan a favor."

"That can't be good." Medusa could only imagine.

"You're telling me, sister." The cicada shifted his cigar from one side of his stylet to the other. "You is a sister, ain't cha? All youngsters look alike to me. I have a hard time telling the difference between guys sometimes. Must be because of the compound eyes, or something. Anyhow, Zeus and Satan didn't want to take the risk of me spilling the beans to the wrong party."

"Then why did you choose me?" Medusa was growing irritated with the bug.

"You look different. 'Medusa was the one that was cursed,' they said. I can see a curse a mile off." The bug studied her and nodded when he finished his inspection. "Cursed, ain't cha?"

To hear what she'd been fearing spoken out loud shocked Medusa. "What?"

"Curses, blessings, touched by a god or goddess, it leaves a mark, don't it? Takes one to know one." The bug flourished his front legs to indicate the whole of him. "Compound eyes sees things different. You have the mark of a god on your nimbus."[7]

Medusa wanted to ask what a nimbus was.

She wanted desperately to ask the bug about the mark he saw.

She was also terrified of the answer he might give.

She tried to keep her voice calm. "What's this big message you have that is so important that you had to travel all the way to the Deep Under to give it to me?"

The cicada looked this way and that, making sure no one was close enough to listen. He took the cigar out a final time and pointed it to the front of the group. "Someone in your group ain't who they says they is." He indicated the others in a broad sweep of his cigar wielding leg. "One of you guys is a mole."

Medusa risked a peek around the mushroom at the others, not quite believing what the bug was telling her. "What could anyone gain by impersonating one of us?"

"How the hells should I know?" The cicada held out his front legs as if he had no idea. "I'm just a bug."

A tremor rocked the ground, hard enough everyone had to brace themselves.

The time to fix the Grand Machine was growing short.

Mopsus grasped his staff and rose up. He called everyone in a loud voice. "A timely reminder we must not get too comfortable. We've rested long enough and should get going."

Medusa froze. *What if it was Mopsus?*

The seer nodded his head as if counting off the members of the group. He must have noticed he came up one short. Before Medusa

---

7. Nimbus: the radiant energy surrounding a living thing. Compound eyes do have some advantages.

could do anything, Mopsus pivoted around his walking stick and started making his way toward her.

"How do I know who it is?" Medusa whispered to the bug. "How do I know this isn't some sort of trick on Satan's part?"

"Fine. Believe me or don't. No wax off my epicuticle,"[8] the cicada said. "That's the message. Do with it what you will."

She could hear Mopsus's footsteps and the click of his staff. Medusa was out of time. "Was there anything else?"

"Good luck, sweetheart." The bug chomped down on his cigar, kicked off of Medusa's shirt, and flew away.

Now Medusa knew something that no one else in the group could possibly know, and she had no idea what to do with this information. She couldn't share it with everyone, least of all—

"A bug?" Mopsus's eyes followed the path of the retreating cicada as he approached Medusa.

Medusa rose from her crouch, nervous. What if Mopsus had heard? What could that even mean? All she knew was it wouldn't help at all to deny something she knew he'd already seen.

"It was a cicada."

"Hmm. Pretty deep in the ground even for a cicada." The seer stared after the retreating bug for a bit, then turned back to Medusa. "This is an unknown place, full of unknown dangers. Even innocuous things may be a bigger threat than one supposes." With that he turned again and went back to the head of the group.

The final statement made her wonder. Perhaps Mopsus, or whoever he was, was hinting at more than she supposed.

---

8. A bug's way of saying "no skin off my nose." Both the bug and human versions of the saying mean you couldn't care less about the decision or opinion of someone else.

CHAPTER 24
WE HAVE TO TALK

THE GROUP TRAVELED CLOSE TOGETHER BECAUSE ANOUP TOLD them it would be safer that way. Mod kept lagging behind everyone else at the rear because Medusa drifted away from the others constantly, almost as if she was wary to be near them.

Every once in a while, he would look over and make sure she knew he was there. She would just smile, nod, and pick up the pace.

She looked like she was thinking pretty deep thoughts.

The others were paying attention to the strange world being revealed around them. The jungle filled a huge cavern that must have stretched hundreds of miles from edge to edge. The mushrooms and ferns abounded in an astounding variety. Hundreds of colors and a cornucopia of smells overloaded and assaulted the senses.[1] There were some kinds of flying animals in what passed for the sky. Anoup told everyone to pay them no mind unless they were the really big, triangle-headed ones. When those flew above, he made the group hide under the nearest giant mushroom.

And there were things that chittered and scurried and clawed all about just past the fringes of the path.

"This looks like a fairly well-traveled path," Three observed. "How come we aren't seeing any animals on it?"

"We're bigger than most of the animals in the jungle, and we're traveling in a group," Anoup explained. "Most of the bigger ones don't know what we are, so they're steering clear of us too. Also this

---

1. The original cornucopia was created accidentally when the infant god Zeus broke off one of the horns of his nursemaid Amalthea. And you thought your nephew you babysat that one time was a handful? Try caring for a toddler that could rip you limb from limb.

isn't a regular jungle. There are a lot of things here from myth and legend."

"They all died and went into the afterlife?" Mod asked.

"Actually, there's a huge difference between the underworld and the afterlife." Anoup tried to explain. "Just because something is underground doesn't mean that it's dead."

Mod gave the youth a quizzical look. "I don't quite understand."

To Mod's surprise, it was Medusa who spoke next. She hadn't said a word to anyone since the break a couple of hours earlier. "I get what Anoup is saying. There were things that called the underworld home before it became the realm of Hades. The dead aren't the only things that reside underground. The mushroom people seemed lively enough in their kingdom. The titans aren't dead, just banished." Medusa pointed out. "Most of my family is exiled down here too."

Mod hadn't ever realized that. "Your family is here?"

"I'm not really close to any of them. I mean, they're my brothers and sisters, nieces and nephews, but . . ." She looked like she was having a hard time just thinking about them.

"We can try to look them up on the way back, if you want to," Mod suggested.

"I'm afraid it might feel just like coming home," she whispered to herself.

Mod didn't like the sound of that. "Are you okay?"

She looked shocked that he'd overheard. "Sorry. It's just my father." Medusa shook her head. "The last time I saw most of my family I was a teen, brooding and deep in Melancholia's dark grasp.[2] Dad and I didn't get along. Really didn't get along. The last time we fought, the powers that be had to get involved. I left before I saw all of the fallout. I don't think visiting with any of my family would be a good idea."

---

2. Melancholia: Greek goddess of petulant, broody teenage girls. *Melancholy* translates in Greek to mean *black bile*, and that describes Melancholia's outlook on life pretty spot on. Think Wednesday Addams as a Greek god if you will.

"Sorry to hear that." Mod didn't really understand. He loved his family and enjoyed his time with them. It must be pretty bad if Medusa didn't even want to bump into any of hers.

"Not your fault." She exhaled slowly. "You're not missing much. Some people are just cursed by the fates not to be part of civilized society."

It sounded as if she meant more by that then she was letting on, but Mod didn't press her about it.

Not everything stayed out of the path of the group. There were a couple of times Anoup had the group stay still while a herd of huge fungivores[3], some sort of mix between a horse and a chicken[4], made their way through the jungle ahead of them. The animals were docile for the most part, but they were large enough that they could crush any member of the group should the animals panic and stampede.

"Do these animals ever cause a problem?" Mopsus asked.

"Not unless you have the misfortune to spend the night under the mushroom they chose to roost on" was all Anoup said in reply.

A small, hairy, lizard-like something rushed out of the undergrowth and nipped at the dog, probably because D'art was the member of the group closest to it in size and the one lowest to the ground.

The furry toad scrambled away, but not fast enough to dissuade pursuit.

D'art howled and would have gone after it, but Anoup latched onto his collar before the loyal beagle had taken a step.

The group all turned and looked in the direction the fur-toad disappeared in. The ferns and vine-like fungus shook in dozens of places. Two or three of the fur-frilled toads stuck their heads out and hissed at the dog.

---

3. Fungivore: an animal that subsists on fungus and spores for its diet. Yes, this is a real word. I didn't just make it up.

4. Hippalectryon: a mythic beast with the front half of a horse and the back half of a rooster or similar fowl. It's like the gods decided to create something akin to a turducken out of live animals, and it got out of hand.

"Pack hunters," Anoup said. "They're only a problem if you get a few hundred of them together."

"A few hundred?" Mod's eyes grew wide.

"We probably ought to go," Anoup urged the group to get out of the area.

Everyone, Mopsus included, decided that was a pretty good idea.

"How long have you been here, Anoup?" Three asked.

"Nine days doth Thoth toil, and on the tenth[5] he rests." Anoup recited some saying he must have learned as a child and shrugged. "Is it the first week or second week of the month? Seems like a while, I guess, but it could have just been a couple of days. Time seems to move differently down here. I was following someone I thought I knew, and I got lost. That's how I wound up here. I spent most of my time in the jungle and in the fringes of the Mushroom Kingdom. That's how I know which things to avoid and steer clear of in the Deep Under. I didn't go into the Mushroom Kingdom proper until just before I met you, thinking being around mushroom people was better than being alone. Shrooms don't take to strangers too quick, but I think they started to get used to me. You learn to be wary of the things in the Deep Under pretty fast, and the Shrooms are wary just like everything else."

"We're glad you're here to help guide us," Mod said.

D'art jumped up and gave Anoup a playful nip. The boy smiled, clearly glad to have others around him, and continued to search the jungle for threats.

"We haven't seen anyone else," Three said.

"Shroom people don't much like the jungle," Anoup answered. "They keep to the city and the caves and spaces on the other side. The jungle is the dividing line. Their territory doesn't come this way. Shroom people don't do much fishing or sailing on the sea either.

---

5. Ancient Egyptians had ten days in the week. Just imagine our Friday being hump day, with four more days of work to go before your one day weekend and you can envision how much their work week would have sucked.

There's things that call the sea home that the Shrooms don't like, or they don't want to deal with, so they both kinda leave each other to their own."

"But this is the way forward?" Mod asked.

Medusa reached into her pocket and pulled out the Orphic tablet. She looked at it briefly and put it back into her pocket before anyone else could see.

D'art took a sniff of the air and gave a confident bark and pointed his nose down the path.

"D'art thinks so." Anoup ruffled the fur behind the dog's ears. "He can't wait to find what the delicious smell is at the end of the trip."

Mopsus looked a bit annoyed at the youth but didn't address it. Then the seer turned his eyes to the dog, and the dog returned the gaze with a tongue hanging out of a happy grin.

"There are other paths, paths that are better known and tried, but getting to them is hard from here," Mopsus said. "It would waste too much time if we tried to use them."

"Anoup and the beagle are leading us well. We should keep going this way," Medusa said as she gave the seer an odd look.

Mopsus grumbled and once more huffed and scrambled to be in front of everyone. His walking stick beat an angry rhythm in the gravel as he took the lead. Everyone gave the seer his space and then followed after. Mopsus tearing ahead in one direction and Medusa pulling back from the others, the group was drifting apart.

Mod studied Medusa for a while as they walked. She looked a bit jumpy and nervous now. Earlier when the rock ceiling had collapsed, it had been almost as if she didn't care what happened to her.

That thought scared Mod a bit. He pushed a bit faster to catch up to Medusa.

She smiled as he approached. It didn't look as if she were still as angry with him. Her eyes darted to the front of the group and looked as if she contemplated saying something to Mod. Then something overshadowed that intent and stilled her tongue. Her smile dropped, and she started to turn away.

Mod caught her by the elbow before she could make it very far.

She looked a bit mad at that, but she stopped short of pulling away from him. For the first time since this whole thing had really started, she didn't look away.

"We need to talk," Mod said.

Mopsus, Three, Anoup, and D'art all paused.

"Preferably with a bit less of an audience," Mod added.

"I wouldn't recommend leaving the path," Anoup warned.

"I agree with the youth on this," Mopsus said.

"We don't have to leave the path. It's just—" Mod began.

"We'll be fine," Medusa said to the others. "Go on ahead. We'll stay within screaming distance."

"Works for me." Three grabbed Mopsus and Anoup by the shoulder and pointed them back down the path.

D'art looked between the two groups for a second, but quickly decided that he'd rather be with Anoup as he caught back up with the youth after a couple of energetic, gangly puppy bounces. Mod smiled at that. Anoup was young enough that the companionship would be a good thing for both the youth and the dog.

When the others had made it far enough ahead to be out of hearing distance, Mod pointed his chin after them. "Shall we?"

Medusa started walking; Mod fell in step right beside her.

They walked in silence for a minute or two. Mod felt it was necessary to give Medusa a bit of time to adjust to the thought of discussion after all the time they'd put it off.

"Not like you to take the initiative," she said in a hesitant voice, head down slightly as she studied the path. "Is this the real Mod I'm talking to?"

That was unexpected.

"I don't know who else I'd be?" Mod's brow furrowed as he pondered the question. "Is this hypothetical or theoretical?"

"Yeah, you're Mod all right." Medusa sounded relieved. "I don't know what you stopped to talk to me about, but it was good you did. I have something to tell you."

Mod hadn't considered there might be multiple pressing subjects for them to discuss. He'd only had his concerns about her on his mind.

"Please," Mod invited her to speak.

"You first," Medusa said. "I'm still trying to figure out what to do with my bit of gossip."

"Gossip?" Mod asked.

"Literally flew at me out of nowhere," Medusa explained. "Would you trust something insane sounding if it were told to you by a bug?"

Mod studied her with more than a hint of concern.

Medusa waved it off. "Never mind. We can talk about it later. What was it you were going to say?"

Mod waited a moment, unsure if he should go ahead or not.

Medusa stared at him, expectant.

After a while he finally relented. "I've had time to think. About what you said about us. I don't move very quickly when I don't have all the information or when I haven't had a chance to think about things. I'm a bit thick in the head."

That made the corner of her lips turn up in a wry smile. "I've noticed."

"I meant about relationships. I've never had one. I mean, I have friends and family and . . ." Mod felt a flush rise in his cheeks. "I don't know what's happening between us or not, because I have nothing to judge it against. I can't see things from your perspective. I don't know enough about you to know what you might be feeling." It was hard for him to say. Now he felt a bit feverish.

Medusa stopped walking. "I've never seen your face this red. This is really hard for you, isn't it?"

"A bit." Mod gulped. "But I needed to say it. I want to know what's going on with you and me—with us." He stumbled over the

215

last word and had to force it out. Mod hunched his shoulders forward to hide the sweat breaking out in his armpits.

She started as if to speak but held it back.

"Did you want to say something?" Mod asked.

"Are you sure you're Mod?" she asked.

He panicked. The way she delivered the question made it hard for him to tell if she was joking or not. "I think so. I don't know how to verify my identity, besides reciting results of the experiments we were both present for."

"The last jab was rhetorical. We both know the gods only made one of you." She shook her head a bit as if surprised. "It was just unexpected, you talking like this. You have a puzzle to solve and a perilous journey to get there. You have to fix the machine that runs the world. All of that is going on and you're thinking about me?"

"You're important to me," Mod responded.

Medusa stopped walking once he said it.

I've said the wrong thing again.

He'd already started the conversation. There was no going back now. "I think I know some of what made me the way I am. I'd like to share it if you'd care to listen."

"Oh, Mod." It was all she said before she gave a stunned nod for him to go ahead.

"I lost my mom when I was three. It messed me up. I can see things in other people that I want—relationships and love and close-ness—but for the life of me I can't figure out what I need to do to get them. There's always the fear of losing someone I can't bear to lose hanging in the back of my mind, and in a lot of ways it has crippled me. At least emotionally and socially."

"I don't think you're crippled, Mod," she said in a subdued voice. She wasn't looking at him as she reached out and put her hand on his arm. She let her fingers linger for a moment before she gave a nod toward the group up ahead. "I can't see the others anymore."

She pulled her hand away, but Mod could still feel the touch. They both started walking down the path again. Medusa still had her head down, but she stepped a bit closer to him. Mod wasn't sure what that meant, but in his heart he thought it was good.

Mod continued, "When Doug found me and his parents, Aoug and Elpis, took me in, it was the best thing that could have happened to me. The unconditional love my brother has for me was the healing comfort and protection that saved me. I don't think I would be me if it weren't for Doug.

"And my parents? Seeing the relationship that exists between Aoug and Elpis was a revelation. In my mind that's what a relationship needs to be. Mom and Dad are so devoted to each other and work so well together, it's hard to imagine them apart. They each have different strengths and roles, but they are partners that compliment and support each other. They're a perfect example of what the union of man and woman is capable of.

"Elpis and Aoug are also the exception to the rule. In all the marriages and partnerships I've observed, I've never seen another relationship like theirs until—"

"Until Doug and Larisa," Medusa answered.

Mod nodded. "Another exception. I'm so glad they have each other."

A thought occurred to Mod. It sounded stupid and sappy in his mind, but he really wanted to say it. "Maybe the exceptions happen when two people really see and care for and help each other?"

There were a few more steps before Medusa gave another slow nod. "Maybe," she whispered.

Mod's mom and dad had always said that things left unsaid led to the greatest regrets. Mod had said all he could at the moment. Mentally he was exhausted, and he didn't know what to expect as a reaction, but at least he'd tried.

They walked in silence for a while.

"I was born to monsters. You know this," she said to Mod.

Mod nodded and stayed quiet while he waited for her to continue. It took a while. The silence was hard, but he resisted the urge to say anything.

"Home life was not comforting, to say the least. There was passion between my parents from time to time. But anger, hate, hurt, and manipulation were the bread and butter of my upbringing, and I saw that spread to my siblings and their partners as our family grew." She stared at the path ahead. "I kept on getting stuck with my nieces and nephews, Echidna's kids, babysitting little monsters[6] when I wanted to be doing other, more normal, young person things. I did what I was told because it was expected of me, and my parents would punish me if they thought I didn't pull my weight. That's why I decided that I didn't ever want to marry or have a family. I dedicated myself to Athena and chose a celibate life." She paused for a second, her voice bitter when she spoke again. "And you know how well that turned out."

The name of Poseidon didn't leave her lips, but it hung as a curse in that ether nonetheless.

"I had a curse that turned people to stone, but my life has made me just as cold and unyielding as rock in more ways than one," she admitted.

"You aren't stone," Mod said. Just saying it didn't seem like enough, but he didn't know what else to say. Another few yards of the path passed beneath the feet of the pair with no talking.

I should hold her hand.

His palm was sweaty, and he was more than self-conscious about it. Nevertheless, Mod reached over and took Medusa by the hand.

Her hand was limp in his grasp for a while. And just as he felt it was too awkward and he should let go, she tightened her grip against his fingers.

When she finally turned to look at him, he could hardly see her because of the tears in his eyes. Mod sniffled and gave an awkward grin. "If I ever run into any of the jerks that hurt you, I'll punch them in the nose for you. I'm not very good at violence, so they'll probably mop the floor with me, but still."

---

6. Literally.

Medusa laughed then choked back a sob. "Oh, Mod. You stupid, innocent boy."

"It wasn't a joke. I was serious." Mod was confused. That wasn't the response he expected, so he didn't quite catch the tone of her reply. "Stupid and innocent is good, right?"

Medusa laughed, choked back a sob, and laughed again.

She pulled up close to Mod's side and leaned her head against his shoulder. Mod put his arm around her back in a loose hug.

"You're my friend, and I need you and love you more than I can say." It felt very weird for Mod to say that he loved her, but it was true.

"I do need a friend," Medusa said as she straightened. She reached out and took hold of his hand again as they continued walking down the path.

"I don't know what this"—he wiggled a finger on his free hand back and forth gesturing at the two of them—"is going to be. I know it feels right to have you beside me. Let's get through the rest of this thing with the world ending, and then we can see where everything stands."

Medusa laughed. "Dinner and a dance after the end of the world, then?"

Mod chuckled. "Not quite how I would have put it, but it sounds like a good plan." He tugged her hand and pulled her forward a bit quicker. "Shall we join the others?"

"Like I was saying when you walked up to me, I do have something else I need to talk to you about," Medusa said as she tugged on his hand to slow him just a bit. "It's about the others. Zeus thinks one of them might not be who they say they are."

"You spoke to Zeus?" Mod asked, wondering how that could have happened.

"He sent a bug. A cicada." Medusa paused. "Actually, Satan sent the cicada to deliver the message to me at Zeus's request."

Of all the things Mod could have heard today, this was probably the most unexpected. "I've heard from Hephaestus that those two really don't like each other. If Zeus is working with Satan, they must think this is really important." Mod nodded. "What do we do about it?"

They rounded the next bend in the path and the rest of the group stood just a few meters before them at the edge of the Mushroom Sea.

Mopsus approached them probably to discuss what the group should do next.

Medusa smiled, shrugged, and shook her head. "We'll have to figure it out later."

Mod swallowed hard and tried not to look like he was keeping a secret. He gave an awkward grin to the seer as he approached. "I guess we will."

CHAPTER 2J

THE LARGEST BOWL
OF MUSHROOM SOUP
YOU EVER SAW

THE TREMORS STILL CAME AT REGULAR INTERVALS, BUT THE effect of them was somewhat less now. You could see the ripple of each tremor from the faltering Grand Machine in the form of tiny waves that radiated outward over the surface of the sea.

Mod and Anoup were skipping mushroom caps over the surface of the water. If they timed it just right the mushroom bounced along the peaks of the waves and skittered farther than it would have otherwise. They'd perfected a side-throw that really sent the mushrooms far away from the shore.

"Salt, water, mushrooms," Mod observed after a particularly impressive throw. "Add heat and we're making soup."

"Needs more mushrooms," Anoup laughed as he launched another cap into the wet.

There were reptile-like things in the shape of birds in the sky, and what appeared to be fish and shellfish and such in the water. If there wasn't the unimaginable vault of stone in the place of a sky, it could be any sea from up on the surface.

Medusa wondered how that same mechanical skipping of the universe might affect the things that called the waters of this part of the Under their home. She reached into her pocket. "Don't feed the fish."

Mod paused before he chucked another mushroom into the surf.

"I don't think the tablet is talking about mushroom caps," she said to Mod.

"Better safe than sorry." Mopsus glared at Mod and Anoup. Mod tossed the cap in his hand up the beach, and Anoup reluctantly let his fungal discus fall. "What does the tablet say now?"

"Same as before. Don't feed the fish." Medusa shrugged. "That's all the instructions the Orphic tablet gives about the sea."

"That doesn't help much, does it?" Three asked.

"Prophecy and vague forewarnings rarely do." Mopsus went forward and struck the water with the end of his staff. "No boats or ships, just how are we supposed to pass over these cursed waters."

"I hear that if you hit a sea with a staff just right, the waters part and you can pass through on dry land," Anoup snorted.

Mopsus didn't think it was funny.

"Sorry I said anything." Anoup flinched from the seer's anger. "It was an Egyptian joke."

"I thought it was funny," Mod whispered as he nudged Anoup in the ribs.

Mopsus ground his teeth and shook his head. "Does the worthless golden tablet have a suggestion on how we should get across?"

The golden plate shimmered and morphed. When Medusa looked at it again, it said:

Learn the breaststroke.

Probably best if I don't share the discovery that the Orphic tablet has a sense of humor.

"Nope. Nothing." Medusa shoved the plate back into her pocket before anyone else could see the writing. She pointed out over the waters in an attempt to divert attention from her glowing pocket. "Any idea how big it is?"

"I walked from that way when I came." Anoup pointed to the left. "It took a long time."

"Perhaps the other side of the sea is shorter?" Mod suggested.

Anoup shook his head. "I don't know."

"Across the sea is the best way, or the plate wouldn't have warned us of the fish." The seer was frustrated. "A day, or a week, or a month of rafting or sailing? We're running out of time. We have no way of knowing without going ahead and just setting out on it."

D'art sniffed the air then gave a couple of quick barks.

"D'art says the center is getting near," Anoup translated. "The smell is stronger, despite the apparent vastness of the sea. Too bad we haven't found any papyrus growing here. We could make a pretty decent skiff if we only had a good bullrush marsh around."

"We must rely on what's available. We could build a raft from the mushroom trees," Three suggested. "Many of them are big enough for logs to make a sizable raft."

Anoup giggled and grinned. "On a raft we would look like a cracker floating above a giant bowl of mushroom soup."

Mod fist-bumped Anoup. "Good one."

Mopsus did not look amused.

Three patted Anoup on the shoulder. "I thought it was a good joke."

"Building a raft will take forever." Mopsus snarled, frustrated, and stuck. He gave no suggestions or alternatives to shorten the trip. "Time is of the essence. We must hurry if we're to achieve our goal."

Medusa had an idea. "Mod, Three, and I will start on a raft. It should only take a few hours." She put the seer, youth, and dog in another group. "You others go and scout the shore that Anoup doesn't know. If the smell gets stronger for the dog, we'll know that way is faster. Then you can come back and get us, and we'll all walk. If after a couple of hours the scent hasn't increased and you come back, we can launch the raft when you return."

"Is that the best you can come up with? That would be a total waste of time." Mopsus fumed.

For being the seer that was supposed to be leading them, he wasn't being very insightful—or supportive for that matter.

"With Daedalus's schematics, I could probably try making us all wings out of wax and feathers," Mod suggested. "Then we could just fly above the sea and make better time."

The seer looked like he was hesitant to even ask, as if he already knew the answer to the question. "Do you have Daedalus's schematics?"

"No," Mod admitted with a shrug. "I know the basic concept though, and I might be able to extrapolate design possibilities once we gather sufficient supplies to build wings for all of us."

"You utter fool! Where would we get wax down here, and as to feathers, unless you want to go wrestle with the big goose/hippo hybrid we passed half a day ago. The suggestion is nothing but sand thrown to the wind. Which leaves us with our only options being floating on a hastily constructed raft which will surely drown us or tromping along the sand, which I have had more than enough of already." Mopsus regripped his staff with a harsh snap, whipped around in a huff, and started off down the shoreline. "Stupid, worthless, son of a shoe,"[1] the seer growled in a harsh whisper.

The rest of the group stared after him, Anoup a bit more wide eyed than the rest.

"What?" Medusa asked the youth.

"Is calling someone a son of a shoe in Greece considered bad?" Anoup asked of the others.

"Not particularly, no." Medusa thought it odd that the seer had said that as he left but didn't really put much thought into it.

"Why would someone get upset about being compared to a sandal?" Mod asked.

"It means something you shouldn't say in front of your mother where I come from." Anoup squirmed. "I guess I better head after Mopsus then." Anoup didn't look like he wanted to be alone with Mopsus. But he gave a quick whistle to D'art, and the two of them headed after the seer.

Mod gave Three a long look, then turned to Medusa with a question in his eyes.

Medusa nodded. "I'm pretty sure the bug wasn't warning us about her."

---

1. Don't ever associate anyone with the bottom of a shoe in Arab, Hindu, Buddhist, or Muslim countries unless you want to start something. This is about as insulting as you can get.

Three stopped rooting around in the compartment in her forearm where she was looking for a tool. "What about me?"

"Medusa had a warning from a bug about a mole that might be out to jeopardize our efforts," Mod explained.

"Bugs and moles are aiding and undermining us?" Three found what she was looking for and pulled out the coiled loop. "Is this another one of those weird, whodunit puzzles that Aesop is always trying to get us to play?"[2]

"Deadly serious," Medusa confirmed. "Zeus thinks the fate of the universe is at stake."

Three uncoiled her small, two hand chainsaw.[3] "Well, let's get to assembling the raft. If we don't get to the center of the Grand Machine one way or another, a saboteur won't need to sabotage, will they?"

The raft went together quickly. Strips from the ancient mushroom's leathery caps were cut and braided to create rope. The trunks of the treelike fungus were sizable enough to create a firm footing for the deck of the craft.

Medusa directed a discussion of the most recent complication as they assembled the craft.

"Mopsus has been off since he first got here," Mod pointed out. "He's forgotten or misremembered things he should know, like my name, and doesn't have the same insight he had from our last outing."

"He's also out of his element and under a lot of stress," Three said as she secured the packs of supplies to the mast in the center of the deck. "Not really a combination noted for bringing the best out in people."

"He almost killed the dog." Medusa completed a paddle, gave it a good swish through the air to test it, then placed it on the identical

---

2. The Whodunits of Aesop never gained the same notoriety as the Fables.

3. The chainsaw is just a chain with saw teeth on it. Pulling back and forth with each hand holds the chain against the tree and creates the cutting motion. It isn't a full powered, two-stroke model from Husqvarna. She isn't Bruce Campbell, you know.

paddle she had fashioned earlier. "Three had to rescue D'art from Satan's frozen hole[4] when Mopsus bowled him over."

"Both of which can be explained away by the situation and circumstance." Three said in defense of the seer. "You flesh and bone people do odd things under pressure."

"Fair point," Medusa admitted.

"But then, Mopsus did almost bury you in a landslide." Three reminded her.

That could have been happenstance again, but the counts against the seer were adding up.

"But we've been with Mopsus since the very beginning of this quest." Mod tied one of the last decking logs to the top of the raft with a complicated knot. "When could someone have had the chance to replace him?"

"Which throws suspicion on Anoup," Medusa said. She didn't feel like the boy was the threat to the main group, but they had to look at all the options.

All the options?

Mod and Three could just as easily be the ones in disguise, but Medusa felt she needed to trust somebody. She felt certain it wasn't either of her friends.

But what if she were wrong?

Stupid Satan. This is why you did this, isn't it?

"Mod, what is my favorite food?"

"Oh, gods, is this a test?" Mod panicked. Medusa could see him racking his brains.

Three helped him out. "Bad breath squared," was all she said.

Mod calmed visibly. "Garlicky garlic cheese. How could I forget?" He put a sour look on his face and waved his hand in front of his nose for emphasis.

"Closely followed by cheesecake." Three added.

---

4. Satan's frozen hole would make a pretty good non-swear swear. It would still probably get you into trouble if you use it in front of your mother, though.

"If Mod had remembered without a sciences-based mnemonic I would have worried. And Three knew the mnemonic to give him, so I know you're both okay. Sorry. I just had to be sure." Medusa shook her head to get the doubt out of her mind.

Mod nodded. "That was a good test. But just to be sure, what's my favorite–"

"Pancakes with the crust cut off," Medusa and Three said in unison.

"I wouldn't ask mom to do it for me if she didn't like doing it." Mod grunted and turned back to his work. "Well, it appears we're all who we say we are, so it has to be one of the others. Anoup seems to have been pretty forthcoming about everything so far." Mod forced an upright for a railing into the hole Three had bored into the deck for it. He used a crudely fashioned mushroom mallet to hammer a few wedges into the space at the base to make the support tight.

"My money is on the dog." Three finished carving out the rudder for the raft and held it up to admire her work. "What is he hiding behind that lolling tongue and those cute, adorable little eyes? When he begs for treats, is he really just searching us for weakness? Has he weighed and measured us so he can finally strike and end us once and for all?"

Mod and Medusa stopped working and stared at the automaton as if they couldn't believe what she was saying.

"I've been studying cynicism and satire with Diogenes. He told me to question and disbelieve everyone." Three narrowed her eyes and glanced suspiciously first at Mod, then at Medusa. "In fact, either of you might be the one we were warned against."

Three's eyes widened in apparent realization. "Oh my gosh! It could even be me?"

That was met with a moment of dead silence from the others while they watched Three try to glare menacingly at herself as if to convince herself to tell everyone what she knew.

"Are you serious?" Mod asked when the eye squints of Three bordered on the absurd.

Three smiled, jumped up to her feet, and fitted the shaft of the rudder in its support. "Not in the least. But in whodunits the culprit is almost always the one you least suspect, like the fox in Aesop's fables."

"It's almost always the fox that is the villain in Aesop's fables." Now Mod looked really confused. "Isn't it?"

"She's teasing you, Mod." Medusa knew Three was just poking fun at them. The automaton didn't always place the same weight on impending danger that mortal men and women did.

"My point is, the trio of us work well together." Three gave the rudder a good shake to see how it handled its seating. "We know there's a threat. We can look for it and protect the others if we see it."

Medusa nodded in agreement to Three then let her eyes shift to Mod.

Mod had a curious look on his face. "The only one that needs to be put in danger is me. I'm the one that needs to fix the Grand Machine."

"And you need us to get you there." Medusa reminded him. "The path ahead isn't just a stroll in the Elysium Fields, you know."

Mod nodded and tried his best to smile to convince her he agreed with her.

Mod always was a terrible liar.

He'd watched his brother leave everyone else behind to protect the ones he loved, and now Medusa was sure that Mod was contemplating the same thing.

We're just getting things worked out, Modifixeus, so don't you dare try it. I won't let you.

Medusa might have said something to that effect right then, but she was interrupted before she could speak.

"The others are back," Three pointed her chin down the shore at the approaching figures. "I guess you'll have to figure out who is trying to sabotage you on the safe, not limiting or dangerous at all, confines of a small raft on a sea full of unknown dangers."

"Thanks, Three. You really put this all in perspective," Medusa said with a sinking feeling in her gut.

CHAPTER 26

NOT REALLY THE BEST OF FAMILY REUNIONS

MOD TRIED HIS BEST TO HOLD THE RAFT STEADY, BUT WHATEVER it was that attacked the craft had sheared away most of the rudder.

"Where in the hells did they come from?" Anoup screamed.

D'art bounded from one side of the raft to the other and tried to attack whatever was attacking his friends the moment the beasts appeared.

The long-snouted, wide-mouthed creature slapped the raft with its tail.[1] The blow caught D'art and flipped the dog to the other side of the raft with a yip and a cry from Anoup. Anoup scrambled after the dog and grabbed him by the collar. D'art lost a good portion of his bravado and let the boy hold onto him.

Another strike from below sent all the passengers on the raft violently to the left. The makeshift sail billowed out as it was pushed into the wind and threatened to overturn the raft.

Mopsus slammed against the railing and had the breath knocked out of him. "Come close to me, you foul breathed son of a crocodile," he wheezed as he held his staff out over the waters with one hand.

The next time Wide Mouth poked his head up, Mopsus jabbed the thing in the nostril with the metal butt of his staff.

Wide Mouth croaked in anger and dove beneath the choppy water.

Mopsus doesn't seem so incapable now, Mod thought.

Mod and Medusa both headed to the mast and pulled down the patchwork mushroom skin canvas just in time. Something under the

---

1. This is what everyone thought was the Ichthyosaurus from *Journey to the Center of the Earth*. The 1959 version.

water grabbed a loose rope and tore the canvas away, dragging it down into the water.

Luckily no one got dragged down with it.

"Awe, man," Three said, dejected. "Do those monsters know how hard that was to scrape and sew?"

"Maybe they'll get tangled in it and drown or something," Mod said hopefully.

"Typically, water monsters don't drown in the sea," Medusa pointed out as she picked up an oar.

Mod picked up the other one and held it at the ready.

Anoup dragged the dog to the mast next to Mopsus's pack and wrapped his arm around the mast, his free arm clinging tightly to the dog. For his part, D'art held onto the youth as tightly as his four legs would allow.

The frying pan and reset club appeared in Three's hands. "Not a lot of reach with these. Especially if I can't get too close to the edge."

"What happens if you get too close to the edge?" Mopsus backed away as if now all too aware of what might happen should he fall in.

"I'm not terribly buoyant," Three pointed out the obvious. "Should I happen to go into the water, I sink like a millstone."

"You can't swim?" Medusa asked as a fin appeared to the east of the boat.

"I walk upon the bottom of lakes and seabeds very well, thank you very much," Three snapped back.

"Buoyancy versus density," Mod said. "Three is denser than all the rest of us put together."

Three glared at Mod.

Mod shrugged an apology as best he could while holding an oar outstretched with both hands. "I could have phrased that better. Sorry." He swung at a scaled flipper as it broke the surface. "My actual point being, Three is made of heavy ceramics and metals. Those aren't typically materials noted for being used as fishing bobbers."

"Speaking of fish." Three jumped to the side and took a swipe in the air as the long-necked member of the water monster duo swung its head over the edge of the raft.[2] She struck it a glancing blow with the frying pan.

The animal stopped its swimming for a moment and zeroed its gaze on the woman who had just struck it.

"I may have just made a tactical error," Three said as the aquatic dinosaur lunged forward.

Long Neck tried to sweep the deck with his throat. He hit the main mast with a sickening crack about a foot above Anoup's head.

"Damn," the monster swore as it pulled back from the splintered mushroom trunk. "That hurt!"

Mod and Medusa shared a look.

"That isn't a regular beast," Mod said.

Medusa shrunk down a little bit, probably stunned with the realization of what she was most likely dealing with. "I think these are my nephews, the toddlers, Bub and Tug."[3]

Long Neck squared in on Medusa with a sneer. "Huh. Thought you looked familiar. Unexpected and short reunion, huh, Auntie M.?"

"Which one is which?" Mod asked as he pointed the business end of his paddle at whichever one was closest.

"Bub is the one with the long neck. Tug is the one that has to have everything explained to him."

"We're twins," Tug lifted his head out of the water and sneered with his wide, long mouth. "No one can tell us apart."

Bub frowned and shook the head perched atop his very long neck at his brother.

---

2. This one is what everyone thought was the Plesiosaurus from *Journey to the Center of the Earth*.

3. The children of Echidna and Typhon, Bub and Tug have been described as sea serpents that attacked the Trojan priest Laocoón at the end of the Trojan war. There were rumors that these two were sent by Poseidon or Apollo or Athena to punish the priest, but the truth is they were just wild kids that constantly got into trouble and Laocoón happened to be in the wrong place at the wrong time.

Medusa rubbed her eyes hard before she looked at them again. She was probably hoping she was mistaken in what she saw.

The names meant nothing to Mod, but she referred to these huge beasts as the toddlers, which meant they were much smaller the last time she saw them. He had to think about it, which was hard with everything going on around them. "Babysitting? These are the ones who made you not want to have a family?"

"Yeah, these are the ones." Medusa covered his face with her hands.

"Looking at them, can you blame her?" Three asked.

"So rude!" Tug yelled.

Bub swept the deck again, this time missing the mast and striking Three with a solid crack. He immediately shrieked and rubbed the back of his skull with a long flipper. "Hitting that woman hurt. Was she made out of rocks or something?"

Three went flying and landed with a quiet kerplunk about fifty yards from the raft. She sank from sight as soon as she hit.

"Three!" Medusa lunged against the railing, her arm outstretched.

"She'll be fine," Mod tried to reassure Medusa. "She's mechanical. She doesn't have to breathe air. We'll just have to find her once we reach the shore. She'll be fine." Mod repeated the last part partially because he was trying to convince himself, even though he was confident he was telling the truth.

The monsters rose up over the surface of the water and gaped at each other.

"That voice. That isn't—" Tug's eyes gaped wide. "Aunt Medusa?"

"Try to keep up, brother." Bub jutted out his lower jaw and glared at everyone on the raft.

Medusa returned the glare in full, fists clenched and trembling as she roared at both the boys. "I swear, Bub and Tug, if you have so much as hurt a hair on the head of my friend I will—"

"She's gonna turn us to stone!" Tug screamed.

"Get a hold of yourself." Bub slapped Tug upside the head with the flat of a long flipper. "If she could 've turned us to stone she would have already done it." He used the tip of the flipper to direct the other monster to face Medusa directly. "Take a look at her. What do you see?"

"She's wet."

His brother slapped him again. "Her hair, you idiot."

"It ain't snakes." Tug's jaw gaped in shock.

"No snakes, no stone, you hear me?" Bub turned a cold eye toward his aunt.

"No snakes, no stone. That's a good . . ." Tug looked conflicted, like he suddenly realized something. "Sacred Typhon fewmets![4] If Pa finds out we attacked kin, we are gonna be in so much trouble."

Bub turned to his brother and got a wicked look in his eye. "Well, what if Pa don't find out?"

His brother looked like he wasn't tracking.

"There's only the four of 'em," Bub continued. "The day we can't eat four people will be a sad day indeed."

"But Medusa's kin." Tug didn't look so certain. "We can't eat kin, right?"

"That's all right. I got you, Bro," Bub said. "I'll eat her first, and then you won't have to feel guilty."

He rushed at his aunt, giving no sign of hesitation.

Mod batted Bub upside the head with the oar. The force and sweep at the end of the long paddle was enough to daze the creature.

"Hey, you can't fight back. It ain't fair." Tug half beached himself on the edge of the raft farthest away from Mod as he tried to bite him. When that didn't work, he moved to the closer targets of Anoup and D'art. He inched closer and closer to Anoup and D'art with every clack of his jaws.

Mod closed the distance, struck Tug across the beak with the flat of the oar, then jabbed him in the eye with the blade.

---

4. Sacred Typhon fewmets: Holy Crap

Tug let out a pain-filled croak and rolled back into the sea.

"Why are they attacking us?" Anoup asked.

"Because we're here," Medusa answered as she dug into her pocket and pulled out the Orphic tablet. "As long as we stay on the raft will we be all right?"

How should I know?

Medusa shook the tablet in frustration. "That's not helping! How do we beat them?"

Drive them off or fight. They're Typhon's children. They share their father's weakness.

Something bumped hard against the bottom of the raft and lifted the whole craft off the surface of the water. The braided mushroom ropes stretched but held. The raft smacked back down to the sea with an erratic slap that nearly threw everyone from the deck. The logs and decking were all considerably looser now. The mushroom floats swayed and creaked against each other.

Medusa called out to the others. "Bub and Tug share Typhon's weakness. We can use that to beat them or drive them away."

"Typhon?" Mopsus laughed. "Typhon has no weakness. Zeus barely defeated him the last time they fought by . . ."

Everyone on the raft zeroed in on Mopsus's pack at the same time.

"Zeus's lighting." Mod fought hard to reach the pack as the deck heaved and shifted under his feet.

"Careful!" Mopsus warned. "The effects of lightning striking water can be disastrous to anyone unlucky to be caught in the blast to say the least. I should be the one to do it." The air crackled around Mopsus's staff as he made his way forward. He didn't take more than a step before the seer was knocked from his feet by another strike on the underside.

Mod had seen enough of the effects of electrical current in Hephaestus's forge to know there were dangers to all of them if he did this wrong. But what choice did he have? Mod pulled one of the crackling lightning bolts from Mopsus's pack and held it ready to throw. He was surprised at how cool to the touch the weapon was.

The twin sons of Typhon hit both ends of the raft from below. The raft bucked again, lifting high off the surface of the water.

The logs gapped in the middle of the deck.

Mod had a mostly unobstructed view of the twins below.

He'd never get a better chance.

Mod aimed for the gap and threw the bolt as hard as he could. It expanded and blazed to life as it left his hand, growing so bright and hot that it filled the space beneath with light and thunder.

Mod, Medusa, Mopsus, Anoup, and D'art were all tossed in different directions as the raft came apart in midair.

CHAPTER 27

GETTING MORE THAN
YOUR FEET WET

It was all oddly quiet.

Being so close to the lightning blast when it destroyed the raft had stolen the sound from the world.

As Mod flew through the air, bits of debris tumbled about him. The odd light of the Deep Under glinted and flashed off the surface of the broken water.

The destruction of the raft churned the sea and created great plumes and jets of spray where little details were lost in the chaos. Objects of different sizes and weights struck the water in a haphazard sight of overlapping splashes.

Mod's head felt as if it would soon explode. In trying to save everyone he'd probably just doomed them all. Medusa, Anoup, Mopsus, and D'art were all going to die by drowning in the center of Mother Gaea.

What have I done? The thing Mod had feared most his entire life was realized as he landed in the water with a harsh splash. *I'm going to die the same way my mother died.*

He'd seen his birth mother drown when he was only a couple of years old. It had taken years and the love and support of his adoptive brother Doug for Mod to overcome his fear of water, only Mad hadn't overcome his fear at all. He'd only managed to hide it. His fear was back, and it terrified him.

Mod froze, panicked, and dropped below the surface of the water.

It was only as the water closed over the top of his head that he realized, after a lifetime of thinking he feared the water, that it wasn't the water he was scared of. He was scared of separation. He'd lost his mother to drowning. He'd lost his brother to marriage. *And now?*

He thought he would struggle to swim to the surface. He was surprised to find that he was wrong.

"Medusa!" he screamed as his head cleared the sea.

He wasn't sure if he loved her or if she was his friend, but he knew for certain that it couldn't end this way.

Mod sputtered and swam along the surface. He couldn't see anyone else among the wreckage of the raft as he treaded water.

There was no way he was going to track them down from here on top of the sea.

Mod filled his lungs with air and ducked far below where the chaos of the fight couldn't reach. The waters were cluttered and churning just below the surface, but the view improved as he pushed himself deeper.

No sign of Medusa, Mopsus, Anoup, or the dog.

Mod could see the outlines of large shapes slipping through the murky depths though. The light in his eyes turned red. Bub and Tug had survived the bolt of lightning. Now they searched through the wreckage for anyone they might have missed.

Mod hadn't experienced hate and anger since the pirates took his mother from him. It didn't matter that they were Medusa's family. They had just hurt Mod's. Revenge was something that had never occurred to him before. And even as angry as he was, it didn't feel like the right thing to try right now.

But if they kept coming for him, it didn't matter. There was no way Mod could search for the others with Bub and Tug threatening and hunting him while he worked.

But if I can take them out of the equation?

Mod dug furiously in his pockets as he hoped beyond hope that the thing he searched for was still there.

His fingers closed about a control and the loop of wire attached to it.

Mod turned to face the two leviathans underwater as he waved his arms and legs and did everything he could to attract their attention.

The two beasts seemed to recognize the motions of the frantic prey in the same instant. They spun about and raced each other to be the first to reach the chewy, crunchy treat as it writhed and panicked.[1]

Mod fiddled with the controls on the device in his hand and snapped the wire out to its fullest extent.

Come and get me, poor, defenseless little Mod, he thought.

Bub and Tug bumped and jostled each other as they rushed forward, dead on target, as their jaws gaped wide and wanting.

Mod switched on the portal, and the two beasts wedged into it with a force that sent them, Mod, and the device skipping and twisting in a vortex that spanned dozens of yards underwater.

The twins slipped and struggled against each other in the frame that was too small. Bub slid through the doorway first, and Tug, having much wider flippers, snapped the wire of the device as he was pulled through.[2]

The resulting explosion tumbled Mod head over heels out of the water. He landed on his back hundreds of feet from the ruins of the raft.

His breath was knocked from him, and he began to slip quietly into the sea.

Mod would have let everything go then, knowing that at the very least the monsters from below could never attack his friends again.

A frantic waving from a half-submerged log caught his attention.

───────────────

1. "Adrenaline adds a flavorful edge to the meat." If you ever hear this, politely decline the meal if you can. Nothing good comes from this kind of lead in. Trust me.

2. Bub wound up in the UK, while Tug dropped in a lake in what one day would be California. Bub appeared inside a rock, and wasn't nearly as old as the scientists thought the remains were when they found him. Tug was luckier but is now being exploited to unwittingly help a local artist sell hand-made creations touting the beast on Etsy.

Mod raised his head out of the water. It took a second for the liquid to drain from his ear canals so he could hear again.

Mopsus was rising and falling with the swells. The man screamed at the heavens, or at least at the vault of rock that hung over the head of the mushroom sea. "I did not come this close to righting this wrong to be finished now! I swear, Ptah, you shoe, you dirty filthy son of a shoe, should the abominations you created choke me down, I will rip myself from their gullets and tear apart every living thing until I am avenged!"

Mod had never heard of Ptah, but the shoe insult was one the seer had used before. Mod still didn't understand why being a shoe, or the shoe's offspring, was bad. But whatever it meant, Mopsus sounded pissed.

Mod was just relieved that the seer had survived. It raised Mod's hopes about the others.

The wreckage of the raft was spread out too far for Mod to see all of it now. And to search for any of them, he'd have to swim closer.

Mod set off toward the seer.

Two sets of eyes are better than one.

CHAPTER 28

PRAYERS OF DESPERATION

Somehow Medusa managed not to lose the Orphic tablet in her grip. "Fat lot of good you did me."

I did my best. There were a lot of variables to consider.

She felt like flinging it into the sea. But it did have a point, so she tucked it into the pocket in the front of her dress that Mod had sewed for her.

Mod.

She didn't have time to look for him now.

Medusa could just make out what she thought was the form of someone hanging off of debris rising and falling with the surface of the sea.

She wiped as much water from her eyes as she could and looked again.

D'art had the collar of Anoup's shirt clenched between his teeth. The dog kept scrambling back on a twisting piece of decking as he tried to keep the youth's head from slipping under water.

With a whine and a yelp, D'art lost the tug of war and they both tumbled back into the sea.

Medusa was an excellent swimmer. She dodged the bits and pieces of raft bobbing about in the swirling mess and caught Anoup before he could be dragged too far under. He was heavier than he looked, but she managed to pull him up and drape him over a couple of logs that were miraculously still lashed together. She hit him on the back until he coughed up a lungful of sea water. He took a couple of ragged breaths, coughed, and spit up a bit more from his lungs, then flopped hard onto the surface of the logs.

D'art popped back to the top of the water a couple yards away, and the dog paddled over to her.

"Well, that's two down." Medusa grabbed D'art by the collar and helped him scramble up on the log on a spot next to Anoup.

The youth and dog safe, she scanned for whatever else she could see just around her.

No one else was close to her on the surface. A dark shape searched and grew larger in the gray waters under her feet.

Medusa braced for what she knew would be coming.

For the first time since she had lost it, she wondered if her curse might have been able to help her.

It was a stupid thought, and she rejected it immediately.

She was just about to ask the Orphic tablet for advice when the dark shape down below was joined by another. Bub and Tug rushed off in a path away from Medusa so fast that they left twin wakes on the surface of the water heading toward a target on the other side of the wreckage.

The monsters had found one of the crew.

There was nothing Medusa could do.

She watched, expecting the bloody red froth to break the surface as her nephews attacked and tore apart whoever was unlucky enough to be their prey. She didn't want that to happen to Mod or Mopsus. No one deserved that.

She choked back a little sob and wiped the tears from her eyes as best she could.

There was a brilliant flash of light from below. The sea erupted. A huge wave hit her and threatened to capsize her little vessel. She managed to ride it out, but it pushed her away from the rest of the wreckage of the raft. She could hardly see any of the bits and pieces anymore except for the part she was next to.

There were a few more large ripples that radiated from whatever had happened, then the sea calmed and the waves of the attack stilled.

Medusa had to know what happened. She turned to leave, intent on swimming until she found Mod or whoever was in the center of the flash of light. But the second she let go of Anoup, he slipped back into the water.

D'art tried to hold him up, but the youth was just too heavy for the beagle.

She couldn't rescue anyone else if it meant she left the boy to drown by her absence.

She waited.

There were no new attacks. She had no idea what it was he'd done, but Mod had to have driven Bub and Tug off. *Mod, please be all right.*

"Zeus, if you can hear me, please watch over Mod." She looked around at the unbroken sea around her. Zeus was a god of the skies, so the likelihood of him hearing her, especially in this situation was next to nothing. And Medusa wasn't even sure if a prayer could make it past the barriers that blocked Hades and the underworld from the rest of the universe. If any message would get through to a god, if any god might be able to help, it would have to be a god of the waters that resided in the underworld.

Medusa did something she never would have considered. She trembled as the thought worked its way forward, and she feared it, just as she knew that making it real by speaking it aloud would give her power.

It had been a very long time since she had prayed to anyone. But she would humble herself and ask for any help, if it meant saving one of her family.

One of her *real* family.

Ceto and Phorkys were both primordial sea gods, so they should be able to hear her if she spoke to the water. "Ceto, Mother, hear me. Phorkys, Father, hear me. Someone I love is in need and I can't help him. Please watch over him. Give me the strength and a path to be there when he needs me the most. Please."

Her head hung lower and she continued, "Mother Ceto, Father Phorkys, I would pray to Nereus, old man of the sea, and Oceanus, the river that circles the world, but they won't be able to hear me. Mother Ceto, Father Phorkys, one I love is in need. Please guide my hand forward so that I may see him again."

Medusa began to sob, not believing what she was considering saying next. *For Mod, my friend, my chosen family, I will do this.*

"Mother Ceto, Father Phorkys, I know when I left I said I would never speak to you again. Forgive me of my pride and my anger. Mod needs me, and I need him—I *need*—" She tumbled over the words, the end of the plea leaving her throat raw as she wailed to the heavens. Rage, sorrow, and hope filled her to the point of bursting then fled her in one overwhelming rush.

D'art must have been swept up with her emotion. He threw back his head and howled, his sorrowful braying giving deeper meaning to Medusa's plea.

And as soon as her cry ended, a weight lifted off her shoulders. Letting go of hate and anger was a freedom she hadn't expected. She was no longer prisoner to any god's name. She was no longer prisoner to the curse and harm brought to her by circumstances she could not control.

Medusa started to weep, full body wracking sobs that burned down to her very core. She let go of the guilt she'd carried for what the curse had wrought. She could feel the need and weight of the hatred of herself go.

For the first time she accepted the truth that her curse was gone.

Her body was weak. Weaker than she'd ever been since she was a child. She was aware she was still sobbing, but the tears flowed out of her and took with them the pain and judgment she had hidden in the dark corners of her soul.

The next thing she felt was the tender attention of D'art as he tried to lick her tears away.

Medusa laughed and hugged the dog. She cried a bit more until it seemed as if she might never have any more tears to shed.

D'art was quiet and still until she finished. When she was through, he gave her a final lick on the nose.

"Thank you." She scratched him between his wet ears.

One of the oars she'd used against her nephews popped up in the water next to her foot. Medusa wasn't sure if it was a coincidence. She grabbed it, wiped her nose on the back of her sleeve, and turned to the only other conscious member of their craft.

"Well, dog, which way do we go?"

D'art sniffed the air, then turned just a bit to the right and gave a small bark.

She used the paddle as a rudder and turned the makeshift raft until it was pointing the right direction.

Before she started rowing she looked at the dog again. "D'art, where's Mod? Do you know where Mod is?"

D'art sniffed the air again, and once more barked in the same direction.

Medusa wasn't sure the dog had understood.

She pulled out the Orphic tablet. She was going to ask it what direction to go, but instead she asked, "Is Mod okay?"

You'll find him when it ends.

"When what ends?" she asked. "Is Mod okay?"

The golden surface shimmered, started to write something, then changed its message when it was halfway finished.

Follow the dog.

The golden surface shimmered, the words vanished, and the plate was clear again.

She tucked the tablet away.

D'art pointing the way at the head of the makeshift craft, Anoup secured and safe in the center, Medusa dipped the paddle in the water and pushed all of them in the direction D'art had told her to go.

CHAPTER 29
SELF-MEDICATION, SERVICE ANIMALS, AND CHEESE

"Hey, Medusa."

Someone gently shook Medusa on the shoulder.

"Medusa?"

The grip on her shoulder tightened, a bit more insistent. Then a long tongue licked her across the nose.

I hope that was the dog.

Medusa cleared her wet hair from her view.

D'art was in her face. He wagged his tail, gave a small happy yip, and threatened to kiss her face all over again.

Medusa scratched the dog behind the ear as she raised her head and blinked the sleep from her eyes. She could see Anoup, looking much more alert now, standing over both her and the dog.

"You're awake. That's good. D'art and I found somebody." Anoup and the dog both took a step back.

Three sat no more than a few feet away, perched on a gnarled stump of drift mushroom as she peeled a long curved yellow fruit.[1]

It took Medusa a second to process what she saw.

Medusa jumped to her feet as well as her weary legs would allow her and threw her arms around her friend. "Three! Oh, my gods, I thought I'd lost you."

---

1. Long curved yellow fruit? A Banana? "Bananas?" You say? "The author is bananas! Putting bananas in ancient Greece is bananas!" I'll have you know the consumption of the curved yellow fruit is mentioned in early Greek, Latin, and Arabic writings. Alexander the Great saw bananas on an expedition to India and thought enough of the fruit to mention it in his record. And this isn't ancient Greece, this is the center of the universe, so who knows what kind of weird, exotic fruit just happened to fall down a crack and flourish in Mother Gaea's nether regions.

Three hugged her back. "I was fine. Your nephews left me alone once I sunk to the bottom."

Medusa pulled the hug tighter. "Oh, my friend, how did you ever manage to get out of the sea?"

Three squirmed a bit under the increased pressure of the embrace. "You're not usually this affectionate."

Medusa smiled and buried her face against Three's neck. "I'm just . . . It's good to see you. Really good to see you."

Three tightened her grip against her friend, giving her a reassuring squeeze. "It's good to see you too. I'm fine. It just took a bit of time. I found the underwater slope that pointed up and hoped it went in the right direction. I climbed until I reached the shore." She gave Medusa a pat on the shoulder and pushed her gently away. "I walked along the beach until I found you here sleeping."

The curved yellow fruit that had been squashed between them fell to the ground.

Medusa looked at it. She'd never seen the like of it before. "What is that?"

Three shrugged. "I have no idea. It looked like a fruit of some kind, and I thought you might want to have a bite of something that wasn't mushroom based for a change. Anoup liked them. He ate six of them."

"Seven." Anoup patted his round belly and pointed at the pile of peels on the ground. "And just for your information, they are much more palatable if you remove the skin."

Three jerked a thumb in Anoup's direction. "D'art and the boy wonder found that out the hard way."

Medusa looked down on the curved yellow mush sadly. Her stomach growled. "And I squashed it."

"Probably still good to eat, but if you want an unsquashed one, I found more." Three reached behind the stump and pulled out another handful of the yellow fruit.

D'art came up and gave the smooshed fruit a lick. He shook his head as if he still didn't really like it. But he must have been pretty hungry because he cleaned the mess up rather nicely.

Medusa took an unsquashed fruit. She peeled it the way Three showed her and nibbled off a tentative bite. It felt and tasted a lot like the custard used in galaktoboureko.[2]

"Where did you find this fruit?" Medusa took another, larger bite.

"You see a lot of things when you walk ten or twelve nautical miles along the bottom of the seafloor," Three said as if it were nothing.

"Fair enough." Medusa continued eating, then she stopped as something more important than food occurred to her. "Have you seen Mod?"

Three pointed to the right. "About a mile or so that way, there are prints from both of the men."

"There's lots of things down here." Medusa looked down at a huge number of what might actually be goat tracks crisscrossing the beach. "How do you know it was Mod?"

Three shrugged. "Two sets of human-sized footprints, with one of the sets of prints making an extra mark every time Mopsus leaned on the staff. It was them, all right."

Medusa almost broke into tears. "Mod is alive." Saying it was too much for her to take. She started to cry as she jumped to her feet. "We have to follow them. Now!"

Three shrugged. "We can't. The way behind them was blocked. Mopsus is really good at collapsing unstable caves."

A tremor shook the ground around them. There was the sound of more falling rock off in the distance.

"More rocks keep falling all the time without Mopsus's help now," Anoup observed.

"We need to catch up to them. But if the path they've taken is

---

2. A Greek dessert made with a crust of layers of crispy phyllo, a custard filling, and drizzled with melted butter.

blocked . . ." Medusa pulled out the Orphic tablet. "Can we catch up to Mod?"

The tablet shimmered.

They are on the easiest path. You can't follow.

"We have to get to the center of the universe to save Mod. If something happened to him because I wasn't there, I'd never forgive myself." Medusa's shoulders slumped a bit before the gold surface shimmered and morphed again.

The path of the blind, that next passes time, is the best option you find. Follow the dog.

"That's what I needed to know. Thank you."

The tablet blushed.

"D'art, this is all on you, buddy." Medusa scratched the dog under the chin and gave him a confident nod. "Find the yummy smell at the center of it all."

D'art yipped and sniffed the air. After just a bit of searching, he zeroed in on a path that headed off to the right. He took off running with everyone else close behind.

The path turned and led them down a wide tunnel away from the sea. The tunnel wound back and forth, then ended in a wall with a crevice leading through it, a huge boulder partially blocking the opening from view. Inside the crevice was a large cave that appeared to only have one entrance and exit.

D'art had led them to a dead end. D'art didn't seem defeated however. Instead, he was somewhat distracted by other smells in the room. Still he went straight and true to the far wall opposite the entrance and scratched at a small crack near the floor.

Anoup hurried up behind the dog and crouched down beside him. "This was once an opening, but a boulder about the same size as the one we passed on the way in is blocking this side." Anoup rose up and held his hands out like he didn't see a way past it. "There has to be another way."

D'art scratched at the floor, digging a small divot in the dirt before he hit stone. It was just enough to stick his nose in the hole but no more.

The dog seemed insistent that the blocked off area was the way they needed to go.

Maybe there is something here we aren't seeing?

Medusa searched the wide area inside the cave. There was something akin to a corral that occupied a large portion of the room. It looked like a farm or ranch or some such. There were signs of animals and their caretakers everywhere, but no livestock or shepherds were here now.

Medusa wasn't scared of sheep, but here in the Deep Under, with all the things that might be lurking about somewhere, there had to be a keeper. A keeper in this part of the underworld would likely be something to worry about.

They needed to find a way past the rock blocking the way forward soon.

There were animal droppings in the fenced off area, and they didn't look or smell like anything Medusa was familiar with. "These look like the leavings of sheep or goats, but they smell off somehow." Medusa wrinkled her nose.

"Maybe it's because the animals are fed different foods than the animals on the surface you're used to?" Three ran her fingers through a trough filled with extremely long, dried mushroom stems and caps mixed with some sort of dehydrated seaweed. There was some sort of herb there as well, but the automaton didn't seem to know what it was.

There were piles of animal droppings molded into impressions in the stone floor until they had formed chips that looked like plates several feet across. A huge pile of the dried chips stood stacked against the cavern wall.

Three shrugged. "Nomads and shepherds use animal dung as a

fuel source for fires. That could be what this is for."

There was a huge fire pit across the way, so the automaton was probably correct.

Off to the side a series of odd, woven troughs were lined up next to animal droppings of a slightly different composition. Medusa couldn't quite place the smell, and she didn't feel like investigating too closely. There was a substantial amount of something compressed and drying in each one. At the end of the progression of drying troughs, there was a large stack of the dried pressed logs stacked like cordwood.

"It smells foul, whatever it is." Medusa took out the Orphic tablet because she didn't want to be around the smelly barnyard any longer than she had to. "How do we get past the rock at the end of the cave?"

Have the blind move it.

That wasn't very encouraging.

"Let me give it a try." Three went over by the dog and the youth and put one hand in the hole the dog had excavated and braced herself against the floor and the wall.

She heaved. The rock moved, but only enough to know it could be moved.

"I'd have to have at least one of my siblings with me to help me move it." Three sounded pretty certain. "I guess we need to find another way."

D'art looked insistent, so Medusa pulled out the Orphic tablet. It shimmered quickly and flashed a quick message.

If you take another path you won't be there in time.
Have the blind move it.

"The dog and the tablet agree." Medusa pointed at the boulder blocking the way. "This is the way forward, but I don't know what blind mover the tablet is talking about."

"So we can't go back, and we can't get past this boulder." Three was quiet as she pondered for a moment. "Maybe the blind mover is something that can't see, like a lever, or some sort of mechanism to release the door?"

They searched the walls. If there was a hidden release, they couldn't find any trace of it.

While Medusa searched the walls of the cave, a new smell hit her, and it was strong enough it made her wince. Medusa pinched her nose. "High and holy heifers of Helios, that is potent."

Anoup sniffed the air. "Cheese? Or soiled foot bindings of a mummy." He took another deep sniff. "Possibly both."

Medusa looked at Three and blinked hard to try to clear her watering eyes. She scanned about until she found the most likely source of the smells. There was a large, solid ledge with half a dozen huge identical clay jars capped off with leather tops held in place by cords. "I found the source of the cheese smell. There's also ten leather bags over here filled with the stuff."

Three was next to her in a second. Three pressed down on what looked to be the oldest bag, and the curd and whey squeaked in protest.

A fresh wave of fermentation vapor hit the air. The smell and sound in conjunction was almost too much to take.

"Please don't do that again," Medusa asked.

D'art, however, was suddenly very interested in the stuff.

Medusa unplugged her nose and took another sniff. The unsavory bouquet in the air was still just as potent, but somehow transformed. It was now totally different, as if the new stench had displaced the old, so the saturation point was still roughly the same. Now it just smelled like a rodent that Medusa was unfortunately familiar with.

"You haven't seen any skunks in your observations of the Deep Under so far, have you?"

Before the automaton could answer the question, sounds came from the open end of the huge cavern.

Something, or a whole lot of somethings, were coming their way.

"Hide," Medusa hissed in a quiet whisper.

Three grabbed Medusa and led her up to a shallow depression hidden by the shelf of a calcite flow and two huge stalactites. D'art and Anoup raced to join the women in the hiding place a moment later.

Whatever was coming in was the source of the smell, a herald that announced the arrival of its maker.

It was a solid enough smack to the senses that Medusa almost passed out from it. The room obviously didn't have enough ventilation.

A shadow darker than the air outside filled the entrance to the cave. A red-tipped, white cane the size of a pine probed about the entrance.

Confirming the entrance was clear, the giant stepped into the room, cane in one hand, a leash tied to a ram wearing a service animal vest held in the other.

A slew of smaller shadows bleating in maniacal fits and bursts followed right behind him.

"Sure is nice to be here, by myself, in a place with no squishy little human Nobodies[3] to mess with me or my precious Meloi Khryseoi. I should've moved years ago," the giant said to himself as a bunch of fat, neurotic-looking lambs and ewes staggered into the cave.

The giant leaned over and sniffed each of the sheep as they stumbled past and called them each by name starting with Alexandra and ending with Zona.

To Medusa it was a bit of a relief to see sheep that weren't some sort of fungal/mushroom hybrid. It was obvious the animals were cared for, but the lack of sunlight and open air seemed to be taking a

---

3. When Odysseus blinded Polyphemus, he said his name was "'Nobody," so when the giant called out to his neighbors complaining and trying to get help, he sounded like an idiot. Polyphemus hates Nobody, because Nobody ruined his life, and the blinded cyclops will kill Nobody if he ever happens upon him.

bit of a toll on them. They looked like the golden sheep from topside, but their colors have changed significantly from a long time in the depths of Mother Gaea. They had a decidedly green-ish, grayish cast to their coats from being in the cold damp and not getting enough, or any, sunlight. Their eyes had enlarged to magnify any light they chanced upon[4]. Sheep just weren't meant to be kept in the bowels of Mother Gaea.

The ram with the service vest came in last. He stumbled and snarled as he tripped and ran into everything in the path. "I need a hit, man. I'm freaking out!"

"Hush, Butacidas,"[5] the giant said as he rolled a huge rock forward to seal off the only open exit from the cave. But it also must have uncovered a chimney of some sort. Air started to flow from the room, and the pervasive smell eased by a fraction.

Medusa didn't feel the undeniable need to puke every time she breathed.

"Well, now we know there wasn't a secret lever or release to move the rocks out of the cave entrance," Three whispered to Medusa.

"Quiet, Three," Medusa gave a quiet hiss. "This is bad, and I'm trying to figure out a way to get out of here."

The chimney was probably out. Medusa had no idea how slick the sides would be with the soot and grime from the cave, but she suspected it would be a mistake to even give it a try.

As the light in the room grew brighter, Medusa and the others saw how shallow their hiding spot really was. They were growing more exposed with every giant sheep chip the cyclops threw on the fire.

Not that the cyclops could see any difference.

"The single-eyed giant is blind," Three whispered to her compan-

---

4. Their offspring look more and more like Gollum with every successive generation.
5. The name of a Rhegian Greek slinger who served during the Syracusan-Rhegian War. Also the name of a sheep.

"At least we know what blind guy the golden tablet was referring to." She raised up and waved her arms to get the giant's attention.

Nothing.

Medusa pulled Three back down to their hiding place. "It doesn't matter if the giant can't see you because his seeing-eye ram can," Medusa hissed.

"What's a sheep going to do?" Three whispered back.

The ram did look in the women's direction and narrowed his eyes. Luckily, he hadn't been shorn in a long time, so his line of vision wasn't exactly unobstructed.

"I'm going through withdrawals, so I might be seeing things, man," the ram said to the giant. Then the ram gave a sniff in the air. "I'm also smelling something I'm not used to. Something I haven't smelled since we were up on top. Can't quite place it though. Maybe if I had a hit?"

"Quiet, Butacidas," the giant said to the ram. "You'll get your treats soon enough."

The giant went about the cave as if he knew every inch of the space. He stuck a fork into a pile of dried stockfeed and put some in the corral for the sheep. He pulled a huge waterskin from his shoulder and filled a bath-like rock that had been hollowed out for the sheep to drink.

The ewes and lambs all filed into the corral, and the cyclops closed them in.

His flock taken care of, he went over to the oldest of the bags of cheese and pulled out a huge, stinking curd. "Ahh. Nice and warm and squishy. I love a good cheese."

Medusa and Anoup both almost retched. D'art gave a little bark of anticipation.

"What was that? You want some?" the giant asked the ram.

The ram shrugged. "I'd rather have a bit of *herb* myself."

"Herbs and cheese. Hmmm." The giant scratched himself with his free hand as he made his way back across the room and sat down against a few boulders that had been shaped into a sort of couch. He let out a contented sigh, took a squeaky bite of fetid cheese, and tucked his free hand down the inside front of his belt.

The ram went over to the dried logs and clamped down on the most desiccated of the lot with his teeth. He lifted the thing up and trotted over to the giant like a dog bringing his master a bone.

"Blind cyclops. Cheese. Sheep. Cave. Well this is unfortunate." Medusa knew without a doubt who the cyclops was. "Polyphemus. Of all the bad tempered, cannibalistic wastes of life to stumble upon here." She craned her neck over the lip of their hiding place and looked at the ram. "On the plus side, the ram may not be a talking ram after all."

"Why is that?" Anoup asked.

"One of the interpretations of Polyphemus's name is 'many-voiced.' I think he's the one making the ram appear to talk," Medusa explained.

"Like how the dolls in the puppet shows talk during festivals back in Egypt?" Anoup asked.

"Sure. Why not," Medusa answered.

"And this helps us how?" Three asked.

"I have no idea," Medusa admitted.

"Perhaps the ram is a physical object that Polyphemus projects his subconscious on, so the ram reacts to stimuli that the cyclops wouldn't normally perceive yet is still relevant and pertinent to his life and survival, and the cyclops, though his unseen talent has found a way to give his subconscious a voice," Three said.

Medusa just gave Three a long gaping stare.

"What? I told you I've been studying with a lot of different philosophers." Three explained.

Medusa just shook her head. "That's pretty out there even for most of the philosophers I know."

Three craned her neck over the top of the rock for another peek. "He doesn't look so bad. His size reminds me of one of my fathers."

"This guy ate one of Mod's uncles," Medusa whispered. "He may look like Talos, but in no way is he anything like your father."

Polyphemus took the proffered log from the ram and stuck an end into the fire. After it caught, he pulled it to his lips and took a long, slow drag.

"Well that is just vile," Medusa said under her breath.

Polyphemus huffed the smoke back and held it in. "Hup. Hup. Hup." With a long, drawn out sigh, he exhaled in the face of the ram.

That just made the ram more anxious.

Polyphemus held up a finger for the ram to be patient. "Amazing how the hemp and mushrooms are concentrated by passing through the digestive system of an ewe, ain't it?" He took another drag before he passed the joint off to Butacidas.

The ram balanced the huge roach between his front legs before he clamped the end between his teeth and sucked in for all he was worth. It took several hits before he began to relax. "Yeah, man. That's the stuff."

"Once they get the munchies, we are so boned," Medusa whispered.

"Bones?" Three asked. "That's a phrase I'm unfamiliar with."

D'art perked up at the mention of bones.

"D'art is good with either some bones or a bit of cheese," Anoup said in a soft voice.

"Not bones, boned." Medusa corrected. She pointed at herself, then at Three, then held her hand out, fingers outstretched, and shoved it palm forward first very close to her own face and then palm forward very close to Three's.[6]

The gesture was something Three and Medusa had seen before when two sailors had gotten into a disagreement. The crews of both ships got involved after the gestures were exchanged. The resulting riots lasted for three days and destroyed two ports and a fishing village.

_____

6. It just goes without saying that you should never do this to a Greek. You may think you're just telling them to speak to the hand, but I guarantee it is so much deeper and more insulting than that.

Three looked like she got the point, and it looked like Anoup did too.

They all huddled a little lower in their hiding place.

Polyphemus's eyebrow rose high and contented on his forehead. "Hey, man," he said to the ram, "you hungry?

"Crackers would go really well with this cheese. I always have the best ideas once I medicate."[7]

"We're out of crackers, man," the ram said.

The giant took another puff of smoke, followed by a bite of cheese. "I'll make due."

Medusa clenched the Orphic tablet that had led her here so tight, her knuckles turned white. "How do we get out of this?"

The sheet of gold just continued to say the same thing.

Blind the one who cannot see.

"Thanks for the help, you wretched sheet of gold," Medusa hissed.

The Orphic tablet gave her a thumbs up.

The giant smacked his lips and started to rise. "Bit more cheese. See if I left something crunchy laying about to munch on. Let's see what we got."

"Yep. We're boned," Three agreed.

Suddenly the ram started freaking out. "The smell! I'm tripping man. I recognize the smell."

"Calm down," the giant said. "There's nothing here. How are you supposed to act as my service animal if you're hysterical?"

"Wolf!" The ram was frantic. "Wolf!" The ram started clutching at his throat. "The wolf is gonna get me. I'm gonna die." He started making choking sounds. "Trapped in a cave with no escape. Anxiety. Can't breathe. Need air flow."

---

7. Putting cheese in the cracker hadn't been thought of yet. That particular innovation would have to wait centuries until Cheez-Its are invented in Dayton, OH in 1921.

Wolf? Three mouthed to the others.

Air flow, Medusa mouthed back with a smile. *How do you blind a seeing eye ram so he can see?* And then she answered it. *Blind him with the scent of the predator he's most scared of.*

They all turned at once and looked at D'art.

The dog looked rather proud of himself.

"Huh." Three risked another look at the ram, who staggered about and scratched at his throat with his front hooves. "Maybe the cyclops isn't projecting his voice and subconscious, and the ram really can talk and is scared of the dog."

The ram rolled on his back and jerked his stiff legs in the air.

"Oh, for the love of—knock it off!" the blind cyclops said to his companion.

The ram's tongue lolled, and his eyes bulged out. "Everything is growing dark. Maamaa, is that you? Maamaa!" The ram reached up his front hooves for added dramatic effect.

"Gaea's soiled knickers."[8] Polyphemus swore and rose from his couch with a weary sigh. He made his way to the door he'd come in at and easily moved the stone aside.

That gave Medusa hope. At least this way the group had a way out.

"Wolf. He's gonna get me." The ram covered his eyes with his front hooves. "Tender little me, brought down by a vicious killer in the prime of my life."

"I'm going to have to cut down on your medication, man." The cyclops shook his head as he moved to the other side of the cave. He rolled the final door closing off that end of the cave with a huff. "There. Now you have a cross breeze going on. You satisfied?"

"It's helping man, but I still smell the wolf." The ram peeked between his hooves at the shelf of rock the group had all hid behind.

D'art rose up and stared at Butacidas. The dog pointed his right

---

8. It is a swear, but it sounds dirtier than it is. Gaea's knickers are soiled with soil.

paw at his eyes, then turned it so it pointed right at the ram, then turned his paw back to point at his eyes again.

The message was unmistakable.

"You're watching me? I don't see you man," the ram blubbered. "You aren't real."

"How in the world can you help me see things if you're freaking out like this?" the exasperated cyclops asked.

Slowly Medusa and the others made their way to the door.

Anoup carried D'art, and D'art kept making threatening gestures to the ram.

"I didn't see nothing." The ram had rolled into a fetal position and was trying his best to suck on his hoof. "I didn't see nothing."

When they were out the door, Medusa reached over and scratched D'art on the ears. "Good boy. You were the hero we needed just by being there."

CHAPTER 30
WHAT'S THE PASSWORD?

LEAVING THE OTHERS HADN'T BEEN RIGHT. OR IT HAD BEEN.

Mod wasn't sure what he thought. He'd wanted to go and search for the others. Mopsus had said there was no time. Mod knew Three would be all right. Finding her was just a matter of time.

Mod hoped that Anoup and the dog had found a way out of the sea. He hoped that he'd acted quickly enough to keep Medusa's nephews from hurting anyone.

Most of all, Mod hoped he'd saved Medusa.

They'd come to a point of understanding. She'd opened up to him. He'd opened up to her. The friendship, the relationship, seemed good, and he expected that it might only get better from there.

And then the trial by sea had happened, and Mod had used a magical tool in a manner it had never been intended to be used. Somehow Mopsus and Mod had made it out of the sea. Somehow Mopsus had convinced Mod the best course was to move forward.

"We will find the others," the seer had insisted, "but we must first assure ourselves that the way forward is clear."

Mopsus said he knew the way. The seer had been very persuasive, insistent. Mod finally agreed just so the man would stop hounding him.

They left the beach and the sea behind. They found a small passage in the wall of the dome that encompassed the sea that looked well-traveled and started down it just to see how far it went. The pair hadn't scouted down the path very far when the cave entrance behind them collapsed.

Mod, a few yards further ahead on the path at the seer's insistence, hadn't felt a tremor. Mopsus had narrowly missed being crushed by the slide that had come down and sealed any hope of backtracking.

It didn't stop Mod from scrambling and trying to dig through the debris. There was just too much stone and dirt, and it was too unstable. Mod considered using his portal device until he realized he'd destroyed it getting rid of Bub and Tug. And Mod couldn't fix the portal without the tools in his shop. There was no way back.

Mod was struck on one side of a wall with the seer, and the fate of Mod's friends lay somewhere in the unknowns on the other side.

Mod cried and beat his fists against the tumble of rocks. He only stopped because Mopsus grabbed his hands and reminded him that he was still needed.

The pain from the cuts and bruises on Mod's hands and arms brought a bit of clarity. It had been stupid to hurt himself for nothing like that. If he'd injured himself too much, Mod would've doomed everyone in the end unless Mopsus found a way to fix the Grand Machine without him.

That didn't seem very likely.

So now it didn't matter what Mod felt. The center of the Grand Machine lay somewhere down the path ahead, and the only way he could save his friends and everyone else he loved was moving ahead and fixing the machine they all believed that only he could fix.

Mod had never been much of one for faith and hope. He still offered a little prayer to Elpis to know if Medusa and the others were still alive.[1]

After he'd prayed, he felt a peace that told him that Medusa and the others must be all right. It didn't rid him of all his fears, but it did allow him to move forward.

Perhaps it was for the best. There was probably danger ahead, and Mod didn't want to risk the lives of his friends anymore. Mopsus

---

1. Elpis is the name of the Greek goddess of hope. Elpis is also the name of Mod's adoptive mother. The reassurance from either one would greatly ease the anxiety and worry Mod is now experiencing.

was most likely the one that the bug had warned Medusa about, so Mod didn't want Medusa and the others around until he knew what the seer was planning for sure.

Not that there was much Mod could see the seer doing. The world was ending; Mopsus was taking him there to fix it. Doing anything beside that would be insane, right?

Besides, the final task of righting the Grand Machine was meant for Mod and Mod alone.

A new tremor ripped through the planet's core, sending a shower of debris raining from above. The grit and gravel falling were partially blocked by two huge rotating, burning wheels up above.

The goddess strapped to one of the wheels spat out a pebble that had stuck in her teeth after the tremor ended. Her companion strapped to the other wheel just shook his head to clear off the pile of dirt that had covered his face.

Whatever the pair had done to deserve such treatment, Mod was pretty sure the punishment was overkill, and being pelted with rocks and grit could only be making it worse.

Mopsus paid no heed to the deities trapped on the dirt-caked rotisseries above him. He was picking up speed. The center of all had to be close. For the first time on the entire journey, the seer appeared to know exactly where he was going.

"Smooth sailing from here on out, I assume?" Mod asked.

"What? Oh, yes." Mopsus seemed to have forgotten he was traveling with Mod. "The end is close." Mopsus leaned into his staff and picked up the pace. "I will assume there are still safeguards barring the way yet to overcome, so nobody must be counted an ally until I have achieved my goal."

My goal. Interesting choice of words, Mod thought.

It was almost as if the seer didn't care that Mod was here.

"There should be a door ahead that leads the way to a large chamber just beyond." The seer looked nervous and excited. "The center of all is in the room just beyond that final chamber. That large chamber before the center will be guarded by one most feared above all." He hitched the pack filled with Zeus's unspent lightning bolts higher on his shoulder. "I am ready for such a confrontation."

Mospus was confident in his stride and choice of direction no matter how the way ahead branched or turned.

They passed by a basalt column that looked suspiciously like the frozen visages of the damned. Mopsus stepped over a broken stalactite lying in the path. He looked down and giggled at it as he did so.

Mod glanced at the broken piece of calcite. He didn't see any reason why the chunk of rock was amusing.

There was a huge part of Mod that was warning him that the seer was only keeping Mod around because he was an engineer, one of the few who might be able to fix the Grand Machine. With the others around, Mod would have been worried about them because he now was pretty sure Mopsus would consider them expendable. Mod didn't want to contemplate what dangers the seer might be able to justify if he felt he needed to.

Was Mopsus only concerned with saving his own life? A while ago Mod would never have suspected him to be that selfish of a person.

Or how anyone could be such a selfish person.

Mopsus plowed ahead, leaning heavy on his walking stick, the thing striking the stone with such urgency that its metal tip sparked and crackled from time to time. It didn't seem like the seer really needed the stick for walking.

Why is the stick even here? Heck, why am I even here?

The answer to why he was here was probably obvious enough. *It's in my name, isn't it? Modifixeus, a combination of the words* modify, *meaning to alter or tweak, and* fix, *meaning to rectify or repair.*

Mod shook his head.

He didn't know if that was really what his name meant, and it didn't matter really, did it? *They expect me to perform a miracle and save all of creation.*

"I don't like going on without the others," Mod said out loud and out of the blue. It shocked him a little bit that he'd said it.

Mopsus stopped suddenly, bringing them both to a halt. "You want to go back and find the others? You think the task before us will hold off if we search? Fine. If you are to be our guide, then tell me the path we must take to get to them? What trials must we face to do so?" He glared at Mod as he leaned heavily on his staff and dared the other man to answer.

Mod was silent.

"The way forward is shown to me. The way back is not. I want this over just as much as you. I'm sick of being told what to do and when to do it. I just want this all to end." Mopsus looked justified and turned back to continue on his way. "I really don't care at this point whether you come with me or not. Go, find your friends, I'll be at the center of the Grand Machine where I am meant to be."

"So you're just going to let me go find the others?" Mod called after the seer.

Mopsus didn't answer, which just made Mod worry. Why, after all this time, did the seer not want the engineer here to fix the grand machine? After a second of thought Mod hurried after Mopsus. Mod's friends were important, and Mod didn't want to leave Mopsus alone because he was becoming concerned about what the seer might do if someone wasn't there to stop him.

The old man was driven to get to the center of the world, no matter who tagged along for the trip. He'd said he wanted Mod there, and now he couldn't seem to care less. Mopsus seemed to feel no loss for the others that had been left along the way.

Mod was sure he wasn't seeing the whole picture.

Get to the center of Gaea. Fix the Grand Machine or don't. If there really is only one more task to go then the whole thing should be over soon, and I could leave the seer and hopefully never see the man again.

Cautiously Mod moved forward.

After a few more steps, they rounded a corner, and the seer cursed and flattened himself against the wall. He pushed Mod back with his free hand and craned his neck around to study what he'd seen.

"There's the shade of a hero up ahead," Mopsus said to Mod as he looked back over his shoulder. "The guard that opens the final gate that leads to the waiting room before I get to the center of all. We might just be able to use him to get past the final hurdle I'm expecting to encounter before we get to my goal." Mopsus grinned. "Do not underestimate or antagonize him," the seer advised. "He is very dangerous."

"Good to know," Mod said.

"Just a final word of warning. I think the guy's crazy," Mopsus said with a wry smile.

The way he said it and the look on his face were not reassuring.

"I guess we'll just have to see, won't we?" Mod held his hand out in front of him and invited Mopsus to lead the way. He wanted Mopsus out where he could see what the seer was doing.

Quietly the pair inched around the corner.

The way ahead was blocked by a pair of massive stone doors. A giant of a Greek sat on a broad, bench-like toadstool. Stripped to the waist, wearing only a skirt, belt, sandals, and a sweatband that read *Bring it!!!*, the giant Greek stared at the closed doors and argued with himself.

The huge eagle tattoo that spread across his back from massive shoulder to massive shoulder shifted and rippled as the man made a point, flexed his shoulders so it looked like the raptor shifted to the left, and then made a counterpoint that shifted the bird back to the right.

"*Odysseus* should have the armor. He went to *Academy*." The last word was emphasized with an implied sneer. "He's so fancy—so well spoken! Why don't we all just line up and smooch on his finely toned ass? Muw, muw, muw." The giant made slobbery, kissy sounds.

The eagle shifted back to the left. "You could have shown him, but you ran yourself out of options when you ran yourself through with that sword, didn't you, smart guy?"

The giant poked at his chest, where his fingers wiggled through a hole and protruded out of his back directly between the eagle's feet.

"Clean through and through, ain't it?" The giant gave a maniacal laugh. "Bet you old *Odysseus* couldn't have stabbed himself directly through the sternum that good."

The eagle came to rest in the center, the fingers poking out the back retreated, and the giant let out a loud sigh. "Damn you, Hector! You couldn't have given me a gift card to a spa or something?[2]" He held up a sword, regarded it, and tossed it to the side where it clattered to the ground.

The eagle shifted to the right. "Can't stab yourself with a gift card, can you?"

The bird went just as quickly to the other side. "Oh, you'd have found a way."

Mod stood in wide eyed shock of the shade as he continued to argue with himself. "This is the one who is going to help us?" Mod whispered.

Mopsus nodded and gripped his staff tightly.

"He doesn't seem like he's quite all—" Mod started.

"He's not. He's as mentally brittle as a loaf of unsoaked *paximathia* under a chariot wheel.[3] One of his last acts while living was attempted revenge against all those he was allied with and an attempt to slay them all. It's very likely he could try something similar to us. We can't trust him at all, but I think I can bring him over to our side rather easily. We might be able to kill two birds with one stone."

"Uh, are we sure there isn't another way around?" Mod whispered to Mopsus.

"There is no other way around. If approached properly, I believe

---

2. At the end of a day-long duel Hector and Ajax exchanged gifts as a show of goodwill. Hector gave a sword to Ajax. Ajax gave Hector a girdle. It was a nice girdle. A manly girdle. Hector thought it was a great gift. A manly man, secure in his masculinity, can wear a girdle without being self conscious in the least.
3. *Paximathia*: A traditional Greek hard bread similar to biscotti, best consumed by soaking to soften first. Mopsus is basically calling the man crackers.

the shade will aid us, as a distraction at least if not something more." Mopsus shrugged and pursed out his lips just a bit. "He is searching for a challenge. Those that fail are often enticed by the possibility of righting wrongs and redeeming their name. Look at him. Study him. He will ally with you if you do nothing but speak his name."

"How am I supposed to know his name?" Mod was flustered. "I never met the guy."

"He's famous in Greece," Mopsus said with a sly grin. "Think about it. One of the last things that stands between me and my goal is you speaking this fallen hero's name."

"I'm telling you there's nothing familiar—" Something clicked in Mod's head.

Mod squinted and studied the man a bit more: the broad shoulders, the eagle tattoo, the need to redeem his name.

He remembered a couple of the cyclops in Hephaestus's forge discussing the Trojan war as if it were a sporting event. Mod usually didn't pay too much attention to that kind of talk because he couldn't care less, but he paid enough attention to some of the highlights just to glean a name or two so he wouldn't sound like an idiot when the other men were discussing manly things.[4]

One Greek in particular shone as a hero until he got miffed at being passed over for the MVP award.

In an uncharacteristic show of awareness and bravery, Mod stood and spoke. "Ajax?"

The giant tensed up and sat straight-backed on the toadstool.

"Someone has said my name?" he blubbered.

"It is you." Mod took a couple of steps closer. "Ajax, isn't it?"

The man raised his fists to the heavens. "My name! Someone in the vast planes of the underworld has recognized the mighty, worthy Ajax?" The man with the eagle tattoo turned around.

---

4. It didn't work. Mod couldn't tell the difference between a pankration and a pentathlon, but the men he hung around with thought his lack of understanding despite the effort he put forth was endearing, so they let it slide.

"Hi." Mod waved at the hulking man. "I'm Mod, and this is Mopsus." He indicated his companion. "And we need you to help us get to the center of the Grand Machine."

"You spoke the name of Ajax, freeing Ajax, so Ajax is beholden to you, but"—Ajax narrowed his eyes—"there is a great danger between here and the nexus."

Mod nodded, unsure why he'd suddenly taken the reins on this when Mopsus stood right beside him. "We know."

"I could let you pass and will should you ask it." Ajax sighed. "But you will only perish once you have passed the doors. As I said, the danger is great."

"How can the danger be greater than you, oh mighty, godlike Ajax?" Mopsus gave a slight bow.

Ajax stood and flexed. "Very dangerous. Most likely you won't make it past without the aid of a great hero." He considered for a moment then nodded. "But Ajax is quite the hero, is he not?" The Greek got a maniacal gleam in his eye. "If you seek access to the center of the Grand Machine, Ajax will give it to you."

"Why do guys like this always refer to themselves in the third person?" Mod asked the seer.

Mopsus shrugged.

Ajax shook his head. "Ajax is not one of the uneducated, heathen masses. Ajax has speaking skills and even graduated with a public speaking degree from the Lyceum. It has just been so long since Ajax has been unbound so Ajax can hear and speak the lovely name of Ajax."

Ajax reached for the lever but hesitated. "But Ajax is not supposed to open the door without hearing the name of . . . It is a password, a safeguard, so that none but those who know and say the name may have access beyond this point."

"Then I will whisper it, this one last time, so that you may open the doors, regain your honor in battle, and never have to hear your enemy's hated name again." Mopsus leaned in close, looking very much the part of the fox being given access to the henhouse, and whispered, "Odysseus."

Ajax narrowed his eyes, hit the lever, and whispered under his breath. "Ajax will never hear your cursed name again, *Odysseus*, you cheater."

Ajax bent down and picked up his discarded sword and flicked the thing from side to side as he limbered up and stretched. "The way is all but clear. Ajax must just deal with a bit of housekeeping so that you may be on your way. A worthy challenge, to be sure. Ajax backs down from no challenge." Ajax puffed and postured and walked up to the doors he'd previously guarded to throw them open in a grand, over the top, manner. "And there is no challenge that is prepared for the awesome might of Ajax, he who is mightier than Grease!"[5]

---

5. Never met a dish he couldn't lick clean.

CHAPTER 31

KEEPING TIME

MEDUSA LET D'ART LEAD THE WAY. HIS STATUS WAS ELEVATED by his lording it over the seeing-eye ram, but the way forward had the walls pinch in. The feel of the place changed, becoming dark, closed, and more claustrophobic.

A tremor, bigger than any Medusa had felt before, tumbled the whole cavern back and forth. The tremor filled the air with a haze of dust. It took a bit of time for everyone to get their balance as the aftershocks hit and diminished in power. The end of everything must be getting close.

"We need to hurry," Medusa said to the others.

The light ahead dimmed. It became difficult to make out the path more than a dozen yards ahead.

Medusa had a hard time making out any of the details of the passage. "There's something old here." The air of the place wasn't unwelcoming, rather felt of something long unremembered and alone that it had forgotten how to welcome guests. "Something has been trapped here for a very long time."

She pulled out the Orphic tablet.

Give Time what was lost.

It was a short message. It felt as if it contained more information than it appeared at first glance.

They ran in silence, tremors happening at a more regular basis stealing away the desire to talk with each other.

It wasn't very long before the path ahead was littered by things Medusa couldn't identify at first. As she drew closer, the images clarified into bits and pieces of skeletal remains. At the first widening of the path, there were tens and dozens of leg bones of beasts unknown etched with lines at regular intervals down the length of the bone. The bones had odd markings around the ends, as well, using differing colors and patterns. Some were marked with red rings, some with blue lines; some had green bands, others a track of black dots. And there were still more with combinations of the other markings. They had been rifled through and thrown here and there in a haphazard fashion, as if someone or something had been looking for something specific they hadn't been able to find.

Medusa pulled out the Orphic tablet. "Are we in danger? What are all these bones?"

Gather the collection. Put like with like. Find the missing piece.

That would take time, and the tremors were a constant now. Medusa wasn't sure if she should hurry ahead or do what the tablet suggested.

She looked about at the mess of bones. "Collection? How do we find out what piece is missing? Do we have time?"

The golden surface was insistent.

Gather the collection. Put like with like. Find the missing piece.

"And then what?"

Give Time what is lost.

"There's patterns and colors on these." Anoup pointed at some of the bones. "I think I recognize what these are. These are calendars, and they get put on a wall to make a kind of record of what has passed." He pointed over to the wall. "I think they go on the shelves and displays over there."

"Let's gather the ones with the same marks and put them together."

The group sifted through the scattered piles. Several of the bones were hidden off the path, covered over in rock and dust from a collapsed display. D'art was able to sniff them out. Medusa dusted those off and placed them in the empty spots of the displays.

Another huge tremor hit and brought everything they were doing to a stop for a minute.

There was a sense of urgency when they could finally get back to the work. When they were finished, every spot was filled.

"That's all of them," Medusa said, confused.

D'art sniffed the ground. He became very interested in a very old, small pile of dust and rocks that had crumbled off to the right of all the displays.

They were still missing the piece they had to find. Perhaps the clue would be in the things they had already discovered.

Medusa looked at the neat and tidy shelves and displays that now held the bones. Aside from the markings that were used to identify each grouping, she hadn't paid all that much attention to the identical etchings on the bones. She picked up one of the bones and looked at it. There were twenty-nine full marks on each bone, with a half mark near the end.

Medusa put the bone back and picked up another. Twenty-nine and a half marks. All the other bones had the same number of markings.

There were thirteen bones on each shelf or display, and there were hundreds of displays. Medusa hadn't realized how much work organizing them had been.

"Lunar calendars," Anoup clarified for the others.

The dog started digging in the pile he'd found. It wasn't long before he uncovered a rough shelf carved out of the same brittle stone the cave was formed of. The dust around the shelf had solidified into a type of flowstone or mortar. D'art's claws started raking the surface of the pile without digging any further down.

"Let me." Three's hands and fingers were tougher and stronger than anyone else's. Bit by bit she carefully chipped away at the hardened mess.

Under the crumbling remains of the shelf, there was a nub of bone poking up through the soil. It had been there long enough that the dust had settled and solidified around it. It took care and patience for Three to dig it out in one piece.

It was less decorated and etched than the others and looked to be the oldest of the group.

"That must be what Time has lost," Medusa said.

"It's been here a while." Three handed the bone to D'art. "Here you go, buddy. We never would have found it if it hadn't been for you."

The dog took it gently in his mouth as if careful not to mar it with his teeth. He made his way back to the path and stoically continued on.

The dog's nose led him on as if the bone in his possession was important or special somehow.

Medusa and the others followed. Another large tremor hit, and Medusa picked up the pace.

The path narrowed considerably, then widened and branched as it entered into a huge chamber. There were eight pits arranged in a huge circle running against the walls of the cave. It took only a few glances and comparisons to see what the pits represented.

"Phases of the moon," Anoup said to the others as they rushed past.

The dog followed the path that ran right through the center of the pits and exited the chamber on the far side.

There was another room just a bit further along. This one was filled with things even Medusa recognized immediately.

The earth shook, and some of the things sitting on shelves in the room before them clattered to the floor.

"Sundials."[1] Anoup said.

Three nodded. "My fathers use these quite often."

The mix and manner of them was quite varied. Stone and bone and wood made up the simplest of them. They grew progressively more complex the deeper into the chamber they went. The final examples were made from finely wrought gold and silver, with precious gems embedded in the metal bases to mark the passing of each hour.

The next room held something different and more advanced. "Water clocks,"[2] Three exclaimed. "My fathers love these. All the moving parts and pieces are powered by the measured downflow of water."

The water in the reservoir splashed over the side, driven back and forth by the motion of the earth beneath their feet.

There were also hourglasses that used quantities of sand to count off varied measurements, sticks of incense created to burn for precise intervals, and candles scored to mark the passage of the hour. The most elaborate candles were marked with a nail or piece of metal that would fall out and drop like a mallet to a revolving bell plate placed below once the flame freed the mallet striker from the wax.

The evolution of the devices happened quicker now, the space between displays growing shorter with each room they passed into.

Something called seconds was displayed in the next room.[3] Why anyone would need to measure the passing of a moment so small, Medusa had no idea.

She did observe, however, that the smaller tremors were now hitting within a matter of seconds.

---

1. The first real sundials were Egyptian. There were also representations from the Babylonians, the Greeks, the Chinese, and the Meso-Americans on display in the room.

2. An Egyptian creation, the water clock was one of the first devices that allowed someone to tell the passage of time without the use of sun or moonlight.

3. English Philosopher Roger Bacon came up with this one. He used the slivers on Ptolemy's subdivided globe as units of time equal to $1/86,400$th of a solar day.

Huge machines with cogs and wheels came next, gongs and bells calling out the passing of an hour one quarter at a time. Except they were all ringing sporadically from the motion below. The machines grew smaller and more complex, the fine tooling and craftsmanship almost beyond anything Medusa could comprehend.

D'art stopped at the next chamber in the cavern as if waiting for the invitation to go ahead.

Medusa didn't want to rush in until she knew what she was dealing with. The room was filled with dust and haze, but she could make out the hunched form of an old man in a wheelchair bent low as he worked on some sort of crystal on a leather topped bench.

The old man manipulated the device he was working on with delicate tools.

A tremor shifted him to the right, and he cursed as a small screw dropped, fell to the work surface, and bounced to the ground falling somewhere far off and out of the old man's reach.

"Bullocks and Lions! The damn machine won't work without that tack!" The man scanned around the floor. "It was your doing, wasn't it?

Medusa panicked for a second, as she thought the old man had just accused her or someone in the group of losing the small screw. She held out a hand and signaled everyone to stay still until they figured out who they were dealing with.

"Chaos? You didn't answer me, damn you!" The old man swept his hand across the benchtop, scattering the rest of the clockwork to the floor. "Are you listening now? Is that enough of a mess to get your attention? You let them put me here, where I don't belong and where I can't leave." The old man gestured rudely at the wheelchair. "Hobbled and crippled by what you've hidden from me, I can't do anything but measure the endless as it continues its cruel work."

The old man straightened up and glared about the eddies of haze that filled the room. "Chaos? Are you there?

"What do you expect, Chronos?" The old man muttered ruefully to himself. "Chaos won't act as predicted. He's Chaos, after all."

277

Chronos moved the chair a bit on its wheels so he could look at the parts he'd strewn on the floor. "Days and hours and seconds wasted." He sighed.

The room shook and the scattered pieces rolled around in little circles.

"Where are you, Burt? I need a hand. I dropped a whole mess of things. And I can't move down to get them myself, so the blasted things might as well be on the peak of Olympus." The old man grunted and hung his head a bit as if in frustration.

"Burt? Cuckoo? Are you there? I've gone and done it again."

Something small flitted in the shadows. It followed a slow spiral that got tighter and tighter as it surveyed the damage. "Good gods, bad gods, and those with a foot in each camp, you've made such a mess." A small clockwork bird popped upward in the center of the spiral in a wide, high sweep toward the ceiling of the room. The bird reversed course just as quickly and darted back down to where it landed on a perch near the old man. "I told you I wouldn't pick it up again if you did something like this."

"Please, Cuckoo," Chronos begged. "I was frustrated and made a mistake. You know there's no other way to keep myself in check."

"So stop making time, you jackass." The bird cocked its head to the side and regarded the old man.

The old man growled. "The biggest mistake I ever made was you, you ungrateful plonker. Some helper you are." Chronos's face turned sour. "I've half a mind to take the parts from you to replace the missing ones."

"You'd have to catch me first, wouldn't you?" The bird lighted off of his perch and flew temptingly close to the old man. "Get up. You can do it! Are you a god, or aren't you?"

"God? Don't make me laugh. I'm not one of those spoiled, bratty infants. Even if I had my leg, I'd be hard pressed to catch you, you little twit, and you know it." There was a hunger in the old man's eyes at the temptation. "Are you actually Cuckoo, or are you that insuffer-able womanizer trying to trick someone into a tryst?"[4]

"I'm not a shapeshifter. I'm just Burt." The bird landed on the perch again.

Medusa had watched enough. "Before this goes any further, may I interrupt?" Medusa asked.

The floor shuddered again, and the focus of the room shifted from the parts on the ground to Medusa and the others.

Burt cocked his head to the side as he looked at the new arrivals. "Visitors? How unexpected."

The old man straightened up and looked over his shoulders. "Hmmm. I haven't had a good visitor over for a nice meal in a long time."

Medusa wasn't sure if she and the others had just been invited to dinner or as dinner.

Best not to get too close until we are sure.

Medusa and the others didn't move from their spot at the entrance to the chamber. "I am Medusa, and my friends are Three, Anoup, and D'art." She pointed to each one in turn, then reached down and scratched the dog between the ears. "We've been separated from our friends and are trying to find our way to a meeting spot to reunite with them. Would it be improper if we were to ask for passage through your residence on our way?"

Chronos said nothing for quite a while, as he stared at the group with the dog standing at his doorstep.

"Burt?"

The bird cuckooed and laughed. "You're not seeing things. They're really there."

Chronos nodded slowly, then pulled the back of his hand across his lips as if he were salivating just a bit.

---

4. The cuckoo is sacred to the goddess Hera, so Zeus transformed himself into one to trick her into a relationship. The ruse must have worked, though one has to wonder how a cuckoo could put the moves on a woman and have her take it seriously enough to turn into something real.

That is a tad disturbing.

"We're trying to get to the center of the universe," Medusa clarified, as if anyone would travel this way to get to someplace other than that.

Burt cocked his head to one side as if taking stock of the pair, and then cocked his head to the other side as if to verify. "The quadruped is too small for his parts to be of any use, but maybe the youth or either of the women might be able to work?"

Chronos stroked his beard for a second as if contemplating. "These new model parts are almost never compatible." He pursed out his lips, then shrugged. "Either way, compatible or not, at least I'll get a meal out of the deal."

With that pronouncement, the way behind Medusa and the others clanged shut with finality.

CHAPTER 32

PLANETARY CORE SMACKDOWN

TYPHON, THE EMBODIMENT OF POWER AND TERROR, A MONSTER who fell just shy of defeating Zeus in the war between the gods and the titans, filled most of the chamber just beyond the doors. Hundreds of heads and eyes and arms covered a trunk the size of a mountain.

Mod's eyes went wide in shock. He'd known Medusa's brother-in-law was scary and huge, but the scope of just how immense and terrifying he was seemed to have been lost in the description. "How is Ajax supposed to defeat that?" Mod asked the seer in a quiet voice.

"He probably won't, but a distraction at the right time will allow us to slip by," Mopsus whispered back. "Using Ajax just means we're more likely to get past Typhon unscathed."

They didn't need to whisper. Ajax rushed out hellbent on attacking the monster. He didn't even wait to hear if there was a plan.

"For the glory of Greece, baby!" Ajax, sword poised and gripped tightly with both hands, threw himself off a ledge at Typhon. "Hells yeah! Ajax bets you Mr. Smarter-than-thou wouldn't 'ave been able to do this!" Ajax stabbed the sword deep into Typhon's belly and hung on as it sliced a line down the gargantuan monster's gut.

Typhon slapped Ajax away with a hundred hands. Each back-hand struck the shade in rapid succession that sent him into the great cavern wall. Ajax hit the rock with a wet splat and slowly peeled off to fall to the cave floor hundreds of feet below.

Mod and Mopsus turned and looked at the monster with dread. Typhon would make short work of them now that Ajax was out of the way.

The body of the Greek warrior jerked. Ajax coughed, spit up a couple of teeth, and leered hungrily at the giant he was battling. "That all you got, no nuts?"

"How is he not dead?" Mod asked.

"Shade," Mopsus replied.

Mod nodded, impressed by Ajax's tenacity. "Can't die because he's already dead."

Ajax rose up, leaned back on his heels, and laughed. He sent a bloody wad of spittle in Typhon's direction. "Today is a good day to die!"[1]

"Don't do it," Typhon warned. He looked at Ajax with most of his sets of eyes, but still spared a few pairs to watch the seer and Mod at the entrance to the chamber.

Ajax picked up his sword and launched himself at Typhon a second time.

Typhon plucked the Greek out of the air, held him tight with many arms, and ripped off both of Ajax's hands.

Ajax screamed as he dropped to the ground. "Cheater! How is Ajax supposed to beat you in a fair fight if you rip off Ajax's hands and you"—he squinted up at the giant monster with two hundred arms as if he were doing a quick calculation—"have at least a dozen of 'em?" Ajax rose up to his feet and started kicking dust on Typhon's shins.

More of Typhon's heads turned in Ajax's direction. He was only keeping track of Mod and Mopsus with two or three heads now.

"Well, I was saving this for something special, but I guess now is as good a time as any. My plan was to just chuck as many as we needed at the monster as we ran, hoping to hit the monster and at least stun him and to give us enough time to make it to the door, but now we have a delivery system." Mopsus reached into his pouch and

---

1. The phrase has been uttered in one form or another many times in history. It is most frequently attributed to the Oglala Lakota war leader Crazy Horse or his contemporary Oglala Lakota chief Low Dog, but we all remember it now as uttered by Worf from Star Trek.

pulled out two sparkling lightning bolts. He appeared to be trying to get Ajax's attention. "You, idiot!"

A dozen of Typhon's heads turned in the seer's direction. Some of the monster's eyes squinted as they tried to determine what the seer was holding.

Ajax wasn't getting the message. Now he was running against Typhon's shin and biting the giant on the ankle.

"Ajax! A gift from Zeus," Mopsus cried in a voice loud enough to fill the hall.

Recognition drew all of Typhon's faces around. The giant moved toward Mod and Mopsus with fear in his many, many wide eyes.

"Ajax, it is now or never," Mopsus shouted.

Ajax hacked several times as if he tried to expel the ankle hair or something similar that tickled the back of his throat. One final mighty cough did the deed, and he was able to look up and clue in.

Mopsus didn't hesitate. He dropped Zeus's lightning bolts down into the pit.

Hundreds of Typhon's hands rushed forward to stop the gift a fraction of a moment too late.

Ajax leaped as high as he could, his arms outstretched in a heroic pose he must have practiced a thousand times before, and both of the lightning bolts clicked into place on the ends of his arms.[2]

All of Typhon's dragon heads swiveled, his attention now fully focused on the electrified Greek.

"Are you sure giving that kind of power to a maniac like Ajax is a good idea?" Mod asked.

Mopsus shrugged. "Not my problem. My goal lies just beyond in the smaller chamber behind Typhon."

Ajax's eyes glinted with a mad spark, and it couldn't all just be attributed to the six hundred million amps coursing through his

---

2. Much like the way Bruce Campbell's chainsaw clicked into place in the theatrical masterpiece *Army Of Darkness*.

body.[3] "Recognize these?" He twisted the sparklers in the air for Typhon to see.

Typhon took a step back.

Ajax clicked the lightning bolts together over his head. The connection fried him a little and straightened his hair, poofing it out in an Afro. "Ajax fears no man, nor beast or evil, brother! There's a smackdown coming hard and fast from these thirty-two-*daktyloi* pythons!"[4] He kissed one bulging bicep then the other then launched himself at Typhon and buried both prongs of the lightning bolts deep in Typhon's foot.

The giant stiffened and started to make little spastic noises as his multiple jaws clamped shut. Speech and movement were impossible as the shade of Ajax tased him.

"Serves you right for not speaking up at the beginning," Mopsus said as if he spoke to the monster. He let out a little happy chuckle and started forward and tapped Mod on the shoulder to follow as he went. "Now, while the two idiots are engaged."

Mod followed him, unsure why the look on Mopsus's face disturbed him so much.

Typhon continued to pop and sizzle.

"How would you handle this, Mr. Smarter-than-thou?" Ajax snorted and pushed the crackling bolts deeper. He pulled the prongs out, gave Typhon just a fraction of recovery time, then forked the giant in two different spots. "You wouldn't, ha! Ajax is the better man."

Ajax's theatrics were lost on the giant, and a smell, not unlike uncured, flash-roasted calamari, filled the air.

Mod threw up in his mouth, just a little.

The air cleared once they'd made it a bit further on.

Mod and Mopsus made it into the final chamber, and Mod could

---

3. The average lightning bolt is three hundred million amps, and Ajax is holding two. This is simple math for most people, unless they went to a charter school.

4. 1 *daktylos* equals about 1.93 centimeters, which is about .76 inches. Basically 24 inches. If you get the reference, it's time to take your multivitamin.

already see the hub of the wheel holding the universe together was falling apart.

"All the warnings that I've given you, they've all led to this." Mopsus turned around and put on a hand on Mod's shoulder. "There was something I saw in you, the potential you have is great. After all this time, I just had to make sure. Can you fix this Mod?"

Mod surveyed the damage. It was a lot to take in. There was no way to shut off the machine to repair it, which made everything more complicated. "I've never done anything quite like this before. Even with Hephaestus, I've never worked on a machine even approaching this. This is big. Really big."

He looked at the debris in the chamber and decided what might be useful and what needed to be cleared away as a hindrance. If he had access to his shop back home fixing this would be a challenge just due to scale, but here? He refined his definition of tools down to the extreme basics, reevaluated what he could use from the chamber, and did a few more calculations in his head.

Mod folded his arms and walked around studying it more. It was immense, but the movements and interactions were all fairly simple. And the central gearing that powered everything else was small enough it almost looked possible.

"Mopsus, I don't think there are many who could fix this machine, especially with the supplies I have on hand and the condition of the machine." He looked up at the interconnected cogs, wheels, and gearing, and could see the timing he would have to use to make everything work. The rotational window needed to make a repair was short, only open for a few seconds each time. Mod took a deep breath and let it out in one long sigh. "I don't think many could fix it. But I can."

Mopsus put his hand on Mod's shoulder and gave him a reassuring pat.

"That's all I needed to know."

Mopsus's smile tipped up at the edges as he pulled Mod closer.

Mod felt a sharp pinch, and then the sensation flared as if a burning brand had been sealed in his chest. All his breath left in a rush, and when he tried to inhale, his lungs refused to fill again. The white hot weight in his chest amplified as if it were tearing at something vital. It pulsed and flashed until Mod was sure there was nothing but pain and heat left of him.

Mopsus backed away, the previously hidden dagger buried up to the hilt in Mod's chest.

With the realization of what had happened, all of the pain and heat rushed out of Mod in an instant. He staggered at the sudden cold that took him yet somehow remained standing. Mod looked Mopsus in the eyes.

Mopsus patted Mod on the shoulder again, laughed in Mod's face, and pushed him away with a sneer.

"I knew you couldn't be Mopsus," Mod gasped.

"You knew I wasn't the seer, and yet you still followed me willingly? Ha! You really are a blind, pathetic fool." The seer dropped his disguise, his face elongating and distorting until his profile took on the shape of an aardvark. His body morphed and twisted as well until he was all godly muscle and sinew. "Mopsus was left unconscious in a bathroom stall back in the bar right after Zeus gave him this charge. What better way for a criminal to make his way back to the scene of the crime than disguised as the one sent to fix it?"

"Not Mopsus." Even seeing it with his own eyes, knowing it was true, it was still a hard thing to accept. Mod tottered a bit to the side. "I preferred the disguise instead of whatever in Tartarus you look like now."

"Mopsus is a doughy, ugly, pitiful thing." The aardvark shook his arms and shoulders to loosen up. He stretched and flexed and drew back his lips to bare his teeth in a wicked grin. "My true visage is glorious, is it not."

"I'd say no." Mod's knees buckled but he remained upright. "There's not enough lipstick in Greece to make your disfigured pig face pretty."

"Cruel, but you've just been stabbed, so I'll let your insolence pass." He grabbed Mod by the front of his chiton and pulled him close, his sharp teeth so close Mod turned his head aside to avoid the beast's snout. "My given name is Set, and I am a god most wronged. Today I have my final vengeance." He hit Mod in the chest again, driving the blade deeper.

Mod staggered back, his hand reached up and he grabbed the hilt of the knife with a tight fist. "Why?" The blade was deep, and Mod could feel his heart struggling around it.

Set sniffed the air. "Smell that? That's the smell that enticed the dog forward. That's the smell of my heart sizzling." He pulled back his lips from his canines in a vicious smile. "That is how little the gods of the beginning cared for me, that they ripped out my heart and used it as a spare part in the vile little experiment they call creation.

"I can still feel it, burning and turning and rubbing inside the center of the machine. Can you imagine that? What it would be like to have your heart used and abused like that, hurting and praying that someday it will fail. Hoping beyond hope that someday you will die? No more. I'm taking it back now."

"My heart for yours." Mod choked. He was dying. At least this way his death would mean something. At least this way he might be able to save his family and friends.

Set shook his head. "Sorry. Just wouldn't be the same. You're not a god, kid. Besides, I'm pretty sure your heart is damaged."

Mod stumbled forward, falling to his knee only to pivot and tumble backward. "Who fixes the machine?" He gasped as it became harder and harder to breathe.

"No one." Set reached down and pulled the dagger from Mod's chest. "I don't think the gods could have fixed it. But you"—he pointed the tip of the bloody dagger at Mod—"were special. Were." Set tossed the knife aside.

Mod tried to reach for the dagger to do something to give the others a chance. Medusa might still find her way here, and with the help of Three, she just might be able to do something to save the Grand Machine. Mod's fingers clutched for the blade, but Set had tossed it too far away. He needed another weapon. The toy from his childhood was in his pocket. Mod grabbed it, intent on bludgeoning Set with it or throwing it at him. The sphere tumbled from fingers too weak to hold onto it and rolled out of his reach on the floor of the chamber.

"Gadgets and possessions are just traps, really. No need for such burdens where we're going." Set rose and dropped his walking stick to the floor. "It's time for all of us to be unfettered from this miserable existence, don't you think?"

"Oh, gods, I'm sorry." Mod choked and flinched from the pain. "Doug. My family and friends. I've failed them."

"Sputter and spew all you want. It's over." Set turned to the center of the Grand Machine. "I've got things to do."

"Medusa." Mod smiled at the thought of her, but his feelings were more complex there than they'd ever been. He didn't know what to think. He didn't know if she'd be saddened or relieved at his passing.

The smile slowly dropped from his face.

"No sense running," Chronos said. "Only one way in and one way out, and both those ways are shut."

"There is a third way," Burt the cuckoo mentioned. "The stew pot is the escape route most eventually wind up taking."

A tremor stronger than any Medusa had felt before shook the room and almost sent everyone sprawling.

Time is almost up.

"No one leaves via the exit, so why don't you save us all a bit of hassle and just climb into the cauldron?" Chronos spun his chair around to face Medusa and the others. His arms and left leg were corded, stringy muscle while his right leg spun and twisted as if it were nothing but a hunk of boneless flesh connecting the foot to the knee.

It acted like that because it was exactly what it was.

"All those bones at the beginning of your cavern." Anoup's eyes widened like he was shocked. "Those were human legs?"

"Human?" Chronos spat on the ground. "How dare you? My tastes are so much more refined than that. I'm still going to eat you, but I won't enjoy it nearly as much now."

"He'll probably enjoy eating you more," Burt said as if he confided in them, like he'd just let Medusa and the others in on a proprietary secret.

Chronos wheeled himself closer as he licked his chops. Anoup looked panicked. Three looked intrigued. The dog seemed oddly calm with the bone in his mouth.

Medusa wasn't sure how long she would let this go on. She decided this was probably far enough. "Chronos, right?"

"Arg! I'm going to eat you up like a tender vittle." He made clawing motions with his fingers and gnashed his teeth dramatically.

The only one reacting to the threats was Anoup, who had a very recent and traumatic interaction with another gullet not very long before. "What are we going to do?"

In apparent response to Anoup's question, D'art sat back on his haunches and wagged his tail, the bone held tightly in his mouth in front of him. He wasn't scared of the approaching old man at all.

"No fun if you don't try to run," Chronos said. He looked disappointed, like he wasn't getting the right reaction.

"It's a pretty good joke," Medusa said. "The only problem is, we already met Kronos, and he already tried it with us."

"Anoup and D'art were not happy with the interaction." Three put her hand on Anoup's shoulder to steady him.

Chronos dropped his clawed hands. "Already met Kronos, huh?" His face fell into a pout. "I waited and thought about that joke for a long while, and all that effort goes to naught." He threw up his hands, frustrated.

Chronos huffed and turned away from the group. He mumbled and muttered to himself as he went. He rolled his chair over to the leather-covered workbench, where the wheels actually slid into divots worn into the stone floor that jostled the old man slightly as the chair settled. Chronos sniffed, his shoulders slumped, and he leaned his head over the top of his bench.

After a few moments, he started to gently weep.

"I didn't mean to make him cry," Medusa said to the others.

D'art woofed around the bone in his mouth.

Burt the cuckoo flew over beside Medusa and landed on a shelf just out of reach. "He's sensitive. And he doesn't always know how to act because he doesn't get a lot of visitors. Most of the time he only gets to talk to me, and I'm as annoying as heck. I don't even like being around me."

"Normal social interaction doesn't involve threatening to eat the visitor at the end of the visit," Medusa pointed out.

"You met Kronos, huh?" Burt asked. "Which ones of you did he eat?"

Medusa pointed at Anoup and the dog.

"I see you passed through the experience okay." Burt cocked his head to the side as he studied the young man and the dog.

"Please don't say *passed*." Anoup paled just a bit.

"We'll, you don't have to worry about Chronos here. He isn't like his nephew, eating people left and right." Burt hesitated, cocked his head to one side, and added, "Mostly."

"It was a joke." Chronos sniffed and wiped his nose on the back of his sleeve. "No one can ever keep the names Chronos and Kronos straight. Me, Chronos, I'm the father of time and space, contemporary of Chaos himself. My grandnephew, Kronos, he's the one that thought the nursery room in his house was a buffet. We're two totally different people with different standards, but no one cares enough to put in the effort to distinguish between us. I'm trapped, here below the realm of Hades because of a paperwork error. They thought I was Kronos, and no one bothered to listen to me when I said they were making a mistake."

"So you were trapped in the underworld due to a clerical error?" Somehow that didn't sound right to Medusa.

"Clerical error? Who knows?" Chronos threw his hands up in exasperation. "The gods are prideful if they're anything. Once they make a mistake, they think the easiest course is just to ignore the problem they created. So here I sit, unloved and forgotten, bearing the curses and swears aimed toward someone with a similar sounding name." He shrugged. "So what can I do except try to make the most of a hard situation? Not that anyone cares that it brightens my day a bit if I use humor to try to lighten an awkward introduction."

"Joking about eating us was a tad extreme for a first meeting," Medusa said.

Burt flinched at that. "Your sense of humor gets a bit skewed when you're stuck in a solitary cell talking to your bird for eternity."[1]

"Gets lonely," Chronos sniffled. "I was only having a laugh."

D'art wagged his tail and slunk a bit closer to the god of time. He held the bone in his mouth up high for the god to see it.

Chronos squinted in the dog's direction but said nothing.

Perhaps Chronos couldn't see the proffered bone because of all the tears in his eyes.

The dog looked a bit discouraged to not have his gift recognized. He acted insistent though and scooted closer so he was almost in grasping distance of the god's claw-like hands.

That worried Medusa a bit, but she trusted D'art's instincts.

Anoup shuffled a couple of steps closer, and Medusa let him. He didn't look as scared now, and he was focused on helping D'art. "Perhaps if you were to try interacting with visitors without suggesting activities that could cause them mortal harm?" Anoup leaned to the side and crouched down to try to get in Chronos's line of sight. "Like invite them to participate in a game of Senet or Mehen or such?"[2]

Chronos sniffed again and coughed. He glanced at Anoup without raising his head, his eyes red-rimmed and weepy. "I don't know what those words you just spoke are."

"Games? Hounds and jackals? Twenty square? You know, games?"[3]

Chronos shook his head. "The only games I know about require running and jumping, and I . . ." Chronos indicated his boneless shin.

D'art edged closer until he was right next to the old man. He nudged Chronos with his nose.

Chronos looked down at the dog. "What do you want, dog." The

---

1. Not a euphemism.
2. Senet and Mehan are ancient Egyptian board games. Can you call it a board game when it is played on a ceramic coil representing a snake god? Anyway, they were played by two to four people, appropriate for ages 3+.
3. Chronos would be in a much better mental state had he found out about solitaire or Tetris or Minesweeper. Those games have wasted billions of man hours since they were created.

old man's bushy brows peaked up and his eyes went wide. "Is that . . .?"

Anoup scratched D'art on the back of his neck. "D'art thinks that the bone felt lonely. He said it needed to get back to you."

It took a bit for the offer to register. After a quiet moment, Chronos put out a hand. D'art dropped the bone in Time's palm.

The old man's lower lip trembled. "Thank—thank you." He had a hard time speaking. "It-it's been a long time."

Chronos placed the length of bone against his boneless shin. The flesh rippled and swelled against it, the foot and knee pulling away from each other as the flesh flattened and stretched to accommodate the length of bone that had been missing for so long. Skin crawled up the sides of the shinbone like a tree engulfing a fencepost, and after a minute or two the flesh on either side met in front of the bone, pulling it fully inside.

There was an audible click and a pop, and Chronos let out a long, drawn out, sigh. His reboned leg was now a perfect mirror of the other.

He placed one foot on the floor, then reached out a tentative toe with his newly restored leg. Chronos pushed up out of his chair and stretched to his full height. The old man let out a hoot that scared everyone in the group. Then he laughed and started to do a little jig. Ironically, the embodiment of time had a terrible sense of rhythm.[4]

The sight of him dancing was one of the happiest things Medusa had ever seen.

"Haha!" Chronos fell down to his knees and kissed the dog on the nose. "Thank you, my four-footed friend. A billion seconds of thanks![5] Of course you may all travel through my home on your way to the center of the Grand Machine. Though I'm afraid the trip will

---

4. My wife can't keep a beat or hold a tune. When she sings it is pure and true, and I find it very endearing.
5. That's almost thirty-two years worth of gratitude.

be a very short one. The machine has failed. It's in the process of ripping itself apart."

A bigger tremor than all the others ripped through the room. A huge fissure opened in the space right between Medusa's feet.

"We're too late," Medusa lamented.

Chronos cocked his head to the side and knitted his brows in concentration. "Maybe. Maybe not." He shuffled into a dark corner and pulled out a treadmill. It was layered with dust several inches thick. "Haven't used this for a while, because of, well, you know." Chronos swept the dust off from side to side and stepped up onto the device.

He held onto the rail and started to push the tread backward.

The crag in the floor sealed up as if it had never been there before.

"Did you—" Medusa gasped.

"Turn back time?" Chronos beamed. "Pretty handy trick, isn't it?"

Three looked about at the de-destruction happening around her. "Wow. Deja vu."[6] Then her brow knit. "Wait. You just did something that had an effect on the Grand Machine but not us. How did you do that?"

Chronos shrugged. "You don't think about taking a step or picking your nose, but you do it anyway. Care to explain the mechanics behind that?"

Three looked like she was going to argue, but then she just nodded and pursed her lips. "Touché."

"Can you take us back to before all of these tremors began?" Medusa asked. "Can we fix this all before it starts?"

Chronos shook his head. "This thing is dangerous. I only have the strength to push things back a few minutes at most, but can you

---

6. Three learned French from one of those philosophers she's been studying with. The philosophers group in Greece had a pretty good teacher exchange program going on with a place called Babel.

imagine what would happen If I went too far, or stumbled and the treadmill kept on going? Or, primordial heavens forbid, had someone like Hermes or a speedster got on it?"[7] He wiped his nose on the back of his hand and huffed as he started running backward. "Best I can do is give you a couple minutes, just enough to get to the center before everything goes kaput."

"We'll take a couple more minutes," Medusa said as she braced herself. "Give us what you can, Chronos."

---

7. Barry Allen first used a similar device in The Flash #125 issued in 1961. It has been used for good or ill in many comics and movies since.

CHAPTER 34

AN URGENT DREAM

MODIFIXEUS COULD FEEL THE OCEAN SPRAY ON HIS ARMS AND face. For a second he was worried he was back in the Mushroom Sea, but when he opened his eyes, he saw the ocean and boats from his dream.

The toy from his childhood was in his grasp. But his fingers encompassed it, and the hand he saw was the hand of a man. Not the child, but an adult walking in the memory of a child. Or was it a memory?

His young and beautiful mother was there, sitting on a high piling at the end of the dock, kicking her legs out and feeling the breeze, very happy and very much alive.

The pirates, the people on the dockside doing business, the faceless inhabitants of the town living out the day, weren't there. It was just Mod and his mother.

She patted the pilon next to her.

He hesitated. It was worth it to wait, to take in every detail of the face and person he hardly remembered.

She patted the seat next to her again, insistent, as if to say time grows short.

Mod got up and walked toward her. It was odd, to see her like this, carefree and happy. So many of his memories of her were tinted dark by how she'd died, but none of that fear or hurt was with him now.

His mother continued to look out at the horizon, a smile creasing her face. Her smile grew more content as he approached, as if she were just happy to be in his presence.

"Mom?"

"I've waited for this moment for a long time. Let's just savor it for a second."

"Is a second long enough?" he asked glibly.

"It depends on how long you want a second to last," she replied.

The small drop of water in the air before Mod stopped and hung suspended in space and time. It didn't shift or drop no matter how he looked at it or moved around it.

There were other droplets suspended in the air as well. Mod walked around them carefully, as if he might snap the string that held them aloft if he went the wrong way. He could see the force that would propel them forward were they not frozen in time, and the movement and distortions of the air that would have beckoned it forward.

Which was odd but somehow not unexpected. Mod studied the water. He was transfixed on the complexity of the drop, the makeup and composition of the thing, and how it reacted with the atmosphere, light, and forces around it.

He turned to his mother, amazed and dumbstruck. "Mom?" He finally managed.

She held up a finger to stop him from saying anything else.

"The water isn't the only thing you perceive in detail this great." She swept her arm out before them in a great sweep that encompassed the world and more. "Take it in. Just a moment. Then tell me what it is you see?"

Mod sat down next to her and looked in the direction she faced. It was hard to look away from her, to look out at the world and see the way things worked within it.

He did it anyway.

Mod observed the way the line of waters curved at the horizon, a seemingly straight line that dropped ever so slightly at the edges. He knew the horizon line was an illusion of perception. There was more to what was seen than the average person realized. Once you knew there was more, you could see the truth and fact of things so much more clearly. From that drop in the horizon line, he was able to calculate that Gaea had a circumference of 40,075 kilometers.

His mother nodded, though he'd said nothing. "Go on."

Mod looked at the rising moon. He was able to account for the refraction and magnification of the atmosphere at that angle and could tell anyone who asked that the circumference of the moon was about 10,900 kilometers, and that the path it tracked around Gaea in its orbit was 384,000 kilometers, give or take.

His mother nodded again and gave his hand a little squeeze.

Mod was able to see the effect the weight of the moon had on the waters before him, tugging individual particles this way and that, so they crashed into and pushed the water drops next to them. He could see how they interplayed with the debris in the water, the resistance they had to overcome on the ocean floor to move one way or the other, the energy needed for a single drop to break from the others to become the spray that landed on his face.

He looked over at his mother.

She looked back at him and smiled. "Are you beginning to understand? The Grand Machine is beautiful."

The magic of the moment was broken at her mention of the machine. "The Grand Machine is breaking. And I'm lying in a pool of my own blood. I tried to save everyone. Instead I let myself get killed. I've failed."

She cupped his cheek in her hands, pulling his face about so he had to look at her.

Suddenly feeling as if he were little again, Mod tugged on his Momma's hand. "I wanna go."

"Just a minute, Modifixeus." She used his full name just as she always did when she was serious. "I told you it would only be a minute more. You can be patient for a minute more, can't you? Your understanding is so much greater now because you are beginning to see, and the need is great. And in the makeup and operation of the Grand Machine there are allowances made and precautions set in place for when the need is great."

Her eyes bored into him. He couldn't look away if he tried.

He didn't know if he wanted to walk away or not. He knew what was coming next, though he didn't understand it or any of the ramifications, but a stronger part of him wanted to understand.

Mod always loved a challenging puzzle.

"There are safeguards in place to stop a catastrophic malfunction." He gulped and swallowed hard, not quite believing what he was about to say. "I'm the safeguard."

"No. Not a safeguard, my son." She smiled a sad smile as if she regretted that his time of innocence was over. "You are so much more than a safeguard." She took her hands from his face and held the toy of his childhood out to him.

Mod looked at it and saw it for what it was for the first time.

"Go," she said, "use your mind and be the man I know you to be."

He didn't want to leave her, but she seemed insistent.

He closed his eyes, and she was gone.

And then Mod opened his eyes to the end of the world.

CHAPTER 35

PULL THE PIN, COUNT
TO FIVE

The service entrance to the Grand Machine was long, and Medusa could only see a fraction of what was going on down the narrow way.

They ran as fast as they could.

The tremor that had hit when Medusa and the others were in the bone calendar room repeated itself and knocked Medusa off her feet.

Three helped Medusa back up, and Anoup and D'art ran on ahead.

Medusa looked up just in time to see an aardvark-faced someone she'd never seen before using Mopsus's staff as a lever to pull the pin from the center of the Grand Machine. It still took time for the aardvark-faced man to pull the pin, but Medusa and the others were just too far away to stop him.

There was a moan on a cosmic level, as the universe and everything within it started a slow, ever widening, spiral from the center of intended place and purpose.

"Oh," The aardvark-faced man cried as tears of joy welled in his eyes. He held out his hands and spun around in a little dance mimicking the motions of the dying reality. "I can't believe this is real! After so long, it is really, finally happening. Just one thing left to do." He bent down and pried on the cover for the track that kept the bearings surrounding the now absent pin in place.

Medusa watched as Anoup and D'art ran into the center chamber just ahead of her.

Anoup dropped his disguise, turning into the same type of animal-god hybrid that was moving the pin, only with a snout more sleek and a face more black than the other man. "You! Father, how could you?" Anoup, now with the head of a jackal, launched himself at the aardvark-faced man and knocked him away from the hub of the Grand Machine. "I will end you, Set!"

The two grappled, but Set easily freed himself from Anoup's grasp and overpowered his smaller attacker.

Medusa and Three stood there stunned, possibly overcome by the odd powers in the air as reality began to twist and fray from the center. Or maybe it was from seeing Anoup now also had the head of a jackal.

"Anubis?" Set laughed and spun and threw the younger god to the ground. "I thought I recognized the scent of my son! No matter the face you wear or the ways you try to hide, it is almost impossible to cloak yourself from the man that sired you. You did very good. I had my suspicions, but I was never sure enough to confront you on our journey here. You somehow still found your way to the center of all. I'm impressed, yet maybe I shouldn't be, taking into account the birthrights inherited from your sire." Set grinned, pleased with himself and his prowess.

"D'art just followed his nose," Anoup said. "Your heart stinks of burning pork."

"Where is Mod?" Medusa demanded.

Set ignored Anubis as if he were nothing and turned to face Medusa. He gave her a little bow and grinned. "He arrived just before you, but I'm afraid that Mod is going to miss the show."

D'art barked and yelped at what looked like a pile of rags crumpled on the ground. Medusa couldn't bring herself to believe what she saw when she looked where the dog was pointing. She turned back to Set and gaped at him with horror in her eyes.

"Oh, yes. You aren't mistaken." Set twirled his right hand in a little flourish until the motion ended with his arm pointed at the blood-soaked form lying on the floor.

Her anger made her want to tear Set to shreds, but anger and revenge could wait. "Mod!" Medusa ran forward and slid on the slick next to the body. She cradled Mod's head in her arms and screamed in rage at the one who'd attacked him.

Set laughed and turned from them as if they all meant nothing.

Three and D'art put themselves between Set and the Grand Machine. When Set turned to deal with them, Anoup went wild. He bit down on Set's upper leg, his teeth sinking to the bone. Set tossed back his head and howled.

The world spun half a degree off as if on cue. With a grinding sound, the central track full of bearings buckled and twisted. Some of the bearings ground against the others and bound the main wheel of the universe for a moment.

The universe shuddered and stopped for a second. "That hurt!" Set screamed as he lashed out at everyone around him.

Medusa shielded Mod from the fresh wave of debris that fell then pushed Mod's hair out of his eyes when the tremor stopped. "Mod!" He wasn't responding to her. Medusa pressed her hand to his wound in a futile attempt to stop the slowing flow of blood.

The center of the universe crumpled a bit more. The cover on the small track that housed the central ring of bearings popped off. Shiny metal balls and a steaming, smoking heart spilled out onto the floor.

"Set—" Mod choked up a mouthful of blood.

"Don't try to talk." Medusa sobbed, and her bloodied hand pressed uselessly against the wound in Mod's chest. "We'll deal with Set. You just hold on."

"Set is heartless," Mod managed, his voice faint and tired.

"Set's a monster." Medusa's hand moved, but no new blood issued from Mod's wound. His heart wasn't pumping strong enough anymore or the supply of blood had run too low.

Mod struggled and raised his head off the floor. "Set's heart." With evident effort he brought his hand up and pointed at the pile of bearings being expelled from the center of the Grand Machine. "Set needs his heart."

"Mod, don't try to speak," Medusa cried, not understanding what he meant.

Set recovered enough he swept Three and the dog out of the way and slammed his son against the machine. Dazed, Anoup's grip on his father faltered. "A noble attempt offered too late, my little one! No one can help you now." Set clamped his hand on the back of his son's head and pried.

Anoup yelled and released his father from his bloody teeth.

Set's hand went immediately to his son's throat, and he lifted Anoup high into the air so his feet couldn't find the ground. A smack from a cast iron frying pan sent Set tumbling head over heels. Three stood over the god as if daring him to try to get up.

Mod's voice was growing thin, and it was hard for Medusa to hear him over the renewed fight that involved Set, Anoup, Three, and D'art. "Set needs his heart. We can't fix the machine while he's going crazy like this."

"How do we put his heart back?" Medusa looked like she couldn't believe she was having this conversation.

"Just get it close to him." Mod coughed and closed his eyes. "The heart knows where it belongs. Set doesn't understand, because he has no heart."

"So we just give him what he wants?" Medusa brushed the tears from her eyes as she shook her head.

Mod nodded. "Trust me." He put his hand over hers and closed his eyes.

"Mod?" Medusa screamed and shook him.

Mod shifted his head in a slight nod from where he lay on the ground. "I'm still here. Just do it."

It seemed crazy, but Mod was so insistent Medusa couldn't ignore his words. She cradled Mod's head gently as she lowered it to the ground. Then Medusa rose up, more determined than she had ever been in her life. "Three!"

The automaton looked over her shoulder as she did her best to keep Set pinned in a double armed headlock. Anubis and D'art were unconscious on the ground beside her. "Kinda busy."

"Hold Set." Medusa commanded as she dove for the pile of bearings. "Set's heart is in that pile of rubbish near the center. Mod said he needs it back."

Three looked confused, but she went with it. "Change of plans, jackass." She hauled back and lifted Set high into the air.

"You'll burn for this!" Set tried to electrocute Three. He gripped her forearms tight and sent every volt of his power into her.

"The ceramics in my skin make me a poor conductor," Three said as she shrugged off Set's most powerful attack and hoisted the god higher. She turned and faced the pile of debris.

Medusa tore into the pile of bearings. One on the bottom was crushed and bruised, and it beat angrily when she touched it.

Looking like it was burning in Medusa's hands, Set's heart thumped and smoked as if in anticipation. The heart was full of pain, and it passed off as much of it as it could to anyone who held it. Medusa fought against it and didn't let go. She held the heart up before her and turned to Three.

"I'll kill you for this!" Set snarled at the both of them.

"Awe. That's not nice," Three fell forward and pushed Set in front of her, right towards Medusa's waiting hands. "Have a heart."

"You fools!" Set cackled and howled. "That's what I wanted all along." He laughed harder until the heart came closer and started exerting its influence upon him. "Something is different. This isn't the way it is supposed to be." He writhed and squirmed. The look of anger on his face was replaced with discomfort and then fear. "Stop. It hurts. Get it away from me!"

"Was this what you were looking for?" Medusa cried as she forced the beating heart against Set's chest. "It cost far more than you will ever know."

The heart flared and burned hotter than ever, but the pain was mental and emotional. Medusa ignored the feelings passed on to her and pressed harder. Set screamed and cried out as Three struggled to hold him from behind, her weight and strength making it impossible for him to break away. He fought against her at first, then shifted his efforts into getting away from his heart. "It hurts. It hurts! You don't know what you're doing."

"How do we know when the heart goes home?" Three's joints in her arms and wrists creaked and popped from the stress she exerted against the force trying to throw her off.

Set took a large gulp of air, and then cried as if the heaviest burden in the world was on his shoulders—or in his chest. Set fell forward, a dead weight in Three's strong arms.

"That's probably got it," Medusa said as she backed away. Her bloodied hands dropped to her sides in exhaustion. The pain she'd felt while holding the heart was gone, but the memory was slow to fade.

Three released her grip on Set. Then she rose up and stepped away. Set rolled back on his knees. He teetered for a bit and stabilized. Then he just sat there for a moment.

Anoup and D'art both came back to at the same time. They shook themselves and rose up. "What happened?" Anoup asked.

"Set finally got what he wanted." Three explained.

Medusa turned and ran back to Mod.

The main gear that held the wheel of Gaea to the universal hub turned and slipped a bit further off center.

"What have you done?" There was a pause, and then Set's voice grew louder and more desperate. "What have *I* done?" Set wailed and tore at his chest. "Get it out—get it out! I don't want it. I don't—" A great sob racked his frame, and he fell forward on his hands and knees.

He hung his head in shame for a long while, as the universe grew more and more unstable.

After too long, Set raised his head just enough to sway from side to side and surveyed the ongoing damage.

"It's done." Medusa said as she leaned over Mod, her tears raining down on his face.

"Thank you," Mod whispered in a thin, reedy voice. "Set won't be a problem now." Mod let out a long sigh and grew still.

"No. No, no, no, no." Medusa turned to Anoup. "You're a god. Fix Mod."

Anoup shook his head. "I'm sorry."

Medusa turned to Set, still shaking on all fours. "You did this. Please."

The shame on Set's face was painful. "I can't. I don't know how."

"Fix *Mod!*" Medusa demanded.

Anoup came over and put his hand on Medusa's shoulder. "It's been too long, Medusa. Mod's gone. I'm the god of death, and I've never heard of any mortal stabbed through the heart lasting this long."

Set looked over his shoulder. "Oh, gods and primordial forces, what have I done?"

"Yep. You pretty much boned us all," Three said without a hint of sarcasm. "I just learned that phrase recently. I used it correctly, didn't I?"

No one answered her.

Three looked over at the gears and wheels separating from each other. "Yep. Boned. I'm pretty sure I used that phrase at the proper time and in the proper manner."

Medusa kissed the back of Mod's hand and gently laid it on his chest. "I'm so, so sorry, Mod." She rose from his side and leaned heavily on Anoup.

Anoup held her up, a wide-eyed D'art pressed against his leg.

"I didn't know," Set stammered, then corrected himself. "I mean, I knew, but without a heart I just didn't . . ."

Three waved it away. "Not much we can do about it now, and not much worrying about it either. The universe is gonna fall apart in a few minutes."

Dust and grit fell in an offbeat cascade from the roof of the chamber. The sounds and energy of destruction were building to a crescendo around them.

"Not long now," Three said.

"You're right. I should have it fixed up in just a minute."

Medusa recognized the voice. She'd heard it for what she'd thought would be the last time just moments before. She didn't dare turn around for fear she was imagining things.

Mod's hand brushed the side of Medusa's cheek, and she couldn't ignore it anymore. She turned to look at him.

"You are so very pretty when you're crying." He said as he smiled at her. "I never noticed it before, but—"

Medusa staggered, took a step back, then wailed and threw her arms around Mod.

"You're dead. I saw you. I held you." She blubbered and cried into his chest.

"I don't understand it all just yet, but I have things to do." He gently pried her away and smiled at her.

"You were dead," Medusa repeated.

Mod straightened his chiton and probed the hole in his chest with a finger. "Huh, go figure. I'll have to patch that up later."

The others gaped at Mod, not quite understanding how he could be standing before them.

"I stabbed you through the left atrium," Set stared wide eyed at Mod. "You should be stone cold and bled out by now."

Mod searched about the ground as he looked for something. "You lived without a heart for how long?" he asked Set rhetorically.

"You were dead." Medusa sobbed. She would have fallen, but Three caught her under the arms and held her up.

"We'll talk about it. I promise. I just need a minute. You all won't be safe until I'm done with the Grand Machine." Mod must have found the two things he was looking for. He picked up the toy from his youth that always seemed to be on his person and Set's walking stick.

Mod turned to Set and held up the staff. "Can I use this? What I'm about to do may mar it, maybe even crack it, but I need it to fix the machine."

Set reached out and ran his fingers along the surface of the staff like he wanted to pull it close and protect it. It was evident to anyone who saw how conflicted he was to even have someone else touch it. "Why would you even ask my permission after all that I've done?"

Mod looked him in the eyes. "I can't feel right about using it without your permission."

Set's lower lip trembled as he dropped his gaze and nodded. "Yes. Break it if you must. Please use my staff to fix what I have broken."

"If anything happens to the staff I will repair it for you, I swear." Mod dropped his head in a slight bow as he acknowledged Set's sacrifice.

The Grand Machine had started to smoke at the core. There was a new tremor, and the machine shuddered and couldn't seem to get back into any sort of recognizable or smooth rhythm. After another shift, the screeching of something broken filled the air, and the chamber they all stood in began to fracture in a large screw pattern.

"Is that really Mod doing this?" Medusa asked as she rubbed the tears from her eyes on the back of her sleeve.

The group, D'art included, all nodded dumbstruck. Three was the only one to speak. "I don't know how, but he is."

Mod pointed up at a nub on the wheel then to a support it passed as it rotated. "Anoup, when this bump lines up with this strut I need you to clap your hands like this." He tucked the staff under his arm and the bearing in the crook of his elbow. Mod clapped each time the two points passed each other. "Can you do that?"

Anoup nodded and clapped.

"Good. Keep doing that. You'll know when to stop." Mod walked forward to the center of the destruction. He used the sharp end of the staff to spear the bearing track through the center, then threaded it through to the wheel that operated Grand Machine.

Mod started to rotate the staff in time with the turnings of the failing wheel, hauling up every time Anoup clapped. At just the right moments, he would apply a bit of pressure. With each successive revolution the wheel moved closer and closer back to track.

The hard tremors and grinding sounds grew more subdued. The rhythm of Anoup's clapping became more even and consistent.

A few more twists around, and the main wheel holding Gaea slid back almost onto the post it had fallen off of.

Anoup stopped clapping and Mod nodded his approval.

"Can you all hear it now? There's a cadence to the machine, an underlying tempo." Mod pounded his fist against his chest. "You feel it." They all nodded when Mod looked back at them and smiled. "Count with me. One, two, three, one, two, three." He kept bobbing his head in time with the counting as he spoke. "It's like a dance, and the whole of everything created is a part of it, stepping in time, the smallest unit interacting and intertwining with all the bits and pieces around it to create a whole greater than the sum of its parts. Feel it. This is the music of the universe working." At the moment when it was right Mod threw his weight against the staff.

Gaea now rotated back in place, although loosely because the bearings and the cover that held them in place hadn't been put back yet. Mod rotated the staff in a huge circle to keep the central wheel positioned where it needed to be.

"See the wide sweep around the place where the center pin goes? Everything is being held in place because I'm keeping it centered with the staff, but I can't stand here and row forever." He grinned and pulled his childhood toy from where he stashed it in his pocket. He held it up so all of them could see. "Bearings like this go in a circular track surrounding the central point. They take up the empty space in the track and rotate against the pin to keep it in place. I need seventeen more of these."

Three picked up a few. Set filled his arms. Medusa and Anoup each grabbed a couple. D'art tried his best, but he could only really pick up the one in his mouth.

Mod put the bearings back in place, but they needed the cover on the bearing track to keep them from falling out again.

Mod threaded the cover over the top of the staff and slid it along the length until he could push the cover up against its seating. Then he pulled the walking stick from the center of it, turned it around, and hooked the head of the cane inside the inner lip of the hollow shaft. "A bit of leverage at the right time." He rotated the staff so the crook stayed hooked, and the back side of the curve put pressure on the plate.

Three revolutions and the bearing was back in place, the cover secured, and the whole thing was working smoothly again.

Mod pulled the staff from the shaft and put the thin end of the staff back as a temporary pin. He watched just to make sure everything was adjusted right, then held out his hand. "Anyone seen the real pin lying about?"

It was right at Set's feet. "It's bent." Set said with a shudder. "I tried to pull it and a god named Thor tried to hammer it back in place."

Three clapped her hands together and cackled. "I told you you'd need to bring along the trustiest of multitools at the beginning of this." She held out her hand to Set. "Give her here, sport."

Set bent over and picked up the pin. He held it out to Three warily.

Three placed the pin between her knees and grabbed the head of it with both hands. She twisted her arms one direction and bent her hips and knees the other. When she offered the pin back to Set it was more or less straight.

"How did you—" Set gawped.

"It's all in the core[1]." Three flexed her arms and struck a power pose. "My workout routine is pretty intense."

Openmouthed, Set held out the pin to Mod, but Mod stepped back and made enough space for Set to move forward. "Put it right." Before the others could protest, Mod turned to them. "I need you to trust me."

Anoup still started forward to stop his father until Medusa put a hand on the youth's shoulder. She shook her head at Anoup, and he took a hesitant step back. Medusa looked at Mod, sure she under-

---

1. It was a subtle joke very well timed and appropriate. No one present got it but Three was proud of it nonetheless.

his intentions even though the thought made her nervous. "Mod knows what he's doing." She nodded to Set. "Go ahead."

Set's bottom lip trembled as he knelt down beside the wheel. He fumbled with the pin and almost dropped it. There were so many tears in his eyes it took him three tries to get the pin lined up with the hole. The pin worked into the slot, fitting as well as it had on the first day it had been used. Set pressed against it with all his might and the newly straightened pin seated all the way down.

Everything worked the way it should for the first time since creation.

Mod held a hand out to Set and helped him stand up. "This is yours," he said as he extended the hand holding Set's staff out to him. Set looked hesitant to take his staff back. When Mod pushed it forward, insistent, the aardvark-faced god finally relented.

Then Mod wrapped his arms around Set in a big hug. "Well done."

Set looked petrified for a moment, his arms and staff sticking awkwardly out to the side.

Medusa watched as the look on Set's face changed. His lower lip trembled, and his brows knitted. *Set has never been hugged before.*

Set's staff clattered to the ground, forgotten as he hugged Mod back. Set buried his face in Mod's neck as he cried. "Thank you."

A service truck blipped into existence, its tires narrowly missing Set and the others. Medusa read the words *A to Ω Mart* on the side of the truck. A service tech stuck his head out the window. "Huh, nothing out of the ordinary here. Must have been a mix up in the messaging from dispatch." With that he tipped his hat at the men, women, and the dog he'd narrowly missed with his vehicle and blipped back out of existence.

"Who was that?" Medusa asked.

Set laughed and gave a relieved sigh as he fell against Mod and cried again. "Does it really matter?"

"I guess not." Mod clapped Set on the shoulders and helped him stand taller. "Are you all right, my friend?"

"I'm better now." Set laughed as his face split into a tear-filled smile of joy. "Better than I've been since the beginning of the world."

CHAPTER 36

THIS IS THE BEGINNING
OF A BEAUTIFUL-

THREE DIRECTED SET, ANOUP, AND D'ART TO THE MAIN EXIT TO the chamber at the center of the Grand Machine. "Come on, guys. I think we need to give Mod and Medusa a moment or two."

When the others had left the chamber Mod looked at Medusa and wondered what it was she was thinking. He understood so much more now than he did before, but whatever was going on behind her eyes was still a mystery to him.

Well, not everything. Just one look at her and he could tell that she wasn't mad at him anymore. Probably. The truth was he didn't know, but he thought he might finally be learning. She wanted to talk to him again, so that was something.

Medusa came up to Mod. "While I care that the Grand Machine is fixed, I'm more glad my friend is alive." She put her hand on his chest. "You were stabbed through the heart."

He nodded. "So it would seem."

"You didn't die," she said.

"Also accurate," Mod said with a grin. These were easy questions, and he knew the answers to them.

Medusa looked into his eyes, relief and curiosity mixed equal parts within them. "So, you're not a god that you know of, but probably not just a normal human either. What are you?"

That question was a little bit more difficult. "I don't know. I'm starting to have some ideas. I guess we'll just have to figure it out." She smiled when he said *we'll*, meaning both of them together, which Mod interpreted as a positive thing. Unless she interpreted *we'll* as a larger collective, meaning him, Medusa, Three, Set, Anoup, and the dog. Should he include Set, Anoup, and D'art? They were newer to the group but still very important. He probably should include them, but it would be best if he could just focus on him and Medusa for a while. She touched his cheek and brought his focus solely back to her.

"So you just saved the universe," Medusa said.

Mod shied away from the praise. He didn't think he'd done anything special. "I just fixed something simple. It wasn't a big deal." He was sincere in his thinking. "I never would have made it if you hadn't gotten us past all the dangers to get here."

She shook her head as she patted his cheek and pulled back from him, an odd look in her eyes Mod hadn't really seen before. Medusa's smile didn't falter, but she did look down when the silence stretched on just a bit too long. She put her hands behind her back and scratched awkwardly at a pile of debris with the toe of her sandal.

Mod started to speak, then hesitated while he considered, then started to speak again. "It feels like I should be saying something poignant or memorable, but all I can think to say is that I'm glad you're here."

"I'm glad you're here too." Medusa stepped forward, gave him a quick hug, then stepped back again.

Mod remembered looking up at her as he was dying and thinking she was the most beautiful person he'd ever seen. She looked even more beautiful now when she wasn't crying and screaming, even though she was still streaked with his blood. He took in the vision of her face and smile, seeing her in a way he'd never seen her before. He was very content in this quiet and intimate here and now.

Then a mote of light caught his eye, and his attention drifted just a bit above her head as something distracted him. "Huh. How interesting."

Medusa raised her head, curiosity in her eyes. "Do you see something?"

Mod reached up and touched the point of light. He drew a line with his finger, unzipping the fabric of something hidden in the air. A razor-thin frame appeared large enough for Mod and Medusa to walk through side by side. It was like the portal, only not, and Mod hadn't needed a tool to make it.

"Impressive." Medusa looked a little dumbfounded. "Although I have no idea what it is you just did."

"I don't quite know what it is I just did." He grinned and shrugged. "I have a lot of new things I'm starting to figure out."

"A brand new Mod?" Medusa asked.

"Not new, but . . . Can I show you something?" Mod asked as he extended his hand.

"Are you asking me to go somewhere, like a date?" Medusa teased.

Mod pondered what she'd asked for a second before he gave a small nod. "It's special, and I can't think of anyone else I would want to share it with more."

Medusa reached out and took his hand. "I'd love to."

"But if this is going to turn into something let's take it all a bit slow, okay?"

Mod wasn't sure exactly what that meant. "Sure. I guess."

Medusa nodded and they both turned until they faced the rectangle transition that hung in the ether.

"Is this like your portal?" she asked.

"Yes," he said, then paused and added, "and no." He didn't know quite how to explain it. "When I was dying, or whatever it was that happened to me, I was pulled into something or someplace I knew. I didn't know what it was, and I still don't have it all figured out, but I think I can get back there. This is the first time that I've tried to go there under my own power, without having something pull me to it. I think it's a little bit like putting a portal in time and space, so you can visit a memory. And like a portal it has to be to a time and place that I'd been before."

They both stepped through into a beautiful summer day. The sea was shimmering from the light shining down on it. A cool ocean breeze brought the mist of the sea into the air, making the air moist and pleasantly aromatic.

"This is beautiful. It's just this is all a bit overwhelming. A second ago we were in the center of everything, and now?" She looked about like she was searching for something familiar. "Where are we?"

"This is the place that Doug and his parents found me, on the day that my mother died," Mod said in a soft voice. He wasn't sad, just a bit reflective in the moment.

Medusa put her hand on his upper arm. "Are you okay?"

He gave a slight smile and a gentle nod. "It's soothing to be here. This is a good moment."

"It is nice," Medusa said as she turned around and took it in. "I feel so calm, and at peace. I can see why you wanted me to see this. Is this real?"

"I'm really not sure, and I guess it would depend on your definition of what is real, so I'll have to leave that one to the philosophers." He studied the minute details of the time and place he'd once been a part of. There was no way he could have paid enough attention as a child to remember this many tiny variations and nuances. It must be more than just what he'd perceived when he was younger. "I can do things here that aren't normal, like this." He mentally adjusted something, so that Medusa could see the spray of the sea freeze in time, so she could watch the sun sparkle through the drops of water suspended mid flight from all angles as she walked around them.

"It's like a scattering of diamonds hanging in the sky," she marveled.

"I'm glad you like it." Mod watched the twinkling lights about him. "I thought it was pretty too."

Mod led her along the shore to the dockside and then down the dock. "I see things differently now. Almost too much information to take in. I see the things that make up the world, and how they work with and affect each other. I was shown it first here, and I'm trying to figure out what all of this means.

"I know I can see things from all directions at once, but I don't think I can understand them by myself. I need someone to make sure I'm understanding what I'm experiencing, to let me know if it causes me to consider doing something I shouldn't. Set didn't have a heart, and he almost destroyed the world because of it. I don't know what I'm missing, but I don't want to hurt anyone just because I thought I was doing the right thing when I really wasn't."

Mod reached out and took her by the hand. "I don't know what all of this means, but I think we can figure it out if you'd help me?"

Medusa nodded and patted him on the back of the hand she was holding. "I'll be right here."

There was a woman sitting on one of the pylons on the dockside. She rose to greet them as they approached.

"Medusa, this is my mother." Mod indicated the woman.

Medusa looked at Mod for a second and slowly shook her head as a wry smile spread across her face. She let go of Mod and reached out and gently took the woman's hand in her own. "Pleased to meet you."

Mod's mother inclined her head slightly to Medusa and smiled.

Medusa slid an arm around Mod's waist as she turned to him once more. "Meet your mother? What happened to taking it slow?"

Mod was confused. "What do you mean?"

"Oh, Mod." Medusa pulled up close and put her head on his shoulder.

Join the Cursed Dragon Ship Newsletter

Want more just like this one? Sign up for our newsletter so you don't miss out on the adventure. You'll get:

- A free book for signing up
- Advanced notice of new releases
- First word of books on sale
- Opportunities for free books
- Most up-to-date information on author appearances.

We're busy and know you are too. We won't send more than one newsletter a month.

Register below.

ACKNOWLEDGMENT

So many people believe that writing a novel is an act of one, as for me, I can tell you that is absolutely not the case. There are always people who have cheered me on and encouraged me, but there are a few in particular I would like to thank.

To my copy editor, Birdee, I would like to say how much I appreciate you making me look like I actually understand the English language. You are a master, and I am thankful to know you and have you apply your skills to my benefit.

To the CDS crew and my fellow CDS authors, you have given me the friendship, encouragement, and support I needed when I doubted my abilities and those applications for bagboy at the local grocery store started to look a little too enticing.

Thanks to Kevin Pettway for opening the door and encouraging me to join this fabulously eclectic group. You and Lena are my Florida family now whether you like it or not.

Thanks to my brother James for encouraging me to keep working on this crazy idea that started as a joke and became so much more.

And I would be totally remiss if I didn't offer thanks to Kelly. She has been my voice of reason when my weird imagination wandered too far, she has offered clarity when I was stuck in the smoke and fire of creation and destruction, and she has put up with my crazy ideas even when it has meant a greater workload for her (those cursed footnotes). In the world of Greek Myth, Kelly is my Athena. She sprang into my life far more intelligent than I am and has steered me emotionally and intellectually in the right direction ever since.

ABOUT THE AUTHOR

Jeremy Brundage has worked as a stone mason, a carpenter, an artist, an animatronics engineer, and more. He is working on several projects with his brother James A. Owen for Coppervale Studios and assists in creating armor for the SCA at Windrose Armory.

Jeremy writes comedy, fantasy, and science fiction, sometimes combining all three.

Join his newsletter to keep informed.

https://jeremybrundage.com

 facebook.com/jeremybrundage

Did you miss book one?

Doug must complete twelve tasks to win the respect of his future father-in-law the king. Sounds easy except Doug sells yogurt, doesn't know how to wield a sword, and has no idea what he's in for.

Another Title by Cursed Dragon Ship

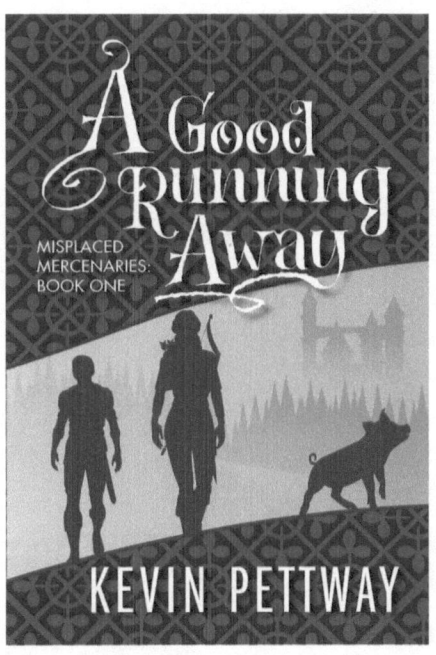

Stealing the cash box of your mercenary unit as you run away probably isn't wise, but it sure is funny.

www.ingramcontent.com/pod-product-compliance
Lightning Source LLC
Chambersburg PA
CBHW061631190726
48289CB00006B/1558